THEIR FATE WAS ENTWINED WITH THE STONES

Doug smiled and shook his head. "I'm not an Abo, and neither are you, so they wouldn't want us snoopin' around their sacred stones. Your dad had a real interest in findin' the place, just like you. He said the stones are the heads of tribal elders from back in the Dreamtime. Their memories are in there, all locked away in stone forever."

"So you've heard of it."

"Yeah, I know about Kukullumunnumantje. Never seen it, though. No white bloke ever has. You don't want to get involved in Abo stuff, Val. Might even be dangerous. It's all they've got left, their secrets."

"My father . . . they killed him, didn't they, because of what he knew."

"Coulda been suicide, like they said. There's no way to prove any of it."

"But it could have been that. . . ."

"Mighta been. That's why you ought pack it in, Val, and not go lookin' for the place anymore. Might be bad news for you if you ever did find it."

"But I found it once. . . . "

"Pure luck. Give it a rest, Val. It's not for us."

BOOKS BY GREG MATTHEWS

The Further Adventures of Huckleberry Finn

Heart of the Country

Little Red Rooster

The Gold Flake Hydrant

One True Thing

Power in the Blood*

The Wisdom of Stones*

*Available from HarperPaperbacks

THE WISDOM OF STONES

GREG MATTHEWS

HarperPaperbacks
A Division of HarperCollinsPublishers

HarperPaperbacks *A Division of* HarperCollins*Publishers*
10 East 53rd Street, New York, N.Y. 10022

Copyright © 1994 by Greg Matthews
All rights reserved. No part of this book may be used or reproduced in any manner whatsoever without written permission of the publisher, except in the case of brief quotations embodied in critical articles and reviews. For information address HarperCollins*Publishers,*
10 East 53rd Street, New York, N.Y. 10022.

A hardcover of this edition was published in 1994 by HarperCollins*Publishers.*

Cover illustration by George Angelini

First HarperPaperbacks printing: May 1995

Printed in the United States of America

HarperPaperbacks and colophon are trademarks of HarperCollins*Publishers*

❖ 10 9 8 7 6 5 4 3 2 1

PART ONE

HAD HE NOT BEEN BLIND, M'linga could have seen more songs than most men are accustomed to hearing. Below the rock escarpment where he sat, M'linga's country stretched for more journeyings than any man, even if he lived to be as old as M'linga, could ever hope to walk. All of its pathways could never be known by one man, nor all of the songs that made those places be sung again in a lifetime. A man who could not die might walk forever on a journey from one place to the next, in the endless walk-about that was each man's task in life, and even that deathless man could never know all of the places in existence, even though every place was within walking distance of the next place, which was easily crossed to reach the next, and the next. It could never be done, not even by an undying man.

This had been told to M'linga when he was young, and could see and walk for himself the extent of just that small piece of country belonging to the Pitjantjatjara. To visit and revisit the places made by song, long ago in the Dreamtime, was the purpose of a man. M'linga had visited those parts of the country made available to him by his strong legs and the years of his life, and had sung again the songs that made those places, sung them so many times he could still feel the places still, though his eyes now were blind. There could be no forgetting, not while the songs remained in his head. M'linga had already passed on many songs to the younger men, in preparation for his own death. This was the thing for which he lived. When all of the songs were learned by others, and the places made by those songs perpetuated by younger throats, he could allow himself to die.

But there were things behind his eyes now that had never been sung, things for which there was no place, no song, and these things puzzled M'linga. He would speak of them when he understood why it was that the unsung things were entering his head. He sat by the escarpment's edge, feeling his beard stir in the hot wind from the desert. The unsung things were doubly strange, in that they concerned whitefellas. Every part of M'linga's naked skin felt the wind from his country, and its familiarity was a comfort to him in this time of puzzling things. M'linga did not like whitefellas; they were a songless breed of creature quite unlike true people, even though they possessed arms and legs and heads. Without songs to bind them to the place of their belonging, they could never be truly human. Whitefellas had no country of their own and so had come to M'linga's country to try and make it theirs, so ignorant were they of the songs that made such a thing impossible. Without the songs of creation and existence in their heads, the whitefellas would not last for long and soon would be swept away again, back to the songless place behind the sky where they had come from.

No, he had no liking for them, and so M'linga was ashamed at the presence behind his eyes of the whitefellas, two of them, and the whitefella woman too. One of these men was known to his tribe by blood, but the woman was not. The other whitefella man was far away but drawing closer, coming from the sky's far side on a whitefella ship as white as clouds.

It had been his custom, from the very beginning of the voyage at Southampton, to walk four times around the deck daily. Clive had maintained his regimen even during a rough crossing of the Bay of Biscay and had enjoyed the exercise thoroughly while traversing the Mediterranean. He had breathed the sand-laden air of Suez and the Red Sea and been invigorated by the stiff breezes of the Indian Ocean, with their occasional scentings of hot places beyond the horizon. Then he was laid low by a stomach complaint in Bombay, and Clive was unwell for some time, unable to maintain his four-times-around daily constitutional. Lacking the strength to walk any worthwhile distance, he nevertheless struggled topside each day and found a deck chair from which to survey the tropic skies and flying fish, and forced himself to be content with that.

There had been speculation among the passengers concerning Clive, especially when it was learned he had inherited an enormous tract of land in Australia. Women in particular began to find his habit of keeping himself to himself intriguing. They had, until learning of his estate, assumed he was avoiding social contact with the rest because he was shy, or because he lacked the ability to chat in a friendly manner. Once his true condition was revealed (to a particularly insistent fellow, who, by Naples, could no longer tolerate Clive's secretiveness), it was seen that there had been a misinterpretation of the young man; he was neither shy nor standoffish, but superior to the average passenger by reason of his wealth. Those women aboard who clearly were too old for him began thrusting their marriageable daughters forward for Clive's consideration.

By the time Bombay was reached, Clive had become overburdened with female attention, although he did nothing to encourage it, and his illness in that port had come as a perfect excuse to isolate himself again. He was suffering also from a faintly guilty conscience. His inheritance in northern Australia—Redlands—was of a size he had been unable to determine in his correspondence with the solicitor in Darwin who had written to inform him of his prize. An assumption on the part of his fellow passengers that the place was of typically antipodean vastness ("big as all the British Isles put together" was the expression that circulated) was not corrected by Clive. He rather hoped they were right. There was also the common presumption that his huge holdings were dotted with sheep, since this was the one product of Australia all English persons were familiar with. Again, Clive contradicted nothing, even though the solicitor had mentioned cattle and rice farming in the area. If his fellow passengers wished to cast him in the role of wool baron, Clive was unwilling to disappoint them.

In fact, he knew almost nothing of Redlands or the place called Northern Territory, inside whose tremendously long boundaries it lay. There was a Kiplingesque romance in journeying to the world's far side that Clive found irresistible. It would be an adventure of some kind, he was sure, even if his concept of such things had been formed exclusively by his own bookish ways rather than actual experience of extraordinary things in his life.

Clive had been a teacher in London when the solicitor's letter came, and a particularly miserable member of the profession. He loathed the dreary grammar school in Clapham, was bored to the point of screaming with the pipe-smoking denizens of the staff room, and had never once found, in all of London, a woman with whom it might be possible to fall in love. Clive was too young for the life of stultification into which he had fallen, and the letter, arriving on a rainy afternoon in January, had meant nothing less than delivery from hell.

There had been no one to wave good-bye from the docks; Clive's parents both were dead, and now his mother's brother was dead also, in faraway Australia, and by his dying had set free his unhappy nephew.

Clive was recovering nicely by Singapore, and the women who had refrained from making nuisances of themselves out of sympathy for his fragile condition now returned to court his favour. He had informed nobody aboard of his former profession, hinting instead that he had "dabbled in this and that, bit of an amateur good-for-nothing, I suppose." This good-humoured evasiveness suggested a life of unhurried comfort, supported by cash from an endowment of some kind that allowed Clive to do as he pleased. Clive's one indulgence before boarding the ship had been to buy some expensive clothing, and this served to perpetuate the myth that had grown to surround him. He would reach Australia with very few pounds remaining in his pocket but with expectation of riches to come. While permitting himself to enjoy the attention paid to landed gentry such as himself, he was wary still of overconfidence, a telltale slip of the tongue that might lead to unwelcome exposure of his true self. It was almost a relief to be approaching Darwin at last. He had successfully fended off all proposals of marriage, even offended some women by his outright indifference to them.

When the ship at last dropped its anchor, Clive had become something of a pariah. He was the only passenger disembarking, and there was some delay in raising his trunks from the hold. The captain informed those going ashore for a few hours of tourist exploration that they would have to travel by launch, the ship being unable to tie up to the jetty; a wharf labourers' strike was in progress. Clive was left behind as the first launch departed, and barely was able to join the second. On the five-minute trip across the harbour, nobody spoke to him, and Clive saw that he had departed from the good graces of his fellow passengers even before landfall. But it no longer mattered.

It was while he attempted to lift his trunk unassisted from the launch to the wharf, some four feet above his head, that Clive became alarmed. The trunk he struggled with was the lighter of the two he had brought from the ship, but he could barely lift it to shoulder height. The launch was not pitching, in fact the water was perfectly smooth, but he could do nothing with the trunk at all except let it slip from his shoulder three times in a row, watched by an amused crewman at the tiller. Every other passenger had already climbed a wooden ladder onto the wharf and begun walking along its considerable length toward the low, scrub-covered bluff overlooking the harbour. The air was rich with the smell of tidal mudflats and an overall odour of tropical decay.

He removed his hat, the expensive white panama purchased in Singapore in anticipation of Australia's legendary sun, and mopped his brow several times with a handkerchief. The crewman was smiling, it seemed to Clive, and presumably was reluctant to assist him because he was no longer a passenger. It was not the first time Clive had detected a subtle sneer on the collective face of the crew, and he decided that such disregard for the needs of a paying passenger was intolerable.

"I don't suppose you could possibly lend a hand, could you?"

It sounded less stern than he had hoped, and the crewman's smile widened as he stepped forward. The lighter trunk was hefted with ease up onto the timbers above, and the second followed with barely more than a muted professional grunt. Clive was impressed despite himself.

"Thank you so much."

The crewman shrugged, smirking broadly. Clive turned from him in some embarrassment and climbed the ladder to join his belongings. The launch's idling motor was shoved into reverse; it backed away from the wharf and was thrown into an expert arc to retrace its passage from the ship, cool and white against the sea a quarter mile offshore. The other passengers were a distant knot at its landward end. No one had stayed behind to help him or wish him well in his new life. He was angry over his isolation, angry also over the crewman's smirking strength and the humid air surrounding him with its foetid embrace—the root, he was sure, of his awful sense of dislocation and impotence.

No trolley or cart was at hand to make the shifting of his trunks easier; and Clive sat on the larger of the two, absorbing this latest insult to a new arrival. It was not the beginning he had anticipated. He felt weak, horribly wet, and disappointed in the extreme with the country he had chosen to live in. Virtually his last pound had gone into bringing him halfway around the world, and here he sat, stranded and alone on the end of an inhospitable wharf. He supposed that regret over his foolishness in having come so far was childish, given that he could not simply turn around and go back.

His erstwhile fellow passengers were trailing up what appeared from that distance to be a rough path. Buildings of some kind could be glimpsed above the trees atop the bluff, but Clive was in no hurry now to be among them. He stared instead at the many smallish craft pulled up onto the muddy beach on either side of the wharf, not one of which impressed him with its appearance. He assumed they were workaday fishing vessels and dismissed them; his predicament demanded something with wheels, not a hull.

Staring again along the wharf, he now noticed a figure seated on a piling two thirds of the way from shore, a faint haze of cigarette smoke hovering around its head. If this was a seaman of some description, or an unloader of ships, Clive might learn from him the location of a trolley for his belongings. He stood and began walking, determined to make a stronger impression on this fellow than he had upon the crewman who had set his trunks on the wharf.

Approaching him, Clive braced himself for this, his first encounter with an Australian. The smoker on the piling wore heavy lace-up boots and a pair of filthy khaki shorts, a sleeveless undershirt of dark blue or black—Clive could not be sure, since this was even filthier than the shorts—and a felt hat with shapeless brim and crown, the band darkened by sweat. The shoulders, arms, and legs of the smoker were nut brown, and his unshaven face was pinched in to keep hold of the twisted stub of cigarette between his lips to the last puff of paper and tobacco. A tiny nubbin of greasy whiteness was extracted and flung away as Clive stopped before him.

"G'day."

Clive translated this foreign word and realised he had been wished a good day.

"Good . . . good afternoon. I wonder if you might know where there's a trolley to be had in the vicinity."

"Got one near the shed."

Clive saw a small galvanised-iron building where the wharf met land.

"There?"

"That's it. Should be round the side."

"Thank you."

He walked on, found there was indeed a wooden cart with a handle behind the shed, and began dragging it back along the wharf. When he reached his informant, he was joined for the remainder of the walk to his trunks, although he had not offered an invitation.

"You from England?" asked the man beside him. Clive judged him to be somewhere in his mid-thirties. Clive was twenty-nine.

"London."

"Comin' ashore for a while, eh?"

"Pardon me?"

"Got your boxes with you. The others didn't."

"No; they're all going back aboard later on."

"Doug Farrands."

A brown hand reached for Clive's pale fingers. He accepted it and felt his palm crack uncomfortably in a grip too strong for mere friendliness.

"Bagnall. Clive Bagnall."

He took back his throbbing hand. It had been some ritual intimidation, he was sure, the mocking of an old-worlder by a colonial, and Clive resented the handshake for its bogus message of good fellowship. He wished Farrands had not accompanied him.

The squeaking of unoiled wheels behind them and the raucous screech of hovering gulls were noise enough for Clive to hide behind until the trunks were reached. Farrands lifted both onto the trolley with little effort, although the second trunk clearly gave him pause. "What's in this one, bloody bricks?"

"Books, actually."

"Yeah? What are you, a teacher?"

Clive was horrified at having been found out so soon but was unable to formulate a lie quickly enough.

"Well . . . I used to be, as a matter of fact. But not anymore," he added, sounding ridiculously defensive even to his own ears.

"What are you now, then?"

Farrands's unsolicited curiosity was uncouth in the extreme. Clive took several breaths, then decided to stun his audience with nothing less than the truth.

"I'm a planter," he announced, "or will be quite soon."

"Planter?"

"A rice planter."

"Got yourself a bit a land in the Top End?"

"I'm sorry? Top end?"

"The Territory."

"Oh, yes, I see. Yes, in the Northern Territory. Not too far from Darwin, actually."

"Got a name, this place?"

Clive surrendered to a full accounting of himself.

"The property is called Redlands."

"Not bloody Redlands. Not old Perce's place. Perce Burridge?"

"My uncle on my mother's side. Do you know him?"

"Well, I did. He's dead now. Did himself in about five months ago, back when the Wet was just gettin' started. Suicide month."

"I'm sorry?"

"November. Drives some blokes crazy, all the moisture in the air before the first big storms. Pressure on the eardrums, barometric pressure, they say. Probly bullshit, but there's always a coupla blokes go round the bend in November. They tell you what he did, old Perce?"

"I was told . . . some kind of hunting accident."

"Nah, not him. Perce never hunted for anythin' except a

reason not to chuck it all in and bugger off back south. He was from Melbourne, he said, but he talked a bit like a Pom; not as much as you, though."

Farrands picked up the trolley's handle and began pulling it along the wharf. Clive took the handle's other side, determined not to appear weak. He was beginning to feel a little panic-stricken over this stranger's acquaintance with his uncle; what kind of social contacts had Uncle Percy been subjected to before his death?

"You didn't say what he did," Clive coaxed.

"Set up a shotgun on a chair and tied the trigger to the doorknob, then yelled out for someone to open the door. Copped it right in the chest. Poor bloody Abo that opened the door went walkabout. Can't blame him, poor bastard. Perce probly didn't pay him off first, either. He was a tight old bugger—no offense."

Clive was appalled. "Why would he do such a thing? I thought . . . the letters he sent my mother were rather cheerful, as I recall."

"November," Farrands repeated. "Anythin' can happen then. Course, he wasn't makin' a go of the place, so that's what did it, everyone says. It's happened before, lotsa times. Bloody hard country to make a livin' off round here."

"Look, this isn't some kind of joke, is it, because I'm the new chum?"

"Nah, I wouldn't joke about somethin' like that. Bit of a shock, eh."

"The solicitor's letter said he died from an accidental gunshot wound."

"Nothin' accidental about it."

"Perhaps it was to spare me any unnecessary . . . sorrow."

"Knew him, did you?"

"No; we never met. My mother had several pictures of him."

"Why didn't he leave the place to her, if he was gunna leave it to anyone?"

"My mother died some time ago."

"Went and put me foot in me mouth, didn't I. Sorry, mate."

Clive's irritation with Farrands now was tempered by a sense of awkward kinship thrust upon them both by virtue of Farrands's acquaintance, however shallow, with Percy

Burridge and his role of messenger bearing bad news to the young heir of Redlands. Events were unfolding for Clive with the headlong inevitability of cheap fiction.

"The place . . . Redlands: is someone looking after it? I suppose things are a bit of a mess with no actual owner present. Or is the staff . . . umm . . . the hired hands or whatever you call them here . . . have they been looking after things, do you know?"

"Nah, don't think so; not that I heard about anyway. I don't go inland much, meself. . . . You have to go in there."

They had reached the galvanised-iron shed. Clive now noticed the words CUSTOMS HOUSE in peeling paint along its front. He noticed also the sudden swarm of flies that began tickling every exposed inch of skin. He swatted ineffectually, to Farrands's obvious amusement. "Wouldn't bother if I was you; they only come back a second later."

Clive pulled the trolley through a doorway barely wide enough for it, hoping for relief inside, but the flies and Farrands followed him in.

"Got a customer for you, Frank," Farrands told the individual in uniform who was seated behind a long table. "Mate a mine, Clive Burridge from England."

"Bagnall," corrected Clive, producing his passport.

Farrands addressed the customs official again. "Come all the way out here to inherit his uncle's property—Redlands."

"Arr, not Redlands," Frank sympathised, raising his eyes from Clive's picture in the passport to compare it with the original. "Doug give you the hard word yet?"

"I'm sorry . . . the hard word?"

"I told him; don't worry. He knows what's what now."

Frank casually stamped a page in Clive's passport, then peered at the trolley with little interest. "Anything in there that shouldn't be in there?" he asked.

"I already made him throw the opium overboard, Frank."

"Doug's a funny bloke," said Frank, his eyes returning to Clive. "Redlands, eh."

"Might take him out there meself," offered Doug. "Got a few quid to hire a coupla nags, Clive?"

"I . . . yes. With the trunks, though, couldn't we take a taxi?"

"Arr, no, mate," said Doug, and Clive was surprised to see

that he and the customs officer were sharing smiles like idiotic schoolboys. "Don't reckon we can, not a taxi. Couldn't take a tram, either, could we, Frank, eh."

"Don't think so," agreed Frank, handing back the passport. "Or a plane."

"Nah, couldn't do that, not out to Redlands."

"Then just to a hotel," said Clive, sounding a little desperate. He could see nothing humorous in the exchange, wanted to crack the two grinning heads together like bothersome pupils, but Clive had never done such a thing even to boys and knew himself incapable of handling fully grown men that way, no matter how deserving they might be of such punishment for their treatment of him. He regarded them both as imbeciles. Farrands presumably had an excuse, since he appeared to be some kind of loafer or layabout, but no representative of the Australian government should have conducted himself in as lackadaisical a manner as Frank. It was apparent no search would be made of his trunks; Frank's hand was lazily waving him through the shed toward another door, on the far side.

"Better give him a hand up the hill, Doug. Big trunks like them in heat like this, a fella could do some damage."

"Bugger that; he's only got books, mostly. Can't you confiscate his stuff so he doesn't need to take it anywhere? Just till he sorts himself out, all right?"

"Could do," mused Frank. "Just temporary, though."

"There y'are, Clive, all taken care of."

"Put 'em in there." Frank indicated a corner of the room enclosed by walls of wire mesh, inside which stood metal shelves awaiting contraband. Doug was already yanking at the trolley's handle. Clive allowed his belongings to be taken from him and placed under official lock and key. A dull headache was massing for its initial assault behind his temples as Doug led him out of the customs house and up toward the town, their shadows in the fierce afternoon light made ragged at the edges by an entourage of flies.

"Looks to me like you need a cold beer, Clive."

"I need somewhere to sit down."

"Right-oh, a bar with tables. We've got a coupla them, but you pay extra for the poshness."

"I just want to sit somewhere out of the sun. . . ."

"No worries, Clive mate; just foller me."

The path rose and leveled, offering Clive his first real look at the town. He had not been expecting much in the way of grandeur or architectural excellence, but it was difficult to suppress further disappointment. The street before him was wide and dusty, the building facades on either side protected from the sun by deep verandahs and canvas awnings. The remarkable thing about many of them was the material from which they were constructed; Clive had never considered sheet metal as suitable for inclusion in anything built for human habitation, but the predominant feature of what Doug Farrands announced, with some pride, to be Cavenagh Street was the walls, row upon row, of corrugated iron. Some were painted, more were not, but the result was equally awful, in Clive's view. To reinforce the effect, every roof within view was made of the same stuff. It was a tin town, and the air above it danced with reflected heat. Here and there along the street were eucalyptus trees of considerable height, their drooping gray-green foliage creating an impression of utter weariness and lassitude. A dog meandered across the street, the slowest-moving creature Clive could recall ever having seen.

Sensing a little of Clive's mood, Doug assured him, "The Vic's the place for us. Got an electric refrigerator from down south. Coldest beer in town."

"Marvelous."

The Victoria Hotel was reassuringly solid, built of mortar and stone, and Clive was directed by his guide to a table inside, where the move from sunlight to shade lifted his spirits a little. He stared back at the faces staring at him, then was distracted by the appearance of a beer pitcher before him. Two glasses of surprisingly graceful design were set down with a delightful clinking sound beside the pitcher, and Clive, never one to indulge in drink except by dint of social obligation, watched as Doug poured amber streams into both. "This is the stuff. You'll like this."

Clive let the beer slide down his throat. It was cold, as promised, and tastier, it seemed, than British beers, but that might have been sheer thirst influencing his judgment.

"Thank you," he gasped, after quaffing almost an entire glass at one long gulp.

"Anytime." Doug smiled. He had already opened a bar account on behalf of his new friend, assuring the proprietor, who had grown over the years to distrust Doug's own declarations of intent to pay, that the bloke in the corner with the sheila's hat and the worried look was a dinky-di English lord visiting Down Under to check up on his estates.

"Not a bloody Vestey, is he?" asked the publican. The Vestey family of British meatpacking millionaires was heartily loathed by many Territorians for having closed down its local processing and shipping factory when the price of beef had tumbled on the world markets fourteen years before, in 1925.

"Nah, not one a them bastards," Doug had told him, "but he's got quids on him."

Doug drained his own beer and poured again for them both. Revived somewhat, Clive lifted his glass. "Cheers," he said.

"Down the hatch."

The pitcher was drained as if filled with lemonade, and Doug fetched another. Clive, by that time, was disposed to think of the Australian in more friendly terms. True, the fellow's blunt intrusion into Clive's affairs had been mildly obnoxious at first, but Clive was prepared to grant that this was probably the colonial way, a simple directness of manner that he would learn to appreciate in future.

"What kind of work do you do, Doug?"

"Sheller."

"Sorry?"

"Pearl sheller. Slice the oysters open and check the buggers for pearls."

"Really? How fascinating!"

"Nah, not after a while. You might find a couple or three pearls in a whole season sometimes. You can get lucky, though. Last year I found nine beauties. The best one went for two thousand quid at the dealer's. He said it'd go for around five thousand over in your neck a the woods."

"London?"

"Yeah, or Holland. Paris too, I think. Where they make all the fancy jewels for rich bastards."

"You must be a bit of a rich bastard yourself, finding pearls like that."

Clive had never in his life addressed anyone as a bastard,

but the term seemed to have universal application in Australia, in much the same fashion as "fellow" or "chap." Clive was unable to enrich the word by imitating its uniquely Australian pronunciation: baah-stud.

"You don't think I was cuttin' oysters for meself, do you? The blokes that own the pealin' luggers pay other blokes to go out and pull up the oysters, Japs mostly, and shellers to split 'em open when they're on deck, fresh outa the water."

"Oh, so it's work for wages."

"Nah, mate, I do it for the glory."

"You don't do any diving yourself?"

"Japs are better than whites at the diving part. Tough little bastards they are."

"So you work for them."

"Bloody hell, no. They work for the blokes that own the luggers. All those boats down on the beach? Pearl shell luggers. The owners don't even set foot on 'em, as a rule. It's all contract work."

"I see. Have you ever thought of working on the land instead?"

"You're not gunna try and sell me bloody Redlands, are you?"

"Oh, no; I was just inquiring. I was going to offer you a job if you were interested."

Doug leaned across the table. "Listen, I don't think I coulda made meself clear enough. Redlands is a dump, Clive, take it from me. Old Perce never should've started bloody rice farming when he knew bugger-all about how to do it, and even if he had've been an expert, it never woulda worked out because he picked the wrong place to do it. He got told, but he wouldn't listen, and when it all got to be too much for him and even his lubra ran off, he went and tied the shotgun to the door, the way I told you."

"Lubra?"

"Black velvet."

"Pardon?"

"Your uncle Perce had a lady friend to snuggle up to. Word was he had more'n one, come to think of it. They all shot through in the end. He really liked the last one, though, I heard."

"An . . . Aboriginal woman?"

"Too right. There's practically no white women up here in the Territory, so most blokes go for the dark, or else do without. The Chinese keep holda their own, and the Japs don't bring any women down here with 'em when they sign on for pearlin'. They go for the blacks too, then they pack up and go home with their wages when their contract's over and done with. Bet they don't let on to their wives and girlfriends what they did while they were down in Aussie."

"How very . . . expedient."

"So don't go and get yourself all worked up about Redlands bein' yours, because it's nothin' you could do anythin' with anyway. You'd wind up the same way Perce did."

"I don't think that's a foregone conclusion at all, if you don't mind my saying so."

"I don't mind. It's your beer."

"Is it?"

"What I mean is," Doug hurried to explain, "the land up here's worthless, most of it. Dry as a bone for half the year and a swamp for the other half. You just can't do much with a place like this. There's been gold strikes, but that's all behind us, and there's cattle stations about as big as bloody England, but even they sometimes come close to goin' under. Mozzies and flies in the bush, snakes too, poisonous buggers most of 'em. Sharks in the sea, and jellyfish that'll sting you to death, plus saltwater crocs that'll take your leg off at the hip, no worries. It's tough country, hard yakka all the way."

"Yakka?"

"Work, mate, bloody hard work, whatever a bloke turns his hand to."

"Why don't you leave?"

Doug reared back, his expression hurt. "I was born here, that's why. A bloke doesn't shoot through just because everything isn't perfect!"

"Of course. I wasn't thinking."

"I mean, I can understand you comin' out here from England and that, who wouldn't, but a Territorian can't do it, see?"

"Yes . . . that is, no, he can't, I suppose, not if he doesn't want to. . . . This beer's stronger than you might think, isn't it?"

"Nah, not really. You'll get used to it."

"I think I need something to eat."

"The Vic's got bonzer food. Just ask for anything, a pie or a sandwich. You're lookin' a bit crook, Clive."

"I think I'm going to be sick. . . ."

"That'll be the heat. Happens sometimes."

The empty pitcher was thrust under Clive's chin just in time to receive back what it had so recently dispensed. Doug had moved with such adroitness none of the nearby drinkers was aware of Clive's embarrassment. Doug returned the brimming pitcher to the bar, leaned over, and poured it into the drip tanks beneath the serving spouts. To the barman he said, "There was a bloody fly in that lot."

"You coulda fished it out."

"It already had a shit. Ever try to get holda flyshit?"

"You're not gettin' a free one."

"Who asked for it? Give us a fresh supply, and throw us a coupla ham sandwiches too."

"That English bloke know you're throwin' away beer he's payin' for?"

"Course he does. Come on, come on. A bloke could die a thirst in here."

Clive ate his sandwiches, grateful for Doug's attention to his needs. He supposed he had found a friend, although he had not been attempting to find any such thing.

"I'd put you up at my place if I had a place," Doug was saying, "but I never did have enough sense to save me pennies and put a roof over me head. Arr, I dunno, maybe I never wanted to. Who needs it, eh. I spose it'd come in handy in the Wet, though, havin' a roof to keep the rain off. No pearlin' durin' the Wet, because a the weather. Rough seas stir the water up so the divers can't see a bloody thing down there."

"What do you do when you're not opening oysters?"

"Sometimes I do odd jobs around town, or a bit a station work. I'm not a bad horseman when I wanna be. I don't like cattle, though; stupid bastards they are. They say sheep are worse, but no one runs sheep up here. They're so close to the ground they drown in the Wet—no joke."

"Why don't you get your own pearling boat?"

"Me? Those things cost thousands a quid. I'd have to crack

oysters for about fifty years and save every penny to buy a boat. Not bloody likely. I might be able to swing a job for you if you want."

"I expect I'll be busy with Redlands, getting it back on its feet, so to speak."

Doug shook his head and poured himself more beer from the fresh pitcher. "I keep tellin' you, there isn't a thing you can do with a shitty place like that. Might put a few head a cattle on it, but not enough to make a livin' from. It's not big enough, fair dinkum, Clive."

"I'll have to see it for myself."

"Course you will. Only sensible to run your nose over the place. I just wouldn't want you goin' out there with big expectations or anythin'."

"I've always considered myself a realist."

"I know a bloke we can hire a coupla horses off tomorrer, or we could take a truck if you want."

"I rather like the idea of riding. I do appreciate your help."

"Anyone'd do it, even for a Pom. No offense, mate."

"None taken."

"Want me to fix you up with a room here? The Vic's the best place in town. They won't rook you if it's me that does the arrangin'. Someone new to the place, they're liable to charge him double and he wouldn't know the difference, Aussie quids not bein' the same as English quids. Did you change your money over yet?"

"In Singapore."

"Want me to book you in, then?"

"If you like, yes, thank you."

"A bloke needs a mate in a hurry sometimes."

"Indeed."

It was not until the evening, which came spilling from the sky with a swiftness Clive still was unused to, that he learned Doug had arranged for a double room, with himself as tenant of the second bed. But by then Clive was too tired to question anything his guide saw fit to set up on his behalf, and approached his bed with a yearning for its softness that saw even the draped mosquito netting as a romantic prop. He was in the antipodes, the other end of the world, and he must adapt to its peculiarities if he was ever to find success there.

2

CLIVE AWOKE TO FIND his new friend snoring freely, still
dressed, lying with his head at the foot of the bed, his boots
gracing the pillow. It would have been unkind to disturb Doug
while he was in such deep repose, so Clive dressed and went
down to the street, too hung over to seek breakfast as yet, but
fit enough to explore the town.

Wandering up one street and down the next, moving farther
from the harbour, Clive found that Darwin was not so rudi-
mentary an outpost as he had thought. Many of the houses,
bungalows for the most part, were brightly painted, and any
dwelling with a yard was partially hidden by the fantastic plant
life there. Darwinites were more proud of their gardens, it
seemed, than of their homes. The palm, in all its varieties of
frond and bole, was everywhere, and larger yards were overshadowed by huge banyan trees, every bit as venerable and
dignified as English oaks. There were brilliant patches of purple bougainvillea and jacaranda, a myriad of creeping vines, all
in splendid flower, and any number of strange shrubs that
defied Clive's meagre knowledge of botany. The houses themselves were without pretension, boxes with rooves of tin, nothing more, despite their coats of paint; places in which to shelter
from the elements. Their windows were plentiful, equipped
with tilting panes to allow free passage of air, and always
fronted by fine wire mesh to keep out insects. Clive saw no
neat floral beds, no constricted window boxes or potted plants
lurking behind windows; anything that grew did so outdoors,
across as wide an area as it could creep or spread, and the
heavy perfume drifting into his lungs made Clive a little sick.

Doug had talked the night before of Darwin's exclusivity in

the Territory, its claim to importance as the sole deep-water port, its pride in the longest wharf in the north, and its heterogeneous population of races, the thing that, above all else, made Darwin what it was: "a humdinger of a place, bit of everythin' thrown in." There were lesser towns to the south, Doug admitted, but none was more than "a flyspeck" until a traveler should reach Alice Springs, "the Alice," six hundred miles away. The country between the coast and the interior was deemed by Doug to be "a big red desert, and it's worse on the other side of Alice, a thousand miles a nothin' straight down till you get to the ocean. You'd have to be an Abo to like it." By this and other comments, Clive had been made aware that the great Australian emptiness began, abruptly and without restraint, where the streets of Darwin ended.

He returned to the hotel and found his room untenanted. An enquiry at the desk led him to a nearby restaurant, where Doug sat feasting on steak, eggs, bacon, and chips, a meal that caused Clive's diminishing queasiness to return. He ordered toast for himself, and a cup of tea.

"Hardly enough to keep you goin'," was Doug's observation.

"I really couldn't manage any more than this."

"Been walkabout?"

"Yes. Darwin's quite a pleasant town, if you look closely."

"You bet it is. Got the nags all set for us, just down the street."

"Nags? Oh, yes, for the trip."

Clive found himself wishing he had opted for a truck instead, but was disinclined to talk of it, given Doug's effort in making the arrangements.

Clive had not ridden since childhood, and that had been twice around a tiny pen on the back of a docile pony led by a fairground lad. The horses Doug had hired seemed intimidatingly tall and rangy to Clive, but he mounted on the third attempt, and they set off with a packhorse in tow. Doug had purchased supplies for the trip by establishing an account on Clive's behalf at a store on Smith Street. It was easier, allowing himself to be directed by Doug Farrands, then to be obliged by his own ignorance to make clumsy attempts at organising himself and his needs.

"Coulda got a truck if I asked around a bit," said Doug,

"but the track's a bit rough out to Redlands. It was the last time I went, anyway. Nags are better in the bush, in any case. No need to change their wheels, eh?"

"I prefer it this way, really. Were you there often?"

"Nah, just now and then. Old Perce's second lubra was related to a friend a mine, so I'd stop in now and again just to see how things were goin'."

"You have Aboriginal friends?"

"Yeah, one or two."

"Do they work on the pearling boats?"

"The owners want Japs and Malays mostly. They're more reliable. They only hire whites to open the oysters, though. They don't trust anyone but a white man not to palm the pearls. Bloody silly if you ask me. Whites aren't any more honest than anyone else. I can't say that out loud, or I'd be out of a job. I'm on the *Irish Rose* this season, not a bad place to be. She's in dry dock for a bent propeller shaft repair job, or I wouldn't be takin' you out to see the sights like this."

"I don't want you to put yourself in any kind of jeopardy regarding your job, not for me."

"Arr, they'll be bangin' the shaft around another few days yet. Know what bent it? A bloody whale."

"No, really?"

"They come up real close, some a them, like they think a pearling lugger's another whale, and they can bugger the hull if you don't bang pots and pans to frighten 'em away, or else they get their flukes caught in the air lines and drag a diver this way and that, then pull the lines right outa the helmet without meaning to. Seen that happen a coupla times."

"What happens to the diver?"

"He drowns if his lifeline's been cut as well as the air. Can't pull him up again, see. Nothin' you can do. Those Japs are brave little bastards. I wouldn't be a diver for quids."

The country beyond Darwin was red, the color of bricks at sunset, the red of dried blood, redder than earth had any natural right to be, in Clive's opinion. There was very little undergrowth, and the trees were spaced some distance apart, as if unwilling to encroach upon their neighbours. They were gum trees for the most part, their trunks pale and smooth beneath sections of darker bark in a perpetual state of being shed like snakeskins, to lie in brittle heaps upon the ground. Their foliage of elongated leaves rustled very little, since there was not the slightest breeze, once the sea was a mile or so behind the travelers, and these forlorn clusters rang with the various cries of birds so well camouflaged Clive could not see them. In between the gum trees, equally well spaced, each from the other, were tall plants of spindly appearance, terminating in fronds that drooped every bit as much as the boughs of gum leaves overarching them. Doug said these were sand palms or pandanus palms; he had heard them referred to by both names and seemed disinterested in the finer points of botany.

The impression Clive received, as they proceeded along the track, was of a forest that could not make the effort to become thickly mysterious, that wished to conceal no secrets behind its endless repetition of itself, gum tree after sand palm after gum tree, to a point where the eye could no longer discern the interstices between them. It was a disquieting place, the loudest noise a constant droning of flies, millions of them, it seemed, all intent on penetrating the eyes and nostrils of horses and riders. They were a permanent hovering cloud that reduced conversation to the barest minimum, since there was the very real possibility of swallowing several of these buzzing, insistent nuisances in the passing of just a word or two. Such intense proliferation of so common a life form shocked Clive as no amount of twining boa constrictors, had he seen any, would have done.

He had, he supposed, been expecting some kind of jungle this close to the tropic of Capricorn, but the blunt Australian word "bush" best served to describe the dreary sameness of what he saw. Uninspiring, seeming to drowse beneath the sun, it was a place of continual self-replication. Whichever way Clive turned in his saddle, the view was the same, and he came to understand, without any advice from Doug Farrands, that a man straying from the track would become disoriented almost immediately, surrounded as he was by a mirror image of tree upon identical tree. It was, in its unprepossessing way, a landscape of insidious threat. He told himself he must be on his guard against its appearance of blandness, the half-awake menace of its tall and slender trees with their invisible birds, the choking miasma of flies, and the heat that rose around him like the breath from an opened oven.

They dismounted at noon to eat, an occasion for much frustration, since flies insisted on accompanying food into the mouths of both men. "You've gotta slip it in fast," Doug advised, "and do a quick spin at the same time. Throws the little buggers off when you do that."

Clive did as he was told, pirouetting full circle several times while shoving bread and cold meat between his teeth. The stratagem seemed partially successful, and he was about to spin again when he saw Doug laughing silently. Clive felt himself flush to a shade even darker than the heat and his exertions had already made him.

"Nobody does this really, do they?"

"Well, no," Doug admitted, "but it was worth a try, I reckon. If it hadda worked, you coulda told everyone you invented it." Noting the bleakness of his friend's expression, Doug added lamely, "You've gotta have some fun out here, or you'll kill yourself."

"Does it have to be fun at someone else's expense?"

"Fair go, Clive. It's not like anyone's watchin'."

"I believe I'm ready to ride on now."

"No hurry. Your uncle's place'll still be there."

"It's *my* place now, whatever its condition, which I doubt is anywhere near as bad as you've tried to make out."

"No need to get cranky."

"Redlands belongs to me."

"No one said it doesn't, mate."

"You've tried to make me believe it isn't even worth looking at ever since I bumped into you. Are you working for someone who wants the property? Has someone discovered gold there?"

"Gold! Christ, Clive, I reckon the sun's done you in. There's nothin' at Redlands you'd wanna look at twice, and that's dinkum."

"I'll make up my own mind. You don't need to take me there if you don't want to. Is this track the one I follow all the way?"

"There's a coupla turns here and there. Better stick with me, Clive. I couldn't handle me conscience if you got lost or snakebit or somethin'."

"I won't do either of those things. You seem to think I'm a complete idiot because I'm English. Try and imagine how you might feel in the middle of London."

Doug shook his head and turned to the horses. He mounted and began ambling in the direction they had been following all morning, and soon passed from sight around a curve in the track. Clive waited for several minutes, listening to the harsh and continual screeching of cicadas in the bush. When he was satisfied his point was made, he struggled onto his horse and rode after Doug, but not so quickly there was any chance of catching up with him too soon.

It had not been made clear to Clive exactly how far from Darwin his new estate lay. As the sun began sliding behind the trees and shadows lengthened, he felt the first stirrings of doubt. Doug Farrands was twenty yards ahead and had not turned once during the long afternoon to see if Clive was still behind him. The behaviour of both men struck Clive now as childish. His hope, when sailing away from England's shore and the dreary grammar school to which he had lost a small portion of his soul over the years, had been never again to witness the pigheaded truculence of children. They both had behaved badly, and the situation should not be allowed to endure a moment longer.

He hurried his mount along and caught up with Doug as a flock of several thousand black cockatoos passed screaming above the treetops, then wheeled as one to select boughs and branches for the approaching night. "Much further?" he asked, as if these casual words were not the first he had spoken in over six hours.

"Won't get there tonight," Doug told him, accepting the offer of friendship again. "Be sometime tomorrer, probly in the afternoon. Ready for camp and some tucker?"

"Rather."

"Here's as good a place as any, I reckon."

Clive participated in the gathering of wood for a fire, but left to Doug's experienced hands the arranging of sticks jammed into the ground to support two mosquito nets. "Careful when you get under this," he was warned, "or it'll come down on toppa you and the mozzies'll drain you dry before you can set it up again."

"I'll slide in like a shadow."

Doug produced sausages from the bag of supplies. "Better eat these before they go off. After this it's tinned stuff and damper till we get back."

"Damper?"

"Flour and water. Tastier 'n it sounds."

"Won't there be anything at Redlands—garden vegetables perhaps?"

Doug laughed. "Clive, you're a funny bugger, all right. Veg-gies . . . " He thrust sticks inside two sausages and handed one to Clive. The sunlight was almost gone by then, and the first hummings of mosquitoes drawn to the rich smell of human skin could be detected in the vicinity of the ears, the first subtle prickings felt along exposed forearms and around the neck and throat. Clive slapped and swatted with mounting annoyance.

"Come around this side a the fire," Doug advised. "They don't like the smoke."

The sausages spat and hissed, then were eaten with many indrawn breaths to cool the meat. "A banger isn't quite a banger without mash," Clive complained.

"Shoulda spoke up sooner. There's spuds in the tucker bag too. Dunno how you'd mash 'em, though. I was gunna chuck 'em in the coals later."

"Fine." Clive slapped himself across the cheek. "The smoke isn't working."

"What you need to do is tobaccer. Cigarette smoke puts 'em off more'n wood smoke. Ever done the deed with lady nicotine, Clive?"

"My father gave me his pipe to smoke once. It made me vomit."

"Bugger a pipe. I'll make us both roll-ups, and we can blow it down the mozzies' throats, make the shitty little bastards cough, eh."

Clive watched as Doug's fingers assembled, as if by sleight of hand, two slim paper tubes crammed with the pungent brown stuff from Doug's leather tobacco pouch.

"There y'are, good as a ready-made any day. Put it between your lips and suck, as the bishop said to the actress."

Clive accepted the cigarette and tipped his head toward the burning twig offered by Doug. The aroma of burning leaf was more pleasant than the acrid taste of it once he drew smoke inside his mouth. His lungs welled up in protest, and breath exploded from him in a series of hacking coughs.

"Just blow it out again if you can't keep it down. It's for the mozzies' benefit mainly. Garn, have another go at it. Take little puffs."

Clive achieved moderate success before long, despite his streaming cheeks and the fire in his chest, but the mosquitoes continued to plague him.

"They know you're a beginner, Clive. You'll need to practice. Ready for another dick on a stick?"

"Please . . . ," croaked Clive.

At the end of the meal, Doug rolled more cigarettes. This time Clive took occasional swigs from his canteen while he smoked, and soon, by squinting his eyes almost shut, he was able to surround his head with a cloud that did indeed seem to lessen the maraudings after his blood.

"Are those some kind of night birds I keep seeing?"

Swift patches of darkness were flitting among the white trunks of gum trees that surrounded the fire like frozen spirits.

"Flyin' foxes."

"Foxes? Are you sure you don't mean flying pigs? Or pink elephants?"

"They're bats, big ones. Got a long furry face like a fox. Country round here's swarmin' with 'em. Harmless."

They threw their stubs into the fire together.

"You'll have to teach me how to roll a smoke, Doug."

"Right-oh. You'll pick it up quick as a wink."

The coals were embedded with potatoes. Clive felt surprisingly hungry still.

"Do we have butter?"

"Nah. It woulda turned to python piss before lunch. Have to have your spuds without. You're in the bush now, mate."

"Do we . . . is there any toilet paper?"

"Toilet paper! Jeez, Clive, we haven't even got a bloody newspaper to read while you're droppin' anchor."

"Well . . . what do I use?"

"Dunno. Might have to be the five-pronged bum scrubber God gave you."

"You're joking, aren't you?"

"That's how they take care of it in other places. Mohammedans, they use their left hand for nothin' else. Makes 'em keep their nails trimmed."

"But . . . isn't there some kind of grass I could use? There has to be grass!"

"Plenty a sword grass round, I spose. Wouldn't recommend it for arse wiping, though. Liable to cut yourself a second crack that way, mate."

"Well then . . . what?"

"Clive, you're lucky you came out here with a pal. Take a dekko in the sack."

A roll of toilet paper was produced. Clive was absurdly grateful. He stood and began walking away from the firelight, followed by advice from Doug not to park his bum on a bull ant's nest, nor to step on a death adder.

When Clive returned, the potatoes were dug from their bed of embers and split open, the steaming paste inside scooped out with spoons. "This is . . . bloody good," said Clive, testing the waters of the vernacular.

"Too right it's bloody good. I'd call it bloody bloody good."

"Do all Australians eat like this?"

"Only the bushies. Down Sydney and Melbourne way, the nobs eat fish eggs and hummingbird cocks, stuff like that."

"I'm sure."

"I heard about a bloke that ordered a meal in a Swanson Street restaurant and got shitty when they said they never had any fresh lark's balls. He went away happy, though. They wouldn't let him leave till they dished him up a big helpin' a fried kidneys, the chef's specialty, they said."

"What's so startling about that?"

"The poor bloody chef had to operate on himself with a coupla dull spoons and a bent fork to get 'em!"

Clive nodded slowly. "I see."

"No need to laugh or anythin'."

"I suppose not."

"Crikey, don't you Poms appreciate a joke when you hear one?"

"When we hear one, yes."

"Wait till you have a go. See if I laugh."

Third and final smokes were lit from a fire now little more than glowing coals. The moon was near full, its light making the gums whiter than they had been by firelight. Watching the sky, Clive asked, "Where's the Southern Cross?"

"Over there—see it?"

The crooked cross of the antipodes winked and glimmered above them.

"Ah, yes. Someone pointed it out to me aboard ship after we left Singapore. It's brighter down here. Really, it's rather beautiful."

"That's why it's on the flag. Should be all that's on the flag. The guverment oughta get ridda that bloody Union Jack stuck up in the corner like somebody's nose rag. Nothin' personal, Clive, I just don't like to see a chunka some other country's flag takin' up space on ours."

"I suppose it's there for historical reasons, the founding of the colony by Britain, et cetera . . . "

"Like buggery it is! It's there to make us feel like they own us!"

"Oh, I don't think so, not in the way you mean. . . ."

"Exactly that bloody way! We oughta rip that Union Jack outa the Aussie flag and chuck it back across the water where it belongs. The Southern Cross, pure and simple—that's all we need."

"Well, yes, I can see your argument."

"No more bendin' over backwards for Mother England is what I mean. We've done enough a that. Me dad got blown to bits in France for king and country. What the fuck's France got to do with us, eh? England wants to fight Germans, right-oh, go and fight the bastards, but leave us out of it. He never shoulda signed up and gone over there. None of 'em should, not back then and never again, by Jeez, I don't care if that bastard Hitler wants to fight the bloody war all over again. It's got nothin' to do with us!"

Clive said nothing, made uncomfortable by such raw feeling.

"Sorry, mate." Doug smiled. "Got carried away. Dong me on the head if I do that again."

"The news in Singapore was that Hitler isn't really as much of a bully as he sounds. He's just a windbag who likes the attention he gets. Another European war is unthinkable. Everyone learned that lesson from the last one, I'm sure."

"Hope so."

"I believe I'm ready for some kip."

"What's kip?"

"Sleep."

"Yeah, me too, after I wave the wand."

Doug rose and urinated at the campsite's farthest edge, singing off-key while he did so. Clive carefully lifted the edge of his mosquito netting and wormed his way inside. The thin blanket beneath him did little to lessen his discomfort. He listened as Doug positioned himself beneath his own netting, some yards away. Clive was wearing what he had worn now for two days, including his underwear; a change of clothing lay in the customs shed back at Darwin. His entire body itched with sweat and insect bites, and the flesh of his buttocks and back already was sending signals of distress. He supposed he should have been unhappier than he actually felt, given the circumstances, and to distract himself from his various torments, Clive asked himself why this should be so. After ruling out the contentment of his stomach and his anticipation over at last seeing Redlands for himself the next day, he concluded that he felt as he did because he was that lucky man, the friend of a new friend.

"Good night, Doug."

A faint snoring came to him above the sounds of the bush. He tried to see the Southern Cross through the mosquito netting inches from his nose, but the gauze was of too dense a weave.

"How far now?"

It was already well past noon, long after the hour Doug had said would place them within sight of Redlands.

"Look down at your boots," said Doug.

Clive saw his reddened shoes, wholly unsuitable for riding, and the equally reddened iron of the stirrups. "Well?"

"You're lookin' at what's yours."

"Pardon me?"

"The ground under you, that's Redlands."

"This? Here?"

"That there. I reckon we crossed the boundary 'bout a half hour ago. Should be comin' up on the place pretty soon."

"Wonderful!"

"Yeah, well, save your wonderfuls till you get an eyeful. It's not Buckin'ham Palace, mate, believe me."

The landscape was subtly altered from that which they had ridden through the day before. The gum trees had thinned, and the sand palms, and the earth between those that remained was redder, Clive reasoned, because there was less detritus fallen onto it from fewer trees. It did indeed seem to be a red land, much more so than before, and he felt his heart quicken. The area ahead was visible now, a sudden opening-out of the bush, and then the trees ended. Both men stopped their horses. A plain of brownish grass stretched before them for a mile or more, before surrendering to a further line of gum trees. Sensing that this was a moment of some significance, Clive turned to Doug.

"All this here," said Doug, "if Perce had've been as smart as he thought he was, it'd be rice, not bull grass. This is all dead stuff. Come the Wet, it'll be six, eight foot tall. Practically need a bloody scythe to get through it."

"This is where the rice should be?"

"Everyone told him how it'd be—too wet in the Wet and too dry in the Dry. He tried building mud walls to hold the water after the rains stopped comin', but it all just evaporated, the little bit he managed to save, and when the rains came back they swept everythin' away in about two minutes. It's a floodplain, that's the official name for it. You can't grow crops in a place like this. Everyone told him."

"I'd like to see the house."

"That's about all that's left to show you Perce was ever here."

The track they had been following for most of the day, a barely discernible set of wheel ruts worn into the earth, led them across the flat plain and around a promontory of trees intruding upon it, then aimed itself again among the whitened trunks and the forest floor of twisted bark. A dark-brown wallaby—the thirty-seventh they had seen since their journey began, by Clive's reckoning—watched them pass by without exhibiting the least fear. Clive felt anticipation rising in him, but it was not as satisfying a sensation as he had expected. They rode through a broad clearing dotted with fifteen-foot-high termite mounds, granular eructations of orange-red, their weathered crenellations and spires pointing toward the sun. Clive thought of Crusader castles subjected to a million years of aging, and felt a kind of depression begin to settle around his shoulders. This place had been ancient before his uncle arrived, with his plans for scientific farming and material success, and would be in existence, Clive was sure, centuries hence, utterly unchanged.

"There y'are."

A low ridge of red sandstone rose beyond the trees. The horses splashed across a shallow stream and up the far bank. "Flyin' Fox River," Doug said. "Doesn't look like much for now, but when the Wet comes, it runs like a bastard clear through to Van Diemen Gulf, straight north." They passed through some undergrowth made thicker by its proximity to year-round water, and Clive was at last able to see what it was he had been granted by death in the family.

The single-storey house had been built on top of the sandstone ridge, on a broad flattened section much bigger than the dwelling itself. "Floodwaters won't come up this high," Doug said. The roof was of unpainted corrugated iron, its reddish hue the result of rust and neglect; the walls were of identical material, likewise eaten by tropical rains and sun, and contained not one window that Clive could see. His heart sank. He turned to Doug, who was watching for his reaction.

"It's . . . a tin shed."

"Told you, mate."

"It doesn't even have windows. . . ."

"Don't need 'em, really. Got your air gap along under the roof. Goes all the way round, see."

Between the tops of the walls and the rusting eaves, lost in blackest shadow until squinted at, was a space of some eighteen inches, covered by fine wire mesh. Fresh air and light could penetrate within, while insects, at least those too large to wriggle through the wire screen, could not. It was a practical arrangement, Clive supposed, but its aesthetic shortcomings predominated in his mind.

They rode closer, the horses following a well-worn path to the area of beaten red earth before the door, which might have been termed a yard. The door itself was corrugated iron, punctured by several bullet holes, as were the walls, Clive saw, now that he was closer.

"Was the place attacked?"

"Perce did that himself, probly, kinda like kickin' the dog when you're in a shitty mood, y'know."

"Shoot his own house?"

"Probly happened in the last Wet. Pretty normal behaviour. Knew one bloke chopped up his kitchen table with an axe, then he tried the same thing with his missus, but she shot through. Last he ever saw of her. Think she went walkabout with some of the rellies."

"Rellies?"

"Relatives. She was an Abo. This bloke I'm talkin' about was a combo."

"I'm sorry? Combo?"

"White fella with a black gin, like Perce was, and plenty more round here. Might wind up that way yourself, Clive."

They dismounted. "There's a bit of a stockyard around the corner," Doug said. "I'll put the nags in. You take a dekko inside. Watch where you step—might be snakes in there since Perce vacated the premises."

Clive approached the door and lifted a metal latch. The corrugated sheet swung out on creaking leather hinges, revealing another door behind it, this one of fly-wire mesh. He pushed it open and went inside. The house consisted of just one room, without dividers of any kind. The floor was earth. There was not a single stick of furniture. Clive stared at the enclosed space, which was lit from all four sides by the gap between roof and walls. There was in the air an odour of liquor and sweat and something else, an almost palpable taste of what Clive interpreted, given his disappointment, as despair. This was his inheritance, bestowed on him by a man he had never met, an Englishman who had not seen England in thirty years. Was it a joke of some kind, an acknowledgment that Percy was unable, as a representative of civilisation, to alter in any way the place he had come to civilise? Passing on a tin shed and unusable land to a nephew could be interpreted only as an exercise in wry malice, unless the man had become deranged before he died. Clive did not know if the will had been made early on, while Percy presumably entertained high hopes for Redlands, or later, after it had become clear the enterprise could never be anything but a failure, like the man himself.

Doug came inside. "Home sweet home, eh?"

"No snakes," was all Clive could say.

"Coulda been worse. Bugger-all flies too. I think Perce

musta put a few quid into new fly wire before he finished himself. Place doesn't look too bad at all."

"There's nothing here. . . ."

"Musta had visitors. Stuff left lyin' around in a place with no locks, it's like a nice fresh turd for flies. Course, he mighta taken it out and burned it all himself—you never know. A bloke'll do funny things when he's made up his mind to end it all."

"I can't possibly . . . *do* anything here."

"Could run a few head a cattle if you wanted to. There's permanent water pretty much all through the Dry. You'd lose a lot of 'em to Blighty, though."

"Blighty? Is it a disease of some kind?"

"More like a pest. He's a fuckin' big croc that lives round here. Perce tried a coupla times to shoot him, but Blighty's a hard bastard to do in. The Abos reckon he's a spirit croc or somethin', because he's never taken one a them but he's croaked half a dozen white blokes. Just coincidence, I reckon. He's a big bastard, though, twenty-five-footer at least, about as big as they come. Saw him meself for about two seconds a coupla years ago. Looked like a railway engine someone left on the riverbank. I took a potshot at him but I missed, and he was off the mud and into the water like a rocket. Yeah, maybe you oughta forget the cattle too."

"Then what have I got? Why did I come all this way?"

Doug raised his shoulders. "Bit of a bloody cruel trick Perce pulled on you, if you ask me. Like I told you, mate, it's good for nothin', basically."

Clive went to a slender metal beam supporting one corner of the house and idly scratched rust from it. "Why is everything made of iron? Wouldn't it have been easier to chop down trees and build a timber house?"

"White ants."

"White ants?"

"Termites. They eat anythin' that's made outa wood. Give 'em enough time, and they'll eat a place down to nothin'."

"I don't have any money left."

"What, no cash?"

"Nothing. I couldn't even begin setting Redlands to rights if I wanted to, assuming I could think of a reason to live here."

"'Bout the only reason for doin' that'd be you wouldn't

need to pay rent. Perce owned the place outright. Musta had a few quid on him when he came up north."

Clive turned abruptly and went outside. Doug followed, and together they stared from their low elevation across the treetops to the floodplain beyond.

"Have I seen everything, all the land?"

"Nah, not by half. It's all the same, though, mostly scrub and bull grass. I can show you the rest if you want. Perce rode me along the boundaries a long while ago."

They began walking around to the stock pen for the horses.

"You seem to have had quite a bit to do with Uncle Percy," Clive said.

"Well, it's like I told you—Perce's second lubra was half-sister to someone I knew. Abos like to keep in touch with all their family, even if they're scattered around like leaves, so every once in a while I'd bring Mandy out to have a chinwag with Beth. That's their white names. Couldn't pronounce their Abo names."

"This woman you knew was . . . Beth's half-sister."

"That's right. I can hear your brain tickin' over, Clive. Yeah, Mandy was half-caste. She was me missus without benefit of clergy, like they say. Yeah, I'm a combo, just like Perce, or was. She's dead now, Mandy. She was a bonzer girl, I don't mind sayin'. We had a kid too, a little yella-fella. That's what they call a bloke with a touch a the tarbrush. Beaut kid; called him Brian. Still bump into him now and then. See these posts?"

They were standing by the pen. Doug crumbled flakes of rotten wood from the fence posts. "That's what your white ant does."

"May I ask how Mandy came to die?"

"Arr, she went back to the tribe to go walkabout, and there was a fella claimed she was his, Abo fella, and he kicked up a fuss when she turned him down. A lot a the young girls get promised in marriage when they're still little tykes—it's a tribal custom, see—and Mandy had got away from the bloke she'd been promised to for years, while she was with me, but when she went back with her own people this joker turns up outa the blue and says it's time she made herself available. She told him to bugger off and he kidnapped her along with a coupla pals of his, and they took her off into the bush. They musta been pretty hard on her, turned her mind or something, because she disappeared for a few years up into Arnhem Land. That's east of here, real rugged country, no whites at all there. I was away at sea when this was happenin', so it took a coupla months for me to find out. The police wouldn't do anythin', seein' as she was an Abo. Strictly tribal business, according to them. I didn't hear anythin' more for about three years, then I heard she was back round Darwin way, but when I found her she was a different person, gone in the head, drinkin' booze, just a completely different girl, looked about twenty years older too. She reckernised me, but she wouldn't let me touch her. Jeez, it was bad, what happened. After that she drank herself to death. Just as well Brian got left behind."

"Does he live with you?"

"Nah, with rellies, down Katherine way, that's south a here. The government wanted to put him in a mission school, but I sneaked him away. They like to take as many half-castes as they can lay hands on and stick 'em in those places so they start spoutin' hymns and turnin' their backs on their own kind. I wasn't havin' any a that bullshit, so I sent Brian away with Mandy's tribe. They've brought him up their way, sort of. None a the blacks live like they used to anymore. We've pretty much buggered 'em up, but anyway, I'd rather have the boy livin' out in the desert on kangaroo and goannas than carryin' a Bible. He's better off where he is, I reckon. Course, there's some who'd disagree about that, but I don't lose sleep over it."

"You didn't want to raise him yourself?"

"Come off it, Clive. I haven't even got a bloody house, and never have. Fact is, I'm a bit of a no-hoper. Bit a pearlin' for half the year, and bugger-all for the rest. You're not lookin' at one a the Territory's best citizens, mate, I don't mind sayin'."

"I'm not criticising you."

"I know that. No harm done."

"Shall we make an inspection of the property?"

"Nothin' else to do while we're here."

They untied the horses, mounted, and rode away.

Doug had not exaggerated the sameness of the country around the house. For mile after mile they rode, circling and returning to the central point of the sandstone ridge. Only two features of note roused Clive from his general silence. The first was a scattering of termite mounds, which unlike those already seen, were neither red nor bulky. They were of grey soil, never more than a yard across at their base, tapering to a knife-blade thinness at the tops, some feet above the heads of the mounted men; and every mound faced in the same direction, like a collection of gigantic, illegible gravestones.

"Magnetic termites," Doug explained. "They always build on a north-south line, so their mounds don't cop too much sun through the hottest part a the day. Clever little buggers. Handy things to find if you're lost in the bush without a compass."

The second feature was Blighty's Pond, so termed by Percy, according to Doug. It lay a half mile or so from the house and was perhaps fifty feet across and twice that in length. "When the Wet comes it'll be part a the river again. They say Blighty never leaves it unless the Dry's so bad his pond gets down to a coupla inches. Crocs can migrate overland if they have to. They'll go as far as the sea to get enough water for a splash and a kill."

"But he's in there now?"

"I dunno. Go for a paddle and find out, eh."

"No, thank you."

They watched the pond's dark surface, made darker along its margins by overhanging trees. Not the slightest ripple disturbed its placid calm. Doug rolled smokes for them both. A jabiru swooped down and began daintily to wade through the shallows, extending its long neck and beak to stab at the bottom. "He's askin' for trouble doin' that," said Doug. "Blighty doesn't like anyone else fishin' his billabong."

Clive waited with some excitement for the sudden flurry of foam, the lightning-fast attack of the behemoth, but the jabiru continued to wade and lunge as before.

"Could be Blighty's already had his lunch."

"Speaking of which, we seem to have neglected food today."

"Yeah, time to boil the billy."

While they built a fire, Clive asked himself what possible use his property might serve, now that he understood its limitations. He could think of nothing. Had a notion come to him, he could not afford to implement it in any case. On the voyage from England his plans had been vague, since he was unsure what type of farm it might be that he was inheriting, but there had always been the certainty of success. Now there was nothing. The one bright spot in his new gloom, Clive saw, was the unlikely friendship he had formed with Doug Farrands. If they had not met on the wharf, everything that he had discovered since then would have been rendered so much darker.

"Doug, why were you on the wharf two days ago?"

"Flies. The further you get from land, the less they bother you. 'Bout halfway out along the wharf's where they start leavin' you alone."

So his good fortune in the midst of discouragement, Clive learned, was the work of flies. "What's the joke?" asked Doug.

"There isn't one."

"Used to know a bloke made a habit a standin' there with a big grin on his face when there wasn't anythin' to grin about. Very successful he was at it too. They promoted him to the laughing academy, last I heard."

"I need to find a job. I have to."

"They've got a school in Darwin. Might get a job there."

"I will never, never again teach a class. I'll dig ditches before I set foot inside another school."

"Bit of a crook job, was it?"

"Do you know what the little shits used to call me, to my face? Not Mr. Bagnall; oh, no. Baggers."

"Baggers? Doesn't sound too bad. Coulda been shithead or somethin' worse. I reckon you're too sensitive, Clive. Baggers, I mean."

"Never again."

"Diggin' ditches'd kill you in this heat. Better look for somethin' else."

Clive watched the jabiru lift a wriggling frog from the water, toss it into the air, and gulp it down when it fell. He was positive he could see a distinct bulge moving down the jabiru's long and slender neck. "I'm not giving up on Redlands, you understand. I just don't quite know what to do with it at the moment. Some scheme might occur to me later, but I have to eat in the meantime, that's all."

He turned to Doug, who was setting the billy can onto the fire. "You said you might be able to get me a job on a pearling lugger. Were you serious?"

"Might be possible. You never know."

"I wouldn't have any difficulty cutting oysters open and looking for pearls. You could show me the technique."

"Yeah, I could do that."

"A life on the ocean wave! It'd be terrific, I should think!"

"Might not think so for long."

"Let's start back for Darwin as soon as we've had some grub."

"You don't wanna spend the night in the ancestral bloody home? Jeez, Clive, I thought you Pommies were supposed to be traditional-minded."

"I'd like to see one more thing before we go—Percy's grave."

"Arr, bit difficult, that, mate."

"You don't know where it is? Who buried him?"

"Well, some a the Abos that worked for him slung him over a horse and got ready to take him into Darwin. They knew they woulda got into trouble if they hadda just buried him right where he fell. Nobody believes a bloody word Abos say, mostly, even if they don't tell any more lies than white buggers. Anyway, they got him down to the river and were halfway across—this is durin' the Wet, y'understand, and the water was a bit high, and the knots weren't exactly seamen's knots or anythin'—and he came off the horse. Got swept away in about five seconds flat. The river went down again a coupla days later, and some joker spotted Perce 'bout nine mile downstream, so he's the one that convinced the coppers it was a shotgun that did him in, not anythin' the Abos said, but anyway, this bloke didn't bother pullin' old Perce too far up onto the bank right away, stopped to boil the billy or somethin', and when he turned around, the body's gone."

"Rising waters?"

"Hungry croc. Probly Blighty snuck up and took him. He'd a been ripe enough for a croc to eat by then, I reckon. The joker said there was big tracks all over the place. Flyin' Fox River's pretty much Blighty's backyard all the way through to the gulf."

"Good God."

"Yeah, so you can't put daisies on his grave or anythin'."

Clive turned to the pond, half expecting the jabiru to be gone, with perhaps a feather or two floating at the center of silently widening ripples, but the tall bird hunted as before, ignoring the presence of men and crocodile alike.

3

ON HIS SECOND ARRIVAL IN DARWIN, this time from the direction of the bush, Clive was more aware than on the first occasion of the number of Aborigines on the streets. None of them seemed to be engaged in any business that did not involve leaning against walls in whatever shade presented itself, but Clive was not prepared to dismiss them as idle, since a number of white men were similarly occupied doing nothing.

The visit to Redlands had not quenched his spirits overmuch, since the inland dream was now supplanted by one equally vivid: a maritime dream, built around the little Doug had told him of the Japanese and their expertise, and snippets of remembrance from Joseph Conrad and *Boys' Own Paper*. Clive was convinced his temporary calling to the sea would be fraught with adventure and romance, despite Doug's warnings to the contrary.

"It's bloody hard yakka, mate. You'll stink like a dead fish before too long."

"I don't have any choice," Clive reminded him.

"Go and ask 'em at the school, that's my advice."

"That's no choice at all. It's pearling or nothing."

"I'll do me best to get the both of us aboard the *Irish Rose*. You say you haven't got any quids left, Clive?"

"A few shillings, that's all."

"Bit of a problem, that. We have to pay up for the supplies, plus there's the bill at the Vic to settle."

"Can't it wait until we get back to port?"

"Pearlers pay up before they leave. They might not come back, see. Typhoons and that."

"Oh, yes, of course. Well, what shall we do?"

"Negotiate with the owner and see if he won't pay off for us in advance. His name's Moxham. Not too much of a shit for a rich bloke. He's got ten luggers and a pearl shell schooner, all bought and paid for. He knows me, knows I'm good for the work. Might have trouble about you, though."

"Assure him I'm good for the work also."

"Worth a try, I spose."

The horses were returned to their owner, then Clive followed Doug to a squalid office in what was termed the White end of Cavenagh Street, although the building was close to the Chinese end.

"Chinks've been here since the gold rush days," Doug explained. "The Malays and Japs stay on their boats most a the time, except when they come ashore for booze and women and a bitta gamblin'. Mad keen gamblers, the lotta them. Wait here a tick."

Doug asked a white clerk if the boss was in, and was soon invited behind a closed door, while Clive sat in a rattan chair in the outer office of Moxham Ltd., under the disinterested eye of the clerk. Doug had been gone for some minutes when two large young men entered the office. Clive noted that the clerk, moments before almost asleep, was made instantly alert by the presence of these two.

"Old man in?" asked the first of them.

"Got Doug Farrands with him," said the clerk.

"Do-nothin' Doug," said the second, and both laughed. The clerk joined them out of politeness, or so it appeared to Clive.

"Who's this?" the first young man said, looking at Clive.

"Mate of Doug's," the clerk explained.

"The Pommie, eh?" said the second. "Are you the Pommie, mate?"

"Yes, I am. Clive Bagnall."

"Farrands tryin' to wheedle around the old man to getcha a job, is he?"

"I don't know about any wheedling," said Clive. "I've never heard the word before, as a matter of fact."

"Your mate Farrands is the biggest wheedler born," said the second young man. "Wheedlers have to wheedle 'cause they never hold a job for long, so then they have to wheedle around for some soft bugger to give 'em one."

"What's a Pommie like you want a job for anyway? You've got a big property with cattle runnin' all over it, haven't you?"

"Not quite."

"Not quite," mimicked the first, and they both laughed. The identical braying, rather than any close physical resemblance, made Clive realise he was being made fun of by brothers. He disliked them both intensely by then.

The door to the inner office opened, and Doug came out.

"G'day, you two," he addressed the brothers.

"Gettin' your mate a job?"

"Yeah."

"What's a Pom know about pearl shell?"

"Nothin' yet, but he'll learn. Clive, these two blokes are Ken and Les Moxham. You probly think they're rude bastards, and you're right."

"Bugger off, Farrands," said Ken.

The inner office door was opened by a large man of middle age, his head completely bald. "What are you two doing here?" he said. Clive thought at first that Moxham senior was addressing himself and Doug, but his eye was directed at his sons, both of whom had suddenly lost much of their bluster.

"Nothin'," said Les.

"That's what I thought. Get down to the wharf and get something useful done."

"Right-oh, Dad," Ken said.

"Farrands, what are you hangin' around here for? You've got the job, now stop clutterin' up my office. That the Pom?"

"That's him."

"Christ," said Moxham, and slammed his door shut again.

"Waiting for something, Farrands?" Ken's sneer lacked bite, so soon after a dressing-down from his father.

"Just goin', weren't we, Clive?"

"Yes, we were."

They walked to the door.

"Look at 'em," said Les. "Coupla poofters, I reckon."

They walked past the brothers and onto the street.

"What are poofters?" Clive asked.

"Blokes that fuck blokes."

"Oh."

"Those two are real pricks," said Doug. "They'll take over

the business when old man Moxham dies, and when that happens I'll have to get work somewhere else. They hate my guts,
especially Les."

"What for?"

"Arr, it goes back years. I won some money off him at two-
up, and he's the kinda bloke that thinks if he lost it's because
the other bloke cheated. You can't cheat at two-up, Clive—it's
just throwin' pennies in the air. Then I pinched a girlfriend a
his, real nice girl. That got him a bit shitty with me. Anyway,
bugger Les and Ken. The job's yours, workin' right along with
me. You're a bloody oyster opener, Clive, and don't go blamin'
me when you start howlin' about it."

"I shan't do any howling. What are the wages?"

"Never mind about that. Moxham's gunna take care a the
bills before we sail, and if we work like bastards there's gunna
be a bit left over when we come back."

"Thanks awfully, Doug."

"You dunno how awful yet."

The surprising part of his new life was that Clive did not once
experience seasickness. If he had, his misery would have been
complete. The *Irish Rose* was small and cramped, the food con-
sisting of variations on a staple of rice. The company aboard,
Doug expected, was beyond communication, since the Malay
seamen, all seven of them, spoke not a single word of English,
and the vessel's diver, a Japanese by the name of Ishi
Murikama, spoke a pidgin dialect only Doug seemed capable of
understanding. The captain was a Filipino named Diego, fluent
in Spanish and pidgin, and without any warmth for either of the
white men aboard, it seemed to Clive. Doug made it clear that
while only whites were trusted to open the oysters, darker races
were hired for all other tasks solely because they would work
for a fraction of what was typically demanded by whites.

"Charming system of business," observed Clive.

"The school's still there waitin' for you," said Doug.

Of all on board, Ishi Murikama was undoubtedly the most
important, but he did not strut or preen. His presence
reminded Clive of some Eastern monastic order devoted to
betterment through risky endeavor, if such a body existed. Ishi

was at all times serene, a kind of inner calm radiating from him in much the same fashion Clive expected would emanate from a priest of Buddha. Ishi was compact of form, his skin beautifully smooth, his features broadly handsome, the bristling hair across his cranium black as washed coal. His perfectly shaped nose and lips, and his widely spaced eyes, appealed to Clive's sense of the aesthetic. He was tremendously impressed by the diver's comportment, even though it was difficult to forget that even as the *Irish Rose* opened silken seas with her prow, Japanese forces were committing atrocities of a hideous nature in Manchuria and the eastern provinces of China.

"He seems a decent sort," Clive confided to Doug. "Rather noble, actually."

"Ishi's a bloody good Jap, even if he thinks he's a cut above the rest of us."

"Does he?"

Clive had never before considered that non-English races might consider themselves superior. He took himself silently to task for such thoughts and treated Ishi Murikama with the deference everyone else aboard seemed to agree was called for. It was intimidating, in a way, to be ignored by the crew as the lugger sailed north for the newest oyster beds of the Arafura Sea.

If the vessel itself was foul, the sea and air through which it moved were magical in their purity of colour, the limitless reaches of their mutual realms of blue. When the wind blew from the right quarter, it was possible to forget the unfamiliar odors of Oriental spices, the ubiquitous reek of human sweat, the ghosts of a million opened oysters, and the unspeakable stench of the crude hole aft, which all the crew were obliged to use. It puzzled Clive how something through which excrement and urine passed, but which did not gather these for collection or dissemination, could prove so offensive to his nose. The board with its hole was never smeared by any careless user, never moistened by anything but salt spray, so far as Clive could tell; but smell it did, unstintingly, and he hated to squat where so many others had before, to void himself into the deep.

But the sea and sky were sublime. He had not so far witnessed either in a state of turmoil, and knew himself to be in ignorance of their true natures. "You might upchuck like a good'n in a stiff blow," Doug warned, smiling.

"I think not."

"You never know, mate."

The weather was unchanged for three unclouded days, three starry nights of heart-stopping brilliance appreciated only by Clive. The rest of the crew, Doug included, spent the hours of darkness below, pursuing easy wealth from each other's pockets with the slapping down of ivory tiles bearing exotic symbols, a game beyond Clive's ability to understand. He supposed it was his Englishness that made him prey to natural beauty and the sights offered by aloneness under starlight, and did not regret that he strode the decks unaccompanied, almost resentful of the Malay helmsman's occasional hawking and spitting over the side.

Doug approached Clive after midnight. "Thinkin' poetical thoughts?"

"Not at all," said Clive, who had been indulging in exactly that. "Just appreciating the fresh air. Have you won anything?"

"Nah, lost again. I owe those buggers too much. You'd think I'd know better."

"When do we begin pearling?"

"Tomorrer. Got yourself all ready for it?"

"I'm quite prepared."

"Good-oh. Hope your hands are too."

The *Irish Rose* arrived at her destination on the fourth morning. The waters below the hull were of such startling clarity the seabed below was visible from the deck. "Ten fathoms," said Doug. "Looks more like ten feet, doesn't it?"

"It's remarkable. I can't see any oysters, though."

"They're down there, covered in barnacles and weed and that. Ishi'll see 'em easy when he gets down there."

The Japanese was preparing for his first descent, dressing his body in two complete sets of thick woolen underwear and three pairs of heavy socks reaching far above the knees. Warm leggings extending from ankles to armpits were secured by a drawstring, and a bulky woolen sweater was eased over all this. Then he was ready to be assisted by two Malays into the diving suit of rubberised canvas, with its tightly fitting rubber collar and cuffs. A heavy copper corselet was lowered onto his shoulders, surrounding his neck completely. Ishi's head was swathed in two woolen balaclavas, then the massive copper

helmet was fitted into place over the corselet, their matching
slots aligned and twisted together; then secured with butterfly
nuts. Large weights were slung on rope across his back and
chest, and the lifeline of thick rope was passed around the
diver's chest and back and tied under his left arm, so it would
not interfere with his movements. Huge iron-soled boots were
fitted over his feet and buckled. The diesel air pump was
started, and when air began flowing through the hose connected to the helmet, the face plate, freshly cleaned in vinegar
to prevent condensation, was rotated into its slots and fixed
there with more butterfly nuts.

Watching the operation from first to last, Clive was reminded
of a medieval knight being dressed for battle. Ishi Murikama
stood armoured against the cold he would find below, even in
tropical waters as shallow as these. He took his first awkward
step toward the ladder clamped to the vessel's side, turned, and
began descending to the last rung, several feet below the surface. When this was reached, he simply stepped off and fell
slowly through the water, trailing his air hose and lifeline and the
lesser rope attached to his wire collecting basket.

Clive watched the diver sinking straight down, the fore-
shortened figure obscured by a stream of bubbles rising from
his helmet valves. The lines snaking across the deck stopped
as Ishi reached bottom. Peering down, Clive saw him walking
laboriously across the sea floor, a shadowy figure stalked by
the larger shadow of the lugger itself. "We just drift along on
the tide," Doug explained, "and Ishi keeps up with us. If the
tide's runnin' too strong, we start up the engine and set the
screw in reverse to slow us up a bit. He'll stay down there six
or seven hours, probly, without a rest."

"He must have remarkable stamina."

"I reckon Ishi's a bit of a bloody marvel, meself."

The peculiarly bulbous figure below proceeded in what
appeared to be a continuous state of leaning forward from the
waist, his weighted feet barely managing to keep pace. Ishi
bent occasionally to pick something from the seabed and place
it in the basket trailing from his belt. Soon the basket rope
jerked twice.

"Up she comes," said Doug. The Malays pulled it quickly
to the surface and dumped twenty or so oysters onto the deck,

then sent it down again, its wire loop riding the lifeline directly back to Ishi.

"Our turn to earn a quid, mate. Just do what I do, only slower, or you'll lose a coupla fingers."

Clive imitated Doug with care, skewering the fleshy hinge of each oyster with the blade of his knife, separating the halves, and inspecting the jellylike mass within for a pearl before ripping it out to expose the gleaming mother-of-pearl inside the shell. Doug told him that very few shells contained pearls; nor was every shell lined with mother-of-pearl, as Clive soon learned. Those without the nacreous gleam within were thrown onto a separate pile, to be dumped overboard later on. Shells that gleamed in the sunlight mounted quickly behind the shellers, more quickly behind Doug than Clive, who soon was aware of salt stinging the many tiny abrasions in his palms caused by handling each oyster's rough exterior. He wished for gloves of some kind to ease his discomfort but was disinclined to ask.

"Your hands'll toughen up after a week or so," Doug advised.

"I'm all right. God, these things stink!"

"You'll get used to that too."

Clive doubted it, and began breathing through his mouth to spare his nose, then had to stop when his throat became dry. Basket after basket was pulled up from below and dumped onto the deck. Doug's blade seemed to fly in his hands, separating the halves and winkling out the living mass from inside. Clive worked steadily, his pace becoming slower as the first hour's work gave way to the second, then the third. As the fourth hour dragged to a close, he asked, "Don't we stop for lunch?"

"Lunch? No fear. We've gotta keep up with Ishi. He doesn't get any lunch down there, and the middle a the day's the best time for him—more sunlight comin' down and makin' it easier for him to see what he's doin'. Nah, we work straight through on this tub, mate. Shoulda told you that before, I spose."

Clive was shocked that such work as this was expected of him without even the benefit of a cup of tea, let alone something to eat. The pearl shell business was conducted in a setting of great beauty, but its true face was streaked with sweat. His head began to throb. His buttocks ached from the hard wood he sat upon to deal with the oysters, and his face, unshaved since he had come aboard, itched with stubble and peeling skin. His hands by now were in agony, bleeding a little over each new shell. Clive had not felt so miserable since he had been made to stand in a lightless broom cupboard for two hours for having broken his mother's most expensive vase, an object, he now recalled, with mermaids painted on it.

During a lull, when it seemed Ishi Murikama could locate no new oysters, the Malay cook appeared on deck with a pot of what passed for tea aboard the *Irish Rose*. Clive despised the maritime brew's oiliness and its aftertaste of fish and curry, but his thirst outweighed his reluctance, and he drank more than half the pot, then accepted a smoke from Doug. "Life of ease, this," said Doug. "Ishi must be havin' smoke-oh down there. Bearin' up, Clive?"

"Yes."

"First day's always the worst."

"How very encouraging. It would buck me up no end if we found a pearl."

"Could be days before we get one, or weeks, and even then it might be a pissy little squirt not worth two bob."

"But just to see one would be wonderful."

"It'll happen sooner or later. Gotta be patient."

"Do we get a reward of some kind if we find some?"

"Yeah, but it's only a coupla quid. Ishi won't get anythin'."

"Why not, since he's the one who found it and pulled it up?"

"He's not white, that's why not. The owner of this lugger's white, so it's his rules we play by, see. You and me get a little somethin' because we're like him, and the others don't because they're not."

"Not a very fair arrangement."

"Arr, I dunno. The money the Malays make'll support 'em like kings when they go back home, even if it looks like shit to us, and Ishi gets a bloody good wage, him bein' the top dog round here. He'll go home with a smile on his face, don't you worry. It's us poor buggers that aren't gunna go back rich."

"You've managed to make a living at it for a long enough time."

"Yeah, but it's half wages this trip, mate."

"Half wages? Why?"

"Only way I could get you the job. Split me own pay down the middle with you. It's the only way old man Moxham'd let you join the crew, you bein' a raw beginner."

"That's outrageous! It's . . . exploitation!"

"We didn't have to take the offer."

"You should have told me before we started!"

"And then what would you've done, gone and got a teachin' job at the school, eh?"

"Well, I . . . I don't know what I would have done."

"So here we are. Could be worse."

Clive was unsure if he should be grateful to Doug for his sacrifice or angry with him for not having shared the decision before it was made. In essence, Doug was a friend who took liberties with the friendship, for the best of reasons. Clive's English soul was unused to such arbitrary choices, so hastily made. Everything about Doug was too casual, too free and easy; he did not approach life with a serious enough attitude, in Clive's opinion. Doug was sincere enough on a personal level but could not be considered Clive's equal in matters of principle. Clive supposed this was because the man had been born in Australia, and in the most backward part of that backward continent. Thinking further along these lines, Clive saw it was his duty as an educator to instruct Doug by example, and so improve him.

"I should like to be consulted next time a similar situation occurs," he said stiffly, made aware of his own injured Englishness as he did so.

"Right-oh. Arr, shit. Here comes more work to bugger the wicked."

The Malays had raised another basket at last and emptied its contents onto the deck, splashing Clive's left eye with salt water. He reached for an oyster.

At the end of seven and a half hours of continuous gathering, Ishi Murikama signaled that he wished to be raised from the depths. Hauled aboard, he was quickly undressed, too exhausted by then to assist in any way with the removal, piece by piece, of his diving suit and the many layers of clothing beneath it. When finally he stood, naked but for a white loincloth, Ishi went aft for his first relief since descending early that morning.

Doug shook his head in admiration. "Blowed if I know how the Japs can hold their water that long."

It seemed a trivial attribute to base esteem upon, but Clive reminded himself that Doug inhabited a visceral rather than a cerebral universe. He had not been so analytical during the first few days of their acquaintance, and Clive was made aware of a subtle shift in their relationship. Unaccountably, he felt a slight twinge of guilt over the change.

Rice and curry. Curry and rice. Clive's stomach yearned for meat and bread. One of the Malays caught a bonito, and the cook served it up as a special treat. With curry and rice. Clive's hands continued to bleed even as they became hardened to the task awaiting them each day. He had never known any work but teaching and had until now harboured a romantic notion that work, real work performed by the human body, must be an ennobling thing, a source of great pride for the working classes. Now he knew better. Work was hard. Work hurt. Work was not necessarily rewarded with anything like the compensation a worker thought he might deserve. Clive did not like to work. It was a shaming, a belittling experience. He had to resist the ease with which he could have blamed Doug Farrands for his plight, despite the unsettling fact that it had been Clive himself who asked Doug to pursue this option. He was unhappy from morning until night, at which time he swallowed as much of his curry and rice as his digestive tract would allow, then retired to his cramped and reeking bunk, no longer interested in the starry canopy above and moonlight shimmering upon tropical waters.

But then he found a pearl. It happened a little before noon. Clive slit open an oyster no different from any other that had passed through his hands, and saw immediately that this one was not the same. Within the mucilage inside was a lump, a hard lump, and he knew even before separating it from its slippery prison that he had found a pearl of considerable size. When it came fully into the daylight, however, he was crestfallen.

"Is this . . . is it a pearl?"

"Strewth, yeah, and a biggy! Good on you, mate!"

"But it's . . . it doesn't look like a pearl."

The surface of the thing was irregular, its colour more grey than white, and on one side it bore a faint pockmark or dimple. Clive had never suspected pearls might be subject to any kind of irregularity; he imagined they came directly from their oyster lustrous and shining, perfectly formed, ready for inclusion on the necklace of a duchess.

"Hasta be peeled yet," Doug said. "It's probly a real beaut a coupla layers down."

"Peeled?"

"Yeah, like an onion. It's got skin after skin all the way down. That's how they grow, see, from the inside out, skin growin' on skin, and every layer's different, some good and some not so good. You peel away the skins that aren't just right till you get to one that is. Might peel away half a pearl to get it lookin' like it should. That one's a big bugger, though, so even if they have to peel off a fair bit of it, there'll still be plenty left. With a bitta luck it's a five- or six-hundred-quid pearl. For the owner, that is; then the dealer sells it for plenty more. Probly be worth eight or nine times that by the time it's danglin' off some rich cow overseas."

"Gosh, as much as that? What do I do with it now?"

"Give it to the captain."

Diego accepted the pearl without comment or change of expression. He produced a small set of scales and proceeded to weigh it. "Fifty-five grains," said Doug, watching closely. "Told you it's a biggy." Diego thrust a leather-bound book, much dog-eared, at Clive, along with a pencil.

"You have to make a note of it," Doug explained, "so the owner knows at the end of the run how many's been found and how many's handed over to him. Keeps everyone honest. Kinda describe it too, just to make sure it doesn't get switched for another one, less valuable."

"Not a very trusting system," observed Clive, moistening the pencil tip.

He wrote: "Found noon, 19 June 1939, one pearl, large, fifty-five grains, with slight flaw."

"Is that all right?" he asked Doug.

"Practically a poem, mate."

Diego took the book and pencil from him and waved both men from the bridge.

Clive returned to splitting oysters with a fervour he would have thought inconceivable just fifteen minutes before, but no more pearls were found that day, or during the four days following. Then Doug found a small one, and this was entered into the pearl log after being handed to Diego for weighing and safekeeping.

"Not much luck this time round," Doug said. "I don't reckon we're gunna get much of a bonus, not unless you do a repeat performance, Clive."

"I'd certainly love to oblige."

But no further pearls were taken. The lugger rendezvoused with a large schooner, along with the nine other luggers owned by Moxham Ltd., and all the mother-of-pearl gathered so far was transferred to the larger vessel for transshipment to shore.

Working at the task, Clive noticed Ken and Les Moxham aboard the schooner, watching him.

"Like the work, Pom?" Les called across to him.

"Marvelous!" Clive called back.

"Bloody idiot," he heard Ken say.

Doug came over to Clive's side of the lugger.

"Why don't you two bludgers do some work yourselves for once!"

"That's what we're payin' you to do, Farrands!"

"Not you; your old man is!"

"Teachin' the Pom how to be a useless bastard like yourself, are you?"

"No; a useless bastard like you!"

"Get rooted, Farrands!"

"Same to you, if you can find a coupla girls desperate enough!"

The brothers made obscene gestures at Doug, then turned away.

"Charmin' bastards, aren't they?" Doug said.

"Princes, both of them," agreed Clive.

When the transfer of shell was completed, the luggers dispersed once more.

Clive's hands were becoming hardened by salt water and toil, and he was less miserable than before. He considered the finding of the pearl to have been the turning point. Life had not been so bad since then, although he still detested the food and the conditions under which he was obliged to live. He strolled the decks again by moonlight, prepared to savour what beauty was on offer there, and one night approached Doug and Ishi Murikama as they held a stilted conversation near the bows.

"Clive, I've just been tellin' Ishi about your farm."

"Farm?"

"Redlands."

"Oh, yes."

"Farm verra good thing," said Ishi. "My fammery good farmer. No me. No good farmer. Good diver. Verrer good diver. Get money, loss of money."

"Yes, I see. It's not a farm, actually; more of a . . . a property."

"Makes no difference to Ishi, mate. In Japan, any property that isn't in the city's a farm."

"Oh, well, in that case . . . "

"Farm good thing. Make food. No eat pearl, no, no."

"No indeed."

"Pearl good for make money. Loss of money."

"Ah, yes, lots of money."

The same sentences circulated again, then Ishi declared himself tired. "Go sleep now, wake up, go fine more pearl. Make loss of money."

"Yes indeed," said Clive, and executed a foolish bow. Ishi returned it and went below.

"I reckon he likes you, Clive."

"How can you tell?"

"You just can, if you've been round enough Japs."

"Do you ever discuss politics? Does he have an opinion on what his country's done to Manchuria? Does he approve of what the Japanese are doing in China?"

"Never raised the topic. Might be embarrassin' for him."

"I should bloody well think so."

"No need to make it personal, Clive."

"Well, it's an international disgrace."

"So was the big war in Europe. I don't go gettin' shitty with you because England told me dad to go over and fight, and the silly bugger went and did it. You didn't make him die, so you and me can get along. Same thing with Ishi, that's how I see it. No sense in gettin' your balls in a knot over what the Japs are doin' in China. It's got nothin' to do with Ishi, and nothin' to do with us."

"You're in a remarkably philosophical mood tonight."

"Yeah, happens now and then."

"Have you ever considered what might happen if the Japanese decided to extend their conquests beyond China?"

"India, you mean?"

"South. Toward Australia."

"Crikey, what'd they want Aussie for, eh? Nothin' but dust and flies. It's too far away for 'em anyway. China's just across the water, but we're thousands a miles away."

"It might happen. They're arrogant, I've heard. They tend to think they're superior to other races."

"And we've never been like that, have we?"

"I'm not excusing what England and the other colonial powers have done. I'm just saying the Japs could do the same if they wanted to."

"Who'd wanna come this far just for dust and flies?"

"Aren't you proud of your country?"

"Too right I am, but I don't see it as anyone else's prize, not somethin' you'd go to war over. It's too far away, mate, and I'm glad."

Annoyed that his concerns were taken so lightly, Clive turned from Doug. He watched a school of fish leap from the water in a blaze of silver droplets and splash back into darkness. He had thought, upon first observing this phenomenon at night, that the fish were leaping for sheer joy, aiming themselves at the unattainable moon above them; but Doug had informed him that the fish, far from flinging themselves about in a state of ecstasy, were trying desperately to avoid the jaws of their natural predators, who skimmed unseen beneath the surface, about their business of killing.

The *Irish Rose* moved on to new oyster beds farther east, almost to the Gulf of Carpentaria, before Ishi went down again and began trudging along the sea floor. He had been gathering for almost five hours, and sending up little in the way of shell, when the lifeline and air hose suddenly were pulled across the deck, slithering aft. Diego responded to the Malays' frantic shouting and threw the propeller into reverse.

More line and hose were quickly laid out before either could snap under the strain they clearly were under.

"What happened?" Clive asked.

"Ishi's got his lines trapped," said Doug, peering over the side. "Most likely caught on a rock or somethin'. We just need to give him some slack so he can backtrack and untangle himself. Happens all the time."

"Can he see what has to be done down there? He's pretty far down, isn't he?"

"Twenty-five fathoms. Pretty deep."

A Malay watching the water began shouting and pointing. A froth of bubbles was foaming the surface a short distance from the lugger.

"Arr, shit, he's gone and broke the air hose! Wind him up! Wind him up!"

The crew already had thrown the winch into reverse.

"Not too fast! He might still be caught!"

The lifeline reeled onto the winch drum without becoming taut.

"He musta freed it. . . . Good on you, Ishi. . . ."

The disconnected air hose writhed freely beneath the keel, still spewing bubbles.

"He's a goner if we don't get him up in time. . . ."

"But . . . isn't his suit already filled with water? It would come straight through the broken air pipe, wouldn't it?"

"Yeah, but he can shut off the valve, if he's quick enough, and live for a few minutes on the air inside his suit. He has to get hooked up again fast, though. We can't bring him aboard for an hour at least."

"Why not?"

"The bends. Yank him up too fast from that depth, and the nitrogen in his blood'll bubble like soda water and paralyse him for life. If we can get the air hose back onto the helmet, we can park him ten fathoms down for a while and wait for his blood to adjust, then bring him up in stages."

The lifeline winch stopped winding as the ten-fathom mark came up onto the deck.

"How do you reconnect the hose . . . ?" asked Clive, but Doug was already aiming himself at the water. He dived clumsily, and Clive watched his white feet kicking him down into the depths, toward the slowly thrashing end of the air hose. The entire crew watched the bubbles move across to the dim blob dangling below, which was Ishi Murikama. After an agonisingly long moment, the frantic bubbling stopped, and by the cheer that went up, Clive understood that the air hose had successfully been reinserted into the diver's helmet. Now Doug could be seen heading back to the surface, trailed by a steady stream of used air from Ishi's helmet. Clive was dumbfounded at the length of time Doug had spent underwater, surely more than the supposed limit of three minutes.

Many hands reached down to assist Doug up the ladder. He was hauled onto the deck, breathing no harder than he would have after a long run.

"Bloody marvelous!" Clive shouted above the general hubbub. "Bloody impossible too, I would have thought."

"Nah, not when I had me own air supply down there to take a gobful out of whenever I wanted. Only got a bit rough after I plugged it back into Ishi's suit. He looks pretty crook, blood comin' outa his nose and eyes. I reckon he's unconscious. Just have to leave him where he is for now and hope he's not too bad when he comes up."

The crew remained silent for the next hour or more, and spoke only in undertones as Ishi was winched toward the surface by degrees from his ten-fathom detoxification depth. When the helmet's dome rose above the waves, he was lifted aboard. His suit and accoutrements were stripped from him, and he was laid upon the deck. A considerable amount of blood had congealed around his ears and neck, and red strings ran from his eye sockets. Ishi remained unconscious. Diego, after close scrutiny of his only diver, started the engine and turned the lugger for home.

"He's buggered," said Doug. "Ruptured his eardrums."

"Is it a permanent injury?"

"Means he'll never dive again, that's all. Jeez, talk about bad luck."

"Shouldn't we take him below?"

"Nah, stinks down there. He's better off up here in the fresh air. Help me get his bedding up, and we'll put him under the tarp outa the sun, poor bastard."

Ishi was settled near the stern beneath a canvas awning,

still without having opened his eyes. Doug squatted beside him for some time, then went to the rail and rolled himself a smoke. He offered his pouch to Clive, who had learned over the days and nights at sea to roll his own.

"That's that," Doug said.

"The end of Ishi's career, you mean."

"Yeah, and me too, I reckon."

"I don't follow."

"We're goin' back to Darwin. Nothin' else to do without a diver. When we get there, I'm all done with the pearl shell trade."

"You're joking. What else will you do?"

"Dunno, but I'm fed up to the back teeth with this game."

"I see. Well, I don't wish to seem unoriginal, but I believe I'll follow suit."

"Garn, mean to say you haven't been happy doin' this, Clive? Coulda sworn you were whistlin' merrily all the time."

"It doesn't exactly put us on easy street."

"We could always get jobs at the pub, sweeper-upper or somethin'. How's that sound?"

"Not terribly appealing."

"Well, you never know, mate; somethin' might come along."

"But not for your friend."

"Not for Ishi. When he gets back on his feet again, he'll be ashamed about his busted eardrums. He'll feel like shit because he can't dive anymore. He was one a the best, and he knew it. Japs are bloody proud. He's lost more'n his job today."

"Us too, it seems."

"Us too, Clive mate."

Clive placed the crooked cigarette he had made between his lips and accepted heat from Doug's. They smoked in silence for a while, then Clive said, "I've been thinking, actually."

"Yeah? Wanna watch yourself. Get a brain hemorrhage that way."

"No, seriously. It was your diving in and rescuing Ishi that got me started."

"Wasn't me that rescued him, it was the air, and being held at ten fathoms all that time."

"But you were the instrument of deliverance, shall we say. No false modesty, please."

"What's your point?"

"Well ... this is difficult to discuss, but ... you know, Doug, I've always wanted to have a bash at writing. I suppose most people feel that way at least once in their life, but I've had this feeling growing inside me for some time, on and off, and today it ... well, it finally turned into something real, something actual, do you know what I mean?"

"Nah, not really."

"It was when you came to the surface after the business with the air hose. I found myself thinking it was like a scene from a terrific adventure novel. There you were, the dashing hero, risking life and limb to save a comrade in peril, and doing a bloody good job of it too."

"Garn, I'm gonna start blushin' like mad in a minute."

"The point is, why don't I go ahead and write the damn thing. Romance and adventure in an untamed land. Tropical seas, pearl fishermen, a manly Aussie hero, typhoons and a villain or two, plus a bit of lust among the coral."

"You can't lust among coral, mate; it'd cut your bum to ribbons."

"Among the palms, then, and the gum trees and coolibahs and whatnot. I know I can do this, if I can just find enough cash to keep me going while I write the thing."

"Knew there was a catch."

"I'm determined to give it a try, if I possibly can. It won't be great art, nothing for the Bloomsbury set, but by God I'm sure everyone else would wolf it down."

"What's a Bloomsbury set? Dishes, is it?"

"*Beneath the Waves.* How does that sound for a title?"

"Ripper."

"Pardon?"

"Beauty. Terrific. I'd buy it."

"I think it's what I've always wanted to do, really, deep down. Isn't it strange how things happen?"

"You're a peculiar bastard, Clive."

"Thank you."

Ishi Murikama sat on his suitcase at the end of the wharf, watching an ocean liner approach Darwin. He wore his best suit and shoes, and the cotton wadding in his ears was fresh and clean. Sometimes he moaned to himself, alone on the wharf. Soon he would board the liner and be gone, with nothing but shame in his suitcase. His life was an empty place now. He would have to plant rice like a lowly farmer, and his wife's brothers would mock him for having been reduced to their level. It would be humiliation of a high order, a loss of face scarcely to be borne. He had considered not returning to Nippon at all, losing himself in the thousand and one islands between Australia and home, but his honour would not be served that way. He would have to accept with dignity the shame that had been visited upon him.

Footsteps were approaching him from the landward end of the wharf. Ishi felt them through the soles of his shoes, rather than hearing them. He turned to see who it might be and saw Duck and Crive, the Australian and his Englishman friend. Ishi had already thanked Duck many times for what he had done, and did not wish to be seen now, when he was preparing to board a ship for Yokohama, for a lifetime of shame and regret.

"G'day, Ishi mate. Gettin' ready for the trip home?"

Ishi nodded, understanding the foggy tones of the question if not the actual words. He turned to the water, fighting tears that wished to spill from his eyes, still reddened and sore from the pressure sickness that had destroyed his life.

"Got a goin'-away present for you. Little somethin' to make life a bit easier, y'know. Bad luck's a bastard sometimes. Here y'are, mate, and don't spend it all in one place."

Doug opened Ishi's hand and placed in it a pearl. It was not the world's finest pearl, but it was far from the least. Ishi saw at once that it would support him in some style for the rest of his life, if he was not extravagant. He did not understand where the pearl had come from, or why it had been given to him.

"You give to me . . . ?"

"That's right. Clive and me reckon you deserve it, don't we, Clive?"

"Oh, by all means," said Clive, just as puzzled by the sudden appearance of the pearl as its recipient.

"Don't go tellin' where you got it, though. Might get me in trouble, see."

"No tell . . . ?"

"No tell nobody."

"No tell. Thang you . . . Verrer good fren, you."

Doug extended his hand. Ishi stood to shake it, then shook hands with Clive, his eyes smarting with the many emotions he felt.

"Well," said Doug, "partin's a bastard at the besta times, so hoo-roo, Ishi, and take care a yourself."

"I thang you. . . . No forget."

"Me too, mate. So long."

Ishi watched the two men walk back along the wharf. He had been unable to tell them what was inside him, and now it was too late. They had known he could not find the words, and had left him there alone to spare him further torment. They were very fine men. Ishi stared at the pearl they had given him. He held in his hand another kind of life from the one he had, only minutes ago, been contemplating with such sorrow. There it was, in his very own hand—a different life.

"I suppose that was genuine?" Clive inquired, as they passed along the wharf.

"Too right. I wouldn't slip a bloke like Ishi somethin' crook."

"May I ask where it came from?"

"Courtesy a Moxham Limited."

"You stole it."

"I found it. Finders keepers, eh?"

"Bloody hell, Doug . . . ! If you'd been seen, you might be in jail now."

"But I wasn't. Ever notice me scratchin' me ear while we cut the oysters?"

"I can't say I did."

"That's because I did it casual like."

"You hid the pearl in your ear?"

"Bloody oath I did."

"But your chums Ken and Les searched us when we came ashore. They searched us both thoroughly. . . ."

"Yeah, the bastards. First time anyone's ever done that to me, but I had it in the backa me head they'd have a go because a the slangin' back and forth between them and us. I could probly get 'em in trouble with their old man if I wanted to. Old Moxie never searched his shell cutters when they came home. He trusted 'em."

"I know; they're white, therefore trustworthy, or so the theory goes."

"Silly bloody theory, eh? Don't go lecturin' me, Clive. I know I'm a naughty boy. It's in a good cause, though, so I won't go to hell or anythin' nasty like that."

"To return to the point; we were searched."

"But they never poked around where the eye can't see. Know what this is?"

Doug pulled a vulcanised article from his pocket. Clive blushed as he recognised it for what it was.

"A French letter."

"Right, a franger. See what's inside? Not what you'd expect, eh?"

The condom was filled with pearls, small ones, a dozen or more that Clive could see through the milky colouring of the thing.

"You can't just swaller pearls to hide 'em. The acid in your guts eats 'em away. This little beauty kept 'em safe and sound. I reckon we've got a coupla thousand quid here, mate, more'n enough to let you laze around and write your book."

"Doug . . . you stole all these?"

"Moxham won't miss 'em, rich bastard like he is, and if I sell 'em to the right buyer, word'll never get back to him. I know a Chinaman, bloke called Sung Yee, that doesn't care where he gets his pearls. He'll give us a good price, no worries."

"This is . . . you can't do things like this. . . ."

"Jeez, you shoulda told me before, Clive. I've gone and done it now."

"It's dishonest. It's theft."

"Want me to hand 'em back? I'd go to jail anyway, for takin' 'em."

"I don't suppose that would serve any useful purpose."

"Nah, and jail's no place for a bloke that can shit pearls."

4

SUNG YEE TOOK EACH PEARL and examined it carefully, ignoring Doug and Clive.

"Beauties, aren't they," Doug suggested.

Sung Yee shook his head. "See many better pearl. These bad."

"Bullshit, if you'll pardon me Chinese. They're bloody good pearls. Not fit for a queen maybe, but they'll do anyone else, and you know it, so stop bullshittin' and make us an offer."

"Mus consider firs."

Sung Yee rang a small silver bell at his elbow. When his wife appeared, he issued staccato instructions, and she left the room.

"Tea soon," explained Sung Yee. "Make good tea, old wife. New wife not so good tea."

"You have two wives?" Clive asked.

"Two wife better. One old, one young. Better that way."

"I'll bet it is," Doug said. "Now how 'bout these pearls, eh?"

"Too soon, too soon. Firs have tea, then talk. Too big hurry no good. You take pearl, make sorry two big fool?"

"He means Ken and Les," Doug said to Clive. To Sung Yee he said, "Yeah, to make fools of 'em. Wasn't hard, eh, Clive?"

"They're both naturally inclined to idiocy."

Sung Yee found this amusing and rocked his upper body slowly several times, his laughter like the stuttering of a distant motorcycle.

"When old man die, these two fool, they no run business good. No good smart in head." Sung Yee tapped the side of his own shaven head.

"Serve 'em right when it happens," said Doug.

From the rear of Sung Yee's house came female screams.

"Sounds like your two missus are havin' a fight. Better go and break it up, don't you think?"

"No for man to do, stop womans to fight. No to touch. They stop soon. New wife good to fight. Old wife no like to fight. New wife win all time."

"I reckon I'd need earplugs with two wives in the house."

Sung Yee stuttered again.

Tea was brought on a tray and set down before Sung Yee. The tea bearer was not the same woman who had taken the order. Very much younger, she bore the mark of a scratch on her lovely cheek. Sung Yee spoke some honeyed words to her, and she left the men alone. Sung Yee poured tea into bowls. "Old wife make tea," he said. "New wife take tea to me. Old wife no like. New wife take tea all same."

"Equal division of labour," said Clive, and again Sung Yee laughed his stuttering laugh. "You funny Pom. Say funny thing."

"I bet we're gunna laugh like hyenas when you make an offer on those pearls."

"Five hunned pound you say funny?"

"Ha, ha, bloody ha."

"Sis hunned pound."

"Two thousand quid, mate, and they're worth every zak of it."

"No, no. Too much. I give seven hunned pound."

"Nineteen hundred."

"No, no. Too much. Give eight hunned pound."

"Eighteen hundred."

"Nine hunned pound."

"Seventeen hundred."

"Give one thousan pound. No more."

"Sixteen hundred."

"One thousan pound. No more."

"We'll take fifteen hundred."

"One thousan pound."

"Listen, mate, you're not the only pearl buyer in town. We can take 'em somewhere else and get what we want for 'em, easy."

"Nobody give more pound. I give best pound. You take, you see."

"We might just do that, eh, Clive?"

"We certainly will."

"You steal. Nobody want. I give you one thousan pound."

"Tell you what, you robber, you give us eleven hundred and they're yours."

"One thousan fifty pound. No more offer. You take, or you go."

Doug looked at Clive. Clive shrugged.

Doug said, "Sung Yee, I hope your new wife fucks you to death."

"I die happy man," said Sung Yee, smiling.

It was while they were celebrating their new and illicit wealth in a pub that Doug and Clive were made aware of a difficulty neither had expected. The barman, who knew Doug, as did all barmen in Darwin, told him, "There's a geezer lookin' for you and the Pom. Been in here a coupla times since you got back. Probly been in all the other pubs too."

"What geezer?"

"Parfitt, solicitor bloke. Says he needs to talk to your Pommie mate."

"What about?"

"Never said."

"Right-oh, I'll tell him."

"Been a sheila lookin' for him too."

"A sheila? Good-lookin'?"

"They're all good-lookin' round here if they're white."

"She wasn't English, was she?"

"Nah, Aussie from down south."

"Thanks, mate."

When he returned to the corner of the room that Clive was guarding for them both, Doug set a fresh pitcher of beer on the narrow shelf jutting from the wall and leered at Clive. "There's a good-lookin' white sheila lookin' for you."

"A what?"

"Who is she, eh? Haven't got a secret missus have you, Clive?"

"Don't be absurd. Where is she?"

"Not here right now, but she's been askin' around. So's a solicitor."

"Now you're confusing me. What solicitor?"

"Bloke called Parfitt, works just down the street."

"Oh, Parfitt. He's the one who forwarded notice of my inheritance to my mother's old address in London. I suppose I should've dropped by his office and let him know I'm here. He probably doesn't even know I've already been out to take a look at Redlands."

"Might be nothin' to do with that. Might be the little lady's gonna sue you for breach a promise."

"You're being ridiculous. I'll go and see Parfitt now."

"Want me to come along?"

"You look after the beer."

"I could bring that too."

But Clive was already elbowing his way through the crowd of drinkers.

Parfitt was finishing lunch as Clive entered his office. The remains of the pie before him seemed no less untidy than everything else on his desk.

"Mr. Parfitt?"

"That's me. Mr. Bagnall?"

"Yes. I really should have paid you a visit as soon as I arrived, but what with one thing and another . . . "

"Heard about your adventures, going off into the bush with Doug Farrands, then pearling. Life's been pretty hectic for you lately."

"Yes, it has, rather. I suppose you need signatures on legal documents and that sort of thing. I've got some stuff from the solicitors in London, but it's in a trunk down at the customs house. I really must get that back."

"I'd do that, if I were you, Mr. Bagnall, because there's been a bit of confusion about the inheritance. The more paperwork you can produce to verify your claim to the property, the better."

"Confusion?"

"Another heir."

"But how is that possible? I'm Percy Burridge's only nephew, the last in the family line, in fact."

"Well now, that might not be true. Have a seat, Mr. Bagnall. There's always been a bit of a mystery about Perce Burridge. Everyone around here's always known he was English, but before he came to the Territory he spent a few years down south, in Melbourne."

"Oh, God . . . he has a daughter, doesn't he?"

"She's been looking around for you, Mr. Bagnall. She's got papers from a Melbourne solicitor that are every bit as legal as those you have. Seems Perce was married for a bit down there, and she's his legitimate offspring, even if she never laid eyes on him. Valerie Lansdowne. Nice sort of a girl."

"Shouldn't her name be Burridge, if she's Percy's daughter?"

"Lansdowne's her married name. You'll have to meet her."

"Yes, of course . . . This is a bit of a shock."

"I'm sure it is. The whole thing'll have to go through some kind of probate to sort it out. I'm assuming Perce forgot about one or the other will. It wouldn't make sense to let both of them represent his dying wishes, just to create trouble."

"Which will is the most recent? Surely that's the one that counts."

"Yours is, but Mrs. Lansdowne's directly related to the deceased. There's a case to be made for the importance, in a legal sense, of a daughter over a nephew. It might be possible to reach amicable agreement. You're cousins, after all, and Redlands isn't really worth anything."

"I was . . . about to go out there and begin work on a project. I suppose that's all up in the air now."

"I don't know what kind of a project you could work on out there. Rice and cattle have both been tried. There just isn't much you can do with that kind of country."

"This was going to be something quite different. All I need is the house and a typewriter."

"Typewriter?"

"May I know where Mrs. Lansdowne is staying?"

"She's down at the Vic."

Clive stood. "Thank you, Mr. Parfitt. I take it that you'll represent me if it comes to any kind of a legal battle."

"I'll be happy to do that, Mr. Bagnall. You were saying about a typewriter?"

"Oh, nothing. Good afternoon."

"I'm sure you two can work it out."

"Yes," said Clive, but his voice was without conviction.

Entering the Vic Hotel's residence doorway without any plan laid out in advance was probably the worst kind of folly, given the circumstances, but Clive preferred not to wait a moment before meeting his adversary. Parfitt had made no mention of the woman's husband being present in Darwin, so she might, as a lone female, prove more amenable to whatever argument he presented for giving up her share of Redlands without a fight, or at least negotiating a reasonable compromise. He dreaded being met by a wispy creature who would allow him to dominate her completely, since this would eventually bring on pangs of guilt, but that was the type who would provide a quick solution to the problem. Clive supposed he could wrestle with his conscience later, in uncontested residence at Redlands.

"Is there a Mrs. Lansdowne here?"

"Up in room nine," said the large woman behind the front desk. "She's been looking for you. You're the Pom, aren't you?"

"Yes. I'm the Pom. May I go up?"

"Course you can, love."

Clive knocked at the door marked 9 with a faint quickening of his pulse. He was determined to be firm with Mrs. Lansdowne, no matter how pathetic a picture she might present. His future, his sudden resolution to become a writer, was at stake.

The door was opened abruptly, but the woman revealed was far from pathetic. A halo of frizzy red hair stood about her head, making her resemble some pre-Raphaelite goddess. Clive had forgotten somehow that she would be young, several years younger than himself, since Percy had left for Australia shortly after Clive's birth; and he had not anticipated that she might be pretty.

"Yes?"

The Australian twang in her voice sounded incongruous coming from that small and somewhat petulant mouth.

"Umm . . . good afternoon. My name is Bagnall. . . ."

"Come in."

It was an order rather than an invitation. Clive stepped past her, aware of the perfume that could not overcome a slight, but not offensive, odour of female sweat.

"I've been looking everywhere for you."

"Yes, so I heard. I've been away, actually."

"Pearl fishing. Everyone told me about it."

"Really? Pearl *shell* fishing, to be accurate. Any pearls you might find are the icing on the cake, so to speak."

"Did you get any?"

"Well . . . no, as a matter of fact."

"Only the ones your mate pinched. Or don't they count?"

"I . . . what? Who pinched what? I don't understand. . . ."

"You two better hope Moxham doesn't hear about it. He'd get a bit hot if he did, don't you think?"

"I don't know what you mean. I've come to discuss Redlands."

"Clive, isn't it?"

"Yes."

"Call me Val. We're rellies, Clive, so we don't need to be formal, do we."

"No, I suppose not. Who told you about the pearls?"

"Mrs. Christie, the lady downstairs. There's not much goes on she doesn't know about. Your mate's a bit dim if he thinks he can get rid of stolen pearls without word getting around."

"This is awful. . . . I think I'd better go and tell him." Clive began backing toward the door.

"Hold on. We've got some family business to discuss. Have a seat and we can get to know each other. They'll send beer up if you want some."

"No, thank you."

Clive sat. Things were not proceeding as he had hoped. He wondered if Moxham would approach the police with charges in mind. Blast Doug for selling to an unreliable type!

"I suppose you think the place is yours," said Val. She did not seem to be accusing him of foolishness or avarice.

"Yes, since the will handing it to me was written after the will handing it to you. It's a simple question of precedence. The new outweighs the old."

"I'm a bit newer than you."

"I was referring to legal documents. What possible use could you have for a property like Redlands? I've been out there, and I can tell you without exaggeration that it's a small piece of hell. Heat and flies, no amenities at all. The house, if you could call it a house, is made of sheet metal!"

"I can fix it up."

"It isn't worth fixing up."

She wore a cotton dress that fitted loosely, but he was aware of her breasts beneath the pale-blue-and-yellow flowered print.

"If it's so awful, why do you want it?"

"Oh . . . sentiment," said Clive.

"Over an uncle you never met."

"I gather you didn't see too much of him yourself."

"Never laid eyes on the bugger. He shot through before I even popped into the world. I never thought he'd leave me a brass razoo."

"He was a peculiar man, apparently."

"Living with a black woman, they say."

"Yes . . . I was told that."

"I've only seen about five white women in the whole week I've been here. Poor old Perce probably got a bit lonely stuck out there in hell."

"One can understand the situation, I suppose. We seem to be straying from the point. We can't both own the place."

"I might consider sharing it with the right kind of man. That's not a marriage proposal, Clive. I meant sharing as in co-owning, or whatever you'd call it."

"I'd really prefer having the place to myself, frankly."

"You might wind up like Perce did."

"I hardly think so. I wouldn't be there to make a go of it as a farm."

"What, then?"

"I . . . it doesn't matter why I want it. The place is simply mine, legally. Mine and mine alone."

"Well, I don't think so. It took months for the will to find me, and when it did, things weren't too good with me, I don't mind telling a member of the family, so when I found out I've got property in the north, it was like winning Tatts."

"Tatts?"

"The lottery."

"Your husband, is he keen at all on moving up here?"

"I haven't got one anymore. I divorced him a year and a half ago. I moved around a lot after that, so Perce's will went from here to there in the post before it caught up with me. I'm not greedy, Clive."

"And neither am I. It's just . . . I need the privacy and the peace and quiet, you see. I . . . I want to write a book, if you must know, and Redlands would give me somewhere to live rent-free."

"But you and your mate have got all that money from those pearls you pinched."

"I didn't pinch any pearls! Doug took them without even telling me—and that makes the money he got from them his, not mine, so all I have is Redlands, and I want it, without interference or company."

"Gosh, Clive, I always thought what they said about English people had to be a load of bull, but you're not changing my mind at all."

"And what, precisely, do *they* say about the English?"

"They say Englishmen are too stiff-necked to know what's good for them."

"What a charmless observation. Typically Australian. Without humour and without truth." He stood. "I don't think I'll bother continuing this conversation."

"How about if I apologise? I've had a few beers today, Clive. I don't usually drink the stuff, but the lemonade up here's awful."

"Very well, but that doesn't change anything. I hate to be insistent about this, but I want the place to myself, and that's that."

"What's your mate think?"

"I don't see what his opinion has to do with anything."

"Can I meet him? I've heard he's quite a character."

"I really don't see the point." Clive went to the door and opened it. "Please think about what I've said."

"I will if you will."

Clive closed the door on this too-reasonable request. Australian women, he had learned, were as direct, as crude and ungracious, as the men. He supposed he should have expected something of the sort. It was a shame Val was so attractive in a physical sense and so appallingly blunt in her speech.

When he returned to the pub where he had left Doug, Clive found the place in an uproar, with Doug Farrands in the eye of the storm. Doug and a large man were scuffling back and forth within a tight circle of drinkers, who were encouraging both battlers to greater effort and making bets on the outcome. When the large man's hat came off, revealing a bald head, Clive recognised Moxham the pearl shell dealer. Locked in an embrace that gave neither one advantage, he and Doug staggered back and forth across the room, within the shifting circle.

Noticing the presence of Clive, Doug shouted, "Hit this bugger over the head, willya! Better let go, Moxham! Me mate's here now!"

Incredibly, Doug's opponent seemed to hesitate and digest this advice. His arms relaxed their hold, and he took several awkward steps backward.

"Knew you'd listen to reason," Doug puffed. Moxham was far bigger and heavier, and Doug was relieved that the scuffle appeared to be over.

"Don't be a fuckin' quitter, Moxham!" jeered one of the onlookers, whose money had been bet against Doug's chances of success. Several others, who also stood to lose cash, joined in. Moxham ignored the hecklers, his expression more dazed than the inconclusive tussle with a nonfighter like Doug Farrands would seem to warrant. He continued stepping backward until his spine encountered the bar, then he slid sideways onto the linoleum floor. It was apparent to everyone by then that his behaviour was unusual, and the shouting back and forth began to die away.

"Heart attack!" someone yelled, and another voice shouted, "Get a bloody doctor!"

Doug approached the man he had been grappling with and knelt beside him to hold a palm near Moxham's mouth. "Shit . . . I don't think he's breathin'. . . . Hey, Moxham, you can't settle an argument like this!"

A general air of curiosity and mild shame took hold in the bar while everyone waited for the arrival of medical help, although it was clear, following more amateurish attempts to find a pulse or breath, that Moxham was dead.

"I reckon you've done him in, Doug," offered a bystander.

"The silly bugger shouldn't have started something at his age," Doug insisted. "Did I make the first move? He wouldn't take no for an answer. Jeez, what a balls-up."

Clive hovered nearby, unsure how best to offer comfort, not that Doug seemed to require any. The arrival of Royce Curran, Territorial policeman, caused a general parting of the crowd that had gathered around the dead man; only Doug remained close by Moxham.

"He's gone," confirmed Royce, after an examination only slightly less cursory than those preceding it. "Did any of you blokes send for a doctor?"

"Someone went," said a voice in the crowd. "I think it was Dave Coombes."

"Dave's the one that came and got me. Didn't anyone else have the nouse to go for a bloody doctor?"

It appeared that no one had, but it was not difficult for those present to shrug off guilt, since it was clear that Moxham had died quickly.

"You were havin' a barney with him, Doug?" asked Royce.

"He started it. There's fifty witnesses."

"Come in like a mad bloody bull," confirmed a bystander, and a general murmuring of agreement followed.

Royce stood and pulled a notepad from his shirt pocket. "What was the fight about? Was either one of you drunk?"

"I'd had a couple," said Doug, meaning pitchers, not glasses. "Moxham just barged in and started whackin' me around, so I held him off for a bit, then he keeled over."

"He didn't just start punching, did he? He said something to you, right?"

"Well, yeah. He reckoned I pinched some pearls."

"And did you?"

"Come off it, Royce, you know me better than that. I dunno where he got the idea I pinched somethin'."

"You better not have." Royce shook his head, then addressed the crowd, many of whom had resumed their interrupted drinking. "All right, now this time could one of you gentlemen go and get a doctor, and come back with him before dinnertime?"

"I'll go," offered a voice near the door.

"Better get Ken and Les Moxham down here too while you're about it," Royce added, and the messenger was gone, a beer glass still clutched in his hand.

Royce took statements from Doug and several others, and was still engaged in this when the doctor arrived and began his examination.

"Dead," was his succinct diagnosis. "Ticker," he added, for Royce's benefit. "I told him he ought to be taking it easy, but not him; he's got to go at it like a bull at a gate. He was warned."

When Ken and Les burst into the bar, Royce Curran immediately stepped between them and Doug. "All right! All right! It was nobody's fault! Calm down, the both of you!"

"Fuckin' cunt!" Ken spat at Doug.

"You're fuckin' dead, mate!" Les shouted, spit flying from his lips.

"Cut it out, or you'll both get the lockup," Royce threatened. To Doug he said, "Get out of here, and stay away from these two." And to the Moxham brothers: "If you two lay a hand on Farrands over this, it'll be criminal assault, so steer clear of him or I'll have the both of you in Fannie Bay before you can turn around—hear me?"

"He's a fuckin' murderin' cunt!" insisted Ken.

"It was an accident. Your dad had a bad heart, just ask the doc, and for Christ's sake settle down! Farrands, are you still here?"

Doug motioned for Clive to join him outside, and they began walking down the street.

"What's Fannie Bay?" Clive asked.

"Local jail," Doug said. "I oughter wring that Sung Yee's neck. I told him to keep his trap shut about those pearls. Probly the best buy he's made all year, legal or illegal, and the silly bastard has to go and yak yak yak about it. He's about as inscrutable as a bloody parrot."

"This should never have happened. We should have given the pearls back before this got so far out of hand. A man has died. . . ."

"He was pushin' sixty if he was a day, old Moxham."

"That hardly amounts to an excuse."

"Wasn't intended as one. Moxham did it to himself, far as I'm concerned."

"Les and Ken aren't going to let it go at that. They want blood."

"They're welcome to try gettin' it. Stuff 'em both, coupla stupid shitheads. What happened at Parfitt's, anything?"

"Disaster has struck me too, I'm afraid. Percy had a daughter in Melbourne. It seems he left the place to her as well as to me. It's an incredible mess. She's not going to give up on it, either."

"You met her?"

"A very stubborn person. Very Australian."

"Can't be all bad, then. Nice-lookin'?"

"I suppose so, if you happen to like red hair."

"Sweet-talk her into marryin' you; that'll take care a business."

"I wouldn't even need to do that. She offered to share the place with me."

"She what? Crikey, mate, sounds like she's got the hots for you."

"No, I don't think so. She'll get me out there and drive me mad with interruptions and be all kinds of a nuisance. I need peace and quiet. I'm serious about writing a book, you know."

"Course I know. I only pinched a coupla pearls till you told me that, then I took every bloody one I could find."

"Are you saying you committed theft for my sake?"

"Too right I did. You don't have to go down on your knees and act grateful or anythin', but I wouldn't have taken so many if it wasn't for you and your bloody book. Those things take years to write, don't they?"

"Look, you're not really going to create more trouble with Sung Yee, are you? Aren't we in enough bother already?"

"I'll deal with him later. Maybe it wasn't his fault word got around. Might've been someone spyin' through the keyhole or somethin'."

"Valerie Lansdowne told me, and the woman who runs the Vic told her."

"Bloody hell! You can't keep a secret in this town for five minutes!"

"Well, we can't leave, not until this question of who has the legitimate will has been resolved."

"She hasn't been out there yet, has she?"

"No."

"Take her out and let her have a dekko. It's no place for a sheila, is it?"

"I wouldn't have thought so. It's hardly the place for anyone."

"She'll have a snake run over her toes and scream a bit, and that'll be that."

"She didn't strike me as the screaming type, frankly."

"Clive, you're gunna have to trust me. Be nice to the lady and invite her out to what she thinks is hers, or half hers, or whatever she thinks. In a coupla days she'll sell out to you for a few measly quid, I guarantee it."

"It might avoid a costly legal battle."

"Definitely would. I mean, whatta you got to lose? Might even get some romance in, eh?"

"Doug, please understand when I say that your opinions

carry considerable weight with me but sometimes I wish you'd just shut up."

"Arr, you don't mean it, do you, cobber, old pal, mate?"

"Please stop referring to this cousin of mine as if she was nothing more than a tart. I find it offensive, and I'm sure she would too."

"I'll shut up, then. No harm done. If I don't shut up, you might not put me in your book. I'd hate that to happen, Clive. Am I gunna be good-lookin'—you know, the kinda bloke all the sheilas go for?"

"My description will be accurate and realistic. I don't intend to write nonsense."

"But do I get to do the naughty with some sexy sheilas, or don't I?"

"You'll get your foot caught in a giant clam at twenty fathoms and die bravely."

"Jeez, I don't think I'm gunna read this book."

"Others will."

"Says you."

When she met them by prior arrangement beneath a banyan tree in the center of town, Val was prepared for some kind of confrontation. Clive had delivered the message (he had called it "a sensible suggestion, to talk things over, you know") on behalf of himself and the much-talked-about Doug Farrands. Val already had a fair idea what kind of man Clive was and had formed an impression of his mate, solely from listening to Mrs. Christie who ran the Vic. Mrs. Christie seemed to know everything about everyone in the Territory and was happy to share the lot with another white woman.

"You watch out for Doug Farrands," Val had been warned. "He'll try to kid you along just to get his way with you. I don't think he's ever had anything but black, so he'll want to be smoodging around a nice-looking girl like you the minute he lays eyes on you. Don't say later on I didn't tell you."

"I know how to take care of myself," Val had assured her.

"I'm sure you do, dear, but it wouldn't sit right with me if I didn't say me piece on Doug Farrands. I'll say this in his defense—I reckon he pinched those pearls for his Pommie mate, I really do. Doug Farrands could've pinched enough pearls to fill a beer pitcher over the years, but didn't, so he's always had regular work with the pearl shell fleet. He's gone and buggered himself up now. Wages of sin, like they say."

Val recognised Clive's lurching walk while he was still halfway down the street, and the not very tall person with him struck her as a disappointment, following Mrs. Christie's gossip. He seemed much like any other male Territorian, with his slouching manner of carrying himself and his complete disregard for dress.

"Mrs. Lansdowne, may I present my good friend Doug Farrands."

"G'day."

"Pleased to meet you."

Uneasy in his role as outdoor host, Clive moved his feet aimlessly and cast looks of mild agony at his cousin and his friend, neither of whom was aware of his discomfort.

"Clive says we should all go out to Redlands," said Doug, "just so's you know what it is you've got. Or think you've got. What you've both got."

"Sounds fine to me. When do we go?"

"Well," said Clive, "we need to arrange for a considerable amount of supplies to take with us before we brave the wilds, so shall we say . . . tomorrow?"

"All right."

"Game for the bush life, are you?" Doug asked.

"Why wouldn't I be?"

"Just askin'. Gunna be a bit different from Melbourne."

"Good. I need a change."

Doug retreated into silence.

"Perhaps we should all take a stroll and get acquainted," Clive suggested.

"Good idea." Val smiled. "If we're going to share a place, we should get to know a bit about each other. I've shared places before with people I wouldn't want to meet again if you paid me."

"Hard to get along with, were they?" Doug asked.

"Might've been," said Val. "Then again, it might've been me. Everyone's got their own ideas about who's a pain in the neck, don't they?"

"Spose," Doug admitted. Val was proving to be something other than what he had expected.

They drifted toward the Chinese end of town, by accident rather than intent, making stilted conversation every few steps along the way, when Doug saw someone darting down a narrow lane. "Scuse me," he said, and began running after the retreating figure, who, Val saw, was a Chinese.

"I suppose that's the one he sold the pearls to," Val observed.

"Really," said Clive, sounding peevish, "I don't know how crime can flourish in this place. Everyone seems to know everyone else's business. It's ridiculous."

"He's not going to bash him up or anything, is he?"

"Oh, I doubt it. He's not the violent type at all, really; in fact, he's quite a generous sort of chap, when you get to know him."

"Going to stay in Australia, Clive?"

"It's rather too soon to say. It depends on all kinds of things."

"Like me not liking it here."

"I didn't say that."

"Look, I'm not silly, all right? You two want to take me out there and watch me throw up my hands and say, 'Oh, how awful!' Well, I won't. I know what awful is: it's a marriage that goes bad through no fault of your own. Ever been married?"

"No, not at all."

"I'm not, not anymore, and listen, Clive, don't call me Lansdowne, all right? I haven't called myself that since the divorce. I think all divorced women should have their old names back automatically, just to remind everyone they're not married to whatsisname anymore. It ought to be a law."

"Capital idea. Ah, here's Doug back."

"Catch him?" Val asked.

"Yeah. He says his wife yakked about the pearls because she's got a shitty on—I mean, she's not too happy about this other wife he just took on board, a younger one, so she wanted to get Sung Yee into trouble. God knows how it spread from her, but it did. He gave her a good hiding for it, he says."

"Bastard," said Val.

"Oh, I dunno. She bloody near got me killed."

"We were just discussing the merits of divorce," Clive said.

"Sung Yee needs some a that."

"I think his wife does," said Val. "Both his wives."

"Been divorced yourself, have you?"

"Yes."

"Husband a bastard, was he?"

"Aren't they all?"

"I wouldn't know. I've never been one."

"Oh, I heard you had a son."

"Yeah, a yella-fella."

"What's that, a half-caste?"

"He's a bastard too, a real bastard. That's what you're after, isn't it?"

"I wasn't after anything. . . ."

"I'll leave you two to do some cousin talk."

Doug turned abruptly and walked away.

"Touchy," said Val.

"I don't think it was an easy subject for him to discuss. It's different up here, what with one thing and another."

"Look, Clive, I don't give a stuff if he's sensitive. It really annoys me that men like him have it off with Abo women and then walk away from the result. All they want, basically, is a root. Sorry if you're shocked."

"Oh, no, not at all, but you've got it a bit wrong where Doug's concerned. His . . . woman, I suppose you'd call her, was taken from him—kidnapped, actually—while he was away at sea, and it was years before he found out what happened. She died a rather unsavoury death from drink, according to what he told me. I really doubt that it was a casual fling. Doug's something of a diamond in the rough, you see, and it's easy to take him the wrong way on occasion. I shouldn't like to see you two fighting, not if we're going to share lodgings, so to speak."

Val paused while three Aborigines, two men and a woman, passed them by, stick thin, dressed in cast-off white men's clothing. All three were obviously drunk.

"I'm sorry. . . . Ever since I've been up here I can't take my eyes off them. It's awful. . . . They seem to have nothing at all to be proud of. It isn't right to use them that way, is it?"

"Certainly not, but no one man is to blame."

"No one man ever is."

5

A SECONDHAND FORD UTILITY TRUCK was bought with the money Sung Yee had given Doug for the pearls. Since throwing cash around would have confirmed rumours of the transaction that had led ultimately to Moxham's death, the entire amount was handed over to Val, who could, if questioned, say it was part of the inheritance left to her by her father, Perce Burridge. This story was believed by no one, but every store in Darwin was pleased to accept money for the various articles Val requested.

Virtually an entire household was purchased, including furniture and kitchen utensils, hammocks (better than a bed any day, Doug assured Val and Clive), many yards of mosquito netting, tools for repairing the house at Redlands, tinned food for the months ahead, a .303 Lee-Enfield rifle and several hundred rounds for use against Blighty and any marauding water buffalo that might threaten the trio, and a ten-foot dinghy for use in the approaching Wet.

It required two trips in the Ford to transport all this and Clive's trunks from the customs house out to Redlands. The new tenants caused a scandal of sorts by installing themselves beneath one roof without benefit of clergy between Val and either of the men, but the Territory had no historical legacy of prudery by which to measure the arrangement, and the matter became one of conjecture rather than of outrage: was she with the Pom, despite being his cousin, or was she (this was far more likely) Doug Farrands's first white girl? No one in Darwin asked these questions of them outright, but the obvious nature of the public inquiry accompanied the three to their new home like a fourth, uninvited guest.

When they were done with loading and unloading and arranging and storing, their dwelling seemed only a little more presentable than before. Clive had never experienced such crude conditions for living while in England. Val, who he assumed would be aghast at the blow to her natural female instinct for domestic order, seemed oddly satisfied by the result of their labours. "Talk about an improvement," she said, and Clive's spirits sank. Doug was oblivious to his surroundings and appeared resentful only of the work required to establish these rudiments of householding. He called for smoke-oh frequently and made his unhappiness over the presence of Val fairly clear by avoiding her eye and addressing the bulk of his limited comments throughout the operation to Clive.

When it had been done, this transferal to the bush from the coast, all three were at a loss to explain to themselves or to each other exactly why they had done what they did. It was obvious to Clive he could never hope for the peace and quiet he was sure he needed for creative work. He unloaded the only typewriter he had been able to locate in town, an ancient Underwood with several missing keys. "Could be worse," Val said. "None of them are vowels." Doug asked if vowels were really every second letter in the alphabet, or had the person who told him this many years before been bullshitting. Clive set the machine squarely on the new secondhand table, as if its place there should remain uncontested by such paltry devices as cutlery and plates. Val made him move it.

Doug found himself performing unnecessary work by turning continually from whichever direction Val happened to occupy. He knew he was doing it, like a child that turns its back on a parent who has recently spanked it, but he seemed unable to stop himself. Whatever he did, whichever way he turned, she seemed to be there, her red hair thrusting itself into the periphery of his vision like a burning bush, and he became miserable over his inability to change himself, make himself indifferent to her presence. It would have been better if Clive and he had made the move together, without the unwelcome third party, who made herself even more unbearable by ignoring him utterly.

For Val, the establishment of a home at Redlands was a

quiet triumph. She had not thought that her cousin would be quite so obliging as this. A battle of raging words and threatened lawsuits was what she anticipated before Clive knocked on her door at the Vic. She had wanted to meet Doug so that she might know the full extent of her cousin's armament, and found him surprisingly thin-skinned, his resentment of her easily manipulated by ignoring it, or at least pretending to. She was unsure if he disliked her because she threatened to take half of his mate's property, or simply because she was female. Her ex-husband had been such a man, and it had taken Val almost five years to understand this; once learned, the lesson had helped her avoid several potential entanglements since her divorce; beneath the veneer of friendliness, she saw, there often was contempt for her because she was not a man. Australia, she had been taught from infancy, was a man's country, wherein women were required for the breeding of more men. The marriage had been a bitter lesson, and she recognised in herself an unaccustomed hardness as a result. She could not ignore what she knew, however, and so did not attempt in the least to mollify Doug Farrands or encourage him to accept her.

On the evening of their first day together, they lit an oil lamp and closed the fly-wire door against airborne intruders and looked at each other in their primitive domain, somewhat baffled to be there, slightly hurt that the arrangement was less than perfect, and unmindful of where to proceed from there.

"We really should have brought some wine to celebrate with," suggested Clive, his voice brittle with insincerity.

"Beer'd do," said Doug. "No need to get fancy."

"I need some help with my divider," Val said, measuring a length of rope with her arm before cutting it with a heavy knife.

Clive looked at Doug, who stared as if entranced into the lamp's wavering yellow flame. Clive had become aware of his friend's reluctance to accept Valerie Lansdowne as a fixture at Redlands, therefore a part of their own future. It was boorish behaviour, and he made himself appear twice as friendly as he was inclined to be, in order that Val might not consider Clive in the same churlish light in which Doug insisted on placing himself. She was his cousin, after all, and had every right to be with them, no matter how awkward the situation. An Australian girl should be made aware that not all men behaved as Doug did.

"Certainly," he volunteered, and tied both ends of the rope that sectioned off a corner of the only room. It was a simple job, one that Val could easily have handled for herself, and Clive suspected it was a ploy to get one or both of the men to talk to her. Val draped a large sheet across the rope, providing a triangle of privacy for herself, behind which Clive assisted with the rigging of her hammock. When he emerged he found that Doug had silently and swiftly set up their own hammocks in opposite corners, without benefit of privacy sheets. Mosquito netting was arranged over all three, this task being left to a still-silent Doug, since he was more familiar with the tricks of draping and arranging that best prevented the nighttime misery of insect attacks.

"I'm absolutely bushed," Clive announced. "I believe I'll turn in."

"Right-oh," said Doug, without interest. Clive had been very much aware of Doug's disgruntlement over Val since her comment on his son's Aboriginal mother. It had been rude of Val to address the topic as she had, or, at the very least, insensitive. Still, Doug should have forgiven her by now and returned to being his usual jocular self. If the atmosphere enveloping Redlands did not change soon for the better, Clive would have to give both of them a talking-to. He was, after all, the friend of one antagonist and cousin to the other; like it or not, Clive was caught in the middle.

"Me too." Val yawned. "Good night."

Both men responded, Clive with more conviction than Doug.

Secured in his hammock, its nervous swaying diminishing as he lay there, Clive watched Doug alone at the table, smoking yet another cigarette, his form made indistinct by feeble lamplight and the layer of gauze between them. Watching, he came to see that he had not truly known Doug before Val came between them, had taken the man and his moods very much for granted. Now that Doug was unhappy, Clive was unhappy too. Doug had instilled himself somehow beneath his skin, without even trying. Clive fell asleep, his ears filled with the frustrated humming of mosquitoes, his thoughts occupied with waning images of obligation and intent.

The first morning at Redlands was spent doing very little of anything. By noon, Clive became frustrated. "I hate to be a nuisance, but I really do need some time to myself, if I'm to write a book."

"I'll go for a long walk," Val said, without any trace of resentment, despite the approaching hour of maximum heat. "Doug, do you want to show me around the place so Clive can get on with it?"

"Yeah, spose so."

They left shortly after and wandered in the general direction of Blighty's Pond, Doug carrying the heavy .303.

"Has Clive talked about his book with you?" Val asked.

"A bit. He's gunna call it *Under the Waves,* I think. It's gunna be about pearl shellers."

"Might be interesting."

"Might be. He'd have to bullshit a lot, though. Pearl shellin's mainly hard yakka for bugger-all profit. Sorry. Have to watch me mouth."

"I don't care if you swear. Be yourself. I'm going to be."

"Fair enough."

"Why'd you bring the gun? Planning to shoot me?"

"Nah, not unless you get rabies or somethin'. This is for Blighty, if he shows himself."

Clive had told Val of the elusive crocodile, and she had been fascinated. "Why kill him? We just need to be careful around the pond, and he won't hurt us."

"Don't know much about crocs, do you?"

"I'm willing to listen to someone who does."

"First thing about crocs, you dunno what they're gunna do, same as sharks and buffalo. They might leave you alone; then again, they might go for you. Depends on how they feel right then, and nobody knows how a croc feels, ever. Blighty's a man-eatin' bastard, and I'd walk around here a lot easier if he's gone. Nothin' cruel about it. He'd kill me if he got the chance, or you. We're better off with him dead. Abos'll get upset, though."

"Why?"

"Some a them think he's a spirit croc or somethin', you know, gettin' revenge on white blokes for the way we've treated the blacks. They like old Blighty, the Abos."

"Wouldn't it be smart to leave him alone, then? You don't want to go upsetting the locals."

"Better they're upset than one of us ends up as a croc's lunch."

"Do you know any of them, the locals?"

"You mean because I've got a yella-fella kid by a gin?"

"Yes," Val said, aware she was trespassing again, but this time Doug seemed able to talk of it without anger.

"Nah, I wouldn't call meself an expert about Abos. I don't hate 'em like some do. I reckon it's stupid to try and make 'em like us. They're not. They're them. The more we try to make 'em like us, the more pathetic they get, with the booze and the hangin' around doin' nothin'. Every step they take closer to us is bad for 'em. That's why I sent Brian away—that's me kid. He's with some Pitjantjatjara down south a here. They haven't chucked off the old ways yet. Spose it's just a matter a time till they do. I dunno what else to do about him. You probly think I shoulda kept him with me, eh?"

"No; I don't know what you should've done. Do you ever see him?"

"Sometimes. Both of us are wanderers, me on the sea, mainly, and him on land. He's fourteen this year. Haven't seen him since he was eleven."

"Clive . . . told me about Brian's mother. It's an awful story."

"If I knew who the bugger was that took her away, I'd kill him."

"But he was only doing what was right according to tribal laws, Clive said. Aborigine girls can be promised in marriage when they're only little, can't they?"

"Yeah, he thought she was his to take, never mind what she felt about it. Probly can't blame him for that, but I do, anyway. I can't help it."

"Doesn't anyone know who the man was?"

"Course they do, every Abo in the Territory knows, but they're not gunna tell me, are they? They're lookin' after their own, just what I'd do in their place. Can't see Blighty."

They had reached the pond. Its surface lay like black glass.

"We can wait for a bit. He might show up."

They sat on the smooth trunk of a fallen gum tree. Val removed her hat, and Doug rolled a smoke.

"Clive's being very good about me wanting half of Redlands."

"Nothin' much else he can do. Your dad buggered you both up writin' two wills like that. I told Clive he oughta marry you and settle it that way."

"Cousins don't get married."

"Arr, that's right—two-headed babies and that, eh?"

"In any case, I wouldn't marry a man for property. That's disgusting."

"Why'd you marry the bloke you married?"

"I thought I loved him, that's why. Then I found out I didn't. I had a hell of a time getting a divorce. He didn't want to give me one, just because I wanted one. If I hadn't wanted one, he'd probably have turned around and divorced me; that's the kind of idiot he was."

"I wouldn't wanna get married, meself. Hardly ever works out like it's sposed to. I've heard more blokes crackin' their gums about what a rotten life it is. Course, most of 'em were up here on the run from their missus down south. Maybe the blokes that're happy stayed down there."

"Might have. Are you sure there's a man-eating croc in there?"

"He's there somewhere, probly listenin' to us. They've got good hearin', crocs, even if they're underwater."

"He could hear us even if he's down at the bottom?"

"Course he could. He's probly thinkin': Come on, you buggers, it's a hot day, so go for a nice swim, why don't you. Probly lickin' his chops just thinkin' about it."

Val set her hat back on her head.

"Show me some more of the place."

Doug shouldered the rifle and they began walking again. He showed her the strange cities of the magnetic termites, and they watched a four-foot goanna go dashing madly off among the trees at their approach.

"I haven't seen a single snake."

"Most of 'em get movin' once they feel your footsteps

comin'. Not death adders, though. They'll stay right where they are, so you have to watch where you put your feet."

Doug consulted a pocket compass every half hour or so, to Val's relief. The bush surrounding them was so unvarying in character she felt she would have become quite lost if left on her own. Red earth, white trees with pale-green foliage, and a remorselessly blue sky overhead, all of it saturated with the continual buzzing of cicadas and the chattering of wild budgerigars: this was her true inheritance, not the tin shed masquerading as a house. She had no idea what to do with it and was envious of Clive and his book. The uses Doug Farrands might make of Redlands were unknown to her. Val assumed he was here because his mate was and for no other reason.

Doug seemed a lost soul in many ways, without a home of his own, without a family he could acknowledge and live with. The air between herself and Doug had certainly improved, as if he had decided that whatever its cause, the bad feeling that had separated them was no longer worth sustaining. It had been Val's one misgiving about the move to Redlands with the two unlikely friends, and now it was gone. She was also grateful to Doug for having provided them all with money to do with as they pleased, even if it had been the result of theft. She could not judge him harshly, since she was an eager beneficiary of the act, and he had, after all, given the single most perfect pearl to a Japanese diver as compensation for having injured himself. Doug seemed to have no interest in money for its own sake, and so his criminality was on a different plane from that of professional thieves, or so Val lectured herself.

"Hang on," Doug said, pointing among the trees.

Val looked and saw a peculiar structure some twenty yards away, resembling the skeleton of a small house, hastily thrown together, in the manner of something built by children for use as a cubbyhouse. They approached it and saw the thing was assembled from articles of furniture; the base was a table, the next tier a bed frame, the third tier a wooden meat safe balanced on three chairs, the pinnacle of the thing a collection of such articles as salt and pepper shakers and other kitchen utensils. Battered horse harness was looped among the legs and struts, tying the crazy fabrication together. It stood among the gum trees like some domestic totem, made bizarre by its presence in the outdoors, without the walls and roof that would normally enclose its various parts.

"Abos," said Doug. "I was wonderin' what happened to all Perce's stuff."

"Why would they bring it all here and pile it up like that?"

"Dunno. Might be because he killed himself sittin' behind that table there. I'm only guessin'. You'd have to be an Abo to understand it. It's all yours and Clive's now."

"Let's leave it here. I couldn't stand to have any of it back in the house."

Val could not keep herself from examining the tabletop; there was a deep red stain along one edge, with insects that had become mired in it while the blood had been fresh. This was her father's blood, the only part of his physical self left to her. Staring at the table, she felt a sense of dislocation from her surroundings, a rush of anger at the faceless man who had abandoned her, then tried to make amends through his will, and bungled even that effort to atone for his absence.

"I want to burn it. . . ."

"Eh?"

"Burn it all. I don't care who took it or why, I just want to burn it."

"Can't do that, light a fire out here in the middle of the Dry. Could try in the Wet."

"Bugger the Wet. Got any matches?"

"They're stayin' in me pocket. Bit brassed off with the old man, eh?"

"I just want it burnt!"

"Nah. Sorry, Val."

She walked away from the incongruous pile, angry with Doug for refusing her his matches, angry still with her suicidal no-hoper of a father, angry with her ex-husband, who had also disappointed her modest expectations of him. Even Clive, who had done her no wrong, was cast into the boiling bucket of her rage, solely on account of his gender. "Goin' the wrong way," Doug called, but she ignored him, striding away from his voice. Val understood her emotions well enough to know she required privacy for a while. In time the anger would pass, but until it did, the less human company around her the better. And so she walked on, between trees so widely spaced they offered no obstacle, her shoes crunching over fallen twigs and the gravelly red soil beneath.

Eventually she felt the mood pass, and her footsteps, quick with resentment, slowed and came to a stop. It had been a silly thing to do, throwing a tantrum as she had, and Val regretted it now. It had been especially idiotic to behave as she had in front of Doug Farrands, who had done nothing but offer good advice against her wishes to incinerate the sorry pile of furniture. She had made herself look foolish. And she was lost. The bush presented its forlorn stillness all around her, the same in every direction, an outdoor hall of mirrors in which she could see no reflection of herself, only her surroundings, endlessly multiplied. Val surprised herself by experiencing embarrassment over her predicament, even though no other person was there to witness the result of her folly.

Now she had to decide what to do. If Doug had followed her, there would not be any difficulty, but he had not. She supposed her bad mood had communicated itself to him with enough force to dissuade him from trailing after her, and she had ignored his last comment deliberately. This was the result: she was lost; a babe in the woods. It was too ridiculous for words.

"Doug? Are you there?"

Her voice was small, made faint by contrition, and seemed to go no farther than the nearest tree before fading to nothing, leaving not the slightest echo.

"Doug?!"

The birds nearest to her ceased their squawking momentarily, then resumed. Val felt the beginning of panic, a tentative clutching around the heart, and fought it off, even as she turned in circles, looking for some sign that Doug had not allowed her the solitude she had made it clear she wanted. There was nothing. Walking in ever-widening circles, she could not even come across evidence of her own tracks to that particular spot. It was as if her every step had been swallowed the instant her shoe left the ground to take another. Every indication of her passage through the bush had, to Val's inexpert eyes, been erased.

"Hullo . . . ?"

This time the birds paid her no attention, and Val could feel panic returning, its grip more insistent this time. She had been an idiot, yes, but felt she shouldn't be made to die for it. Like every Australian, even those who live their lives in the cities, she had heard stories of death by starvation and thirst and exposure in the bush of her country, where no predators but aloneness and distance would stalk her, and direction was strewn across the ground like fallen bark, pointing every way but the way out, the way home. There was nothing for it now but to attempt the traditional bushman's solution to her predicament.

"Cooooooo-*eeee!!!*" she screeched, and parrots flew from the branches above her by the score, wheeled in unison like brilliant party streamers, and were gone for less alarming reaches of the bush. "Coooooooo-*eeee!!!*" It hurt her throat to make the sound; it hurt her pride to have to.

"Cooooooo-*eeee!!!*"

"Give me ears a rest, eh?"

Doug stepped into sight, seemingly from nowhere, since no tree trunk nearby was thick enough to conceal him, no crooked pandanus so leafy he could have hidden behind it. Val's relief was stronger than her suspicion that she had been under observation for some time.

"There you are," she said, as if it had been he who lost himself.

"Yeah, and I know where I bloody am too."

"Well, you've got the compass, so I'm not surprised."

"Doug's book a rules says you have to hang around the bloke with the compass and not go chargin' away in a shitty."

"I didn't."

"Pull the other one."

"I thought you were behind me."

"I reckon I'll have to be from now on."

"No you don't. I wasn't lost. I thought you were."

His smile was infuriating. "Feel like goin' back now?" he asked.

"If you like."

"This way. Or did you know that already?"

"No need to be such a smart arse."

"If I had a smart arse I'd ask it questions, not sit on it."

"And I wonder what it might say."

"Somethin' long-winded, I expect."

Val laughed in spite of herself and wondered if she wasn't a little hysterical at having been found before too many minutes of fear were endured.

They began walking again, Val insisting that she walk beside Doug, at a distance of some feet, so he would not form the impression she was blindly following him. They continued walking in silence and came eventually to the open lands near Flying Fox River. While they picked their way among tussocks of parched grasses up to their knees, Doug suddenly held out his arm to make Val stop. He pointed across the open space between themselves and the trees. They had come at last to the river, which here opened out into a shallow lagoon, and she saw four or five dark shapes moving along the opposite shore.

"Are they buffalo?" Val whispered.

"Yeah, bull and four cows, I think. Keep walkin', but don't talk loud. They're temperamental buggers sometimes."

The buffalo were wading nonchalantly in water up to their thighs, fat bellies swaying, backswept horns curving toward their spines as they tossed their blunt heads lazily in the sunlight. Val thought them splendid. "They're not as big as I thought," she murmured.

"Big enough to squash us flat if they wanted," Doug said, his voice uncharacteristically low. "Knew a bloke once, wasn't payin' attention where he was goin' and walked into a herd a buffalo, and instead a standin' still and bein' quiet, he starts wavin' his arms and shoutin' like a drunk, and they trampled him to death before he could say Jack Sprat."

"What's that one doing?"

The cow farthest from shore had suddenly begun to thrash about and bellow. Its four companions turned away and stampeded for the trees, leaving it to lunge at the water with its horns, where a floating log, unnoticed before, had surfaced. The end of the log nearest the buffalo cow opened and fastened itself upon the left rear leg, sending blood into the air as the cow attempted to wrench itself free.

"Blighty . . . ," said Doug, and began to run, unslinging the rifle from his shoulder. Val ran with him, several paces behind. The cow's bellowing took on a new tone of high-pitched urgency and terror. The crocodile, monstrously long, its tail thrashing in sinuous curves just beneath the surface, had begun dragging the cow into deeper water. Doug stopped and brought the .303's stock to his shoulder, aimed, and squeezed the trigger.

"Shit . . ."

He worked the bolt to place a bullet in the breech, then aimed again. The shot, the first Val had heard in her life, was explosively loud. Doug swore again and worked the bolt as fast as he could for a second shot. The cow was up to her neck in water fast turning red around her, mouth open in a continuous bellow that had about it an air of hopelessness. Blighty could not be seen at all, his presence signaled by nothing more than overlapping eddies at the rear of the cow, a constant moiling of the redness there. The buffalo now began to snort as the water rose to its nose. Blighty had dragged it to a depth in which its hooves could no longer touch bottom, and the cow became part of Blighty's liquid world, disappearing quickly below the choppy surface, nostrils sending a final spray of blood-flecked mucus into the air. Then the waters were still.

"Bastard . . . ," breathed Doug, lowering the rifle.

"It was so fast. . . ."

"It was him. Nothin' else coulda been that big. I buggered that first shot, and he was already underwater for the second one. A bit closer and I mighta got him."

"The water doesn't look deep enough for what happened."

"Yeah, well, you have to watch out around here, like I told you. There's nothin' that's safe. Christ, I woulda loved to get him . . . wily old bugger."

They watched the lagoon and its motionless red stain.

"He'll take the cow down to the bottom and stick it under a log. Crocs have got grippin' teeth but nothin' to chew with, so they let their meat rot a bit till it's nice and soft. He'll start eatin' what he caught in a week or so."

"Can we go away from here now? I don't like it."

They walked on, following the direction the fleeing buffalo had taken toward shallower waters, and crossed the Flying Fox farther down, barely wetting their feet.

"I thought you said Blighty lived in that other place, Blighty's Pond."

"He does, but he ranges where he wants to, and that means wherever there's water, even places where there isn't. That's what makes crocs so bloody dangerous."

"I want you to show me how the gun works."

"Here." He handed it to her. "The bullets come out this end."

"Don't be funny. I'm not in the mood."

The first two shots served to awaken Clive from something approaching torpor. He had not progressed beyond the title page of his novel before the heat inside the iron house began to sap his enthusiasm for the project. He sat and stared at the sheet of paper on which his story was to begin, and its intimidating whiteness, the broad expanse of its utter emptiness, began to grow as he watched, until the sheet was all that he could see. No words came swimming into his mind, no scenes presented themselves. He had gone no further than deciding to write about pearl shell divers, with a hero based loosely on Doug, but thus far the only incident he had stored away in his head was the timely rescue of Ishi Murikama. Everything else was a perfect blank, like the paper before him.

The second series of shots, shortly after, were enough to take Clive outside, away from the typewriter that squatted so insolently, so unavoidably, on the table. Following the sound of more shots, he came to the river, where Val was firing at a rock the size of a man, twenty yards away. She lowered the heavy rifle as Clive approached, and Doug took it from her.

"Know how to shoot, Clive?" Doug asked, pressing more bullets into the .303's wedge-shaped magazine.

"No."

"Wanna learn? Might need to know one day."

"We saw Blighty," Val said.

"Really? Where?" Clive was instantly envious.

"Back there," Doug said. "He got a water buffalo, dragged it under in less'n a minute. I tried to get him and missed." He offered the rifle to Clive. "Have a go?"

"Rather!"

Clive proved no better at hitting the target than Val. Attempting to show them both how it was done, Doug himself missed two shots out of four. "There, that's why Blighty's alive and well today," he said.

All the ammunition Doug carried having been used, they returned together to the house.

"Got your first chapter done?" Doug asked, smiling.

"No, of course not. It's not like making out a shopping list."

"What's your hero's name?"

"I haven't given him one yet."

"How 'bout Fearless Farrands, sharkbiter."

"I'll let you use that in the book you write."

"Arr, come on, Clive, you know I couldn't write a book. You said you were gunna make your hero like me."

"Did you?" Val asked.

"In a general kind of way," Clive admitted. "This will be fiction, not biography."

"It's because I'm not good-lookin' enough," Doug said to Val.

"I really don't want to discuss it," Clive announced.

"All right, mate, the subject's closed." After a few steps more, Doug said, "Gunna be any dirty bits in it?"

"Please!"

"Leave him alone," Val said, laughing.

"Just tryin' to be encouragin', that's all."

Val said, "Clive, we found the furniture."

"What furniture?"

"Perce's stuff," said Doug. "It's all piled up a coupla miles southeast a here. Abos did it, I reckon."

"What on earth for?"

"Dunno. Could be somethin' to do with Perce killin' himself."

"Are Aborigines opposed to suicide on religious grounds?"

"Wouldn't have a clue."

6

CLIVE VISITED THE RICKETY PYRAMID of furniture several times; he could not have said why. He left it untouched, since none of the pieces was necessary in the house. The sight of such commonplace household stuff arranged in such a fashion unnerved him a little, yet was fascinating somehow. He had made a discovery he assumed Doug and Val had failed to notice, since they hadn't mentioned it, and that was the presence of a small shaving mirror, about eight inches by five, at the heart of the wooden cluster of objects in the bush. The mirror had been struck a blow at some stage and was fragmented in a spiderweb pattern from its center. Clive supposed the striker had been Perce Burridge, the act committed in a fit of self-loathing. Obviously the man had not been happy within himself, since the shotgun solution is the recourse of unhappy men. It drew him to itself on each of his visits, that shattered mirror, and he tried to discern fragments of himself in its triangulated slivers, each holding true to its place within the frame despite the hundred lines of demarcation from its neighbours.

The book was not going well. The book, when Clive forced himself to think of it, was nonexistent. The title, with its trite yet pompous arrangement of words—*Beneath the Waves*— mocked him. He had not even had the courage to include his own name beneath it on the single page he had been able to produce. There was no story; there were no characters, not even one resembling Doug, who was certainly an interesting enough man to be transferred directly to the printed page. But Clive had said he was uninterested in biography, and so the individuals he wrote of would have to come from his own experience or, failing inspiration there, his own imagination. Both repositories proved barren. He could think of nothing, conjure no one from his brain onto the page. His secondhand Underwood sat before him each day. Its letters on their angular arms had risen to smite the paper just fifteen times, then lapsed back into formation to mock him with their stillness.

He was a failure. His reason for being at Redlands was a farce. His friend and his cousin left him alone for the greater part of each day, as requested, and he had produced nothing to make their help worthwhile. They were themselves distractions, Doug and Val. Clive suspected they were making love behind his back. He had cast them out into the dreary gardens of Redlands, and they had become Adam and Eve, he was sure. Sometimes he heard the sound of shots as Val practiced with the rifle, but there were silent hours unaccounted for every day, and Clive, whose imagination could provide nothing for his typewriter to use, was able to create the most lascivious scenarios for the absent duo, and these were fed into the part of him that was able, despite his best efforts at remaining aloof, to become jealous. At times he actually thought they were encouraging him to continue with his futile literary efforts in order that they might have more time together, while he sat before the Underwood in sweaty impotence.

There were never any stray signals between the two that Clive was able to intercept, but he remained convinced his suspicions were grounded in truth. "What have you two been up to?" he finally was able to ask. He expected guilty looks, evasive answers, but Doug said, "I sat next to Blighty's Pond for two and a half bloody hours, waitin' for the bastard to show his scaly snout, but he didn't turn up."

"I went for a wander with the compass," Val told him. "Doug's been giving me lessons in bushmanship. I went solo today and didn't get lost."

Their faces were honest, their replies plausible, and Clive was puzzled to find that he believed them. It was then he realised that his mind had slowly been turned away from its natural interests and acceptances by a green-eyed demon of his own construction, and the demon had stolen into his mind by way of Clive's frustration over the project that had failed before it had even truly begun. Understanding ran through him like cool water, and he said, "Do you know what I did today?"

"No, what?" Val said.

"I . . . stopped pretending to be an author. It's over and done with. It was a brainstorm, nothing more than that. I can't think why I imagined I could do it. What an idiot . . . !"

"Arr, don't give up, mate. You could write a bonzer book if you wanted to."

"It's too soon to stop trying, Clive, really."

"No, I've made up my mind. I don't have it in me. Do you know I've been unhappy since we arrived here? I have, and the blame lies with my own stupidity in proposing something I don't have the slightest talent for. I taught English composition, you see, and the little buggers, all those disinterested boys . . . they absorbed none of it, not a scrap, and I think I despised them a little, their ignorance, their not wanting to know the difference between an advertising slogan for Bisto gravy and *The Iliad*. I knew the difference, but . . . there's another difference, yes, between the ones who make the stuff, the stories and the moments that live on paper, and those who can only appreciate their efforts. Am I making myself clear? I thought I was the former, and I'm only the latter, nothing but a . . . a reader, you see, like anyone else. Bit of a shock to the system, actually. A fellow thinks he knows himself and then finds out he doesn't. Moment of revelation. Bloody awful moment . . . If I could write about that awful pile of tables and chairs out there in the bush . . . tell the story that nobody knows, tell how it got there . . . but I can't. This other thing . . . bloody silly nonsense. Pearl divers. Adventure . . . No, I'd rather do nothing. It's the more honest choice, don't you think?"

Val and Doug watched him, saw the despair twisting his features into a grimace that was intended to be a smile of relief, of self-perception, acknowledgment of folly.

"If you reckon that's what you really want, Clive."

"Are you sure?" Val asked. "You were really sure you wanted to . . . "

"Absolutely and positively sure! I want all this nonsense behind me! I've been an idiot, a complete idiot, but now I know it . . . and I want to stop."

"If that's the way you feel, you made the right choice. No need to talk about it anymore, eh?"

"It just seems a shame . . . ," said Val, but Doug sent her a look that made her stop.

"Thing is," said Doug, "what are we gunna do now? I mean, here we are, all three of us, and not a job between the lot. Maybe we don't need any jobs just yet, with the money we've got left, but if we're out here on a piece a land you two both own, it seems like we oughta be doin' somethin' with it. That's what I think anyway."

"This is my fault," Clive said. "I brought this down on us all. I told you I wanted to do . . . what I wanted to do, and you took some pearls so that I could do it. And now I've let you down. You took a personal risk, and it was for nothing. I apologise to you. Unfortunately, I don't have the faintest idea what we might do instead of . . . what I originally intended, and again, I'm sorry. I'm very bloody sorry. . . ."

"Shit, Clive, put a sock in it. No one's blamin' anyone else. It's just that we're stuck out here in the middle a nowhere with nothin' to do. Even old Perce tried to grow rice, and had a few head a cattle before Blighty took 'em. I just reckon we need to put our heads together and think a somethin', that's all."

"I can't think of anything. I'm sorry. My brain doesn't work, not at all, so you'll both have to excuse me and think of something yourselves."

Clive went outside, close to tears, it seemed to Val. Doug lifted his shoulders helplessly. "Stay here," Val told him, and followed Clive out into the harsh afternoon sunlight.

He had already gone some distance from the house, and she strolled in his tracks slowly, to give him time for recovery. It was clear he had been under self-imposed pressure ever since their arrival, becoming more distressed with every day that passed, while his book refused to be placed on paper. Val followed Clive all the way to Blighty's Pond, and when he sat on the same fallen tree she and Doug had sat on the first time they walked together, she approached him slowly and did the same, making sure she was not too close. He chose not to turn his head and acknowledge her for some minutes, and when he was able to, Clive put a wry smile on his face and shook his head at his own performance back at the house.

"Must be the heat," he said.

"Doug's used to it, but you and I aren't."

"But you're an Australian."

"From down south. It's nothing like this."

They stared across the dark waters of the pond. Cicadas zinged and rasped, filling the air with abrasion.

"I still haven't seen him, old Blighty."

"I don't think I want to again. Doug does. He wants to blow his brains out and skin him and make me a set of shoes and a handbag, he says."

"He seems rather taken by you," Clive said, feeling a familiar and reprehensible twinge. She was his cousin, he reminded himself.

"Oh, I don't know. It's just his way of talking. He's a bit of a skite."

"A what?"

"Show-off. He just says things to make you laugh."

"Nothing wrong with that, I suppose."

"Clive, don't take this the wrong way, but do you really think you should stop work on the book? We've only been here a little while, and it must be hard to concentrate in all this heat."

"No, I really have been fooling myself, I don't have it in me."

"I wouldn't know about writing books, but they do say you're supposed to use your own experience to write about. That way you've got something to say. You just put down what happened to you."

"I'm not interested in autobiography."

"Fine; just change a few names, and it's fiction."

"Nothing's ever happened to me, Val. Coming to Australia was my big adventure, and it's not really so adventurous after all, just a little peculiar for a Pom."

"What about back in England? Couldn't you write about being a teacher?"

"God, no. It would be far too depressing for anyone to read. There's no more boring and frustrating occupation on the face of the earth than teaching, at least for me. No, that's definitely out."

"What about your love life? Everyone's interested in everyone else's."

"Equally boring and frustrating, I assure you."

"You know, Clive, I was sort of looking forward to telling people about my cousin the famous writer. You really ought to ask yourself if you're just in a bad mood over this particular book that you weren't ready to write. There's no need to say you'll never have a go at writing something else, is there?"

"I suppose not."

"So you don't need to be all depressed."

"I suppose I've been a first-class prat. Doug's right, though; we need to find something to do."

"There's no rush."

"No, thanks to him and his pearls. I'm not used to being a gentleman of property and leisure."

"Me neither."

They both laughed.

The next day, Doug decided on a project to occupy himself with.

"We need a new dunny, or at least a new hole. Perce always said he was gunna dig one, but he never got around to it, so I'm gunna do it."

"How are you going to dig a hole without a pick and shovel?" Clive asked.

"I'm not. We're all goin' into town so I can buy 'em."

The Ford was cranked and started and steered along the rough bush track to Darwin. Val began to sing; Doug joined in, off-key, and Clive was persuaded to drown him out. The truck bounced this way and that, upsetting their rhythm and introducing screeches of alarm into their lyrics, but they sang for much of the way to town, in any case, only becoming self-conscious as they entered Cavenagh Street.

A pick and shovel were bought and thrown into the Ford, then Doug proposed a quick beer at the pub. "You two go ahead," Val said. "I'm going to have a chinwag with Mrs. Christie over at the Vic."

"Right-oh, but don't go gossipin'."

"Wouldn't dream of it."

They watched her move away. "All right, mate," said Doug.

"Now the real business can be got down to. Bring a thirst with you?"

"I believe I have, with all that singing."

"Call it singin'? I've heard better-soundin' water pipes in a fleabag hotel."

"You're referring to your own voice, of course, not my choirboy efforts."

"I wouldn't argue with a choirboy, Clive. God might put the mighty finger on me."

"And not before time, I'm sure."

"In here and no more argument."

Doug manhandled Clive inside the nearest pub and elbowed his way to the bar.

"Look what's come back to town like a bad smell!" someone shouted.

"A fart always wants to get back to the arsehole that gave birth to it!" Doug shouted back. "Who wants a bloody drink!"

For several minutes there was pandemonium as beer pitchers were filled and passed around, then Doug held forth on a highly exaggerated rendering of the encounter between Blighty and the water buffalo cow. In this epic of strength and mayhem, Doug's own role was changed from that of witness to participant, as he held on to the buffalo's horns at one end while Blighty attempted to drag it away with jaws clamped around its rear. Blighty only succeeded, Doug said, because his feet slipped from beneath him in the water. "If it hadda happened on land, I mighta been able to pull both of 'em my way."

"I reckon that buffler's not the only thing you been pullin', Doug," suggested one of the listeners.

"Every word I told you's dinky-di! Clive was there so he can back me up."

"Go on, then," Clive was challenged. "Is it bullshit or isn't it?"

"I was certainly there," said Clive.

"Yeah? Doin' what?"

"Doug asked me to hold his hat while he went to the rescue of a lady."

The bar erupted with laughter, and Clive had his first inkling of acceptance among the Darwinites, a pleasant sensation.

"Next time," Doug shouted, "next time I'm gunna fling

meself on old Blighty with me knife, like Tarzan in the flicks!"

More laughter, then a voice said, "Y'oughta fling yourself off a fuckin' cliff, Farrands!"

Doug turned and saw the Moxham brothers at the door. An expectant silence was hastily established in the room. "Now then, you blokes," said the barman, "now then, now then, no high jinks . . . " Everyone waited for Doug's reply.

"You supply the parachute, and I'll do it."

The reaction of the drinkers was louder than was called for, in order that Les and Ken might be goaded to continue their wrangling with Doug; with luck, an interesting fight might develop.

"Been doin' anythin' out Redlands way, Farrands?" asked Les.

"Gunna dig a new dunny. You can help if you want."

Ken said, "What's wrong with the old dunny? Fill it up with all your bullshit?"

Les said, "Probly not all he's been doin' out there. Been doin' the redheaded sheila, I bet, him and the Pommie both."

"Yeah," agreed Les, taking the opportunity to escalate the conversation closer to outright confrontation. "A back-and-front-end job, all at the same time. I reckon she could do that, a slackie like she is."

There was murmuring along the bar now, as the line between banter and insult was crossed. Doug set down his beer, and Clive, taking his cue from someone clearly better versed in barroom etiquette than himself, set his down also.

"Y'know," said Doug, "old man Moxham wasn't a bad bloke, as blokes go, but it's a shame what happened to his wife, turnin' out a coupla dingoes like she did." He continued, "I reckon it's just as well he kicked the bucket when he did, so he couldn't see how low they finally got. Yeah, I'd have to say I did him a bloody favor, havin' that fight that knocked him off his perch."

Les and Ken launched themselves at Doug, and Clive saw that he would have to take part in the ritual bashing the room was primed for. He had never hit another person in his life, and in this, his first attempt at fighting, he presented himself as an open target for Ken's fist. The sudden pain from his split lips altered Clive's tactics as no amount of instruction could

have. It was not just the physical hurt he received that made
him instantly forgetful of his qualms about such behaviour as
this; it was the coarse insult to Val and, in some peculiar way,
the fact that his attempt at literature had failed to flower.
Clive was enraged, an unusual condition for him, and his arms
flailed like propellers.

"Go on, Pom! Hit the bastard!"

Clive took several more punches to the face from Ken
before landing a lucky blow to his opponent's cheek. Ken was
so surprised that the Pom was capable of touching him that he
hesitated, and Clive hit him again.

"That's the way! Get him!"

Doug's efforts at besting Les were less amateurish but
hardly more successful. He had never liked to fight and did so
now only from a sense of powerful tradition; to back away
from known enemies before a barroom audience would have
finished him in Darwin, and very likely the entire Northern
Territory. He fought as best he could against a fighter no better than himself, and they staggered clumsily back and forth
along the bar, bumping several times into Clive and Ken; in
fact, they traded partners for a minute or so before resuming
the fight as they had begun it.

Mutual exhaustion set in before long, and the four men
slumped against the bar, panting and wet from their exertions.
"Beer up!" called the barman, and tall glasses of foaming
enticement were slid toward the fighters. All snatched them to
their lips and drank until the glasses were emptied. It was the
natural pause immediately after, when they each waited for
the inevitable belch that followed such hurried gulpings, that
ended the fight. All momentum was lost as wind passed from
rasping throats, and the barman took advantage of this to
announce, "Beer served in the next five minutes'll be a penny
off!" The bar was swamped by takers, the four battlers separated, and that was the end of the fight. Nobody had won, but
no one had been proved a cowardly dingo. Honor was satisfied. Ken and Les Moxham drifted to one end of the bar,
Clive and Doug to the other, and all were shouted beers by
those among the drinkers who favoured them.

                              °   °   °

Val had been waiting by the truck for over thirty minutes before being joined by the men. They bore the smell of the pub and the bruises from their time spent there.

"Look at you two. What happened?"

"Hit by a bus in Trafalgar Square," said Clive.

"Bloody big bus," agreed Doug, who had never seen such a vehicle except in magazines.

"We taught the driver a lesson, though, didn't we?"

"Gave him a bloody good hidin' he won't forget. I hadda pull Clive off him before the poor bastard had his ears bit off. Real demon fighter when he gets goin', that Clive."

"You both look pathetic. God, you stink!"

"You fart, Clive mate?"

"Don't believe so, old cock."

"Get in," Val commanded. "I'm driving. I wouldn't trust either of you behind the wheel in that condition." Doug reached for the cab door. "No you don't," Val told him. "You can both get in the back, so I don't have to smell you. Go on."

"Crikey," Doug complained, climbing into the truck bed. "You're a bit hard on a bloke, aren't you?"

"Clive, get in."

"Certainly, certainly." Clive was assisted over the side by Doug. "Fresh air and good fellowship, that's what we have back here, isn't it, Doug old pal?"

"Too right. Tons of it."

"Absolutely oodles."

Val started the Ford and drove out of town. She made no attempt to avoid the roughest stretches of track on the way home to Redlands. Via the rearview mirror, she saw Clive vomit twice over the side. Doug emptied himself once.

Work on the new dunny hole began late the next morning. Doug attacked the red earth with pick and shovel as if atoning for past sins, and Clive made a feeble pledge to share the work a little later. The new hole was positioned some ten yards west of the old dunny, a corrugated-iron box standing over an ancient hole filled almost to the top with ancient shit, a paradise for blowflies, a place where humans risked asphyxiation if they breathed through the nose while inside and risked inhaling blowies if they chose to breathe by mouth. A new dunny on the property was certainly overdue, and Val spared her criticism of the men for their drinking and fighting of the previous day in order not to slow them down with talk. Doug's pick flew, and he sank slowly from sight, disappearing completely from view by late afternoon, by which time Clive was sufficiently recovered to assist him from time to time.

During one of Clive's many rest periods, Val approached him.

"Mrs. Christie showed me some newspapers yesterday, Clive."

"Oh, yes?"

"They say there'll be a war in Europe soon."

"Nonsense. Everyone learned the idiocy of conflict last time."

"Hitler says part of Poland belongs to Germany, but England said he can't have it, or something like that."

"Bloody little egotist. Isn't Czechoslovakia enough for him? I suppose it's better to let him have his way, though. Once he gets what he wants he'll shut up, I should think."

"Mrs. Christie thought you ought to know, being a Pom."

"Very decent of her. Not to worry, Val; war's a thing of the past. Political negotiation and bluff, that's the way things are done now. Shooting at each other is out of the question. No country can afford to lose another generation to the bullet, really they can't."

"You wouldn't get involved, would you, Clive?"

"Nothing to get involved in. It won't happen. Hitler just wants compensation for the humiliation of Germany's defeat in 1918. Once he gets it he'll sit back and crow for a bit, then everything will get back to normal. God, it seems like the doings on another planet. Anything happening in Australia?"

"We won the Davis Cup."

"Congratulations. Anything else?"

"The editorials are saying we shouldn't get caught up in what's happening in Europe. It's not our fight, they say."

"Quite right. Nothing's going to happen, in any case."

"Clive!" came Doug's voice from the hole. "Is that you yakkin' up there?"

"Yes!"

"Well, get down here! I'm bloody knackered!"

"Excuse me," Clive said to Val. Within two minutes he and Doug had changed places. Doug swallowed mouthfuls of water from the rainwater tank, the level of which had fallen to its lowest point since Redlands had been reoccupied. He spat out as much as he drank. "Gettin' stale. Might as well drink outa the river."

"Blighty might get you."

"Bastard. I'll get him first. Heard you talkin' to me Pommie mate. What's all this about Europe?"

Val explained as best she could. Doug shook his head. "It better not bloody happen again. I lost me dad last time, for nothin'. Upset me mum up so much she died a few years later. Shitty bloody war. Sorry, Val."

"Clive says it won't happen again."

"Clive's a terrific bloke, but he doesn't know any more than you and me about what might happen over there. He's whistlin' in the dark, if you ask me. Can't blame him for it. I'd do the same in his shoes."

"He's a Pom, though. If something started, he'd want to join up, just because. You know what Poms are like."

"Reckon we'll have to tie the bugger up if the time comes, eh?"

"I can't joke about it, Doug. He's my cousin, and even if he wasn't, I really like him a lot. I'd hate to see him go away and get blown up fighting a war."

"Fingers crossed, for all of us."

The old dunny's rickety structure was lifted and carried across to the new hole and placed with care over it. The hole cut into the plank seat was aligned with the hole in the ground, and Doug invited anyone who felt the need to go ahead and baptise the new dunny while it was free of flies and the smell of human waste. No one accepted his offer, so Doug suggested carrying earth displaced from the new hole across to the old, to seal its aroma forever and "bury as many bloody flies as we can before they wake up to what we're doin'."

The old hole was filled and patted down with the shovel. The air smelt cleaner, and the flies that had escaped burial buzzed around in consternation, their homing beacon gone.

○   ○   ○

She knew why Clive kept his distance; the taboo between cousins was very nearly biblical, its hold on the public consciousness virtually immovable; but why was Doug Farrands not a problem? Val knew he was attracted to her, once their initial antipathy had been resolved without ever truly being discussed, yet he had barely so much as touched her in all the time they spent together wandering through the bush at Redlands. It was all very well to be treated like a sister by Clive, for whom her feelings were sisterly, but Doug was more of a problem to define.

Her divorce was too recent for Val to be interested in a man on anything but a superficial level, certainly one so very similar in some ways to her ex-husband. That man had been something like Doug, until the marriage revealed his actual self, virtually from the day of the wedding. The change in Ted Lansdowne had been abrupt, inexplicable, complete; it baffled her still, but at least she had concluded by now that it was not her fault. It was probably best that Doug made no move to be more than a casual friend; another such disappointment in a man would have been difficult to take. Still, the reasons for his sexual distance intrigued her in an abstract fashion.

It was Mrs. Christie who had provided the clue during their visit to Darwin for a pick and shovel. Doug Farrands, she hinted broadly, was a combo through and through. Exclusive association with black women was not unusual in the Territory and had been considered the norm for as far back as the place had been populated by whites. Mrs. Christie, no raving beauty even in her youth, had been courted like a queen, she informed Val, solely on account of her race. "It's a rarity up here, love, white skin on a woman. Makes the fellas a bit soft in the head when they see it, generally. Now, a nice-looking girl like yourself, it's almost too much to handle, if you see what I mean. They'll treat you like gold because of it, most blokes. No exaggeration, Val: You could have your pick. There's fellas in Darwin that's millionaires, believe it or not. Pearl dealers, they're the ones to go after. Not all of them's old, and not all are ugly, by any means. They'll take you down to Sydney and Melbourne and even overseas. But Doug Farrands . . . no, dear, not for you. Been behavin' himself, has he? That'll be the shyness. Shyness, that's what I said, you being white, and out of bounds, so to speak. Sounds silly, doesn't it, but this place is stuffed with more silliness than you'd find in a circus, I sometimes think. No, he won't go making a nuisance, not unless you encourage him, and you won't do that, will you, dear. Once bitten, twice shy. Save the second go-round for a bloke that's got the wherewithal, if you know what I mean. Shame to throw yourself away on anything less, and Doug, he's quite a bit less, and I say that in all kindness. He's just a big overgrown boy, like most of them up here. Good-hearted, oh my word, yes. Remember what he did for that Jap diver? But not marriageable, dear, not if you want something better for yourself than a bark humpy to bring up your littlies in. More tea, love?"

And so the atmosphere at Redlands had about it a schooldays kind of remoteness between the sexes. There was interest, but it came to nothing, through inexperience. Val accepted it after a while, but could not quite bring herself to look on Doug as her other cousin, even if the thing that drew them together—their casual Australianness in the face of Clive's more intense Englishness—made everyday contact between them as easy and natural as blood relatedness. She reminded herself more than once that as far north as she had come, she was that much further removed from the conventions and normalcy of the south, and silliness (to use Mrs. Christie's word) of one kind or another was bound to flourish. In a place neither desert nor swamp, so sparsely populated it did not qualify for statehood even in a nation famous for its chronic shortage of humans, it was only to be expected that nothing, not even love, would function as it did elsewhere.

Doug had warned her about the change of seasons that drove men to acts of unreasonableness and excess. The gradual shifting from Dry to Wet produced an alteration in the psyche that was almost barometric in its daily fluctuations, and Val thought at first that the thing she saw was the result of pressure on the brain from this phenomenon. But the Wet began in late October, as a rule, and it was not yet September; why did the hallucination visit her as it did?

The moving of the dunny was what began it. Within a week,

Val became aware of the figure occupying the space once enclosed by the box of corrugated iron that now stood ten yards west. When Doug and Clive filled in the old hole, they had piled excess dirt into it, raising the level a few feet above the ground, in the manner of a gravesite, so it might gradually settle over time to become level again. It was over this mound that the figure appeared, and Val was the one who saw it there.

She had no idea of its true nature, since it was seen by daylight, and spirits of the dead are commonly thought to present themselves in darkness. It sat, or rather hovered, a few inches above the mound, in a blast of sunlight so intense the rays appeared to flay it of any real solidity it might have pretended to possess. She thought it was a mirage born of heat and her own mind's reaction to the century-topping temperature that day. A sitting man was perched in the air where once a toilet seat plank had been. The figure wore shorts, although these were draped around its clumsy boots, and a shirt with the sleeves torn off, and a wide hat that cast its features in deep shadow. Its knees were spread widely apart, and its hands rested firmly on those knees. Val was reminded of a photo she once had seen in a picture book, of a statue from the time of the ancient Egyptians, a pharaoh seated in just such a stern and uncompromising stance upon his throne. Val rubbed her eyes, then turned again to the mound, to find it empty.

When she had seen it three times in five days and was convinced the thing had reality of a kind, she told the men. They went to stare at the mound but saw nothing on or above it. "Are you positive it was there?" Clive asked.

"Yes. Sometimes it's more solid than others. Its shorts are down around its ankles."

"It's Perce," said Doug. "He's sittin' where he always sat. He had guts made outa concrete. Used to sit out on the dunny for hours sometimes, waitin' for the gravy train. Used to leave the door open so the blowies wouldn't mob him to death. It's him, all right."

"A ghost?" Clive was skeptical.

"First one I ever heard of that liked hangin' around the thunderbox. Trust old Perce to be different."

"I won't accept it until I've seen it. Val, are you absolutely certain?"

"I don't know what it is, but it's there," she insisted.

She saw the thing again two days later, and without taking her eyes from it, scared that distraction would rob her of its presence, she called for Doug and Clive. They saw nothing, even as Val told them the vaporous entity was right there before their eyes. Doug approached the mound and walked through the somnolent sitter without being aware, through any of his senses, that he had done so, and Clive did the same.

Val could not explain it in any other terms but blood. "I'm his daughter. I suppose daughters are closer to fathers than nephews are, or friends. I can see him, sort of. He's really there, and if the both of you don't say you believe me, I'm going to get very shitty about it."

"Can't have that happen," Doug said. "I believe you. How 'bout you, Clive?"

"Well, I daresay there's merit to such sightings," he admitted, "since they seem to happen all over the world, in every era and culture. 'More things in heaven and earth than are dreamt of in your philosophy,' et cetera. I'm certainly not going to accuse anyone of fibbing."

"Thank you very much."

Clive was in fact slightly jealous that it was Val who apparently had been visited, like Hamlet, by the ghost of her father.

7

THE TREES WERE MOTIONLESS. Distances were guessed at by how distorted an object might be when viewed through the squirming waves of transparent heat; the more convulsive its shimmying movement, the farther off the thing was. The landscape for miles around appeared to convulse between baking earth and an incandescent sky. The bush performed an unceasing dance from midmorning until late afternoon, writhing and shivering as if in torment, every gum tree a soul rooted in hell, until October should come like redemption.

Redlands was roasting. Its tenants lay in their hammocks and thought of ice and cool breezes and far-off regions unacquainted with conditions such as these. The air entering their bodies was arid, without sustenance, inhaled after having passed from the mouth of some invisible dragon. The rainwater tank was dry, every drop of drinking water brought from the Flying Fox, now reduced to a tired trickle. The level of Blighty's Pond had dropped four feet, and the lagoon wherein Blighty had dragged the water buffalo had shrunk to several acres of spongy soil interspersed with tussocks of dying grass. The birds did not bother to make song. The endless dirge of the cicadas was lowered an octave and had about it the dissonance of despair.

"I'd give me big toe for a cold beer," Doug groaned.

"My entire foot," said Clive, who could not quite accept that this, the dry season of the Northern Territory, was called winter in the rest of Australia. Doug had warned him of what was to come when the tropic sun came closer, bringing with it the time of the monsoon. "This is gunna seem like paradise then, mate. There'll be a river a sweat comin' off you twenny-four hours a day. You'll be prayin' for the Dry to come back, fair dinkum."

Val went outside to look for Perce. The phantom had appeared several more times, but of late appeared to have faded somewhat. Val was unsure if relentless sunlight might affect the occupants of whatever plane of existence Percy Burridge currently inhabited, but he did seem to be stripped of a little more substance each time he sat in the air over the mound, now settling noticeably beneath his ghostly buttocks. His hat continued to shade the long face beneath, and peer as she might, Val still could not say with assurance that she knew what her father looked like. He was tantalisingly present yet frustratingly absent, much as he had been in life—often in her thoughts during the years of growing up, never there in the flesh. Val was not one to dabble in the psychological sciences, but she did ask herself, as she watched Perce floating before her, his wispy torso threaded by blowflies, if he wasn't perhaps a reflection of her memory of that time. She did not share this notion with the men, had by that time stopped all mention of the visitor, as their interest in something they could not them-selves see began to wane.

Perce was not there today. Val felt waves of heat come rolling from the redness beneath her, the blueness above, attempting to flatten her between them. She began to walk. Blighty's Pond, a true billabong now, lay stagnating, its leaden surface dimpled by the slow eruption of bubbles from below, as matter on the bottom decayed. Dragonflies darted across the pond like blown scraps of coloured tinsel. Val stood watching for some time, waiting for another glimpse of Blighty, unseen since the killing of the buffalo. The air itself seemed to hum, with a resonance to it that was separate from the dron-ing of flies. She felt herself begin to fall asleep on her feet, or so it seemed. It became difficult to keep her eyes open, and as her eyelids were lowered for longer and longer moments, Val rocked slightly in her shoes, like a tree subjected to the slight-est of winds. Her eyes closed fully now, she felt the ancient heat pass across her skin, the timeless vibration of unseen life in the air around her. The cracked mud beneath her soles seemed to shift and stir, as if straining to break open, split like old snakeskin, and peel aside to reveal newness there of a kind Val knew she had never seen before and might never see again.

She opened her eyes to prevent herself from toppling, and saw the reddish-grey mud on the pond's far shore bestir itself. A long section of the bank beneath the trees was separating itself from the rest, sliding forward like a dragged log. Blighty's stubby legs propelled him in a leisurely sinuous waddle for several yards, then he paused. Val could see one yellow eye caught in sunlight that lanced down through the leaves. The eye shone like a ball of amber, the curved surface in its socket of horn bisected by a thin wedge of darkness, the slit pupil that saw Val, and watched her, as she watched Blighty.

He was a true monster, the sheer bulk of him, even at a distance, seeming to occupy more than mere yards and feet. From the tapering, almost dainty tip, forward along the serrated battlements of Blighty's quickly fattening tail, to the splayed rear legs and the belly so broad it lay flattened against the ground beneath it, to the awkwardly placed forelegs with their fat and pointed claws, the thing was too long for mere lizardry, too predatory in its watchfulness, its complete lack of fear before a human, to be nothing more than a reptile. Its back, encrusted with knobs and further lines of serration, was cracked and mottled like clay gone dry from the sun, but it was the head that defined Blighty's true nature and essence, the massive toothed weapon bulging from a neck wide as its body. His snout lay along the earth, resting against the time for its use, the crooked and wavering line of the jaws pricked along its length with teeth protruding above or hanging below the gums: yellow, pointed teeth in contrast with the greyish skin of his back, the slightly greenish yellow of the underbelly blushing beneath. Blighty sent a chill through his observer, and the unblinking eye of amber assessed Val's reaction to his presence before her, gauging her terror and her availability to his needs. It was not worth his while to do more than be still, since he had been seen and could not disguise his shape or his intention, should he proceed to slide into the pond; and so Blighty remained as he was, content to be acknowledged by his inferior.

Val began walking backward before being aware of it. She

took her leave of Blighty like a fearful messenger departing a royal chamber, unwilling to accept that she had observed the living god and been allowed to withdraw without being struck down. Not until she had backed so far from the pond that trees obscured her view of Blighty did she turn away and begin breathing normally again. Her legs were trembling, her heart accelerating blood through her veins at a dizzying rate. Val wanted to sit and allow herself time to be calm, but sitting seemed too vulnerable a position to adopt, even if she was now quite some distance from the crocodile, and she made herself walk on until a feeling of foolishness made her stop. She was in no danger and must not hurry any farther, she told herself, and eventually was able to do that.

By then she had gone too far into the surrounding bush, gone in a direction she could no longer recall, for an indeterminate time, along a path less than straight. She had once again become lost, and this time there was no one to follow after her, no one she might call for in hope of assistance. Blighty had driven her into a corner without angles, a trap without walls, the open maze of bush that snares the unwary with sameness and repetition, until the inability to choose this way over that becomes the tool by which lonely death is accomplished.

"Bugger . . . ," she whispered.

The sun stood to one side of her, giving some indication of north. Val struck out in the direction she calculated would take her back toward the Flying Fox River, angry with herself for having repeated a part of her recent history she would have preferred to forget. Her mood darkened as she went, along with the light that was to be her saviour; the sun was becoming obscured, its radiance made diffuse by cloud. After weeks without anything in the sky but brassy emptiness, a haze was beginning to seep across the blueness above, filling in the spaces between one tree and the next, building in thickness until the sun was gone, all shadows made indistinct.

"Bugger, bugger, bugger . . . "

If Blighty had not revealed himself; if the sun had not been hidden; if she had only been less stupid, Val might have been walking through the bush for diversion rather than in hope of salvation from her own bungling. Something was racing toward her now—the sound of thunder, faint at first, then building to a cracking, rolling rumbling that was felt as much as heard. It came at Val like stampeding cattle, unstoppable and dangerous, and the haze above darkened in seconds. The land around her was reduced in depth by this abrupt whisking away of light, made flat by a shadowy sky reeling past the tree-tops like aerial waters in flood. Then lightning came, snapping and flashing in patterns of veinous brilliance that lay imprinted on the eye seconds longer than in the air, and more thunder came tumbling from the cracks blazing open and shut with electric suddenness.

A whispering rode through the trees, becoming louder between bursts of thunder; a whispering of wind and leaves in motion, and some other thing that touched her bare arms with tiny fingertips before she knew that rain, last felt two months and two thousand miles south, was falling on the Territory and herself. All but invisible in the afternoon darkness, droplets were making the red soil dance. Val took off her hat, raised her face to the sky, and felt her cheeks and forehead peppered with coolness. This moment was all too short; the shower became a downpour within seconds, the drops so close together and so large it was like being drenched by a bath-room shower. She stood beneath the nearest tree but found that the isolated clusters of eucalyptus leaves gave inadequate shelter from rain. Soon Val was soaked clear through to her skin. The ground as far as she could see was covered with what appeared to be a low red mist but was in fact the parched soil being bombarded with such intensity it leaped into the air several inches before being smacked down again. Val's feet and ankles were already covered with a sticky red spray.

She stayed where she was until it occurred to her that the storm would not pass soon and that what remained of the afternoon would be wasted if she could not use it to find her way home. So she began walking again, her feet sinking a little with each step into the newly liquefied earth, rain dripping from the brim of her hat onto her shoulders, her ears filled several times every minute with more bludgeoning barrages of thunder. As she walked, directing her steps to no particular purpose, she wondered if perhaps her choice to continue moving would only make her more deeply lost than before, and so stopped, then moved on again. It seemed pointless to argue with herself over the precise degree to which she had betrayed her own common sense. Walking was in itself a distraction from a peculiar feeling of blankness that had overtaken her following the encounter with Blighty, then had been swept away by the coming of the rain, and had now reasserted itself. Val walked without bothering to look up, without the least effort to search for even the most insignificant of landmarks. It was as if she did not care whether every step took her farther from any reasonable chance of being found.

And yet she was not unhappy. The despair she had felt earlier, on realising she was again lost, had disappeared for no good reason. Val took an almost childish pleasure in the sucking of what was now red mud at her soles, at the constant pattering of rain upon her hat, at the isolation from adult concerns that her going astray had fostered. She felt, however inappropriately, that she was not lost, not in danger of eventually perishing in the bush; she was looking for something that had no relation to her life until the moment she laid eyes on Blighty, enthroned on the bank of his pond. What it was she expected to find in the course of her wandering in the rain Val could not have said, but she raised her eyes from below her hat brim on occasion to look around with more alertness than before. Nothing revealed itself among the endless crooked avenues of bushland, not even a rainswept termite mound.

Then she stopped. Confronting her was a natural wall of rock, dull ochre in colour, its surfaces awash with rain. The wall rose to a little above treetop height and continued away from her on the left in a gentle curve. She approached the rock and began walking around it and saw it was not one monolithic stone but a collection of similar giants lying cheek by jowl, like massive bubbles blown out together, their various spheres interlocked, melding one curved surface with the next, and the next, the whole thing having been turned then to stone. Val had never seen such a formation before. More than anything else, it resembled a collection of ancient balding heads, haphazardly stacked, the misshapen faces beneath them, near to the ground, looking in many directions roundabout, and deep into the earth as well. Rain ran from these orbed pates in streams and splashed into the muddied redness below.

She walked around the entire thing in less than half an hour, fascinated by its overall structure, its shape suggestive of heaped skulls. When she came again to the place where she had first stood to look up at the rocks, she began circling again, this time with intentions of finding a crevice or pathway up onto the rock domes, in order that she might see above the surrounding bush and find her direction home. Within five minutes she found such a foothold and began climbing. The continuing rain made every step slippery, every shallow hand-hold in the weatherworn rock a challenge even to Val's slight weight as she pulled herself upward; she split several finger-nails in grasping at knobs of rock to support herself, and the toes of her shoes became as scraped as her unprotected elbows, as she slid back one step for every three gained.

Eventually she reached the top of the lowest rock, and from there was able to clamber without too much difficulty to one higher, this having a more gentle slope, and from that to the highest of them all, a glistening red dome, raindrops rebounding from its surface in a fine spray of silver hair. She stood on its topmost point and turned slowly in a complete cir-cle. The trees were all beneath her, even the tallest of them, and their tossing was like the undulation of a grey-green sea. The north was indicated by a line of blue where land became water, and Val assumed this was the approximate direction in which to search for the sandstone ridge where Perce Burridge had built his house of corrugated iron; but the ridge was low, its back nowhere to be seen. She was every bit as lost as before, and could not understand why Doug had never men-tioned the rock outcropping to her as a feature of Redlands and given some hint of its compass bearing. She would give him a talking-to about that when she returned. It was not pos-sible that he was ignorant of its existence, not something as unusual as the agglomeration of stones beneath her.

Sunlight was breaking over the distant sea, making it shim-mer. Val could not guess how far away it might be, although the light reflecting from its surface made it appear closer than it had just moments before, while still beneath rain clouds. If the storm had come from the north, sunshine might advance toward her and allow Val a chance to dry out before she considered what her next move might be. Already there was a faint line of green growing beneath the blue, as the trailing edge of the clouds was pushed south from Van Diemen Gulf. Val felt that by the time sunlight was able to touch her again, some kind of resolution for her dilemma would present itself. The line of green was widening, deepening, moving toward her. The rain had begun to diminish from the moment she reached the top of the rocks. All of this was an omen, she thought, of good luck to follow. She did not usually think in such terms, but then she had never before experienced anything akin to what had happened over the last few hours. Her responses to the situation seemed appropriate enough to Val, and she watched the approach of the sunline with a quickening of hope.

The red stones began to steam from the moment they were exposed to sunlight again, and Val watched vaporous swirlings start to creep and fall down their sloping faces. Each tiny pool of rainwater caught in a dip or hollow sent out streamers of evaporating moisture that licked and curled at the rock and began sliding downward before disappearing into air that now was bright and clear and aromatic with the smell of wet earth and gum trees and even, Val was fairly sure, a salty whiff of the faraway sea. The sun was higher than she had feared it might be; there were still many hours of daylight remaining, but no answer to her predicament had come to Val despite her confidence. She did not want simply to begin walking as before, since that would provide every chance of becoming lost again. Val did not feel lost while she stood upon the stones, since these were located in a very definite place—the place where they were. Her trouble lay in not knowing where, in relation to the stones, the river ran, and without this as a guide, she felt it best to remain where she was until Doug and Clive found a way to locate her. It irritated Val that she was obliged to await rescue like some helpless heroine, but the alternative was foolhardy. She could encourage the men to find her, though, by making the first move that would bring them in her direction; she would build a fire! But she had no matches.

"Idiot!" she chided herself.

Suddenly she was depressed again, an abrupt transition from her optimism during the storm. Val was disappointed with herself for allowing this to happen, and tried to regain her mood of planning and calculation and hope, but it was gone. Something seemed to be invading her, deadening her perception of herself, some outside force that sought to numb the reflexes of survival she would have to depend upon. Val sat on the curved stone beneath her, already warmed by the sun, and tried to feel what it was that had changed within her. She could think of nothing that might be causing this strange enervation of the spirit. It was not a malign influence, nor was it friendly; the impression creating itself behind Val's eyes was of an entity beyond her comprehension, not a single thing but something made of many things, a shapeless amalgam of diverse parts, neither connected nor unconnected, bearing a thread woven throughout the whole: a twisting, twining, serpentine thing without beginning or end.

Her head was beginning to ache, and her throat was dry. Val walked carefully down to the nearest pool formed in a dimple on the rock slope, knelt by it, and drank. Once started, she could not stop, and so drank the hollow dry, pressing her extended lips into the lowest portion of the natural basin until every drop she could have taken was gone. She could feel the water inside her, so much of it that her stomach made a sloshing sound as she stood. Val felt considerably better but awfully tired, as if the miles she had covered in her wandering through the bush had suddenly been multiplied many times over and what she must seek before anything else was rest. It was an overwhelming sensation, irresistible, and she took herself farther down among a confluence of the stones, to a place near the centre of the rounded masses, and lay down there, with her legs extended and her back set against a reasonably comfortable curve of sun-warmed rock. Val removed her hat, folded its battered felt contours into something resembling a pillow, and placed this behind her head. Now she felt able to doze for a while, until it became time to do other things, whatever they might be. She felt sleep beginning to steal through her, a rapid possession passing from her extremities, closing about her stomach and womb like a warm bath, reaching finally for her brain, which it cupped in a palm the size of a continent.

Although her eyes were closed, Val watched as the sun passed from view behind the stones. Even before darkness came she saw the stars begin to form, and watched them turning overhead like a silver wheel. The moon rose like a staring eye and arced slowly above her body. Val knew she was asleep, yet not asleep. The rock beneath her was hard, but she could not move to relieve her discomfort, and the feel of her eyelids resting together, their lashes loosely meshed, caused her to believe that the things she saw before her in the sky were parts of a dream, even the mosquitoes that drank her blood, and the flying foxes that swooped and flitted in their hundreds while she slept and dreamed of men who pranced and strutted and turned their heads like wild creatures, and behind the men sat women, their faces hidden, who knew without seeing what their men were about, and behind these came young men who offered their bodies for ritual scarring; and behind them all was the vortex that forever spins, the twisting funnel leading back through its own intestines to all times gone, all times yet to come, all animals and men contained within it, and entities that were both animal and man, and all things understood, and passed on for relearning. There were trees and stones that talked among themselves, and birds who passed messages between these things and men; and there were journeys undertaken, not that some other place than the place of their starting might be reached, but that all places in between might be revisited and reunderstood by the journeyers.

And the vortex took hold of her and drew her down into itself, along its passageway from time unto unchanging time, and pressed her against itself until all that she knew became not known, and all things unknown to her were revealed; but she drew back from them, the last known thing that held itself inside her a message to herself: that every part of the learning was not meant for her, and to accept it would be to lose the self she had always known; and so she held fast to that last thing inside her, until the new things—which she understood were the oldest of all possible things—were gone from her, leaving only sunlight and shadow in the place of their passing; and knowing they were gone, and her self restored, Val slept a true sleep, the sleep that comes from exhaustion, from battle within the self.

°   °   °

The light streaming in under the roof had about it a cathedral quality, she thought, despite being filtered through fly wire. Val realised she was somewhere familiar but could not identify the iron roof overhead, nor the light that passed through to the inside where flies could not, unless they were unusually persistent. Then it came to her: she was in her father's house, lying in her hammock, but the blanket she had hung to separate herself from the men was gone. It was supposed to be where it always had been, at the periphery of her vision, but it was not, and she turned her head to see what might have happened to it. The interior of the house seemed very large when viewed from this now-unprotected corner, but the sight of Doug hunched over the table in its centre, a cigarette dangling from his lips, made her distress small. She called his name, but her lips would not move. Her throat convulsed, but no sound came from it, and she knew something strange had occurred, some bad thing that had left her helpless, unable even to speak.

"Duh . . . ," she managed to croak at last, and he came directly to her, smiling.

"Don't go gettin' excited," he said. "Want some water?"

She nodded. He fetched a brimming enamel cup and held it to her lips. When she was done with drinking, she allowed water to spill onto her chin. Doug set the cup down. "Better?" he asked.

"Why am I like this . . . ?"

"Coulda been a lot worse. I've seen blokes end up dead in twenty-four hours out there. Good thing the rain came, eh? Get plenty to drink, did you? That's what kept you goin'."

"I got lost. . . ."

"Bloody oath you did. I looked everywhere, but then the rain started. When it cleared up, I fired off a coupla dozen shots. Hear any of 'em?"

"No . . . "

"Better take a compass next time, eh?"

"I was at the stones."

"What stones?"

"Big red stones, big and round, all together."

"Dunno where you mean. Bri and his mob found you east a here, wanderin' around in the bush. That was yesterdee arvo. You walked outa here two days ago."

"Two days?"

"Yeah. No rain, and you woulda been dead, no bull."

"Who . . . who found me, did you say?"

"Brian. Me boy, remember? I told you about him."

"Your son?"

"That's him. Came up to visit me, and be buggered if he doesn't come across you out there, half dead and mozzie-bit from head to toe. Him and his mates brung you back here. Bloody lucky, Val."

"I fell asleep there, I don't know why. . . . Two days?"

"Two."

"Where's Clive?"

"Stuck on the other side a the Flyin' Fox. He got all anxious about what's happenin' overseas and said he's gotta find out what's what. He took the truck to Darwin a bit after you went out walkin'. He probly got there all right before the rain came, but he won't be gettin' back till the water goes down. Clive doesn't even know you went missin'."

"Is this the Wet?"

"Nah; just a bit of a sprinkle to dampen things down before the real stuff hits us. It'll be a few weeks yet. Just a sun shower, that's all."

"I'm trying to remember. . . . I know I walked for a long time, then there were the stones . . . and I climbed onto them to see . . . if I knew where I was, but I didn't."

"No big stones that I know of around here. You musta gone a long way inland."

"No, I could see the sea from on top, and they weren't really very high. It couldn't have been too far."

"Anyway, Brian found you before things got too bad. I was havin' pups, worryin' about you on your tod out there. I'm gunna get you a compass and make you wear the bloody thing around your neck."

"Are you sure about Clive?"

"He'll be jake. Nothin' to worry about there. Want some more water?"

"Yes, please, and . . . I think I'm hungry."

"Stay right there; tucker's on the way. Sweet corn do you?"

"Anything."

Doug turned to the pantry, a collection of canned food on a metal shelf. Val watched him work the opener with an expert hand and dump the can's contents into a tin pan, then set this in the fireplace, a thirty-three-gallon drum modified to contain hot coals. Watching him blow these to life, Val felt a wave of affection for him. He was not educated, but he owned, she had to admit, a true heart.

"Be a coupla wags of a dog's tail," said Doug.

"I can wait. . . . Oh, Doug, I just remembered now . . . I saw Blighty."

"Yeah? At the pond?"

"He was on the bank, the other bank from me, and he just sat there, watching me. His eyes are a horrible yellow . . . and he's bloody enormous."

"The old bugger just keeps growin' every year. The Abos say he's old as Methuselah. Well, they don't say Methuselah, seein' as they don't know about that bloke, unless they're missionary Abos, but they say he's the oldest thing in the Territory, except for the land."

"He wasn't a bit scared of me."

"Why should he be? Would you be scared of a nice tasty sandwich?"

"Oh, don't."

"Here's us humans, inventin' all kindsa gadgets, ships and planes and electricity, and all we are to Blighty is a sandwich. Makes you think, doesn't it?"

But she had fallen suddenly, alarmingly, asleep. Doug hovered over her but was reassured by the gentle sound of Val's snoring, and so ate the sweet corn himself.

She had never been so close to an Aborigine before. Brian was handsome, with just enough of Doug's features to suggest the relationship. His hair was far curlier than his father's, his eyes darker, his teeth whiter. Brian's skin was the colour of treacle and honey. Doug had told her Brian was fourteen, but he seemed much older. He wore nothing but a ragged pair of white man's shorts.

"Orright?" he asked, when Val opened her eyes.

"Yes . . . Are you Brian?"

"Yeah. Pleeztameetcha."

"You found me, Doug said."

"Yeah, me and some others. You were pretty crook."

Val looked for the sunlight that should have been streaming through the wire beneath the eaves, but the walls were dark.

"Did I fall asleep again?"

"Yeah. Dad says to feed you when you wake up. He's not here. Gone down to the Flyin' Fox to see if your cousin's on the other side, waitin' to get across. Water's gone down enough to get the boat over now if he's there. Ready for some tucker?"

"I'm starving."

"Just be a tick."

He moved silently around the lamplit room. "Been makin' damper," he said. "Turned out really good. Some a that?"

"Lovely."

He fetched a chunk, without a plate. She accepted it from his hand, noticing the beauty of his long fingers. Those must have been his mother's hands; Doug's were short and square. Brian squatted again beside the hammock and watched her eat, unselfconsciously close, smiling as she hurried her way through the damper.

"Got plenny more. Want some?"

"Lots."

He fed her again. When she was finished, the empty place inside her filled, Val asked, "Did you find me where those huge stones are, the big round ones all jumbled together?"

"In the bush," said Brian, but the smile was gone.

"I can't remember leaving the stones at all."

"Dunno 'bout stones," he said, avoiding her eyes. He was an amateurish liar.

"I had the strangest dream there . . . but I can't remember what it was about. Isn't that silly?"

"Dreams come and go, I reckon."

"Yes, but this was . . . special. Are the stones a special place?"

"Too right they are. . . . Arr, crikey!" His face twisted

momentarily with anguish. "I shouldna said that. I'll get in trouble now."

"I won't say anything to anyone, I promise."

"They're gunna know I opened me mouth. . . ."

He appeared genuinely worried over his gaffe, so Val reached for his hand. "I promise, promise, promise. I don't know what else to say."

Brian shook her hand in a lacklustre fashion, his face still creased by worry.

"They're gunna know anyway."

"How, if I don't say anything?"

"They just will. You weren't sposed to be there."

"I just found it. I didn't mean to."

"No whitefellas allowed there, see."

"Oh, I'm sorry."

"Not your fault," Brian admitted. "I shoulda never opened me mouth, but. They're gunna know I did. Probly already do."

"I'll say I tricked you, if that's all right."

"Not gunna be orright with them."

"Who are 'they'? The people you came with? The ones who found me there?"

"Yeah. They never liked it when we seen you out Kukullumunnumantje way. . . . Arr, bugger it!"

He clapped a hand over his mouth, whether because he regretted swearing in front of her, or because he had let slip the name of the stones, Val could not say.

"I won't breathe a word. I couldn't even pronounce it, Brian, so don't worry."

Brian turned from her and looked at the door, then stood and went to it. When he lifted the latch and swung the door open, a tall, white-bearded Aborigine was waiting outside. This man and Brian exchanged a few muttered words through the fly-wire door, then the man looked around Brian at Val and opened the door to put his head inside the house. "Orright, missus?"

"Yes, thank you."

"Pretty crook you were." He wore cast-off pants and a bush hat, and his chest was deeply scarred with ritual markings.

"Thank you for bringing me here."

"No worries. Bri lookin' after you orright?"

"Yes, he is."

"Good-oh. Pom's comin' soon, your cousin."

"Has he crossed the river?"

"Liddle bit, he'll be there. Got Doug waitin'. Hoo-roo."

"Oh . . . good-bye."

The tall man turned away into the night.

"Lettin' the mozzies in," said Brian, and closed the fly-wire door, then opened it again and hurried out, following the bearded man, Val assumed. She could imagine the conversation that might occur between them, equal parts accusation and denial, but Brian would not be able to deceive his own people for long; his handsome, open face was made for friendliness and laughter, not lying.

When Brian returned a short time later, Val asked, "Is everything all right?"

Brian shook his head but would not talk. He stood in a corner, the instep of his left leg perched on the upper calf of his right, and did not look at her. Val supposed he had returned to the house only because of Doug's instruction to watch over her.

She got up from the hammock and bent unsteadily to put on her shoes. Her dress, she noted, now that she was closer to the lamp, was filthy. Doug should have taken it off her while she slept, but there were probably all kinds of prudish barriers preventing this. She wanted to change now, but could not do so in front of Brian, and did not want to suggest he should leave, not after having helped get him into trouble with his people. "I'm feeling better now," she said, smiling at him. "It must've been your damper, Brian."

"Dad made it," he mumbled, still avoiding her.

"I think I'll go and join Doug by the river. Want to come?"

"Nah, not allowed."

"Doug said?"

"Nah, other one."

"With the beard?"

"Yeah, got him on me back now."

"I'm sorry."

"Me own fault."

Val left the house and wandered toward the Flying Fox. Some distance away in the bush, she could see a campfire, its light interrupted now and then by figures passing before it. Doug was waiting near the riverbank, the boat ready nearby. A kerosene lamp was near him, but not so close the insects surrounding it would be diverted by the smell of his skin. She sat beside him.

"Feelin' better?"

"Much. Someone told me Clive's on his way."

"Who said that?"

"One of Brian's mates, the tall one with the beard and scars on his chest."

"That's Ranji; he's the boss. Good bloke, if he takes a shine to you. Clive'll be along, if Ranji said so."

"How can he be so sure?"

"Blowed if I know, but they do. Bush telegraph. Gettin' on with Bri?"

"He's a nice kid. You must be proud of him."

"Yeah, I am. He's grown about a foot 'n' a half since last time I saw him. Hardly reckernised him. . . . Here we go, right on the money."

Doug pointed across the river, where headlights were flashing along the track. The sound of the Ford came to them over the water. Doug stood and began pushing the dinghy off the bank.

"I'm coming too," Val said.

"Better not. Blighty's turned boats over before today."

He pushed off from the bank before she could argue. Val watched the truck's headlights stop where the track entered the river. The distance across was not great, probably not more than fifteen yards, and the depth no greater than three or four feet, but the Ford's exhaust pipe and floorboards would have been swamped if Clive attempted to drive across. The current was weak, and Doug was able to row more or less directly across, even if he was taken a few yards downstream at the central point. The headlights were turned off when he reached the far bank, and Val could not see the dinghy clearly on its return trip. When Clive stepped ashore at last, she stepped forward and hugged him.

"There was never any real danger," he said, surprised by Val's gesture. "I suppose you got pretty soaked out here too. Darwin was positively awash, but it's just a 'sprinkle,' they said."

"We had the same thing."

Doug pulled the dinghy farther up the bank. "Tell Clive what happened when you went walkabout."

"Walkabout?" Clive said.

"Oh, it's nothing. I just went for a walk and got lost, then Brian found me."

"Brian? Have I missed out on something?"

Val and Doug told their stories on the way back to the house, Val with considerable circumspection, in accordance with her promise to Brian. Clive nodded toward the fire burning among the trees. "Is that them?"

"That's them," Doug said. "You'll find 'em a bit different to the Abos round Darwin way, more like they're supposed to be."

"Yes, well, I may not get the opportunity to get to know any of them."

"How's that?"

"England's finally at war with Germany. It's official, as of the third of September."

"Oh, Christ," Val said.

"I'm afraid Australia and New Zealand have also declared war."

"Stupid buggers!" Doug threw his hat on the ground, then picked it up. "You're not gunna go back and get yourself shot, are you, Clive?"

"I really don't see that I have much choice. It's my country, Doug."

"And mine, but I'm not stupid enough to join up just because they expect me to. Bugger 'em! It's politicians start bloody wars, but they're not the poor bastards that have to go and fight 'em!"

Val said, "Don't do it, Clive, please. You don't even live there anymore."

"Where I live has nothing to do with it. Both our countries have declared war. Germany started it, not us. Should we simply let Hitler take everything? The Nazis already have Warsaw surrounded. The Poles don't have a prayer, and when he's got Poland he'll go for France, and from there it's just a hop and a step across the Channel. He mustn't be allowed to get away with it!"

"Same old bullshit as last time," Doug said. "I'm not goin' anywhere near it. Bugger 'em all. I don't give a stuff what the Aussie guverment says—it's not our bloody fight. It wasn't back then, and it isn't now. It's all bullshit and flag-wavin'."

"I don't have any argument with you, Doug. You certainly have a right to disagree, but I have the same right, and I simply feel I have to go home. It's a question of England needing me, however trite that might sound to you."

"Bloody hell, Clive, one bloke more or less isn't gunna make a zak's worth a difference. At least give it a month or two to die down. You don't know for a fact what Hitler's gunna do. He might be happy with Poland and call it quits; you never know."

"No, my mind is made up. Really, I only came back to Redlands to let you know I'm leaving. There's a ship due in Darwin six days from now, bound for Liverpool. The property's yours, Val."

"No it isn't. It's ours."

"I can't own something on the other side of the world."

"Then don't leave."

Clive sighed, then stopped walking. They were almost to the house by then. Val could see Brian standing by the fly-wire door, which he had left open, with the lamp inside attracting insects. "Look," said Clive, "I know you don't approve, and I truly regret that you don't, because you're both . . . I just think we're the best of friends, and I hate to split us up, frankly, but there's a bloody war on, don't you see, and I have to be part of it because jolly old England is. What it has to do with Australia, I can't say. That's for you two to work out. I'll just say this: if Australia was threatened with invasion by an enemy, wouldn't you do your best to prevent it? Wouldn't you?"

"Nobody's gunna invade Australia."

"But suppose somebody did."

"Then I spose I'd join up, yeah."

"Thank you. I rest my case."

Clive continued walking and left the Australians behind. They looked at each other, then caught up with him. Val was more upset at the thought of losing her cousin than she had thought possible. They barely knew each other, were quite different as personalities, but superseding all differences was the fact that they were related.

"Can't you wait even a little while, Clive?"

"Six days, that's all. I'm sorry. My mind is made up. Who's that?"

"Me kid that I told you about—Brian. Hey, Bri, come 'ere and meet me mate Clive. He's Val's cousin from England."

"Bloody long way, that. G'day."

"Yes," said Clive, "I suppose it is. Hello."

All four entered the house.

"Jeez, I could use a beer." Doug's tone was mournful. "This is bloody awful, this. First Val gets lost, which is bad, then she gets found, which is good, and it's by Bri, which is bloody good, then Clive comes home and says he's gunna go off to bloody war. That's shitty. Bloody shitty because the Aussie guverment's gone and done what they did last time, which is jump in just because the bloody Poms want us to go and bleed all over fuckin' Europe again. Sorry, Val. And there's no bloody beer this side a Darwin."

"I apologise for the bad news," offered Clive.

"Not your fault you're a patriot, mate. I can understand. I just hate to think a you gettin' hurt. If I was a bullshitter, I'd say go and punch Hitler on the nose, somethin' stupid like that, but I can't, Clive, I just can't bloody do it."

"I think we should change the subject—or, as you Aussies say, the bloody subject—and, Doug, I apologise for keeping this in the dark until now, but I anticipated your misery and my own and did not return to Redlands without provision for it. Observe!"

He took from the inner pocket of his jacket a flat bottle of Corio whiskey. From the other inner pocket he produced a second bottle. From the two outer pockets of the same jacket he conjured two more bottles. Doug's eyes, already moist with emotion over his mate's decision to leave, became even more damp at the consideration shown for his feelings. "Beauty, mate . . . ," he said, and it was almost a sob.

"I consecrate this booze," said Clive, "in the holy name of mateship, and cousins, and sons, and . . . all sorts of things, I suppose."

"Get the bloody corks out," Doug begged, and Clive obliged.

Two bottles were set aside for Ranji and his entourage. Val pointed out that there were at least a dozen Aborigines. "I know it's not fair division," Doug said, "but it's more'n they can handle. Blacks still aren't used to hard grog, so two bottles is plenty. Good thing you got four, Clive. Bri, take these out to Ranji's mob, then come back and take a swig with us. Or both. Depends on you."

Brian left with the two bottles. Val felt acute embarrassment over Doug's instruction to him. Doug saw her face and said, "Whites aren't sposed to give 'em grog at all, so don't look at me sideways like that. Brian understands better'n you and me put together. Nothin's perfect, not round here. All right?"

"Yes."

"Didn't want you thinkin' I'm some kinda bastard."

"I wasn't thinking that."

"Well, you looked as if you were."

"Well, I wasn't."

"Could we begin getting drunk now, please," Clive suggested.

"The Poms," said Doug, with admiration. "Deep down they're practical bastards."

Val drank only a few mouthfuls of the awful stuff from Clive's bottles. It helped to ease her pain over his decision to leave. The men drank quickly, and she watched alcoholic bonhomie take hold of them. Brian went back and forth between the black drinkers and the white, listening but not contributing to the stories being told inside the house as midnight came and went.

Clive's adventures since arriving in Australia were the focus of these increasingly exaggerated reminiscences, from his first encounters with Doug and with Redlands to the pearl-shelling foray and the rescue of Ishi Murikama, the domestic arrangements of Sung Yee, and the advent of Val upon the scene. There were recollections of Blighty, and of Ken and Les Moxham, and the hearty endorsement of a putative meeting among the three. There was a cheer raised over the rescue of Val from the bush, but Brian would only shake his head when invited to give details, and Val herself said she could remember little of what happened. She was, like Brian, an observer, and she could not help but notice that he drank as little as she. Was he under instruction from Ranji to listen to the whites' conversation and report any mention of the stones called Kukullumunnumantje?

Something else occurred to Val, and when Doug went outside to relieve his bladder, and Brian was back at the Aborigine camp, she asked Clive, whose ability to talk coherently was considerably reduced by then, "Is it because the book didn't work out?"

"Parn . . . pardon?"

"Are you going back to England because you couldn't start writing the book? If you were working on that, would it make you stay here, at least until it was finished?"

"Umm . . . hard to say, Unarserable, acshully. Bloody silly idea, be an author. Bloody egotism . . . mm. Better luck with the bloody old sword, eh, than the bloody old pen. Reverse the cleesh . . . cliché. Destiny calls. Clive Bagnall answers the trumpet toot of the motherland, finds glory on the battlefield against the darsa . . . the dastardly Hun. Smack old Adolf in the eye for being a bully, that's the stuff. Miss everyone, nashurally, you and Doug. Here today, gone tomorrow . . . Bloody shame . . . "

"You can change your mind, Clive."

"No, can't do that, even under the jolly old influence. Immovable objeck, you see. War's the irresistible force. Put the two together . . . Boom! No need to look so down in the mouth. Be right as rain, you'll see. Win a medal or two. Dashing hero and all that. Might happen."

Doug had returned in time to hear this. He sat clumsily and said, "You're a bloody idiot, Clive. There's no heroes, not anymore, not in wars. It's all straightforward killin' nowadays, none a your team spirit, hooray for the fuckin' regiment. The blokes with more tanks and planes are the bastards who'll win, not the ones that're right."

"I don't wish to argue."

"Me neither. You can't argue with a silly bastard Englishman who won't listen."

"Nor with a silly bloody drunken Australian who thinks he has the wisdom of the ages in him."

"Who's drunk! You don't know what drunk is, you Pommie galah!"

"I bow to the expert!"

"What's that supposed to mean? Is that an insult or what?"

"Think about it and write me a letter. No, a telegram would use fewer words!"

"Right, that's it! That's a definite bloody insult!"

"Stop it, the both of you!" Val shouted. "What a couple of morons! You might never see each other again, and all you can do is act like squabbling babies! You both make me sick!"

She ran from the house. Clive and Doug looked at each other.

"What'd we do?" Doug asked.

"Upset the lady somehow, I think."

"She's a sensitive girl, Val. Still not used to bein' up north, I reckon."

"She'll make the adjustment, I'm sure."

"Any a that piss left?"

Doug reached for and drained the last of the whiskey.

"I'm the party taking his leave," Clive protested. "That should have been mine by rights, especially since I paid for it."

"Nah, you bought it, but you didn't pay for it. That's pearl money in your pocket, mate. Sung Yee's the one that paid for it, if you're gunna get technical."

"I refuse to continue this ridiculous conversation," Clive declared, slapping a drowsy fly from his cheek.

"No need to punish yourself," Doug said, tossing the empty bottle into a corner.

"I need . . . water."

"Got plenty in the tank now. Be overflowin' in a few weeks, with the Wet comin'."

Clive stood and moved in the direction of the doorway. He failed to see the fly-wire door and walked into it, tearing it from its fragile hinges.

"Bloody hell, Clive—now we're gunna get eaten alive by mozzies! Watch where you're goin', why dontcha!"

"Sorry, awfly sorry . . . "

Doug attempted to set the door back into the jamb but only succeeded in placing a foot through it, tearing the wire screen from its frame. "Fuckin' pissy door!"

He joined Clive beneath the tank. Together they allowed tepid water to run from the pipe onto their bare heads.

"This is somethin' you don't have in England, eh?"

"What?"

"Showers. You don't have 'em over there, do you?"

"We prefer to bathe."

"Yeah, but not very often, that's what I heard."

"Who did you hear this fascinating information from?"

"Some bloke that was over there. The Poms never wash, he said."

"He's a liar, or you are."

"Say that again?"

"We wash as often as Australians, and a damn sight more often than Territorians."

"We've got a dry season here, mate. There's no bloody water half the year, and the sweat comes rollin' off of you the other half. You don't have that in England."

"Thank God."

"Clive, I'm fightin' the urge to give you a poke in the nose."

"Oh, please, don't exercise willpower on my behalf. Do whatever comes easiest, by all means."

"That's another one a those insults, right?"

Clive walked away from Doug, but Doug followed, then went back to turn off the flow of water, and ran after Clive to catch up.

"You've been makin' a lotta these comments lately."

"What comments?"

"Puttin' the boot into Aussie. Lookin' down your Pommie nose at us."

"Really? I thought I heard the same kind of thing from you, and would you kindly stop referring to me as a Pom. I'm sick and tired of it."

"You English buggers think you still own us, that's the trouble."

"I can't think why we'd want to."

Val heard the sounds of talking replaced by the sounds of a scuffle, and came around the corner of the house to find Doug and Clive on the ground, locked in a clumsy struggle for supremacy. Their wet clothing and hair was caked with soil, and their grunting and puffing as they fought was an ugly thing to hear.

"You stupid pathetic shits! Look at you! What a couple of fuckwits!"

This language from Val caused both men to stop fighting immediately. They found their feet with assistance from each other and stood shamefaced before her, faces masked with dirt. Val placed her hands on her hips, the automatic pose of the angry parent who has discovered her children being both foolish and naughty.

"I don't think I can stand to look at you. Here's Clive about to go away forever, and all you can do is pick fights over nothing. I wish I'd never met either one of you."

"Arr, fair go, Val. We didn't do any harm, did we, Clive. You all right?"

"Perfectly fine, thank you."

"A couple of silly kids, that's what you are. . . ." Her voice rose in pitch, and she began to wring her hands without being aware of it. "He's going away to get hit by a bullet, and all you can do is hit him! You're stupid!"

"Me?" Doug asked. "Or both of us?"

"Ooooh . . . get rooted!"

Val stamped away from the house toward the Aborigine camp.

"She's got a real shitty on, looks like."

"Best leave her alone."

"Yeah. Did we finish all the grog?"

"We didn't. You did."

"Good-oh."

Val's anger waned as she approached the campfire. She had spoken to Brian for only a few minutes and exchanged no more than a few words with Ranji. They were people unlike herself, black people, an ancient race, subjugated and cast adrift inside their own country by the whites who had taken everything. Val had been told little about Aborigines during her school years, other than that they had resisted white settlement by spearing the settlers. This act had been presented in her textbooks as both savage and futile, and lessons concerning the old Australians began and ended there. She was embarrassed, in a way, to be approaching them now. They had saved her from her own folly in the bush, and she was beholden to them for it. Val was not ashamed to owe her life to Aborigines; she wished only to be able to understand who they were, if that were possible. Brian was the natural bridge between worlds separated by colour and conquest, and it was for his slender form that she searched as she came closer to the fire.

Clive's whiskey had generated an effect here also. There was an air about the camp of free and easy laughter, its edges stretched beyond mere good fellowship and mirth. The figures around her, dark even by firelight, were clearly drunk, and Val regretted that her first venturing among them should be tainted this way. She was annoyed with Clive for having bought whiskey in the first place, annoyed with Doug for having drunk the lion's share of what was left in the house, then begun his witless brawling with Clive. She was doubly angry with Doug for having given any of the liquor to Ranji and his people, even though she could recall having resented what she regarded as Doug's stinginess over having divided the bottles unequally several hours ago. It was all very confusing for Val, probably the only sober person at Redlands.

"G'day."

Brian was at her side, seemingly as abstinent as herself. Val felt eyes watching her from faces too lost in shadows and darkness to read. She was close to tears.

"Got troubles?" asked Brian.

"Your dad, he's fighting with Clive."

"Arr, it's just the grog. Nothin' wrong with it."

"But your people don't fight for no reason, do they?"

"Too right they do. Get a bottle, there's gunna be fights. Blows over next day."

"I just want it to stop, that's all."

"Me dad, he's always been that way. Him and Clive, they'll be mates again tomorrer."

Ranji appeared at Val's side. "Bit of a ding-dong goin' on, eh?"

Val turned toward the house. "They seem to be less rowdy now."

"Doug, he's a bloke that likes a drop. Shares it too."

"So I see."

"You go on back there, missus. He won't do nothin' bad. Wouldn' hurt a fly."

"In a minute," Val said. She did not like to be told what she ought to do by anyone, black or white, if it should be a man. It depressed her to think that all men, whatever their race, might be fools. Brian was the only one who had not disappointed her that night.

"I came here . . . ," she said, then hesitated. "I came here to thank you again for what you did. For finding me."

"Jus lucky, missus. Coulda gone along liddle bit this way, liddle bit that way, woulda missed you. Jus good luck."

"Was I lying down or walking? I don't remember."

"Lyin' down, lookin' pretty crook."

"On some big stones?"

"Nah, no stones where you were lyin'. Jus fell down liddle bit near some trees."

"That's what Brian said, but I thought I remembered a lot of really big stones."

"Nah, not roun' here. Doug'll tell you. He's been here plenty a times, seein' Perce. No big stones roun' here, missus."

"Can you tell me why my father's furniture was taken away and stacked in the bush, all the tables and chairs and things?"

"Dunno 'bout that. Never seen no tables an' chairs, eh, Bri?"

"Nup."

"Where are you from?" Val asked, determined not to be thrust back toward the house. It was not that Ranji was rude, but she resented being kept from the secret Brian was obliged by Ranji's presence to hide from her. The thing behind Brian's dark eyes was Kukullumunnumantje, and Val wanted to know why, if that was where Ranji and the rest had really found her, they wanted to deny it.

"Down south a bit, Katherine way, Mataranka, Willeroo, all over."

"Come up for some sea fishin'," said Brian.

"See some people up this way," Ranji added.

"Is my father's . . . girlfriend here with you? Doug said her name was Beth. She was half-sister to Brian's mother. Is she one of your people?"

Ranji and Brian exchanged a look.

"Yeah, she's here," said Ranji. "Wanna meeta?"

"Yes."

Brian went beyond the firelight to fetch her. Ranji said, "Doug tell you 'bout Mandy, did he?"

"He said someone kidnapped her and took her away to Arnhem Land, and later she died."

"Yeah, thas right. Shame what happened."

"Doug said no one told him who the man was, the kidnapper."

"Mandy never got kidnap. This fella, she was promise to him when she's a liddle thing, so he come for her, only she's with Doug, an' they got a liddle yella-fella, Bri. Never stopped him, but. Took her off with him. Had a right to, see. That's the old way."

"So you know who he was."

"Might know," admitted Ranji, "might not know. Long time ago, that."

"Is he still alive?"

"Dunno 'bout that."

"Why can't you tell Doug?"

"Police find out, that fella might go in the pokey, up Fannie Bay."

"Doug says the police wouldn't have done anything anyway."

"'Cause Mandy's Abo, yeah, could be right. Doug'd do somethin', but. He liked Mandy. He got on the grog after she died. He'd do somethin', he found out. Give the fella a good hidin' probly. No need for it. It was the grog done Mandy in, not the fella. Wouldn' be fair, Doug bashin' a bloke jus because a fella took his missus like he had a right to do. That's Abo business."

"So you'll keep on protecting the one who took Mandy."

"Abo business, missus. Doug oughta marry a lady like you, then he'd forget."

Val kept the annoyance from her face until Brian returned, bringing with him a lubra far younger than Val had expected.

"This one's her, Beth," said Ranji. "Not much whitefella talk in her. You ask what you want, I'll say what she says, orright?"

Val was frustrated that the exchange would be filtered through Ranji. She could not think where to begin. Beth wore a dress and nothing else and had difficulty looking into Val's eyes. Val put out her hand. Beth took it briefly, and Val felt the hot, dry texture of her skin.

"Do you know who I am?" Val asked.

"I told her you're Perce's daughter," Brian said. "She's a bit shy."

"Ask her why my father killed himself, please."

Ranji rattled off several sentences in rapid-fire Aboriginal. Beth shrugged.

"She dunno."

"Was he unhappy because he couldn't grow rice?"

Following Ranji's translation, the same reaction was given.

"She never talked to him, so she dunno. Bit of a waste a time askin'."

"Doesn't any one of you know why he did it?"

"Coulda been all sortsa things. Whitefellas, they carn take the Wet sometime. Might be that."

"He killed himself because of the weather?"

"Happens."

Val looked at the rest of the group seated or lying near the fire. Most wore the cast-off clothing of whites but were still partially naked, and there were long spears leaning against the pale trunk of a fallen ghost gum. Gypsies without caravans, she thought, but then dismissed the comparison. Surely no European gypsy had ever wandered over so vast a region as the sun-blasted race watching her, or absorbed so little of the stronger cultures surrounding and inundating their own. Ranji was pretending to help her, Brian longing to tell her more if he could, but it was the blandly evasive silence of Beth that represented the gulf between Val and her hosts. There could never be true understanding, never be more than empathy and curiosity in her heart for the tribal civilisation dying even as its fires burned brightly under the stars. Across a chasm carved by time they stared, each at the other, without any inkling of the nature hidden by skin, the configuration of the hidden soul.

8

CLIVE WOKE WITH A HEAD that seemed to have been attached to his neck by nails and barbed wire. He could not recall ever having felt so bad, and he had not even drunk very much, according to his recollection of the night before. Daylight flooded through the opened door of the house; without the fly-wire screen, insects accompanied the brightness inside. Clive remembered in the vaguest terms having walked into the screen and taken it with him for several steps.

Then he remembered why they had all become so very drunk; he would not be seeing Doug or Val for very much longer. He liked them both a great deal and did not relish the leavetaking he had committed himself to. The agony inside his skull was punishment for his having abandoned England and gone down to the other side of the world. England needed him now, and Clive was in a tin shed, shockingly hung over, his thoughts filled with self-pity and sentiment.

Val was asleep in her hammock, but Doug was absent. Clive took himself outside into the full brightness of midmorning and saw his friend lying beneath a tree. Doug was breathing easily when Clive checked for signs of life, and so he left him there and went to the water tank for several mouthfuls of the metallic-tasting stuff. Feeling a little better for this, he wandered across to the Aborigine camp. He had spoken only a few words to Doug's yella-fella son and did not want the boy to think he was aloof, a typical white man who considered himself superior to blacks.

Several bodies lay around the burnt-out fire there, but he could not identify Brian among the slumbering forms who lay

in positions of abandon on the ground. It was not a sight he
found pleasant, suggesting as it did the aftermath of a pagan
orgy (he could see one lubra's breasts clearly), but Clive could
not honestly say that the three whites in the area, himself
included, looked any different that day. It was a liberating sensation, this identification with goings-on he had not left the
house last night to witness, if indeed anything had happened
around the fire while everyone was drunk with his whiskey.
Clive felt some regret that he had not truly savoured any of
the wildness that ran through his imaginings now. He supposed it was probably too late to indulge in such shenanigans
himself, prior to his departure; all the liquor was gone, and he
could not picture himself doing anything outrageous without
the assistance of alcohol. He would have liked to copulate with
a woman of another race or, that being impossible, with his
cousin.

Clive was brought up short by the forbidden nature of
these thoughts and felt himself blush. He excused himself by
reason of his hangover but continued to feel guilty for some
time after, as he walked in aimless circles about the campsite
and the sorry house his uncle had left him. The great adventure was almost over. He had come so far and accomplished
nothing. Now he would have to justify his existence by returning to the point of departure and risking his life alongside his
countrymen. Clive was of a generation weaned from unthink-
ing patriotism by the devastation of the Great War; no intelligent person could possibly have thought after that debacle
that armed conflict between nations was a thing to be rushed
into with enthusiasm. But enter the battle he must, regardless,
or be forever ashamed. Hitler was a loathsome malignancy
upon the face of civilisation, a leering shadow that must not
cast itself across England. Clive would acquit himself with
honour and sweep away the lingering thought of having failed
somehow in this new country.

Perhaps if he had planned to stay on, things might have
been different; he would never know. It was just as well, he
thought, that the impartial forces of personal and historical
destiny were taking him away from the woman he kept
reminding himself was his blood relation. She was a wonderful
girl, although a trifle too salty in her language, and he knew he

would have become deeply entangled in the treacherous web of unrequited love for Val were he to stay on. It seemed logical that she would instead fall into the arms of Doug Farrands, once Clive was gone. Clive had known this from the moment he decided, in Darwin, that the news from Europe was too dreadful to ignore. He had couched his decision in the noble mold of self-sacrifice, of love for and obligation to king and country, but really, it had every bit as much to do with the impossibility of his ever having Valerie Lansdowne, or Burridge, or whatever she termed herself, for his own. It was not to be, so he would go away to war. It was a Victorian concept, but Clive felt quite at home within its familiar embrace; there was nothing to be ashamed of in doing the right thing, especially if it was the only option available.

"Christ, I feel like a stepped-on rat turd. . . ."

Doug was approaching, his hat crooked, his steps unsure.

"Good morning!" Clive was deliberately cheerful.

"For you, maybe. Seen Brian around?"

"No, not a sign."

"Don't be so bloody chirpy. It's depressin' if you feel like I do."

"Sorry, old sport."

"Clive, I'd wring your neck if I didn't like you. Listen, before Val gets up, are you still gunna do what you said last night?"

"I'm returning to England."

He said it as calmly as he could and with more conviction than he felt. It was gratifying, in a way, to see Doug's expression, already creased by indulgence, become even more distraught; Australians seemed unable to keep their feelings to themselves.

"Clive, you're a bloody lunatic."

"That may be, but I'm leaving."

Doug shook his head at such intransigence and went away toward the camp, where several figures were stirring. Clive saw Val step outside the house and look around, her eyes screwed tightly against the sun. He hurried over to her without appearing to do so.

"Up at last!" he greeted her. "About time!"

"Oh, Clive, don't talk so loud. . . . God, I feel awful."

"Have a nice long drink of water. I did, and it helped."

"Where's Doug? Is that him?" She was squinting in the direction of the camp.

"Gone looking for Brian, I think. Care for some breakfast? I could throw some sausages in the pan, if we have any left."

"Please don't talk about food. . . ." Val took herself away to the water tank and doused her head in a practical but remarkably unfeminine way. Clive realised that part of his growing infatuation with Val stemmed from her reactions, her comportment under certain circumstances; she never conducted herself as an English girl would, at least none of the English girls Clive had known. He watched her hair swing in a heavy arc from down near her waist, to slap against her shoulders as she swept her head back, sending droplets flying through the air. He was sickeningly in love with her, and it could not be. Clive had to turn away and stare at the bush and remind himself once again that soon his difficulties here would be replaced by an entirely new set, on a larger stage elsewhere. It could not happen soon enough, he told himself, but was not convinced.

The days left for friendship were passed in a haze of avoidance and unspoken grief. Doug could not beg Clive to stay, but Val could, and did so several times. Doug again ridiculed the notion of rushing to arms in answer to the whore-siren call of Duty, but Clive would not be swayed by either approach. He appreciated their efforts, recognising them for what they were, but held himself up to the critical gaze of faraway peers; no Englishman would allow him egress from what called him, solely on account of the cajolery and snide commentary of ex-colonials. His English blood was what counted, and it was to this he was answerable, come what may; and so the days remaining passed in a mild acrimony, dimming the bright flame of friendship.

Ranji's band disappeared without preamble on the third day after their arrival. Even Brian was gone without a word to anyone. Val suspected they had gone to Kukullumunnumantje, and rather than lie about visiting so secret a location, they left without warning, to conduct whatever business they practiced there beyond the prying of white eyes. She was tempted to search for the place, but the passing of Clive's remaining days at Redlands kept her there with him. She still had not told Doug or Clive of her time among the great stones, in deference to Brian's fear of their discovery. She had hinted to Brian several times that she would like to see the stones again and been met with awkward grinning and few words other than "Dunno what you mean." To win his trust she had spoken in some detail of the day of the storm and how her accidental finding of Kukullumunnumantje had really begun with a walk outside to see if Perce's ghost was seated in the air, following which Val had visited the pond and caught her first long look at Blighty, after which came the storm and Val's losing her way in the bush. Brian had listened to all this with great concentration and had asked for more detail concerning the circumstances under which Val saw, and was seen by, the crocodile. Val had told the story again, and Brian nodded, then walked away from her. He was gone with the rest the following day.

They drove Clive to Darwin, with several hours to spare until the ship anchored in the harbour was to sail. Doug insisted that the approaching moment of separation should be consecrated with beer. Val was against it, but Clive acquiesced, and the unhappy trio entered the Vic, where the clientele, learning of the Pom's departure, toasted him for a brave man and wished him the privilege of killing many Germans, who were, everyone agreed, "the biggest buncha bastards in the fuckin' world." Clive was shouted more beers than he could possibly consume, so Doug assisted him in their disposal, while Val shared her misery with Mrs. Christie.

When the time came for Clive to board his ship, almost a hundred drinkers bore him down the street and along the wharf, determined that the last piece of Australia the Pom should touch before leaving would be a pub floor. They carried him up the gangplank without allowing even the cuffs of his pants to graze its canvas sides, and once he was safely on deck, they retreated and sang several verses of "For He's a Jolly Good Fellow," serenading the Pom from the wharf while Clive stood above them at the rail, befuddled and forlorn, wondering where his cousin was. Doug was there, lost among the crush, but Val was nowhere to be seen. Clive felt inside his breast an awful emptiness begin to shape itself. He had come, he had seen; he had failed to conquer. He had wasted his time, accomplishing precisely nothing. He was a blithering fool, and he was sick over the side, to the cheers of his entourage.

Doug felt tears pricking at his eyes, but would not allow them release with so many men who knew him close by. The foghorn blared, and Doug looked around for Val, whom he had last seen quite some time ago at the Vic. Where was she now that her only cousin was leaving the country—still chinwagging with Mrs. Christie? It was dereliction of duty, in Doug's opinion, and he became annoyed at Val's thoughtlessness.

"Reckon he'll be all right over there?" someone asked.

"Arr, yeah, no worries," Doug assured anyone within earshot. "Old Clive'll shoot enough Germans to stack from here to Berlin. He's a lucky bugger, Clive. He'll be jake."

The ship's funnel was wreathed in steam as its foghorn blasted a lingering farewell. The sea beneath its fantail began to swirl; mooring lines were cast off and hauled aboard, and the tall white wall of the hull began moving away from the wharf, assisted by tugboats. Doug watched its ponderous departure and wished for the first time since driving to town that he might be alone. He had lost a friend. Doug did not expect Clive to live. Clive was too soft, too decent, for warfare. It made Doug want to curse and rant over the way a good mate was obliged by tradition to waste his life.

"No use hangin' around here, Doug boy. Beer's gettin' warm back at the Vic."

"Yeah, right-oh . . . "

The mob of farewellers turned about and streamed in scattered bunches back to the pub, glad to have done the Pom proud. Every man knew the big cities of the south were attracting would-be enlistees from the surrounding countryside and their own suburbs in astonishing numbers, and yet few of the Territorians were considering doing the same. There had been some out-of-work jackeroos who joined, and no one had called them fools. There had been other men who chose to go, almost from the moment word came that another war had begun in Europe, and it was assumed they had done so because they were eager for a fight, being fighters by inclination. But they had all been brawny men, as Territorians were for the most part, and their decision to risk everything had seemed natural, given their strength and the tough way of life they had always pursued. And then the Pom, neither tough nor experienced in the physical roughness of the world, had sailed away to do what many a bigger man was shirking. The thought was there, behind every raucous yell, every bit of tomfoolery engaged in on the way back to the Vic: the Pom had shown them all up.

Doug separated himself from the rest and began looking for Val, worried now that something might have happened to prevent her from seeing Clive off. He asked Mrs. Christie if she knew where Val might be, and was told she was in the best of all possible places, that being any place where Doug Farrands was not. "Eh?" Doug responded.

"Bloody men," said Mrs. Christie. "All you can do is talk loud enough to deafen each other and drink more than you need. The poor thing couldn't get a word in edgeways with you lot screaming and pouring beer all over the place. She's miserable as a wet cat, and it's your fault. You've got no common sense at all, have you?"

"What'd *I* bloody do?"

"Don't even know what I'm talking about, do you?"

"Where's Val, that's all I wanna know."

"Where you're not allowed, and that's that."

"Look, all I wanna know is if she's all right."

"As right as she can be, stuck with you. I'll give you a clue if you like. She didn't even get to say good-bye to the poor bugger that just left. Her own cousin, gone off to get himself killed, and she didn't even get the chance to tell him good-bye. That's what you did, you and your mates. She was in tears over it. Fat lot you care."

"She coulda come along if she wanted. I mean, where else were we gunna take him except down the wharf? There was nothin' stoppin' Val from comin' too."

"Only a mob of prize piss artists and larrikins. It's all been ruined now. He's gone, and that's that."

"Well . . . it wasn't my fault."

"Of course not. Nothing ever is for blokes like you. And another thing, Doug Farrands—it's her place now, Redlands,

even if it's useless, so you can just clear out and spare the girl
any more of that dirty talk that's been going around."

"What dirty talk?"

"Oh, use your brain, if you've got one. You just clear out
tomorrow, or else ask her nicely if she wouldn't mind too
much being made an honest woman of, even if it's only by the
likes of you."

"Eh?"

"You heard."

Mrs. Christie swept away to her rooms, where Doug suspected Val was hiding. The din from the bar came to him
along a passageway, but he was not tempted to join in and
continue the celebration begun by Clive's departure; Mrs.
Christie had given him too much to think about.

When darkness came, Val went to the truck and found
Doug waiting there, fast asleep in the back on a tarpaulin, his
mouth unflatteringly agape. She took the ignition key from his
pants pocket without waking him and began driving home, the
headlight beams lighting up each ghost gum like a spirit lifting
its many arms to frighten the humans bouncing by. Doug
woke up when they were almost halfway home and yelled at
Val to stop so that he might climb into the cab, but she kept
driving, a little faster than before, and he was stuck there
behind her, the soles of his boots often leaving the truck bed's
metal floor as Val steered for the roughest patches on the
track to Redlands.

Arriving home, she parked the truck and got out, slamming
the door with unnecessary force. Doug jumped from the back,
to land on wobbling legs that gave out beneath him. He was
glad Val was not looking in his direction.

"Hey, Val, what's up? Got a shitty on or somethin'?"

She ignored him, went into the house, and shut the door
behind her. The fly-wire screen still lay on the ground a short
distance from the house; Doug had ignored it, deeming the
repair Clive's responsibility, since it was he who had battered
it from its hinges, although Doug was admittedly the one who
had kicked a large hole through it. When he reached for the
door latch to go inside, Doug found that Val had hitched the
leather thong that prevented it from rising. She had locked
him out.

"Hey, Val, let us in!"

"Bugger off!"

"That's not very nice, I must say, comin' from a sheila."

"Get away from me! If you touch that door again I'll put a bullet through it!"

"Arr, come on, don't bullshit. I mean, what's wrong, Val? I tried to stop Clive from leavin', you know I did. I miss the bastard already. It wasn't my fault he left, now was it, eh? You heard me tellin' him he shouldn't go, didn't you?"

"If you don't go away, I'll shoot! I mean it!"

"Listen, it wasn't anythin' I did that made everyone carry Clive down to the wharf. I didn't tell 'em to do that—they just did it! Crikey, talk about layin' the blame where it shouldn't oughta be . . . "

The sound of the Lee-Enfield's heavy bolt sliding a round into the chamber came to Doug's ears, but he could not accept that Val might actually fire the rifle.

"Look, this is bloody stupid—"

The bullet came through the door several inches above Doug's head. He skipped sideways and fell over.

"The next one'll be lower if you don't piss off and leave me alone!"

Doug got to his feet and began walking backward. "You're as crackers as your old man was! Worse!"

"Just go away!"

"I'm goin'! Think I'd wanna be around a ning-nong like you? You're barmy as a bandicoot!"

Where was he supposed to sleep? It was a warm night, but the ground would be hard. Doug went warily back to the house. "Val? Hey, Val, chuck us out a hammock or somethin', eh?" While he spoke, he changed position in case she should shoot again.

"Lie down under a tree, why don't you! Or better still, climb one!"

"Come on, Val . . . "

"Bugger off!"

He slept in the truck, upright in the passenger seat, and saw the dawn come stealing across the sky, a sight he had not witnessed in years. Creeping across to the house, he found the door unlatched and went warily inside. Val was asleep in her hammock, and Doug stole silently across to his own, easing himself into its cradle of rope with the stealth of a burglar.

For several days they barely spoke, then Val began taking Doug's compass and a sack of food and wandering in the bush all day. Doug had taught her how to navigate by compass and was not so much worried she might become lost again as he was made curious by her protracted walks alone. She had given him no clue to their purpose, unless she was simply avoiding his company, a possibility Doug rejected.

"You oughta take the gun if you're gunna go pokin' about in the bush. Might bump into a water buffalo, or Blighty."

"I don't go anywhere near the water, so I don't need it."

"Well, where *do* you go?"

"That's my business."

"I just don't wanna have to go searchin' around for you if you get lost again."

"I didn't have a compass with me that time. I've been finding my own way home since then, thank you."

"I could come along and make sure everything's jake."

"You should find something else to amuse yourself with."

"Not much to do around here."

"You might think about moving back to Darwin, then. Doesn't the pearling fleet need your expert help?"

"Pearlin's just about done for the year. Once the Wet comes, that's the end of it. Probly nobody'd take me on anyway. Everyone knows I nicked those pearls from Moxham, so no joy there. I reckon me reputation's in ruins."

"That's very sad."

"Yeah, especially since I handed all me ill-gotten gains over to you and Clive."

"So now you think you've got a stake in Redlands, is that what you're saying?"

"Might be."

"And you want to stay here."

"Might do."

"Even if there's nothing to do."

"Better'n sleepin' in a holler tree." Doug smiled.

Val looked at his face for a long moment. The silences

between them had been unnatural, given Doug's gregarious nature. He had been punished enough.

"You can stay if you help me find the stones."

"What stones?"

"The place where I was when I got lost. Huge stones, all rounded and lying together like a heap of giant marbles."

"Never seen anythin' like that around here."

"But it *is* around here. I was there. I saw it and . . . felt it."

"That's what you've been lookin' for the last few days?"

"Yes. I want to see the place again. Brian knows about it. I don't suppose I ought to say that, even to you. It's some kind of secret place, I think."

"What's it got to do with Brian?"

"Not just him, all of them, but he's the one who let it slip about the stones. That Ranji said there weren't any stones, but Brian told me they're called Kukullumunnumantje, then he got all embarrassed and shut up about it. What's Kukullumunnumantje mean?"

"Dunno. There's hundreds a different Abo dialects. I only know a coupla words here and there."

"Such as?"

"Arr, nothin'."

"Go on, surprise me with your knowledge."

"Boogoo."

"What's that mean?"

"Bumhole."

"Trust you."

"You wanted to know."

"Will you help me look for the stones?"

"Might not be a good idea. Sounds like it's a sacred place or somethin', like a church'd be to us. If we were churchgoin' types, I mean."

"Doug, I just want to see it again. I don't want to do anything there that might offend Ranji's people. Something happened to me there."

"Like what?"

"I don't know. I fell asleep on the stones, but then something strange happened to me, I'm sure of it. . . . Ever since then . . . sometimes in the middle of the day, it's as if I just woke up, and there's just a taste of it left in my head, whatever it was, just out of reach, but it's not like a dream. I'm remembering, or trying to remember, what happened to me there. So I have to find it again."

Doug said, "Where'd you look so far?"

"That's just it—I've looked everywhere within an afternoon's walk from the house. That's all it took me the first time, and I was probably circling around a bit without noticing, but even if it was in a straight line from here, it'd have to be within a few hours' walk. Except it isn't. I've covered every square yard of the property, but there's nothing to see, and these stones are really big, taller than the trees around them. I don't know what I'm doing wrong. I'm using the compass the way you showed me, and I'm positive I've looked everywhere. But obviously I haven't. It's driving me up the pole."

"What you need's an experienced bush-basher."

"That's you, is it?"

"Too right."

They spent six days quartering and requartering Redlands in its entirety, even venturing farther than the property lines several times, to be sure Val's elusive stones were not somewhere just beyond the precincts of Perce Burridge's domain. "Goin' a bit beyond the black stump today," Doug said on one of these occasions. "I wouldn't normally do that. Normally I'd turn back, but seeing as you're here to protect me . . . "

Val aimed a twig at his head. "Think of a new joke, for God's sake."

"How 'bout this one. Once upon a time there was a girl from down south who dreamed up a big stone castle out in the middle a nowhere, and she tried to find the castle, but she couldn't because it was just a dream."

"It wasn't."

"But all along, the real reason she was out there lookin' for the castle was because she couldn't think how else to hang about with the good-lookin' bloke that was lookin' with her. She was a bit shy, this girl, so she couldn't come straight out and say she fancied him or anythin', so they wandered around in the bush together till they got so old they fell down and the white ants got 'em, and then the ants went home to their great big anthill, which is what the girl really saw in the first place."

"That's stupid. I said find a new joke."

"What's wrong with it?"

"The stones were real, and I don't fancy you."

"What, not even a little bit?"

"No."

"Was it Clive you were a bit warm and wobbly for?"

"I divorced a man who was charming and good-looking. If all that song and dance about love was worth anything, don't you think I'd still be with him? Don't start smoodging around me, Doug, please."

"Anyone'd think I asked you to jump off a cliff."

"I just want to find Kukullumunnumantje. That's all I want. Nothing else."

"So you want me to shut up about stuff like that."

"I want you to help me find what we're looking for."

"Even if I don't think it's there."

"It is!"

"Then why can't we find it? We've been all over the place. Anythin' as big as you said woulda been found by now, so where is it?"

"*Some*where . . . I didn't dream it up. Brian and Ranji knew what I was talking about. The place is real, and they know where it is, but they don't want me to know. They don't want me going back there."

"Then maybe you should do what they want. Sounds like it's their place."

"But something happened to me there, and I want to know what it was!"

"You haven't been invited, Val."

"What's that supposed to mean?"

"You're stickin' your nose in where it's not wanted, simple as that."

"Are you leading me around in circles for them? Did they tell you to?"

Doug smiled and shook his head. "They didn't tell me anythin'. I'm not an Abo, and neither are you, so they wouldn't want us snoopin' around their sacred stones, or whatever they are, anyway. I reckon it's time to pack it in. Might be Abo magic hidin' the place; you never know."

"What magic? Don't tell me you believe in magic."

"A bit, the Abo kind. I saw a bloke die once, out in the

bush. Real old blackfella he was, and he laid himself down to die 'cause he reckoned his time was up, he never said why. I helped him build a humpy for him to die in, and he said he'd go when the sun went down. So I waited there with him, listenin' to him sorta wailin' a song, probly a death song or somethin', and when the sun started goin' down he went all quiet and closed his eyes, and you know what happened then? A bloody huge goanna started crawlin' outa his mouth, a really big one about two foot long, and it came out onto his chest and looked at me, then walked off into the bush. I just about shat myself, watchin' a thing like that, I don't mind admittin' it. You're the first person I ever told about it, and I don't wanna hear you say it's bullshit. I believe you about the stones, because a that old blackfella, so you can believe me about the Abos not lettin' you find the place. It's invisible, see. You'll never find it if they don't want you to."

"Why didn't you tell me any of this before, if you're not making it up?"

"We weren't talkin'," Doug said. "Then when we finally started bein' polite again, I said I'd help you look, just to be friends again."

"You've heard of the place, haven't you?"

Doug looked away from her, then back. "Yeah, I know about Kukullumunnumantje. Never seen it, though. No white bloke ever has."

"So you've been helping me waste my time."

"Sort of, in a friendly way. You don't wanna get involved in Abo stuff, Val. Might even be dangerous. It's all they've got left, their secrets."

"Who told you about it? Was it Ranji?"

"Ranji wouldn't breathe a word about Kukullumunnumantje to a whitefella. It was Perce told me, if you must know. Your dad had a real interest in findin' it, just like you, but he never did. He said the stones are the heads of tribal elders from back in the Dreamtime, all the smart ones who knew everythin' there was to know. Their brains are in the rocks, kind of, thousands and thousands a years' worth a thinkin' all locked away in stone forever. It's like a big bank vault. All the stuff the Abos think is valuable, all their memories, I spose you'd call it, is in Kukullumunnumantje. That's what the name means, Perce said—Memory Stones, or Remembering Stones, somethin' like that, all the things the Abos ever knew about everything."

"Who told him about it?"

"I reckon it musta been Beth."

"Your wife's half-sister."

"I was never married to Mandy, but yeah, that's the one. She was here with the rest of 'em before Clive left."

"I know; I spoke with her."

"Yeah? What'd she say?"

"Nothing."

"Know why that is? Her tongue's paralysed. Never used to be, but it is now. That's why I think she told Perce about Kukullumunnumantje. They took her tongue away as punishment. She probly reckons she got off light."

"You can't just make someone's tongue paralysed."

"You can if you're an Abo and you're a spellmaker. Ranji's father's one a them. His name's M'linga, and he's killed at least two blackfellas just by pointin' the bone at 'em. Once an Abo's had the bone pointed at him, he knows he'll die. It's all in the mind."

Val felt sweat streaming from her brow. She took off her hat and wiped a forearm across her face, then looked up at a flock of pink-and-grey galahs sweeping overhead. The sky seemed to press down upon her, squeezing air into her lungs with its weight, air she could scarcely find the strength to push out again. From far away came the sound of thunder.

"Wet's comin'," said Doug. "This'll be the real thing."

"My father . . . they killed him, didn't they, because of what he knew."

"Dunno. Coulda been suicide, like they said. There's no way to prove any of it."

"But it could have been that. . . ."

"Mighta been. That's why you oughta pack it in, Val, and not go lookin' for the place anymore. Might be bad news for you if you ever did find it."

"But I found it once. . . ."

"Pure luck. Give it a rest, Val. It's not for us."

She stared at the ground. She saw the furtive pattern emerging behind her eyes, the unprovable chain of causation, the only evidence, itself cryptic beyond analysis, a stack of tables and chairs in the bush and the few quiet words Doug had finally let fall. Doug's hand on her shoulder was no more heavy than the burden of atmosphere, reassuring yet remote from her thoughts. Truth had been kept from her, and he was part of the friendly obfuscation, even if he had meant well. She could not decide whether to shake him off or accept his touch. There was a continual grinding overhead now as masses of cloud, seemingly conjured from nowhere, jostled blue-black shoulders for dominion of the sky, and snaking from the darkness came lightning bolts of eye-searing intensity, reaching for the land below. Val felt the first of a trillion raindrops smite her forehead.

"Here she comes," Doug said, withdrawing his hand.

And the rain was there, enfolding them in a torrent so sudden, so intense, Val felt she had been placed inside an aquarium. The air itself was turned to water around them, drenching their clothes through to the skin within seconds. Val put her hat back on before the relentless hammering at her skull could become painful. The red earth danced and soon was saturated, swimming with overflow, creating swirls around their feet. The sky had lowered itself like a descending blanket until the thunder seemed to crack and boom directly above their heads, lightning to leap at them from the treetops. The weight of raindrops was constant, their thrumming numbers across Val's shoulders a steady liquid pressure, pushing her down.

Doug was grinning at her. "Welcome to the Wet," he said.

Val took the compass from her pocket and looked down at its rain-splattered face, then turned in the direction of home. Doug watched her take those first few steps through the red waters streaming across the ground, then followed along behind. He had given her the bad news she needed to know. She would have learned it sooner or later, and it was better that it came from him. He was her only friend now that Clive was gone, so he had to do whatever it took to look after her, even if she might resent his thinking of her as needful in any way. He was her friend, and she was his, he supposed.

When she came through the door, Val went directly to her side of the hanging blanket and stripped off her red-caked clothes. She toweled herself dry but was covered with moisture again in less than a minute, her naked skin beaded like a sweating cheese. She heard Doug come into the house behind her, then go straight out again. They had not exchanged a word on the long slog across the southeastern section of Redlands, through mud and redly running freshets. Val assumed he had hung back from a sense of guilt over having kept from her those things she had a right to know.

She could hear him outside now, singing "Happy Days Are Here Again." Made curious by this, she pushed the chair holding her sodden clothing over to the wall and stood on it to look through the screened ventilation gap along the eaves. Doug was naked also, striding about in the rain with a bar of soap in his hands, lathering his neck and shoulders and arms, bellowing into the downpour, cleaning himself with the unselfconscious attention of a cat. The soap went to every part of him, the suds washed away in seconds by rain. He looked very clean, apart from redness around his feet and ankles, and very happy to be washing himself under the lowering sky, and Val was instantly envious of Doug's state of body and mind.

It had been a personal ritual ever since he was a boy, this washing under the first true rain of the Wet, and Doug had begun it without thinking, so far behind Val by the time the house was reached he had almost forgotten her presence after the long walk home. She was behind her blanket when he entered for the soap, and he went out again with the expectation of a good wash, as was usual at around this time each year. He stepped from his sodden clothing and began applying soap to his nakedness immediately, singing the first song that came to mind, as was also his custom. The rain stung, so hard did each heavy drop strike his skin, but Doug enjoyed this sensation, as a Scandinavian might enjoy whipping himself with birch twigs before a steam bath.

The ritual of the rain was proceeding according to its simple dictates when Doug, usually the sole participant, was joined by Val. Her appearance from around the side of the house, as naked as himself, made Doug stop singing for a moment, then he continued, somewhat waveringly, his hands making an abrupt swoop toward his crotch.

"You dropped the soap," Val said. "Now it's all muddy."

She bent gracefully and picked it up. The bar of redness in her hand was washed back to yellow by raindrops while Doug and Val stared at it. When she began applying it to her body, Doug watched every circular motion the bar of soap made. When she handed it back to him, his hands left their position of modesty to receive it. Val's eyes had looked nowhere but at his face. She began turning away, and Doug panicked, thinking their moment of nakedness together might already be ending.

"Do my back?" she asked over her shoulder.

He did her back. Then she did his. Then they walked inside the house and became lovers under its drumming tin roof, their cries heard faintly by the slim black figure standing among the ghost gums.

PART TWO

PART TWO

9

ROYCE CURRAN HAD BEEN OUT to Redlands only once before, when the report had come in concerning Perce Burridge's alleged suicide. The body was already gone, purportedly taken by a croc after the jackeroo who found it had turned his back to boil a billy, but the description given to Royce had sounded like a shotgun death, all right. Of course, Royce had to take the word of the Aborigines who told him of Perce's act. Royce was confident he could tell when an Abo was lying, and he had not received that impression from any of the blacks still hanging around Redlands. Perce Burridge's lubra had been terrified, though, and had run into the bush when she saw Royce approaching. He had told the others to fetch her back quick, or it'd be worse for all of them, and they had done so. Royce hadn't been able to get a word out of her, but by that time he was convinced it had been suicide, and that was how he made out his report.

All of this was ancient history to Royce Curran. It had been before the war began and so had very little to do with his second trip to Redlands. As he followed the track through what was now Doug Farrands's place, Royce noted the proliferation of cattle browsing among the scrub. Perce had never been able to keep more than three or four before they became croc bait, but Doug seemed to have a magic touch in keeping his herd from the jaws of Blighty. Two years and more ago, nobody in the Territory would have given Doug Farrands any kind of odds on success, knowing him as they did for a casual worker at best, a lazy bludger at worst, but marriage had changed the man overnight, it seemed. There had been many who thought Doug did it solely to get his hands on some property, but there was no denying he had made the best possible use of Redlands since it became his by way of his wife; the cattle were there to prove it.

The Flying Fox was in partial flood, the Wet having slacked off a bit since the Japs attacked Pearl Harbour two weeks before. There was every chance Christmas Day might pass without some kind of watery disaster occurring. Royce stopped his police truck several yards from the water's edge and turned to his passenger, who sat handcuffed beside him. Most policemen would have put an Aborigine in the back of the truck for transportation, and Royce often did that himself, especially if there was a chance of his prisoner vomiting, but Brian had been sober for several days now.

"I'm taking the cuffs off. I don't want your dad seeing you like this. Are you going to behave if I do?"

"Yeah."

Royce set Brian free. They both got out of the truck, and Royce took his pistol from its holster. He fired twice into the air, then they waited for Doug to appear on the far bank. A heavy chain was padlocked around the trunk of the nearest and largest gum tree. The chain lay along the ground like a rusting snake, disappearing into the river alongside the track, both emerging together on the other side. Doug's dinghy was secured to a tree over there, well above the floodline. Soon a figure appeared and waved. Royce waved back. Brian stood without moving at all as his father untied the dinghy and dragged it to the water, then began pulling himself across by way of the chain. The current was swift, even though the water was down, and Doug had to brace his feet against the dinghy's side as the chain was lifted from the bottom by the rush of water attempting to sweep the boat and its passenger downstream. Doug passed the links quickly through his hands and in five minutes was on the western shore.

"G'day, Royce. Brung me a visitor, eh?"

"Might say that. He's been in trouble. Thought I'd take him home for Christmas and let you sort him out."

"What kinda trouble?"

"He'll tell you. Got the kettle on over there?"

"Too right. Step into me Sydney Harbour ferry. How's it with you, Bri?"

"Orright."

Royce and Brian worked the chain, and the dinghy fairly raced back across the Flying Fox. All three dragged it clear of the water and began walking the few hundred yards to the house.

"What's happenin' with the Japs?" Doug asked.

"The bastards sent two of the biggest ships in the British Navy to the bottom, and now they're attacking the Philippines. The Yanks are in a lot of trouble. Everyone says they're finished. The Japs already took Guam, and Hong Kong's been invaded. That enough for you?"

"Shit. Reckon they'll come south and have a go at us?"

"They'll have to get past Singapore first. Your English mate's there, isn't he?"

"Yeah. Had a letter from him a coupla months ago. Two years in the army, and he hasn't heard a shot fired. They sent him to India, then bloody Singapore. Signs up to fight Germans, and it looks like he'll end up fightin' Japs."

"What's the difference? They're all bastards."

"Clive reckons Singapore's a fortress. The Japs'll lose plenty if they try and take it. He's a lieutenant now, so I spose he knows what he's talkin' about."

"Thought about joining up yet, Doug?"

"Nah; not till I can see 'em comin'."

"Might be too late by then."

"How about yourself?"

"Made the offer, got turned down. Stay where you are and keep on doing your job, they said. I reckon if the Japs come this far we'll need more than coppers. One of your special pals signed up a few months ago—Les Moxham."

"What, Ken didn't sign up as well? I thought those two did everythin' except shit together."

"Ken got a bit drunk and fell off a verandah. Broke his leg in two places. He'll catch up with Les when he's mended."

"Doesn't surprise me Les signed up. Pearlin's gone to pot with the war on, and both of 'em put together weren't as smart as their old man was. Army's the best place for smack-happy blokes like that."

"Come on, Doug, you can't knock the Moxhams for doing what a lot of other blokes are doing."

"All right, they're all heroes and I'm not."

"I'm just passing on the news, that's all, not giving lectures."

Royce had forgotten what a touchy bugger Doug Farrands could be.

Doug asked Brian, "What've you been doin' that you shouldn't?"

"Got drunk in town."

"That's a bit bloody stupid. Anyone else with you?"

"Coupla blokes. They never got done, but."

Royce said, "Found him wandering down Smith Street in a daze. Didn't resist arrest or anything."

"You wanna get drunk, you come out here and get drunk where nobody's gunna see you and run you into jail," Doug said.

"I didn't hear that," said Royce. "No liquor for blacks, that's the law."

"He's not; he's a yella-fella."

"Makes no difference. Anyway, it's his first offense, so I went light on him."

"Thanks."

"Keep him out of Darwin's my advice. He could help you out around here, by the looks of it. How many cattle do you have now?"

"'Bout eighty head. They're comin' on strong. Wanna be a jackeroo for your old man, Bri? Keep you outa the way a bad habits."

"Orright."

"You keep your nose clean for a while, and your arrest record goes in the bin," said Royce. "I don't want to see a good kid like you go bad, and neither does your dad."

"No fear," Doug agreed.

Val was by the door, a baby in her arms. Royce hadn't laid eyes on her since her last trip to town, before the baby was born. He had been told it was a girl.

"Afternoon, Mrs. Farrands."

"Hullo. Got time for a cuppa?"

"That's what he braved the ragin' torrent for," Doug said.

"Hullo, Brian."

"G'day."

She had seen him only once during the past eighteen months, when he came to show them his ritual scars, the four lines drawn across his chest with a sharp piece of rock. The split skin had seemed to disgorge fat rolls of flesh to draw attention to the cuts and had healed that way, half an inch thick, like lines of dark paint squeezed from a tube onto his chest. Val had thought these scars of official manhood disfiguring but had admired them anyway, seeing the pride in Brian's eyes. He was less proud today, and she knew Royce Curran had not simply given him a lift along the track to Redlands. She knew the men would already have discussed Brian, and so did not ask. Doug would tell her everything later.

They sat and talked of the war, Royce repeating what he knew of the various battlefronts, near and far. The people of Leningrad were under siege by the Germans and reported to be starving. America had declared war against Germany as well as against Japan. Rommel was in retreat in North Africa, the sole piece of good news.

"So now we're in it, good and proper," said Val. She had listened to Royce with a sinking heart. If the Japs were approaching, Doug would go. She almost hated the policeman for coming to them this way, with the war trailing in his wake like a long shadow. Brian had been Royce's excuse to lay out the unstated reasons why her husband should join in the madness creeping south toward Australia.

"It's in our back yard," Royce agreed, "or soon will be. They're building a road up from Alice Springs to bring troops north, and the air force is sending fighting planes up here as fast as they can. It's just a matter of time now. There's an official evacuation order been given, Mrs. Farrands. All women and kids are supposed to leave the Top End and go south until we know for sure the Japs aren't coming."

"I'm not going anywhere."

"It's an official order from the territorial administrator," Royce said, directing this at Doug, who seemed unimpressed.

"Val's not scared, are you, Val?"

"No."

"It's not a question of being scared," Royce persisted. "It's a matter of sensible precaution. And it's the law. There's a ship in port right now, the *Zealandia*. She'll be sailing for Brisbane the day after tomorrow. You'll need to be on board with your baby."

Val said nothing.

"Evacuatin' the women and kids from Darwin, that's one thing," said Doug. "We're out in the bush here. Redlands'd be the last place the Japs'll have a go at."

"Doug, you wouldn't even know if they attacked, with no wireless."

"I reckon I'd hear the bombs. Tell you what, Royce; seeing as you came all this way to deliver the message, I promise that if the Japs start somethin' in the Territory, I'll make sure Val and the nipper get going south, away from it."

"They're supposed to leave the day after tomorrow."

"I couldn't be ready in time," Val said. Everyone in the room knew this was nonsense; Val's wardrobe and belongings, like that of most bush wives, could be packed into a suitcase or two.

"There's always the rattler," Doug offered. "If she doesn't take the ship, she can go as far south as the railway'll take her. Compromise, eh?"

The baby began squawling for milk. Val went outside and stood by the water tank to feed her. Brian came out a few minutes later and approached without hesitation. Val found she did not mind him watching her nurse, grinning in approval as the baby suckled. If it had been Royce who came outside, she would have turned away instantly to hide her breast, but Brian somehow exuded a sense of interest in the feeding that was entirely asexual, simply the curiosity of one family member to see another, newer member he hadn't seen before.

"Bonzer-lookin' kid. What's her name?"

"Judy. Doug wanted to call her that after his own mum."

"Eh, Judy, I'm your big brother. Bet she wouldn' believe it if she knew."

"She'll know who you are soon enough. What'd Royce bring you out for, Bri?"

Brian explained, his manner slightly embarrassed.

"Dad says I should stay here and be a jackeroo for you and him."

"Do you want to? We need a bit of help now that this one's taking up half my time." Val changed Judy to her left breast. She protested, then began to suck.

"Curran, he reckons he thought of it, me comin' here to work. Dad too."

"Well, who did think of it—you?"

"Ranji and M'linga. They said to come an look after you."

"Ranji?"

"You remember him. He was here that time. M'linga's his dad, real important old bloke. You don't wanna meet him, but. They said Dad's gunna go away soon, so I gotta be here when he does."

"How would they know what Doug's going to do?"

"M'linga, he knows plenny." Brian's smile was now subtly different, almost conspiratorial. Val reminded herself then that she understood virtually nothing of what went on within his head. She was disturbed by his talk of Doug leaving, however unlikely the source.

"He's got a job to do here," she said, "and you can help him."

"Japs are comin', but."

"They might, and they might not. Doug's not going anywhere."

"M'linga says to come anyhow, so I did."

Brian was sensible enough to know he should not be reminding Val of what was soon to happen. She was white, and although she was especially privileged in ways she was herself unaware of, she would not believe anything she didn't wish to believe. M'linga knew what was going to happen anyway. Brian was his emissary and had been told to look out for the woman who had found Kukullumunnumantje, after being allowed to do so by Gulgulong, whom the whitefellas called Blighty. Although she didn't know it, Val was called Missus b'long Gulgulong, or Blighty's Wife. It was M'linga who had given her the name, after being told how Ranji's mob found her sleeping the deadsleep among the stones of remembering. M'linga had said they found her just in time; any more remembering that did not belong to a whitefella woman, and Val would most likely have become a pelican or a jabiru and flown away, never to be Brian's new whitefella mother. The tribe had been watching over Val ever since, and known in advance that she would stay on at Redlands, to be near Kukullumunnumantje, which was her place now, almost as much as it belonged to the Pitjantjatjara. Brian had not been told everything, but he knew where he had to be when his father left home. M'linga had seen it all, even what was to happen to the poor little whitefella kid in Val's arms, Brian's own half-sister.

"Bonzer little kid," Brian said again, staring hard at the reddish hair and sweet round face, so that he might remember the baby well after she was gone.

Royce Curran and Doug came from the house.

"'Bye, Mrs. Farrands. I'll expect you on the wharf in town the day after tomorrow. Brian, you mind your p's and q's and do what your dad says."

Val smiled stiffly. Brian said and did nothing as Royce and Doug turned and began walking toward the river. Curran wasn't a bad bloke for a copper, in Brian's estimation, but he knew less about what really went on in the world than a kookaburra. The two men disappeared around a bend in the river track.

Val covered her breast. The baby was already beginning to fall asleep. Val noticed that Brian couldn't seem to keep his eyes off Judy, and his face wore a wistful expression she had never seen before. She was very fond of him, considering the prolonged absences that stretched between their few meetings. Someday, she hoped, he would trust her enough to tell her about the stones.

"I still look for them," she said, and he looked up, understanding immediately.

"Won't find 'em." He grinned, then added, "'Cause there's nothin' there."

"If I don't find them again," Val said, looking down at her
· baby, "then Judy will."

"Nah she won't."

The flatness of this contradiction made Val look again at Brian. His face had hardened, but there was sadness behind it.

"She might," Val insisted.

"Nah."

Brian turned away, and Val wondered how she had managed to upset him. She would have to be more careful about what she said to him in future, if Brian was to become part of the household.

When Doug returned, she watched his face to determine the likelihood of his signing up. He wouldn't meet her eyes, and Val said, "Did he talk you into it?"

"What, sendin' you and Jude away? Nah, he can't make you do what you don't wanna do, orders or no orders. It's a free country." Doug was watching his son, who was walking away from them. "What's wrong with Bri?"

"I suppose he doesn't like being brought here by a police-man. Think he'll stay?"

"Might do. We could use him, strong kid like that."

"It was his own idea to come and help, he says."

"Yeah, he'd say that. He's got his pride, Brian."

"Do Abos make prophecies?"

"Prophecies? Dunno. Bri said somethin'?"

"M'linga says you're going away soon."

"What the hell would that old bugger know?" Doug said, smiling, but it seemed to Val that the smile was intended to mask some other feeling.

"He's sposed to be a kadaicha man . . . y'know, a magician or witch doctor or somethin'. Load a bullshit."

"You told me once you saw a goanna crawl out of a dead man's mouth."

"Yeah, but it had nothin' to do with M'linga."

"So you're not going away."

"Where'd I wanna go, eh? Got everythin' I want right here, haven't I."

"What if the Japs come?"

"That's another story," Doug said, watching Brian squat beneath a tree with one leg thrust before him, Aboriginal style. "Me missus and both me kids," said Doug. "If old Clive was here I reckon it'd be just about the best Christmas pre-sent a bloke could have, everyone all together."

"The Japs can't get past Singapore, can they?"

"That's what everyone says."

Seven weeks later, Royce Curran came again, this time driving his truck across the few inches of water still flowing in the Flying Fox. He braked in front of the house and was met at the door by Val.

"Morning. Doug around?"

"He's out mustering. Come to check up on Brian? He's been good as gold. Got his own little place now."

Val pointed to the crude shed built a short distance from the house.

Royce shook his head. "Nothing to do with that, Mrs. Farrands. Didn't do what I said and catch the boat, did you."

"Didn't see why I should."

"Well, maybe you'll see now why the order was given. The Japs took Singapore, and they're on their way south. You need to take the baby and get down to the Alice at least, better still Adelaide or Melbourne. It's too risky to hang around here anymore."

"I don't hang around here, Mr. Curran. This is my place."

"I'm just saying it's too dangerous from now on. They could be down on us any day. It's an official order, Mrs. Farrands; all women and kids were supposed to be out of the Top End two months ago. Get Doug to take you into town and get on the train. This time I'm not asking nicely, all right?"

"All right."

"I've got too much on my plate to be wasting time rounding up people who don't know what's good for them. You tell Doug that and get packing."

Val nodded, unwilling to argue. As she watched Royce return to his truck and drive off, all she could think of was Clive. Singapore, the impregnable island fortress, fallen. Had Clive been killed in its defense? She had received no letters from him in almost four months. He had taken to signing himself "Raffles," to hide his frustration at the noncombatant role he had held so far. During his time in Calcutta, he had signed his letters "Clive of India." They had often been censored by military shears, those dwindling letters, increasingly so once he reached Singapore. And now there would be no more of them. Clive was dead or captured.

When Doug and Brian returned in the early evening, they found Val seated at the table, Judy in her lap, the pages of every letter Clive had ever sent to Redlands scattered across the tabletop.

Doug hung his stock whip on a peg in the wall. "What's up?"

Val told him. Doug looked at Brian. "You can take charge of the place for a few days while I get Val taken south."

"How 'bout if the Japs come?"

"Shoot as many a the bastards as you can, then go bush."

"Orright." Brian grinned.

Val said, "I'm not going anywhere."

"Royce said it's official."

"He said that last time, and I didn't go then. I'm not leaving, Doug, and that's that."

"Come off it. Think about the kid."

Val smoothed Judy's hair. "She's safe as long as I am."

"And what happens when you're not?"

"Then I'll think about leaving, but the Japs'd have to be coming down the track. This is my place. I won't leave unless I absolutely have to, and don't think you can make me!"

"No need to bite me bloody head off. I spose we can forget about the train, then. If they come, we'll go overland, on horseback."

"Bugger up the Ford first," suggested Brian. "Don't want no Japs pinchin' it for theirself an ridin' aroun'."

"Know how to take out the distributor head?"

"Yeah."

"That'll be your job if they come."

"Let the oil out, leave the engine runnin'. Bugger it up bloody good that way."

"Don't go overboard, mate. We're comin' back afterwards." Doug sat and picked up several of the pages spread before Val. "Clive'll be all right."

"How do you know? Japs are bastards to prisoners."

"They're not gunna pay any attention to one bloke. They've got too many to see to. There's somethin' like fifteen thousand Aussies up in Singapore too. I bet they're browned off about surrenderin'. Bet it was the Pommies who waved the white flag first."

"Oh, shuttup! It doesn't matter how it happened. I only want to know Clive's all right!" Judy began making sounds of discontent, and Val spoke more softly. "I suppose you're thinking about getting into the forces now."

Doug fiddled with the letters, then let them fall. "Yeah, well, with things the way they are, y'know. It's not in me nature to go joinin' up, but I don't see any way around it now. Brian'll stick around and keep an eye on things."

"Wait and see if they come first. Will you promise me that at least?"

"If they've got Singapore, we're next. Anyone can see that, Val. The longer I put it off, the worse I'm gunna feel about it. I waited all this time, you know I did, hopin' we could stay out of it. I wouldn't do it just for England's sake, but the bastards are headin' here. I can't sit on me bum and do nothin' while there's other blokes gettin' killed."

Val let her chin rest on top of Judy's head and closed her eyes.

"I'll finish up here first, though. Brian and me, we're just about done with countin' heads and brandin'. Just a few more days, a week maybe, then I'll go into town and see if they'll take me. Maybe they won't, you never know. Might want me to keep on raisin' cattle to feed the troops."

"They'll take you," Val said, opening her eyes to look directly into his own.

Doug stood. "Check on the nags," he said, and went outside to the horse pen.

Brian lit a kerosene lamp, keeping his back to Val.

"Is this what your mate M'linga meant, about Doug going away?"

"M'linga, he's not me mate. Don't even like him, but. Yeah, I reckon."

"Don't suppose he said anything about Doug coming back again."

"Nup. He's been lookin' after both a you, M'linga."

"How?"

"No cattle gone down Gulgulong's neck, eh."

"What's Gulgulong?"

"Blighty. He never took no cows, no bullocks, nothin'."

This was certainly true. Doug and Val had several times congratulated themselves on their luck with the croc, once they began in earnest to stock Redlands with cattle. Perce Burridge had failed to keep his herd from Blighty's jaws.

"M'linga told Blighty to let our herd alone: is that what you're saying?"

"Sorta like."

"And why would M'linga do that?"

"He never. Gulgulong done it. M'linga, he jus knows what Gulgulong told him."

"He talks to crocodiles."

"Nah, jus with Gulgulong, an Gulgulong, he does the tellin', see."

"No, I don't see."

Brian smiled at her. "Never mind, but."

Val forced herself to return the smile. "No, never mind."

The noise came to them while Doug and Brian were several miles from the house, mustering yearlings. It sounded at first like thunder but did not travel through the air the same way, and the sky was clear to the horizon. Then the dull reverberations became interspersed with the unmistakable thumping of the antiaircraft guns placed around Darwin following the attack on Pearl Harbor.

"Japs've come, sounds like," said Brian.

"Might just be an exercise," Doug said, but soon they could see a pall of thick smoke rising from the direction of town. "Oil tanks down near the harbour," Doug guessed. When the wind shifted south by east, they could hear the stuttering of machine-gun fire and the droning of aircraft engines.

"Japs," Brian repeated.

"Shit. That's that, then."

Doug felt foolish, waiting for outrage to stir his soul, but nothing was inside him except a great heaviness. Now he would have to go away somewhere and fight and kill, and maybe die. There was no way around it, however reluctant he might be to begin the process of separation from his family and Redlands. Now the war had reached Australian soil, just as everyone had predicted it would, and he could no longer avoid its lengthening shadow. It made him slightly sick, and he admitted, with reluctance, that he was suddenly afraid. Now he understood what Clive had felt two years and five months before. The inexorable current of duty was picking him up even as he sat his horse miles from the conflict, a witness only to the smoke and tumult rising into the air.

Val stood at the highest point on the sandstone ridge behind the house, watching the smoke, listening to the muffled din of battle fifty miles away. Then came an explosion louder than any that had preceded it, a colossal thump she felt through the soles of her feet. Val had been in town two days before, and there had been an ammunition ship in the harbour; so forceful a blast could only have been a bomb strike deep inside its hold, the entire cargo detonating in an instant. A new cloud rose above the trees, whiter than the smudges already there, its crown roiling upon itself like a living thing in torment. Watching it swirl and spill and swirl again as it climbed into the sky, Val felt a sense of dread rising with it, from the pit of her stomach to her unaccepting mind. The war had come, and Doug would go.

She was by the door when Doug and Brian rode up to the house, dismounted, and began unsaddling their horses.

"Get the truck cranked up!" Doug shouted to Val.

"I'm coming too!" she shouted back.

"No you're bloody not!"

"Try and stop me!"

"Just get it started and argue later!"

Val was behind the wheel, Judy in her lap, when Doug and Brian returned from the horse pen.

"You're not comin', not with the kid along."

"She'll be all right. The bombing's stopped. Can you hear it anymore? I can't."

Doug glowered at her, knowing she wouldn't change her mind, no matter how he might yell. "Shove over," he said, climbing in. Brian came into the cab after him, and all four drove to Darwin.

They stopped once, about ten miles out, to listen again for gunfire or bombs, but there was still no sound, only the rising smoke, so dense it covered half the sky. When the main highway was reached, it was already filled with every kind of vehicle, petrol or horse powered, each one crammed with people. There were bicycles and motorcycles. Val saw one man with his possessions stacked in a wheelbarrow. Every turning wheel, every footfall, was directed south, away from Darwin.

"Jesus . . . ," said Doug.

He began driving north.

"You're goin' the wrong way!" someone yelled from the other side of the road.

Less than half a mile farther on, an Australian Infantry Forces truck was parked beside the highway, its driver flagging them down. Doug pulled over, and a sergeant demanded to know where they thought they were going.

"Into town," said Doug. "Where the hell else?"

"All civilians have to leave. The whole place is being evacuated. Turn around."

"Yeah, but we might be able to lend a hand—"

"Turn around now, or I'll confiscate your truck. There could be a Jap invasion fleet already on its way."

"But you don't know that for sure. You're only guessin', right?"

"Look, turn around, or I'll run you in, the lot of you!"

"Keep your shirt on."

Doug began turning the wheel.

"Just a minute," the sergeant cautioned. He was looking at Val, as if noticing at last there was a woman in the cab. "All women were supposed to be gone by now. What's she doing here?"

"She's me missus."

"I said what's she doing here still, and who's the Abo?"

"Me son."

"Funny bugger, eh? Pull over and get out."

"I'm not in the army, mate."

"Pull over!"

The sergeant had a pistol in his hand now. Doug eased the Ford off the highway and stepped out.

"Doug, calm down," Val warned. "He's only doing what he's told. . . ."

"Now then," said the sergeant, "what's the idea, going into town with an empty truck, eh? Going to do a bit of looting, were you?"

"Eh?"

The suggestion was so foolish Doug was nonplussed for a moment, then he decided the insult was too great. He punched the sergeant hard in the mouth, and the sergeant fell, the pistol falling from his hand into the dust.

"Doug! Stop it!"

"You're rooted, mate . . . ," the sergeant said, reaching for the gun.

"Go on," Doug taunted. "Go ahead and shoot me, you stupid prick."

The sergeant got up and aimed at Doug. "You're under arrest!"

"Piss off. You're not a fuckin' copper."

The stream of refugees nearby had halted, and some were crossing the road to see what the disturbance was about.

"G'day, Doug!"

Doug turned and saw Dave Coombes, a regular at the Vic, approaching.

"You're under arrest!" screeched the sergeant. Doug jerked a thumb at him, looking at Dave.

"Listen to this bloke. Thinks he can bloody arrest me."

"Yeah, well, he can, as a matter a fact, Doug boy. Better kiss and make up."

"He's not a copper."

"AIF's got power to arrest you if you're a nuisance. War powers act or somethin'."

"Arr, shit . . . "

"Get over there, you." The sergeant pointed at the AIF truck.

"Look, if you hadn't been such a bloody arsehole, mate . . . "

"Get over there!"

"Better do what he says, mate," Dave advised.

"Tell him to bugger off!" shouted someone who had crossed the road behind Dave. "I saw some a those soldier bastards lootin' in town!"

"That's a bloody lie!" the sergeant yelled.

"Like hell it is! Loading up an army truck with shop goods blown all over the place by a bloody bomb, they were!"

"I saw 'em too!" another voice said. "Bastards! They were takin' stuff out of a house! I saw 'em!"

Val stepped from the Ford. "Stop all this bullshit! There's Japs coming, and all you can do is have a stupid fight!"

"You're under arrest too," the sergeant told her, "and the Abo as well."

"You point that fuckin' gun at my missus again," Doug warned, "and I'll shove it up your arse. I don't give a stuff about your bloody war powers."

"Here comes Royce," said Dave.

A police truck pulled off the highway, and Royce Curran got out.

"All right, what's happening here?"

"None of your business," said the sergeant.

"Bastard started arguin' the point with me, Royce," said Doug. "Told me I was a looter, and we didn't even get anywhere near town." He pointed to one of the bystanders. "That bloke says the army's been doin' a bit of lootin' on their own."

"It's a bloody lie!" the sergeant said again, but he seemed less sure of himself now. The crowd on the side of the road was swelling.

"What's that truck doing here?" Royce demanded. "It should be in town, where it's needed. There's people dying before they can be taken to the hospital, and you're sitting out here with an empty bloody truck. Get it into town and make yourself useful, why don't you."

"Hospital's bombed to buggery," said the man who had seen soldiers looting. "Post office copped it too," said another voice.

"Get going, mate," Royce told the sergeant, and the sergeant got into his truck without another word. As it began rolling onto the road, several onlookers jeered at the driver.

Royce turned to them. "Keep moving! Get as far south as you can! If the Japs land, there's no chance of defending you if you're still here! Go on!"

The crowd began rejoining the stream of vehicles on the highway.

"Mrs. Farrands, why are you here? I've told you twice to get out of the Top End."

"She's not scared, are you, love," Doug said.

"Doug, next time I'll lock the both of you up myself, I mean it. Turn around and head for the Alice. You might take a few passengers in the back too."

"Yeah, but what about in town, helpin' out a bit?"

"It's army and police business now. Darwin's a bloody mess. There's nothing you can do that'll help as much as what I just told you. Get down to Alice Springs, if you've got enough petrol, and get your missus on a train, then hand your truck over to the military. All vehicles are being confiscated, Doug. Use it while you can."

"All right. Thanks for fixin' that bloke."

"You never should've started an argument in the first place. Go on, get moving."

"Anyone need a lift?" Val called, and several people on foot immediately crossed the road. One man dropped his bicycle to make a run for the Ford. A walker picked up the bike and began pedaling.

When eight people were jammed aboard the truck, Doug started the engine.

A man poked his head inside the cab. "How 'bout the Abo rides in the back, eh? That'll make room for one more up here."

"Fuck off," Doug said, and let out the clutch.

"Bastard!" the thwarted passenger yelled. Doug turned the Ford and joined the line of vehicles heading away from Darwin.

"We'll dump this lot at the turnoff and go home," Doug said to Val. "You'll need a coupla bags a stuff to take south with you."

"I'm not going."

"You heard what Royce said."

"I don't care. He can't make me go, and neither can you, not if I don't want to."

"I bloody can."

"What are you going to do, tie me up?"

"I might."

"Look bloody funny, that," said Brian.

"You can't stay at Redlands. I won't be there meself much longer."

"Brian will be, and even if he wasn't, what's to stop me staying there on my own?"

"Japs, that's what."

"They aren't here yet. A bomb attack doesn't mean they'll come themselves."

"Of course they bloody will! What the hell would they bomb Darwin for if they didn't intend invading sooner or later!"

"They bombed Pearl Harbor, but they didn't invade Hawaii, did they?"

Doug set his lips in a line. "You're not stayin' here if I'm not, and that's that."

"All right, we'll stay together."

"That's not what I meant, and you know it."

"Turnoff's comin' up," Brian reminded them.

Doug pulled over and set the brake, then stopped the engine. He got out and addressed his passengers. "Any a you blokes a decent driver?"

"I am," said one.

"Take over the wheel, then. I'm gettin' off here. She's got three quarters of a tank a petrol. That oughta get you to Pine Creek or Katherine maybe, if you go easy on the pedal. Hand her over to the blokes in brown when you're done, all right?"

"Right-oh, mate. Your lady friend and the Abo stayin' on board, are they?"

"She is, he isn't."

"She isn't either," said Val, getting out, followed by Brian.

"Get back in there," Brian told her.

Val began walking along the track to Redlands, Judy balanced on her hip.

"Keys are in it," said Doug, and began walking after them.

"Hoo-roo," Brian told the truck's new driver, and set off too.

"Come on, mate," said someone in the back of the Ford. "The Japs are breathin' down our necks."

"Get a bloody move on!" urged another.

The truck was started and steered into the stream of vehicles heading south.

The walk back to Redlands, without food or water or provisions for camping on the way, took all that remained of the afternoon, and all of the night. They stopped every hour or so after darkness came, to rest their feet, but the mosquitoes bothered them more when still than while moving, so they walked on before they wanted to, just for respite from the biting and whining. Val placed Judy under her blouse to protect her from the mosquitoes, and to feed her while they walked, something she had never tried before. Judy suckled as if they were simply walking around inside the house, and fell asleep after feeding.

Doug suffered most, since he still wore riding boots. He took them off before midnight, preferring the occasional pain of a sharp stone against his sole to the torture of walking one step more in boots that chafed his toes and heels.

"Shoulda took 'em off before we went to town, like I done," said Brian.

"You've got feet like leather. I haven't. I didn't think we'd be walkin' home when we left."

Val said, "You should've driven at least halfway home before you gave the truck away."

"They wouldn't get as far down the road without all that petrol I left 'em."

"If you're going to be a Samaritan, don't go complaining about it afterwards."

"I'm not. You're the one that said we shoulda come halfway home first."

"You're the one with the sore feet."

"Look, just don't say another word to me, all right? I want peace and quiet and no more arguments."

"Suits me," Val said, with a casualness Doug found infuriating.

They trudged on for another hour. The moon was bright enough to light their way along the track. Night creatures fell silent at their approach, then resumed their foraging and hunting when the human footsteps receded.

"Jesus!" Doug yelped, as a particularly sharp stone cut his foot. He sat down in the middle of the track, tearing at his filthy sock, the riding boots dumped beside him in the dust. "Bugger this. Bri, you're half me age. Feel like a fast trot through the bush in the romantic moonlight?"

"Want me to get the horses, eh?"

"Too right I do. Me feet've had it. You get some nags back here for us, and I'll double your wages."

"You don't pay me anythin' now. Two nothin's is nothin'."

"I'll remember you in me will. Go on."

"Won't take long. See yez later."

He was gone down the track without a sound, disappearing in seconds. Doug peered at his injured foot.

"Want me to massage your poor old tootsies?" Val offered.

"No I bloody don't."

"Don't like me anymore, do you?"

"Not with all the trouble you make."

"I just want to go home and mind my own business."

"There's a war on."

"Golly gosh, I didn't know that."

"Royce Curran's gunna be checkin' up to see if you're gone."

"He'll have more important things to take care of."

"You'll wind up in the shit if you hang around here."

"That's your opinion."

Doug refused any further attempts at conversation from Val, his only words swear words, as he slapped at mosquitoes.

Eventually they heard the sound of hooves as Brian returned, mounted, leading two more horses. Doug found he couldn't bear to put his boots back on, even to ride, and so went home with his socked feet in the stirrups. They reached Redlands by dawn.

While Doug slept late into the afternoon, Val spoke with Brian. It was a clear day, the smoke of yesterday's attack swept from the sky, but for a faint smudge from some persistent fires in the rubble of Darwin. They strolled as if by mutual consent in the direction of Blighty's Pond.

"He's really going to go, Brian. He doesn't want to, but he has to now."

"Gotta get them Japs an pay 'em back."

"But I'm not going, not unless there's a real invasion. I just don't see the point in running away just to avoid some bombs, especially way out here. They'll never bomb this place. I just worry about one thing, and that's getting warned in time if the Japs do land and start coming overland. Will your people tell me when that happens, if it happens?"

"Bush telegraph, yeah. Japs come, you'll get told bloody quick. We can hide you in the bush too. Japs'd never get you."

"Good. If you tell Doug, he won't worry so much."

"Got Gulgulong on your side, so you carn get hurt, but."

"Gulgulong? Oh, Blighty. Are we going to ask for his protection? Is that why we're going to his pond?"

"You reckon it's funny. You're the one goin' to water b'long Gulgulong."

"No, I'm just following you."

"I'm followin' you, an Gulgulong's the one said for you to come see him."

"Then I won't disappoint him. Why does Gulgulong like me so much?"

"I got told not to tell."

"By Gulgulong?"

"Nah, by M'linga. He's gunna tell you himself someday."

"I look forward to meeting him. When will he come?"

"Reckon he'll show up when Gulgulong tells him to."

10

THE WET, THE DRIEST ANYONE in the Territory could remember, was over. Doug was in the Australian Infantry Forces, but to the surprise of himself and the delight of Val, he had been posted no farther away from home than Darwin, where he became part of an ack-ack battery along the shoreline of Fannie Bay. The antiaircraft gun Doug's crew was responsible for stood in a shallow hole twenty yards from Vesteys Beach, near the old meat works. The hole was surrounded by sandbags filled from the beach. The gun's long barrel pointed at the sky.

There had been fifteen air raids so far, but none the equal of the first. Whenever Japanese aircraft were sighted, the alarm sirens would howl and P-40 fighter planes would rise from the RAAF airfield that was usually the intended target. When the Japanese were within range, Doug's crew and the dozens of others stationed around Darwin began filling the air with shrapnel until the P-40s began closing with the bombers. Sometimes the ack-ack gunners brought down a Jap bomber; more often they were unsure if they had hit anything at all. When the bombers were accompanied by Zero fighters, the gunners grew more nervous, since these would dive and strafe their sandbagged positions with machine-gun fire. Three gunners on other crews had been lost this way. When each day's raid was over, the ack-ack teams cleaned their weapons and waited for a meal to arrive, in expectation of having to do no more fighting until the next day, or the day after.

It was a monotonous existence, dominated by hours of emptiness. Some of the men were locals like Doug, but most were from the south. The Vesteys Beach gunners were commanded by Sergeant Bambridge, from Melbourne. Bambridge did not like Doug, because Doug would not respond with sufficient alacrity to orders. Bambridge always jumped when addressed by Second Lieutenant Jewell, who visited the batteries at least once each day and expected this kind of professional military promptness to percolate down through the ranks below his own. Private Farrands, it seemed, thought otherwise, and it irked Bambridge that the other men on the crew were beginning to follow his example.

Bambridge had been a Footscray butcher before the war and, when younger, had been a footballer of some repute. He was used to impressing other men with his size, but Farrands, who was only a little bloke, seemed not to care if Bambridge had performed marvels with a football in front of roaring crowds, nor that he owned his own profitable business nowadays. When Bambridge had first boasted of his shop and the rows of first-class carcasses in the cold room, Doug had said, "Arr, so you're a meat-whacker, eh?" and drawn a laugh from the men. Sergeant Bambridge had marked Doug Farrands out for suitable punishment then but been unable in the interim to think of something that would bring pain and humiliation to the Territorian. Ridicule appeared to slide from his tanned back like water.

"Farrands, they tell me the state bird up here's the blowfly, is that right?"

"Absolutely correct. We grow the biggest blowies in the world. They crawl inside the dirtiest dead bums and hatch the rottenest maggots too. We're proud of how disgustin' they are, our northern blowies."

Another gibe, on another day: "Farrands, is it true that all the kiddies born in this place are bastards?"

"I definitely am," said Doug, "and I'll fight any man who says different."

"But they all popped out of tarts and black gins, didn't they," Bambridge persisted.

"Meself," said Doug, "I popped outa both. I'm a medical marvel, they say. Two mums and no dad! Bloody amazin', eh. Oughta be in a book."

Bambridge assigned Doug the worst chores and the filthiest of gun-cleaning duties, but these were performed competently and without complaint. The sergeant valued the prestige he imagined went with his rank, but its attendant power seemed not to have any real punch, at least not when applied to Doug Farrands, and Bambridge became increasingly frustrated by the impasse. He missed his wife and girlfriend down south and had not found the war sufficiently exciting or distracting to make his voluntary enlistment worthwhile. He was glad, though, not to be taking part in the New Guinea campaign; soldiers were reported to be suffering terrible deprivation in the jungles there.

Darwin was an easy posting, despite the regular air raids, and he could have been happy if only there were more women available. There were blacks, and although Bambridge had found himself attracted on one or two occasions to some of the youngest and shapeliest and would not have minded having a go, the gins were officially off-limits. The AIF knew that warnings of venereal disease would not be enough to curb the sexual appetite of some men and had let it be known that the incidence of leprosy among the Aboriginal tribes of the north was high. It was no lie, and it served to reduce fraternisation to a minimum. Bambridge himself believed the warnings and had to satisfy himself with the available white prostitutes, who were beginning to return to town despite the existing evacuation order concerning females. These women were neither young nor pretty, but they made a living from the Australian troops and the increasing number of Americans flooding in.

All in all, the only real thorn in the side of Bambridge was Doug Farrands. Nothing could ease the annoying itch Bambridge felt when looking at the one man who made no secret of the fact that he thought the sergeant was a stupid deadshit.

After the nineteenth raid, a month went by without a single enemy plane being sighted, and the military alertness of the town became more relaxed. Doug sought leave from Lieutenant Jewell and was told that Sergeant Bambridge had expressed a wish to keep him on duty, since he represented the very backbone of the gun crew.

"That's bullshit," said Doug.

"Don't use that language with an officer, Farrands, or you'll be put on report. Sergeant Bambridge speaks highly of you. Don't prove him wrong."

"He's pullin' the wool over your eyes. He doesn't want me to have any leave, that's what Bambridge wants."

"That's a ridiculous accusation."

"You wouldn't think so if you knew him."

"Sergeant Bambridge is one of the best we have up here, and his crew is one of the best, thanks to you, he says. Think about what you're saying, Farrands. Just because you're a local doesn't give you the right to slip off home when there's a bit of a lull in the fighting. Your request is denied."

There was no chance Val could come to town and see him, given the evacuation edict, and Doug began to consider going AWL just to reassure himself everything was all right at Redlands.

The day before Doug planned to sneak away, Brian came walking along the beach behind the rolls of barbed wire.

"What's this nig-nog want?" asked Bambridge.

Brian spotted Doug and waved. Doug went to meet him, smiling.

"G'day, Bri. Everything all right back home?"

"Yeah, she's apples. Just come to let you know we got no worries."

"Beauty. Want a fag?"

"Orright."

Doug began rolling smokes, talking in a voice low enough not to be heard by the rest of the gunners.

"Jude and Val all right, are they?"

"Yeah, bonzer. Missin' you, but."

"Listen, tell Val I feel the same way, but don't go layin' it on too thick. Got enough water out there for the cattle?"

"Flyin' Fox is down, but they're still drinkin'."

"No trouble from Blighty?"

Brian laughed. "Nah. He's leavin' you alone. Mus like you, but."

Bambridge strolled over to them as Doug was lighting their cigarettes.

"This is supposed to be a restricted area, Farrands. You know this boong?"

"He's me son. Don't call him a boong."

"Your son?" Bambridge was stunned.

"That's right. We're havin' a bit of a private conversation at the moment."

"What, you mean you had a boong wife or something?"

"Look, bugger off, all right?"

"Don't get shitty with me, Farrands."

"I need a few minutes for a friendly chat, that's all."

"Fair enough. You go ahead and chat with him. I heard you were a married man, but I never thought it'd be to a black."

"Different wife, see."

"Yeah? You're a fucking dark horse, Farrands."

Bambridge laughed at his own joke, then retreated. Doug could hear him telling the rest of the men Doug had two wives, one of them the mother of the boong he was talking with. Doug drew hard on his cigarette and tried not to hear the snickering that went on behind him.

"I asked for some leave, Bri, but they wouldn't give it to me, the bastards. No more raids, but they want us to hang around all hours a the day and night."

"That's crook."

"It bloody is. I'd give anythin' to come home for a coupla days. You're sure Val's all right?"

"Yeah. She said don't worry 'bout nothin'. Said some lovey-dovey stuff."

"Like what?"

"I forget."

"Bri, you should get married, then you'd remember."

"Might do, one day. That your gun?"

"That's her. Big bugger, eh? We've shot down a few bombers."

"Good-oh. We seen a few Jap planes our way, little ones."

"Zeros. They won't bother you."

"Bloody fast, but."

"Yeah, they are."

"Hey, Farrands," Bambridge called, "your time's up!"

"Who's that bloke?" Brian asked.

"Sergeant. A real dickhead."

"Looks like one."

"Farrands, tell your boong to bugger off!"

"I better shoot through," offered Brian.

"Give me love to Val and Jude, not that Jude'll know the difference."

"Orright. Hoo-roo, Dad."

"See you later, Bri."

Doug watched his son walk away down the beach, then went back to the gun.

"What's it like with a blackie, Farrands?"

Doug looked at Bambridge and gave serious consideration to hitting him.

"No different," he said.

"Was your nig-nog wife a better fuck, though? I heard they're supposed to do it like monkeys."

"Uninhibited like," said one of the better-read gunners.

"That's it, uninhibited," said Bambridge. Doug said nothing, drawing on the last of his smoke.

"Well, is it true or what?" Bambridge insisted.

Doug carefully stubbed out the butt, then settled himself against a sandbag and tipped his digger's hat over his eyes.

"I want the courtesy of an answer, Farrands."

"I'm asleep."

"No you're bloody not. Answer the question, and that's an order."

"Mind your own business, Bambridge."

"If I was an officer you'd get the guardhouse for that comment."

"But you're not an officer, are you. You're a fuckin' sergeant."

"That's better than being a private, Private."

Doug ignored him. Every gunner was watching for what might happen next. They all liked Doug, but now that they had learned he had an Abo son, he had become a man of an altogether different kind to them. Most had never seen an Aborigine until they came north to defend Darwin, but they had heard stories, even as far south as the cities they came from, of men like Doug who cohabited with blacks. They were slightly envious, yet ready to despise him at the same time.

"Take that hat off your face!"

Doug lifted his hat and set it on his head. He stood up.

"Take those stripes off," he said to Bambridge. "I dare you."

Bambridge took off his shirt, smiling.

"You haven't got a prayer, Farrands. I'm bigger, I'm warning you."

Doug sat down again and put his hat over his eyes.

"Just wanted to see if you had flabby tits, Sarge. Thanks for settling it."

The laughter that erupted around the gun made Bambridge furious.

"Get up, Farrands!"

"Nah, not unless it's an order."

"Get up and be a man, if you know how!"

The warning siren began its wailing, and the gunners leapt to their positions. The last raid before the long lull had numbered at least fifteen fighters and twenty-five bombers. This time there were just three Mitsubishi bombers. They droned overhead, weaving through the flak the ack-ack teams threw into the sky, and dropped their bombs over the town, then turned lazily and flew away. They had been in sight for less than ten minutes.

When they were gone, Doug said, "Tojo must be runnin' outa planes."

Bambridge ordered all the spent shells gathered up as usual. Doug waited to see if their confrontation was to be resumed, but the moment apparently had passed. Bambridge did not look in his direction for the rest of the day.

Royce Curran stepped from his police truck and walked over.

"G'day there, Doug."

Doug was collecting the Vesteys Beach gunners' weekly beer ration from the back of a military truck near the Parap rail-yards and loading it into the sidecar of a motorcycle borrowed for the occasion from an off-duty dispatcher, who had been promised a bottle for his cooperation. The beach road was temporarily impassable due to bomb craters, but the motorcycle was able to weave its way through. The beer ration was supposed to be consumed away from the battery, while the gunners were themselves off-duty in the barracks at Larrakeyah, but night duty was arduous, the air filled with mosquitoes, and a blind eye would be turned to the drinkers, who would be issued with only a single bottle each, hardly enough to get drunk on.

"G'day, Royce."

"Keeping you busy?"

"Busy as a barman on a Saturdee night."

"Heard from your missus lately?"

"How d'you mean?"

Doug was instantly alert for some kind of verbal trap; had

Royce learned Val was still living at Redlands, contrary to the government's wishes?

"Went out to your place a few days ago, saw your boy Brian. He said she was down Adelaide way. Just wondered if you'd had word from her."

"Yeah, I did, as a matter of fact. She's fine."

"Good. Listen, Doug, I've been having a word with the AIF brass up here about you. Heard of a mob called the NAOU?"

"No."

"North Australia Observer Unit. Someone down south reckons it'd be a good idea if there was a bunch of blokes in the bush, hidden away along the coast mainly, looking out for a Jap invasion force. They won't come ashore near Darwin, if they're coming, not with the defenses we've got here now, but they might try sneaking in somewhere else."

"Somewhere there's only crocs and snakes to watch 'em land."

"That's it. We need some bush-bashers on the lookout for a secret landing. This is a new idea, still a bit hush-hush. They're on the lookout for blokes that know their way around the Top End, close to the water."

"Like me."

"Like you."

"What's it called again?"

"North Australia Observer Unit. You'd just watch, but you wouldn't attack if you saw Japs coming ashore. You'd report it over the radio and lie low, that's all."

"Observing, eh?"

"Interested? They want locals to lend a hand. Most of the blokes in it'll be city types, green as grass. You could make yourself pretty useful if you wanted to."

"I reckon I could use a break from the ack-ack."

"Thought you might. Brian said you didn't get along with someone there."

"Too true."

"Looks like Brian's doing a good job of looking after the place."

"He's a reliable kid, Bri."

"Lot for one young bloke to handle, though."

"He can do it."

Royce nodded. He had been told by Brian that Val was in

Sydney, not Adelaide, and although Royce believed that Brian was indeed better able to organise his time than the average Abo, he knew now that Val Farrands was still living on the property and had probably nicked off into the scrub when she heard his truck coming. He decided not to make any kind of fuss, not while Doug appeared to be so eager to join up with the NAOU. It was more important, Royce told himself, to get cracking with the observer unit than to prosecute a headstrong woman who probably was in no real danger anyway. Royce's father had once told him a man could never win an argument with a redheaded woman, and Royce was prepared to honour his father's memory by avoiding any kind of strife with the redheaded woman out Redlands way.

Doug's transfer to the NAOU went through in record time; within ten days he was able to tell Lieutenant Jewell he had been promoted to corporal and was leaving the ack-ack gunners.

"Why?" Jewell demanded.

"Top secret," said Doug, handing over his transfer papers.

Jewell scanned them briefly. "This doesn't say where or what you're being transferred to. This can't be right, Farrands."

"Got all the stamps and signatures and whatnots, hasn't it?" Doug pointed to the signature of a brigadier. "You have a word with that bloke there if you don't like it."

Jewell thrust the papers into his pocket. "All right, Farrands, get packed up, but I'll be investigating this just to make sure. Have you told Sergeant Bambridge?"

"I thought I'd let you do that."

"He'll be sorry to see you go."

"I'll be heartbroken, meself."

"This had better all be in order, Farrands."

"It is."

Doug was in the process of dumping his few possessions into a kit bag at the barracks when Bambridge and several other gunners walked in.

"What's this about you leaving, Farrands?"

"Transfer to the secret service. I'm gunna be a spy on a top-secret mission."

"Bullshit. What the hell would they send you to spy on?"

"Gotta count the hairs on Tojo's bum, then burn 'em off one by one with matches."

"Fuck off."

"All right," said Doug, shouldering his bag, "here I go, fucking off as requested. Hoo-roo, you bastards, and see if you can't improve your bloody aim."

He walked out, leaving dissatisfaction and envy behind him in the air.

"Reckon he was bullshitting?" a gunner asked.

The NAOU quickly became known to its members as the Nackeroos. They were few in number, but the terrain they were expected to oversee was vast, extending along the coast from Joseph Bonaparte Gulf in Western Australia to the southern shores of the Gulf of Carpentaria in Queensland. Once unit headquarters learned of Doug's seafaring experience with the pearling fleet, he was assigned to Lieutenant Gordon McArdle's crew aboard a forty-foot ketch, the *Dinwiddie*. This vessel was undergoing repairs in Darwin, so Doug was given forty-eight hours leave before reporting for duty as a seagoing Nackeroo.

There being no means of letting Val and Brian know he was on his way home, Doug accepted a lift on an army truck as far south of town as the Redlands turnoff, fully expecting he would have to walk the rest of the way home, as he had following the first bombing attack. After walking less than a mile along the track, he heard horses approaching, and minutes later saw his wife and son and daughter. He stood and waited for them, hands on his hips.

"How'd you know I was comin'?"

"Brian just knew, don't ask me how."

"Had a feelin', y'know," said Brian.

Doug mounted the horse they had brought for him and leaned across to give Val a clumsy kiss from the saddle, then Judy, held in Val's arm, exhibiting not the least fear at being five feet above the ground.

"She's gettin' to be a real little jilleroo," said Doug.

"Takes after her mum," Brian said.

Val asked, "How long have you got?"

"Two days."

"It's not enough."

"It'll have to be."

They wanted to hear tales of his military life, so Doug invented a few, crediting his gun crew with bringing down the bulk of the Japanese bombers and fighters that had ploughed the red dust and blue seas around Darwin.

"They give you a prize for all that?" Brian asked.

"Yeah, a ticket to join another bunch a bastards doin' somethin' else."

"Doing what?" Val wanted to know.

"It's a secret. If I tell, they'll rip me arms out and feed 'em to Blighty."

"Is it something dangerous?"

"Not for a bloke like me it's not. Can't tell you more'n that."

When they reached home, Brian offered to keep riding and check that the cattle wandering in the bush roundabout were still multiplying.

"Yeah, right-oh," Doug encouraged him, and Brian left the track even before the house was reached.

"Know what he said to me?" Val asked.

"No, what?"

"He said I had first go at you, being the missus."

"Brian's inherited all me tact and charm where the ladies are concerned."

"You know, those are the very words I thought of when I was thinking about you the other day—tactful and charming. That's my Doug, I thought."

"Garn, expect me to believe a load a bull like that?"

"Aren't you tactful and charming, Doug?"

"Nah, but I'm bloody romantic when I wanna be."

Brian spent the first day and night of Doug's leave away from the house, then returned in time for lunch on the second day.

"How's the moo-moos?" Doug asked him.

"Moo-moos are orright; still mooin'. How's you two? Got big smiles, but."

"We're happy," said Val, "that's why."

Brian nodded, less than happy himself. He had met Ranji in the bush the previous day and reported to him the way of things at Redlands. The events M'linga had foreseen were soon to begin. Brian hid his misgivings behind a grin.

Doug and Brian went riding together, shooed out the door by Val. They let their horses amble without direction.

"How's she been, really?"

"Been orright, her an the nipper both."

"Not gettin' all worried about me?"

"Nah."

A little later, Brian asked, "Real fond a the nipper, eh?"

"She's me daughter, the only one, just like you're me only son."

"Yeah, could be anothery, but."

"A brother for you?"

"Be just a half-brother," said Brian, masking his true thoughts with practical analysis. He would not look at Doug.

"Not worried I'll turn you outa Redlands, are you, Bri? I wouldn't do that. There's some that might, but not me. You know that, don't you?"

"Yeah, I know. I know plenny." His expression was doleful.

"Spit it out. There's somethin' on your mind."

"Nothin'," Brian insisted, and Doug knew better than to pursue whatever it was that Brian was keeping from him. He loved his son, but it was not the kind of love most men would have felt toward a boy like him. The larger world beyond Redlands did not approve of the way Doug Farrands bothered to acknowledge he had a yella-fella at all. The other Territorians who had fathered yella-fellas chose not to speak of their progeny, as a rule, unless they were outright combos, living like blackfellas out in the bush. Doug Farrands was different, in that he kept his son close to him nowadays, as a substitute for himself, it was generally reckoned, while he was obliged by the war to be elsewhere. Some respected him for it, and some did not, since that kind of egalitarianism, if adopted by others, might someday result in the blacks being considered legitimate citizens of the land they so clearly had lost to whites.

They rode with him back to the main highway and sat on their horses for some time, watching a convoy of huge American military trucks blasting by on their way to Darwin. When the last one had passed, Doug said, "No need to hang around." He dismounted and handed the reins to Brian; Val's free hand was occupied as usual by Judy. Doug shifted the strap of his kit bag several times on his shoulder.

"Well, take care and that."

"We will if you will," said Val.

"I will, then. Go on. Watch out for things, Bri."

"Yeah, I will."

"Go on, don't wait around. There'll be more trucks comin' through soon. Bastards never stop."

He watched them turn their horses and return along the track. Doug knew he would not see them again for a long time, months at the very least, and could not shake free of the disquieting sensation that when next he did so, everything would be utterly different for them all. They disappeared around a bend in the track and were gone. Doug wanted to run after them but stopped himself; he was being an idiot; everything would be all right. He was part of an organisation that would concentrate on seeking out evidence of a potential Jap invasion along the wildest stretches of coastline in northern Australia. He was no longer in a fighting unit; he had made that very clear to Val.

When another string of trucks came roaring into view, Doug held up an arm in its khaki sleeve and soon was hurtling away from his doubts.

Dinwiddie had a crew of five. Besides Lieutenant McArdle and Doug, there were Ron Mott and Gavin Pritchard, both in their twenties, both Sydneysiders, and Sergeant Phil Duffy from Katoomba, whose task it was to keep the *Dinwiddie*'s twenty-horsepower engine running. There was little formality aboard; the sergeant preferred to be called Duff, and Gordon McArdle quickly became Gordo. Doug was six years his senior and knew the waters *Dinwiddie* made her ungracious way across far better than Gordo could hope to if he stayed in the north for a lifetime. Gordo's maritime experience had been confined to scudding across Sydney Harbour on the weekends in a tiny sailboat and using the ferry twice a day to reach his office in Woolloomooloo, where he ran the advertising department for

Sydney's lowest-circulation newspaper. He was happy to defer
to Doug on almost all matters pertaining to the handling of the
dilapidated ketch that now was his responsibility, and made
light of his rank. Gordo was grateful that he had been posted to
his own country, even if to its farthest and least-civilised region.

Dinwiddie crept along the north Australian coast, diesel
thumping, her purpose being to deliver food and fresh water
and spare parts for radio transceivers to those units of
Nackeroos stationed nearest the sea. With every delivery, Doug
felt himself a little luckier for having drawn such easy duty. The
Nackeroos whose lifeline *Dinwiddie* was had no other task than
to patrol the coastal bush and swamp in search of evidence that
Japanese forces had made a clandestine landing there. They
endured the ringing emptiness of those lonely places, surviving
with a minimum of comfort, and every rendezvous with the
ketch as it thumped its way toward the beach or mangrove inlet
saw them grinning like castaways facing rescue at last.

The shorebound Nackeroos welcomed such ordinary items as
tins of bully beef, having lived for the last two weeks on goanna
and damper; or they might be grateful to receive bags of flour,
damper being the perfect antidote to nothing but tinned beet-
root and turnip. Theirs was harsh duty, second in hardship only
to that of frontline troops. They received mail infrequently,
courtesy of Gordo and his crew, and, having received their supplies, would melt away into the bush and scrub again, to scan the
ground beneath their rotting boots for Jap footprints, and the
northern horizon for the telltale smudges of an invasion fleet.

Crawling from the western observer unit positions to those in
the east, and back again, replenishing her supplies during the
dockings at Darwin, halfway between, the *Dinwiddie* went
about her business without suffering much worse than an occasional squall as the Wet returned. Doug told his cityside crew
members tales of the north, some true and some not, including
many featuring himself as mock hero; then he told the same
tales again and finally learned he no longer wished to be anyone's resident entertainer. The crew noticed his dour mood and
ignored it, once Doug made known his preference for aloneness.

He knew very well why it was that his temperament had
soured; he wanted to go back to Redlands for at least a quick
visit, but no member of the ketch's crew was granted leave,

since every day called for travel to one or another of the strung-out units of Nackeroos requiring more of whatever they had run out of. There were several vessels plying the same waters, serving the same needs, but the distances were great, and *Dinwiddie* was the largest by far of the supply fleet and so could not be spared from permanent duty. Doug was aware the other crewmen also missed their families, but his own was so tantalisingly close, every time the boat docked again at Darwin to take on fresh supplies, that his torment had a special edge to it that only nearness and the possibility of actual accomplishment could bring. He did not go AWL despite the temptation, but his mood did not improve.

A week before Christmas, NAOU headquarters at Katherine were informed by radio that a death from heat exhaustion had occurred in one of the units stationed near the Roper River in Arnhem Land. Gordon McArdle was ordered to deliver a new member to the unit, since his vessel was scheduled to take that course in any case.

The new man came aboard in Darwin along with the usual supplies, and Doug saw a face he had not come close to in some time.

"G'day, mate. Didn't know you were a Nackeroo."

Ken Moxham slid his kit bag onto the deck and stared at Doug.

"You're no mate a mine, Farrands."

"Heard you broke your leg. Mended all right, did it?"

"Would I be here if it didn't? What the fuck are you doin' here anyway?"

"I work here, as the actress said to the bishop."

"You couldn't work if someone winded you up with a fuckin' key."

"There's probly blokes that'd agree with you, Ken, but there's no need to get nasty. Let bygones be bygones, eh?"

"Fuck your bygones."

"No need to get shitty, either."

Ken picked up his bag and brushed past, allowing the end of the bag to bump Doug's shoulder in passing. Doug chose to ignore the provocation.

"It's a small boat and a long trip, Ken. Might as well bury the hatchet."

Ken said nothing, found a doorway, and went below. Doug waited. Ken came up on deck again.

"That's the engine room, mate," Doug told him. "Crews' quarters is through there." He nodded in the direction of another doorway. "Be happy to show you around our little tub if you like."

Ken dropped his bag again and jabbed a thick forefinger at Doug. "You keep outa me way, Farrands, or I'll flatten you."

"Shouldn't live in the past, mate; it's not healthy."

"You worry about your own fuckin' health."

Watching Ken go below a second time, Doug felt a change within himself, a lifting of the depression that had hung over him like a cloud for some weeks now. The cause of the change was Ken Moxham. With a self-declared enemy like Ken aboard, Doug suspected he would have little time for brooding over Redlands. Ken would throw him over the side, given half a chance. A five-hundred-mile voyage with Ken around the top of Arnhem Land to the Roper River would be a challenge, and it revived Doug's spirits every bit as much as a granting of his wish for leave might have. The proximity of someone to hate was similar, in a strange way, to the nearness of someone to love. Doug felt himself come alive.

Although no mention was made of their previous acquaintance by either party, everyone else aboard *Dinwiddie* soon became aware of the enmity between them. It was not that they shouted at or fought with each other in open view. It was the absolute avoidance practiced by Ken and Doug that made their feelings apparent.

Gordon McArdle, on the second day out from Darwin, asked Doug, "Do you and Moxham have a bone to pick, by any chance?"

"More like a whole bloody skeleton."

"Care to discuss it?"

"Nah, not really. Ken's all right if you just remind yourself every now and then he's a real whacker."

"No chance for fisticuffs aboard, I hope."

"Shouldn't think so. Him and his brother both hate me guts. Ken's used to havin' a go at me with Les alongside him. He's harmless enough on his own."

In the evening of that day, Ken and Doug happened to

approach each other from either end of a narrow companionway. Both stopped, each wondering if the other had somehow engineered this confrontation, then decided simultaneously to proceed as they would if the man approaching were simply one of the crew. If the space available had been wider, they might have passed each other by without incident, but the companionway's peeling walls obliged Doug and Ken to slide past in a way that inevitably brought about contact, however brief. Afterward, both would believe the other had swung first. Doug felt an electric tingling as Ken came toward him, and the first unintended brushing of elbows sent a galvanic message to his fists, just as it did to Ken's. They lashed out together, and lost as much skin from their knuckles against wood as against the nearest parts of their opponent.

The thumping and banging of their constrained battle as they blundered back and forth along the companionway brought Duff and Gavin Pritchard from the galley to see what was creating the noise. Gavin hung back, aghast that grown men would want to inflict bodily hurt in that brutal fashion, but Duff, an occasional pub brawler himself, stepped in to separate the fighters, telling them, "Now then, you bastards, there's no need for that—" Ken's closed fist, missing Doug's eye socket, caught Duff under the nose, and Duff suddenly tasted blood in the back of his throat. Broad experience of Saturday nights in Katoomba gave Duff an advantage Ken was not prepared for. Shoving Doug out of the way, Duff struck at the point of Ken's long jaw. Doug recovered his balance in time to see Ken sliding down the wall.

"King hit," Duff congratulated himself. "That bloke's a bit of a prick, isn't he?"

"Born that way, I reckon."

"What's going on here?" Gordo had entered the companionway.

"Ken fell over," Doug explained.

"Really. Did anyone help him do it?"

"No need. Ken's a very talented bloke."

"Help him up, both of you. He's got a hard enough time ahead of him on the Roper without getting there in a knocked-about state."

"Give us a hand, Duff."

Ken was taken through to the crew's quarters and laid on a bunk.

"Looks all peaceful like, doesn't he?" said Duff.

"Never seen him lookin' better," Doug agreed.

Ron Mott peered at Ken's open mouth. "End of his tongue's been nipped off."

"Serves him right," Duff said.

"He'll use shorter words now, I expect," said Doug, and Ron laughed.

"Don't like him much, do you?"

"I couldn't give a stuff about him," Doug insisted. "It's him that doesn't want to leave me alone."

"Think all that blood'll run back down his throat and choke him?"

"Might do," Doug said, but no one turned Ken onto his side.

Doug ran into Ken on the deck after a silent breakfast. Ron Mott was nearby, pegging the crew's laundry onto a rope strung between the *Dinwiddie*'s stumpy masts.

"All right today, Ken?" Doug asked.

"Get rooted."

Doug turned away, unwilling to provoke further strife.

"Your missus, she's the one you oughta be askin' about."

Doug turned back. "Eh?"

"Livin' with a boong." Ken leered. "Talk about low."

"That's me son, you know that."

"Yeah, but he's not her son, is he." Ken looked over at Ron and winked.

Doug took a few steps toward Ken, then stopped himself.

"You're a shit-stirrer, that's all."

"Maybe. I'm not the only one knows about it."

"There's nothin' to know."

"She's not supposed to be there, Farrands. I can see why she stayed on, though, with the nig-nog shaggin' her silly while you're away. Talk about desperate."

"You're a pathetic bastard, Moxham, you and your brother both, just a coupla useless shit-stirrin' bastards."

"She'd be a hot root, takin' on a darkie—"

Doug flung himself across the deck and began punching at Ken, who fought back with as little science as Doug. They rolled across to the scuppers, watched by Ron, the clothes pegs standing forgotten in his mouth.

Gordon McArdle dashed from the wheelhouse. "Stop it, you two! Stop it at once!"

Both men ignored him. Ken, temporarily in the ascendant, was banging Doug's head against the deck.

"Separate them!" Gordon ordered Ron.

"Oughta leave 'em to get on with it, Gordo."

"Get Duffy!"

The fighters were pulled from each other several minutes later, neither one having the strength to win. Duff held Ken, while Doug was restrained by Ron Mott and a reluctant Gavin. Gordon was unsure how best to proceed; this was his first real dilemma since taking command of the Nackeroos' supply vessel. There was cloud forming along the horizon, and the barometer was falling fast; he did not want to be distracted from the handling of his command by the idiotic feud between Doug and Moxham.

"Farrands, you're to remain on deck the rest of the day. You"—he pointed at Ken—"will go below and stay there. I want no further contact between the two of you until we reach the Roper, and not even then, if it can be avoided. Do I make myself clear? One more incident like this, and you'll both be up on a serious charge."

Ken took himself below. Doug refused to answer Gordon's questions concerning the fight, but the gist of the argument was conveyed to him later in private by Ron, who stressed the role Ken had played in instigating it. Gordon was appalled to learn that Doug's wife slept with blacks. Gordon had never seen an Aborigine before arriving in the Northern Territory, and his opinion of those he had seen since was low.

He approached Doug just before the storm swept down upon them, driving the *Dinwiddie* closer to the coastline of Arnhem Land. "These allegations Moxham's been making, Doug . . ."

"Mind your own business, Gordo. It's between him and me, all right?"

"No, it isn't all right. You know better than to start acting this way. You're in the army, even if it's irregular duty. I'm not a stickler for the rules, you know that, but when I ask a question I expect a civil and honest answer."

"Not this time. Sorry, mate. Put me under arrest if you want, I don't care, but if that shithead says one more thing to me—if he looks at me sideways—I'll kill the bastard, so help me. Keep him away from me, Gordo. I mean it."

"Christ, Doug, don't go talking to me that way. If someone hears, I'll have to put you on a charge. I'm your superior officer, after all."

Gordon began stuffing tobacco into his pipe to cover his distress.

"Just keep him away from me," Doug said.

"Well, you'll be needed behind the wheel pretty soon, by the looks of it, and Moxham's no sailor, so he can stay where he is."

"You want to make a run for Blue Mud Bay till this lot blows over?"

"Fine. Take over the wheel and show me the way."

The *Dinwiddie* was anchored fifty yards from shore by midafternoon, protected from the worst of the choppy seas and rising wind by arms of mangrove growth extending into the bay. She pitched and tossed, but the Nackeroos aboard had all known stiffer blows than this, and a card game soon began, to pass the time. Doug ensconced himself in the wheelhouse to avoid Ken, whose own mood was not improved by the enforced separation: Ron Mott began winning money from him.

Gordon McArdle stayed topside with Doug, smoking and watching rain drench the shoreline of mangroves. He wiped sweat from his face and neck with an expensive lawn handkerchief from a boxed set of a dozen his mother had sent by sea mail to Darwin. Gordon watched Doug without appearing to do so. The Territorian interested him. Gordon fancied himself a student of human nature, and he wished at that moment to understand how a likable man such as Doug Farrands could allow his life to include a wife who slept with blacks. Despite Doug's general openness of character, Gordon had never once attempted to find out what it was that made him tick. He knew what made himself tick—a sense of personal inadequacy that had left him stranded in a job he detested. With luck, the war and his ridiculously easy to obtain commission would change all that, if he survived.

"Think it'll last through tomorrow, Doug?"

"Might do. You can never tell, this time a year."

Gordon studied Doug's blunt profile, wondering about the man. He was a bushie, an ocker, but city men like Gordon learned as boys, by way of the nineteenth-century doggerel verse taught in Australia's schools, to admire such types as Doug for their outdoor expertise and wandering ways. Gordon supposed Doug could have been the model for Clancy of the Overflow or the Man from Snowy River, but these were simple men of action, without psychological depth. Gordon suspected there were currents of anger running beneath Doug's sunburnt skin, some private turmoil of the blood hidden away from men like himself. Doug Farrands was a crude enigma, and unless Gordon found the courage to question him on matters that, as Doug had said, were none of his business, Gordon would never learn even a fraction of what it meant to be him. It was a depressing conclusion to draw, and Gordon stared for a long time at the rainswept windows of the wheelhouse and the forlorn mangroves beyond, imagining himself the loser in some nameless, pointless contest of comparison. War, he decided, brought together the unlikeliest of fellows, the kind who never would have associated in peacetime.

"How about some tea, Doug?"

"Right-oh."

Gordon waited for Doug to stir himself and fetch a pot, but Doug didn't move, and Gordon realised, with mounting embarrassment, that Doug had assumed Gordon would do it. Gordon felt the stirrings of anger; Doug was only a corporal, and he was a lieutenant.

"It's not going to bring itself up here," Gordon snapped.

"You said to keep away from Moxham."

"Oh, yes . . . well, stay away from him while you get the tea. He'll most likely be in his bunk, not the galley."

"Might not be. Ken's a big eater, always tryin' to scrounge another pie."

Doug went to the door, left open despite the rain to circulate humid air through the wheelhouse, and stood there for a moment, looking across Blue Mud Bay.

"Sugar and milk for me," Gordon prompted.

"I know."

Doug left the doorway and was gone. Gordon took several deep breaths, uncertain why he had allowed himself to become upset.

The galley was empty, a kettle boiling on the primus stove. Doug made a pot of tea and set it on a tray, with containers of milk and sugar and two cups. He carried the tray carefully topside and emerged from a hatch aft of the wheelhouse. Ken was waiting for him there, a long-bladed knife from the galley in his hand. His slouch hat was off, the rain plastering hair down onto his brow. He said nothing as Doug slowly set the tray down onto the deck.

While Doug was still bent over, Ken ran at him. Doug flipped open the teapot's lid, then took hold of the spout and handle. He pitched the contents into Ken's rushing face as the knife cut into his sleeve without touching flesh. Ken gasped; the tea was far from boiling, but it stung his eyes badly. In the moment he took to hesitate and blink, Doug slammed the teapot into the side of his head. The pot shattered, leaving nothing but a jagged-ended handle in his hand.

"Cunt . . . ," whispered Ken, and swung the knife again. Doug jerked away from its arc, then threw the pot handle at Ken's face. It cut his cheek and fell to the deck. Ken raised his hand to feel the wound and looked down at the blood on his fingers.

"All right," he said, smiling, "you're gunna get it now, all right."

"Cut it out, why don't you."

"Fuckin' little coward, aren't you, Farrands? Don't wanna real fight, do you?"

"Put the knife down, Ken, eh?"

"Down your fuckin' neck, mate. Come on, come and get what's comin', you little shit, you bastard. This'll be for the old man, y'know?"

"I didn't kill him; he had a bloody heart attack."

"Lyin' little pearl-pincher. I've been waitin' for this, hopin' I'd bump into you, and now I bloody have."

"Look, this is just stupid."

"You're the stupid one—" Ken put his boot on the tea tray. It slid across the rain-slick deck, and he lost his footing. Doug rushed at him, reaching for Ken's right wrist to keep the knife from swiping at him again. They traveled backward together, chest to chest, arms locked, tasting each other's breath. Ken's lower back hit the rail, but neither man was stopped; the momentum of Doug's rush and their backward stumbling carried both over the rail and into the water.

They separated instantly. Doug felt his open mouth and eyes fill with warm salt water. He surfaced and began swimming for'ard to the anchor chain, anxious to be back aboard in case Ken was still in possession of the knife. Doug turned once to see if Ken was nearby. There was nothing but the choppy waves and *Dinwiddie*'s peeling hull. He swam on, took hold of the chain, and pulled himself up until one leg could be thrown over the bow.

Once on deck, he saw Gordo looking at him from the wheelhouse. Ignoring him, Doug began working his way along the rail, looking down at the water. "What the hell happened to you?" Gordon asked as the wheelhouse door was passed, but Doug went on without answering, until he had gone completely around the boat. Ken had disappeared.

"What's going on here? What on earth happened to the tea?"

Gordon McArdle was standing beside Doug on the port side, rain dripping from the polished peak of his cap.

"I dropped it," Doug said, eyes scanning the water.

"Dropped it? What, over the side? I saw you climbing out of the water, so would you mind explaining?"

"Moxham's out there."

"Where? What are you talking about?"

"He came at me, and we both went overboard. He's still in the water."

Doug went to the starboard side. There was no sign at all of Ken.

Gordon joined him there. "You mean to say he's drowned?"

"Ken was a bloody good swimmer. . . ."

They both saw the dorsal fin, its crescent slicing the waves for just a few seconds before sliding from view.

"They don't usually come up to the surface when there's a storm . . . ," Doug said. "Too rough and noisy for 'em. . . ."

"Get everyone on deck!"

The crew of *Dinwiddie* watched the surrounding water for half an hour, then was ordered below. The shark fin had been seen only once. There were no visible bloodstains on the surface, but at the end of the half hour it was generally accepted that Ken was dead, by drowning or shark attack.

Gordon ordered Doug to the wheelhouse for an interrogation that could not be heard by the rest of the men. Doug gave an account of what had happened. Gordon began stuffing his pipe.

"This is bloody bad timing. Here we are, delivering a replacement for a man who died from heat, and before we even arrive with him, he's dead too. Bloody hell, Doug."

"Wasn't me that started it."

"I'm not blaming you, but it does place both of us in an awkward spot. I'll have to submit a detailed report. You can't lose a man and expect the brass to shrug their shoulders over it."

"Tell 'em he fell overboard. No need to mention the fight. What's the good?"

"Each and every one of us abroad will be questioned. There's simply no hope of avoiding it. Do you want everyone to lie about what happened?"

"They would if I asked 'em."

"Absolutely not. No, we'll do this by the book. You've done nothing wrong. You were defending yourself against an unwarranted attack; I'll make that perfectly clear in the report. There's nothing to fear from the truth, Doug."

"That's what they say, don't they."

There was an inquiry into the death of Ken Moxham, held at the Larrakeyah barracks in Darwin. A major conducted the questioning, without the presence of any other officer. Gordon McArdle testified to the bad feeling that existed between Farrands and Moxham prior to the incident in Blue Mud Bay. Doug thought he spoke well, and was confident no blame would be laid against him, as was only right. When he took the chair before the major, he was not prepared for what followed.

"You didn't like this fellow Moxham, did you?"

"Not much. He didn't like me, either, or his brother."

"Just answer the questions as I ask them."

The major consulted a sheaf of papers before him in a cardboard folder. An electric fan hummed at the edge of his desk.

"Your statement says you hit him with a teapot, is that correct?"

"That's right; only thing I could lay me hands on."

"Did you hit him hard enough to cause unconsciousness, would you say?"

"Nah, nowhere near it. Barely made him blink, then he came at me with the knife."

"Were there any witnesses to his having a knife?"

"There weren't any witnesses to any of it. Everyone was down below, and Gordo—Lieutenant McArdle, was in the wheelhouse, facin' the wrong way."

"So we only have your word that Private Moxham had a knife."

"It was one a the galley knives. There was one missin', we found out later, so that was it."

"I'll draw the conclusions, if you don't mind." The major looked at Doug for a moment. "What I'm trying to understand, Corporal, is if the blow to the head you gave him wasn't sufficient to cause him to black out when he landed in the water, if not before."

"He was strugglin' like billy-oh when we went over the side. I didn't see him after that. I didn't hit him hard enough for what you're sayin'."

"Then how do you account for the fact that he apparently sank like a stone immediately, without so much as a cry for help?"

"The shark got him, I spose."

"Ah, yes. The shark. Lieutenant McArdle has said you both saw a shark fin for just a few seconds, quite some time after Moxham's disappearance."

"Not so long; a few minutes maybe."

"And you'd have me believe that it was this shark that snatched him."

"Can't think what else."

"Doesn't it stretch credibility to think that a shark might be right beside the vessel, as if waiting for someone to come hurtling over the side and directly into its mouth?"

"Not really."

"You're an expert on shark behaviour?"

"No; are you?"

"Any more responses like that, and you'll find yourself in a court of inquiry far less friendly than this—do I make myself clear!"

Doug nodded, too angry to trust his tongue.

The major went on: "You seem to think this is just some accident for which no one need bear responsibility. To the contrary, there *is* responsibility, and my task is to assign it, if need be—do you understand? Speak, don't nod your head."

"I understand."

"Good. Now that we know the activities and dining habits of sharks are as much a mystery to you as they are to the rest of us, I think we can return to the more likely cause of Private Moxham's death, by which I mean the blow to his head administered by yourself, Corporal. Was the teapot full when you used it as a weapon? A full teapot must carry more of a punch than an empty one, don't you think?"

"I already threw the tea in his face."

"And why did you do that?"

"To make him drop the knife."

"But your statement says you set the tea tray down on the deck."

"Yeah, then I picked up the pot and took the lid off."

"You took the lid off? You took the time, with this fellow bearing down on you with a knife, to remove the teapot lid?"

"The tea wouldn't a come out if I didn't, would it?"

The major considered chastising Doug again, then decided not to. The man was an oaf, coarse-grained and dim-witted, that was clear. He had conducted a vendetta against someone who, in all probability, had been equally lacking in character and intellect.

"Do you enjoy participating in acts of violence, Corporal?"

"Not much."

"But you've had your share of pub fights, I daresay."

"One or two."

"How do you regard your position with the NAOU? Are you happy in your work?"

"I spose so."

"You don't feel that you might better serve your country by rejoining the regular AIF, in one of its overseas divisions?"

"Hadn't thought about it," said Doug, who wanted to do no such thing.

"Then I'll save you the bother. My recommendation in this instance will be to have you transferred to such a division, so your temper might be directed toward the Japanese instead of your fellow Australians."

Gordon McArdle stood up. "Sir, Corporal Farrands has been invaluable in delivering supplies by sea to the various NAOU stations along the coast. He's an old seaman around these parts, sir."

"I'm sure there are others, Lieutenant. This old seaman will take up arms."

He closed the folder. Doug stood up, a crooked grin on his face.

"Want me to kill a few for you?" he asked the major.

The major could not be sure if Farrands was being insubordinate or simply was unable to appreciate the gravity of military justice, even in so unimportant a case as this. The major chose to be lenient. The army needed every man, and this fellow would be wasted in the guardhouse.

"As many as you like, Corporal. Dismissed."

Word of Doug's newest reassignment had come to Royce Curran by way of the AIF officer to whom he had recommended that Doug be made a Nackeroo. Royce made sure his vehicle was available to take Doug home to Redlands on leave before he was sent to Brisbane and then God alone knew where.

Royce drove an American jeep now, his police truck having been strafed into wreckage at the beginning of the Wet by a low-flying Zero. The Yanks the Territory was swarming with nowadays had simply given one of their spare vehicles to him, with a minimum of red tape, even though he wasn't in the military. Royce was impressed by the ease with which the Americans could provide just about anything for anyone at any time, even though he was less than pleased with their off-duty conduct in the pubs of Darwin.

Doug had refused the lift at first, until Royce told him, "Look, I know your missus is out there and has been all along. I'm not interested in moving her. If tarts are allowed back into Darwin, why shouldn't a decent sort like your missus be allowed to stay where she is—that's how I see it. You want that lift or not?"

"All right."

The drive utilised all of the jeep's ability to negotiate rough tracks, and conversation in the open vehicle was brief, as Royce steered through an endless ribbon of red mud.

"I offered to talk to that major," Royce said, "the one that passed judgment on you, but he wouldn't see me—that is, his bloody adjutant said he wouldn't see me. I was all set to put in a good word for you and a bad word for Ken Moxham, but this twerp of an adjutant said it's no go, sentence having been passed, or whatever they call it. Sorry this happened, Doug. They're stupid, sending you away from where you can do the most good."

"They want me to be nasty to the Japs."

"Shouldn't be too hard. Know how many air raids we've had now? Forty-seven. Eighteen bombers came over in the last lot. Know how many planes we had to send up against 'em? One P-40. They say the Poms are sending Spitfires to beef up the air support here. I'll believe it when I see it. All the Yank planes are somewhere else. One bloody flier to shoot down eighteen bombers . . . but he got one, by crikey!"

"Good for him. That's a few less Japs for me to take care of."

Royce negotiated a particularly tricky bend in the track, swinging the jeep around in a red spray of mud. He straightened the wheel, enjoying his skill with the four-wheel drive. Royce knew he was safe from everything but bombs and the casual strafing attacks the Japs sometimes indulged in. Doug, sent into battle somewhere, was far more likely to cop a bullet than himself.

"It's true, isn't it, Doug, what happened? You didn't kill the bugger, did you? I'm asking as a friend, not a copper. I always thought Ken Moxham was a pain in the backside, frankly."

"It was a shark. It coulda been me that got taken, but it was Ken, that's all. Try tellin' that to the army."

"Not bloody likely. I'd rather talk to a brick wall."

"I reckon you'd get more sympathy," Doug said, and smiled for the first time since getting into the jeep.

"Too bloody right you would."

They stopped at the edge of the Flying Fox and watched its waters foaming past. The sky was filled with more rain to come, but Royce was glad of it; the Japs usually flew their missions when skies were clear. He took out his pistol and fired twice into the air.

"Yank ammo," he said, while they waited beside the boat chain that ran into the river. "They put more grains of powder into their bullets. Heck of a kick to it."

Brian appeared on the opposite shore after some minutes had passed, and began crossing in the dinghy, passing the chain through his hands like an expert.

"I won't come over," Royce said, when Brian was halfway across. "I'll come back in two days to pick you up."

"Thanks, Royce."

"Listen, Doug, I know you're a hotheaded kind of bloke and sometimes you've got reason to be, but don't go getting any ideas about going AWL, will you? They've got you by the short and curlies this time, mate. I'd be the one they sent to get you back, and it's not a job I'd like to do."

"No worries. I'll be here like a good boy."

"Say hullo to the missus for me."

"I will."

They watched Brian hauling the dinghy clear of the torrent.

"Looks like your kid's doing all right out here."

"Course he is. G'day, Brian!"

"G'day!"

"See you in two days," Royce said, and turned to walk back to his jeep. It had been a suggestion, Doug felt, rather than a casual assignation. He could see why Royce might worry about him nicking off into the bush, but Doug had no intention of doing that.

"Where'd Royce get that?" Brian asked, watching the jeep spin in a circle and begin roaring back along the track to the Darwin highway.

"Yanks gave it to him. How's things been, with me away?"

"Orright. Val's hidin' with the kiddie. Thinks it's trouble, them shots and that."

"Royce knows she's here. He's known all along, he says. He doesn't care."

"Yeah? Good bloke."

They hauled the dinghy across together and tied its bow-line to a tree just as rain started to fall, then they began running up the remainder of the track to the house. Even as he ran, the hammering of rain on the iron roof came to Doug's ears like the sound of all his yesterdays.

Val was peering from behind a gum tree a hundred yards away, puzzled by the whooping and yelling going on in her front yard. When she saw the uniform she began to run, Judy tucked against her breasts. Doug stood like a statue, arms wide apart to receive them both, his face streaming in the rain.

11

IT WAS DIFFERENT THIS TIME, having him home. He was changed somehow, less prone to making silly jokes, more given to silences that extended until Val broke them. His lovemaking was unusually tender and prolonged, as if Doug required time for his senses to absorb the feel of his wife's body, committing it to memory against a future time of want. He would not talk about his brief stint with the Nackeroos, other than to describe in a few sentences the nature of the work; nor would he explain his reassignment to the AIF.

He preferred to look at his family, it seemed, as if ingesting their presence whole, storing pictures of them against a time when he might not be able to touch their flesh, and it was this staring, as much as the silences, that made Val begin to fear she would not see him again. This time he would be going away to the real war, those places beyond Australia where the Japs held sway.

She took him down to Blighty's Pond, this being a sentimental journey of sorts, and together they sat on the fallen tree they had sat on years before to begin their friendship. Doug looked at the swollen waters, lapping almost at their feet. Judy threw twigs into the shallows.

"Step back a bit, Jude," Doug said, "or the croc'll getcha."

"Don't say that, or she'll get frightened. She's never laid eyes on a croc, believe it or not."

"You haven't seen old Blighty lately?"

"No. Sometimes I think he must be dead, but Brian says he can't die, because he's not really a croc."

"I've heard the same thing from Ranji's mob. I keep forgettin' Bri's half black. I spose he believes a lot a that stuff."

"You told me once you believe some of it. What about Kukullumunnumantje? We never did find it again. You said the Pitjantjatjara were hiding it from us, because it belongs to them. I've been out looking a few more times while you've been gone. No luck, though. Brian just smiles at me when I talk about it. He says Gulgulong doesn't want me to see the stones again, not yet anyway. When he says things like that, I feel like you, like I forgot about the part of him that's Aborigine. He's a funny kid. We get on well, though. I don't want you worrying about us while you're away."

"I reckon I'll be too worried about myself. Sound like a yella dingo, don't I, but I can't help it, Val. I've got a bad feeling about goin' away this time. I shouldn't tell you, I spose. Probly just nerves, eh? It'll be the first time I ever left the Territory, goin' south to the big smoke. Travel's sposed to broaden the mind. Can't say I want it. Gunna be a long way back. Thousands of other blokes have done it, though. I'm not sayin' I'm a special case. It's just a long way, for a long time, I expect."

"You'll be all right."

"Yeah."

They walked on to what they had come to call Perce's Pile: the deteriorating sticks of furniture taken from the house by unknown hands following Perce Burridge's death and stacked in the bush. The wood had been attacked by white ants in the years since then and reduced to a pile of rotten kindling; a few years more, and it would vanish completely. Judy picked up some of the crumbling dust and let it trickle through her small fingers.

"Seen the dunny ghost lately?" Doug asked, as if inquiring about the weather.

"Not since before Clive left. I think old Perce just wanted to hang around for a bit and make sure his kids took over the place the way he wanted."

"Well, at least one of 'em did."

"I dreamt about Clive the other night. He came through the door and wanted to know where all the hammocks went. I told him we got married and got a real bed. Jude's the only one with a hammock now, I told him, and he just said, 'Oh,' and then I woke up."

"Didn't look like a ghost, did he?"

"No; he looked the way he always looked. He wasn't different at all, but I think he was carrying an umbrella."

"Every ghost should have one."

"He wasn't a ghost, Doug. Clive's alive somewhere, I can just tell."

"I'd give six months a me life to have a chinwag with old Clive. I don't reckon I'll ever have a mate like him again, and I didn't even know him for very long. And he was a Pom!"

"Funny old world."

"Too right it is; that's why you can hear me laughin'."

"Don't go getting all down in the mouth, or you'll have me and Brian the same way."

"Sorry."

She put an arm around him, an act he would not normally have accepted. Doug stared at the decomposing furniture before them, returning slowly to the red earth.

"Old Clive," he said, "bloody old Clive."

Brian had gone bush for the first day of his father's leave, then returned, and the three of them planned for Doug's absence.

"It won't be so bad," Doug said, "not now that Royce Curran knows about you being here. At least you can go into town for stores and grub. Watch out, though: Darwin's crawlin' with randy Yanks. They think every woman they see up here's a prossie, and they are, mostly. It's not the same town anymore, probly never will be again. Anyway, Royce'll keep a lookout for you. No one expects the Japs to invade now, that's what everyone says, so just hang on here till I get back—that's all you need to do. Bri, you haven't gone walkabout since you came here, have you?"

"Nup."

Brian had been told not to move by M'linga himself, and Brian was not about to do anything that might get the bone pointed at him. He was as much a part of Redlands now as the trees, until M'linga said otherwise.

"Well, if you get the urge to go for a wander, let Royce Curran know first, all right?"

"Orright. I'm not goin', but."

"You might change your mind; you never know."

"Yeah I do."

"Fine."

Doug looked across the table at his wife. Her forehead was white by contrast with her tanned face, the white of an outdoor worker, habitually hatted against the sun. She did the work of a man, keeping their small herd intact and cared for, assisted only by Brian, and Doug felt guilty for leaving her stranded in a harder life than most women would have cared to endure. He felt sick with love of her but told himself the feeling in the pit of his stomach was cowardice, an unwillingness to go away and perform the slaughter expected of him.

It was all so stupid. If the Germans and Japs had just kept themselves to themselves and not gone stamping all over their neighbours for no good reason, he would not have had to feel as he did. Doug assumed he would never see the Germans; it was the Japs he would have to face, and he hated them already for having upset his life. As a younger man, he might have approached the war with excitement in his blood, instead of fear. He hated Ken Moxham also, for having been foolish enough to die and bring Doug before the major at Larrakeyah. Doug hated the major too, for removing him from the Nackeroos and the Territory without any real justification.

Judy, asleep for her noonday lie-down, stirred in her hammock in the corner, the same curved sheet of string Val had slept upon when she and Doug and Clive first came to Redlands, when she had not even been his friend, let alone his wife. His son watched him, mere feet away, a boy from another time, another culture; Doug's own blood anyway, living in his father's house at last, but the father had scarcely been there to share his life, and now was going an impossible distance from him.

Everything that meant anything to Doug was within reach, yet would be taken from him by that same time tomorrow. He looked down at his hands, resting on the table. Soon they would pick up weapons and begin the killing. Love and fear and hatred: it all washed through him from moment to moment in a whirling flux, as the hour of his departure came rolling toward him from tomorrow, suffocating him. There was nothing he could do.

Val watched the following morning from her side of the Flying Fox as Doug stepped inside Royce Curran's jeep and was gone, taken from her, the last glimpse of him an arm waving from beneath the vehicle's canvas roof. The jeep had disappeared before Brian was halfway back across the river, hauling without enthusiasm on the chain. He tied the dinghy, then joined Val.

"Gone," he said.

"Yes, gone."

"Be comin' home, but."

"How do you know? Did M'linga say so?"

"Too right. He knows."

They turned and began walking together back to the house.

"When are you going to let me meet M'linga?"

"When he says. Carn tell *him* what to do."

"Please ask him anyway. Is it him you go and visit every now and then?"

"Sometime."

"Who else?"

"Carn say. Might get her in trouble, but."

"A girlfriend?"

"Nah!"

"Then who? It's your girlfriend, isn't it? You can tell me— I'm not against it, Bri."

"She's beaut."

"What's her name?"

"Whitefella name's Jess."

"Are you in love with her?"

"Arr, I reckon."

"Then you should invite her around to meet me. I could use some female company."

"She'd be too shy."

"I bet she wouldn't. Give her a chance to make up her own mind. Ask her."

"Might do. Never know, eh?"

"You never know."

"Have to keep it under your hat, but."

"A secret?"

"Someone finds out, plenty trouble, for her, for me. You, maybe."

"Then you'll have to look sharp and keep the secret a secret."

"Reckon," Brian agreed, but he had lost his happiness of a moment earlier.

Near the house, Judy was tottering in pursuit of a small ochre lizard. She looked up as her mother and Brian approached, and changed direction toward them, while the lizard paused with palpitating throat to blend into the colour of the earth.

"Walkin' like a good 'un now," Brian said. "Be goin' walkabout pretty soon."

"She's a little pest, I'll say that. Here, there, and everywhere at once."

Judy fell onto her face and began howling. Val reached her and scooped her up.

"What's all the noise for? You go that fast, and you can expect to fall over."

Val took her inside. Brian followed.

"We gunna do them cows down near the boundary today?"

"Not today. Judy and I are going to go looking for a special place, aren't we, love?"

"Arr, not doin' that again, eh. Won't find it."

"We might. Kukullumunnumantje got found once by me, so I can find it again. I don't care what M'linga says Gulgulong says, or what you say M'linga says. I'm going to surprise you all and find the stones again."

"Won't," Brian assured her, smiling.

"We'll see. You can come with us if you want."

"Got better things to do."

"I'll bet."

It was the only thing she could think of to distract herself from Doug's departure. The signs of approaching rain were not there, and she wanted to walk until her legs felt like lead weights, to forget that he was gone again, this time for much longer. On her occasional expeditions to find Kukullumunnumantje, Val usually carried Judy on her back in an old haversack with leg holes cut into the sides, and carried a small bag of food and water in her hand. Both she and Judy wore hats with fly netting draped from the brim, and shirts with long sleeves. Judy's fat legs were protected by sleeves torn from one of Doug's old shirts and worn as leggings. Doug had said she looked like Tom Mix in them, but such makeshift outfits as this enabled Judy to go anywhere Val felt inclined to take her. With Doug gone, Judy was suddenly more precious.

Val had little real expectation of finding Kukullumunnumantje again. Brian's confidence that she could not, inspired by Aboriginal magic or whatever term applied to their way of thought, was gradually seeping into her own way of thinking, and today she knew why. If Brian was right about her being unable to find the tribal stones, he might also be right about Doug returning home. He had predicted, as mouthpiece of the nearby-but-invisible M'linga, that Doug would be going away, not that such prophecy was in any way unusual during wartime, when men countrywide were leaving home; but Val held these disparate threads together, weaving them into a net to catch her sinking heart, because the things Brian told her were all she had.

He sent postcards occasionally, but they were never informative. First he was in Brisbane, which made Darwin "look like a bunch of chook houses," then in Sydney, which made Brisbane "look like a bunch of termite mounds." He said he missed everyone, he said the weather was a lot easier on a bloke down south, and he said he could say no more, military censorship being what it was.

Val placed the postcards around the walls to remind herself of the places where she had lived during a different life, and she sometimes felt a longing to be back there, in Sydney or Melbourne, even somewhere smaller, in a place with electricity and a flushing toilet and running hot water and shops just around the corner. Remembering it all was like attempting to resurrect a dream that kept sliding away into the fierce brightness of the place where she now lived, with its whirring insects and clouds of tiny shrieking birds, its eternal bush and sky. She supposed she was jealous of Doug, away among the crowds and bustle of civilisation. But these moods would not last; it was him she wanted back, not the tall buildings and busy streets. It was temporary, this separation; M'linga had said so. When Doug came home again, it would all be as before, with the hardships and discomforts of Redlands no less bearable than they had ever been.

By the first weeks of 1943, Val knew she was pregnant. There was nothing to show, but the familiar sickness came to her each morning. By the time the Wet began to end, the afternoon storms weakening, then receding north with the sun, her belly started to swell a little, and she carried herself differently.

"Got a boy comin'," said Brian, who had known even before Val did that life was growing inside her.

"Are you sure it's a boy? I suppose M'linga told you."

"Yeah."

"And Gulgulong told him."

"'Sright. Gulgulong's kiddie, so he'd know, I reckon."

"What? Blighty's boy?"

"Kinda like," Brian agreed. "Won't have no long nose, but. Be a nice-lookin' kid, you'll see. Be a bonzer nipper."

"I'm glad you think so. I'd have a hard time explaining to Doug how I gave birth to a crocodile."

Brian found that funny. "Havin' a bloody croc, eh! Ha, ha! Dad, he'd be a bit shitty, I reckon!"

"Brian, how could the baby inside me possibly belong to Blighty?"

He grew serious, trying to explain. "When he seen you that time, Gulgulong, like you told me about, an then you went bush an found Kukullumunnumantje."

"That's when Gulgulong did it?"

"Made you his missus, thas right."

"That was more than two years ago. I'm a bit late having his kid, aren't I, or are you saying Judy's his kid too?"

"Nah, Gulgulong don't make no sheilas. Got no use for 'em. Gotta be boys. This one, he's the one Gulgulong been waitin' for."

"And will Gulgulong be sending flowers and chocolates?"

Brian found that funny, too, and laughed on and off for the rest of the day. He sobered himself between bouts of mirth by thinking of the hole that had to be made in the world to fit

Gulgulong's boy into, since nothing could be made that did not replace something else that had to be unmade, to make room for the newly made thing. It was a shame the hole would have to be created in the shape M'linga had specified, but if M'linga said it had to be, then it had to be. Brian expected that another hole could be created somewhere else, to fit Judy into, so she wouldn't be lost to the world, only sent elsewhere to make room for Boy b'long Gulgulong.

In May a ten-wheeled American Army truck came grinding along the track to Redlands and stopped at Val's door. A sergeant and a private stepped down as Val came outside. They seemed as big to her as their outsized truck; even the pistols strapped to their waists were big.

"Ma'am?" said the sergeant. "Ma'am, are you Mrs. Farrant?"

"Farrands."

"Oh, scuse me. U.S. Army Air Force, Sergeant Brady, and this is Private Croker. Is your husband around?"

"Not at the moment. Can I help you?"

"Ma'am, we're stationed down Batchelor way; you know where that is?"

"Just down the road a bit from Darwin. There's an airstrip there."

"Yes, ma'am. Scuse me, shoulda known you'd know that. Well, the outfit there, it's got a bunch of us boys that's restless for fresh meat, and we heard this place has got prime beef on it. What I mean is, ma'am, if you're selling, we're buying."

"Barbecue, ma'am," said Private Croker.

"That's it, ma'am. Barbecue, that's what we want."

"How many head do you need?"

"I'd say just a couple for now. Our truck here's not built for cattle."

"We'll come back for more later, if that's an arrangement you could go for, ma'am, if it's high-grade meat like they say."

"Oh, it's good, all right. You two wait here, and I'll round up a couple of beauts for you. Umm, what price? Better get that sorted out first."

"How about ten Aussie pounds per cow. That sound about right to you, ma'am?"

"Fine, but you'll have to take bullocks. We need the cows for breeding."

"Bullocks? That's what . . . , small bulls?"

Val laughed. "It means they've got no balls."

"Oh, yes, ma'am—that's what we call steers."

"Okay by us, long as it moos."

"Shouldn't take long," Val said. "Sorry I can't offer you a beer while you wait—no fridge."

"That's okay; we're on duty anyhow."

"Keep an eye on the kiddie, will you?"

"Sure will."

Val saddled her mare and rode out to the area where Brian had said he would be. The sergeant watched her with appreciation as she rode away.

"That's a good-looking woman for way out here," he said, flipping a cigarette into his mouth.

"Better than what's around in Darwin. She's got one in the oven, though, you can tell."

"So? A man that knows women, Croker, he knows a woman that's got a kid comin' isn't exactly ruled outa the picture, you know, not till she's a lot bigger. I've had women that's pregnant, and they fucked like monkeys. You just have to be a little more careful if they're big in the belly, go in nice and easy from behind, see; they appreciate the thoughtfulness, and an appreciative woman, Croker, she goes to town on a guy."

"Yeah?"

"Yeah." Sergeant Brady ran a match along the big Chevy's fender and held the flame to his Chesterfield. "That one, that hillbilly lady, she's primed for appreciation, take it from me."

"What about her old man?"

"He's to hell and gone, I hear. Killed a guy, they say."

"Yeah? Gimme one, okay?"

Brady extended his cigarette pack to Croker and offered the matches.

"But you don't go worryin' about no husband if the guy ain't there, I don't care if he's Jack the Ripper. A husband gone means a wife alone, and I do mean alone. Put yourself in her place, boy. Here she is at the bad end of shit street, no man and no beer, just a little thing all on her lonesome, then along comes two movie stars like us. You think she wouldn't be interested?"

"Maybe."

"Maybe nothin'. You watch her moves when she gets back, you'll pick up on the little bitty hints she starts to drop. It's in the eyes and the hips, Croker. She starts to battin' the one and swingin' the other, you'll know we got ourselves a hot one."

"Yeah, but you better not try nothing if she don't have the moves."

"She'll have 'em, trust me—I can tell."

Judy stood a few yards away, watching the big men talk.

"Hey, honey," Croker said. "How's it with you today?"

Judy turned her head to avoid his smile, then turned slowly back.

"Cute kid."

"I guess," said Brady.

They waited less than an hour, sitting on the running board on the truck's shady side, smoking and talking of women and barbecue, then they heard the sound of approaching cattle and stood up to see what kind of meat was available to them.

"Shit, she's got a nigger."

"Damn, she does too. Well, boy, some other time maybe. If this beef's A-one, you can bet we'll be back for more."

They watched Val and Brian pen the bullocks, then dismount and come over to the truck.

"I don't have a ramp you can load them up with."

"No problem, ma'am; we're equipped for every emergency."

Brady and Croker dropped the Chevy's tailgate and hauled out what appeared to be a heavily constructed door.

"Got this off a bombed-out warehouse or somethin' in town. We got permission, ma'am. It was just goin' to waste."

"Looks solid enough," said Val, "but they won't want to go up it, not without sides; they'll be too nervous."

"Well, it's just a door, so it don't have sides."

"I'll get 'em in," Brian offered.

"Think you can do it, Sam?" Brady said.

"Me name's Brian."

"Okay, let's see you do your stuff."

Brian remounted and drove a bullock from the pen while Val opened and closed the gate. Barely touching its flanks with his stock whip, he directed the bullock to the rear of the truck.

It balked at the bottom of the leaning door and attempted to swerve sideways, but Brian kept flicking it expertly around the rump until it tried to escape the stinging by blundering up the ramp. Sergeant Brady clapped his hands together slowly.

"Some show. Let's see you do it again, cowboy."

Brian did it again, faster this time. When the second bullock was inside the truck, Brady and Croker tried lifting and sliding the door ramp back into the truckbed, but the bullocks would not lift their hooves to allow this, and finally the effort was abandoned, the door allowed to fall into the dust.

"Ma'am, they look like prime beef to me, and I can practically guarantee we'll be comin' back for more inside of a week or two." He nodded to the fallen door. "Okay if we just leave this piece of equipment where she lays, for next time?"

"All right."

The sergeant peeled two ten-pound notes from a thick roll and placed them in Val's hand. "Ma'am, don't mind my askin', but is there any little item of grocery you'd like to see, any canned goods you're partial to that I could bring along next time to sweeten the deal maybe?"

"Tinned fruit, any kind."

"I'll do my best, Mrs. Farrant, ma'am."

"Farrands. Peaches especially, and pears."

"Peaches and pears, yes, ma'am. Would your little girl there like something sweet? I bet she would."

"I suppose she might."

The tailgate was lifted and latched.

"So long, Mrs. Farrands."

"'Bye."

The truck reversed and turned and was driven away.

"Twenty quid," said Val, staring at the notes.

"Why'd he think me name was Sam, eh?"

"He probably calls everyone Sam. Imagine if they buy two bullocks every second week. God, we'd be rich!"

"Bloody would, but."

The truck returned ten days later.

"Mrs. Farrands, you run the best kinda steers on your place here, just the best—I mean it."

"Went down all right, did it?"

"Croker and me are the most popular guys on base."

"We'll take two more, Mrs. Farrands, ma'am."

"Same price as before," said Brady, "only with a sweetener, like I promised."

He took two sacks from the truck's cab, set one down on the ground, and handed the other to Val.

"There you go, compliments of Uncle Sam."

Val looked inside; there were at least two dozen cans and jars of fruit and jam, according to the pictures on the labels, although the jam was called jelly, for some reason. There were chocolate bars, twisted in the heat, and a bag of boiled lollies in cellophane wrappers.

"My goodness! This is . . . Thank you *very* much."

"Our pleasure, ma'am. You want to send your boy out for a coupla head?"

"Brian's already out. I'll have to help him round a couple up. Make yourselves at home."

Brady and Croker waited until two bullocks were brought back. The transaction was made as before, the bullocks loaded into the truck.

"Mrs. Farrands, the major back at Batchelor wants me to take a good look at your herd and kinda get a feel for a long-term business arrangement with you, plus we had a god-awful time gettin' those steers off the truck at the other end, even after we got ahold of a ramp to ease 'em down on. We sure coulda used your man, here, with that whip of his, so what I figured we'd do is, Private Croker can go on back to base with these two and take Brian along with him to help unload 'em, and then he'll come back to pick me up. Meantime you could show me what's on the hoof in these parts. That okay?"

"Brian, would you mind?"

"Can I see the planes?"

"Up close." Brady smiled. "Ever been inside a B-24?"

"Nah. Like to, but."

"Then Croker'll do his best to get that for you, won't you, Croker?"

"Sure will."

"Orright."

"Climb aboard."

Watching the truck roll away, Val felt a faint stirring of doubt inside her.

"Can you ride, Sergeant?"

"Oh, call me Charlie, Mrs. Farrands; you aren't in the service."

"All right, Charlie. You'd better call me Val, I suppose."

"Val. That's a nice name. I like that."

"Can you ride?"

"Heck, I'll come clean, Val. I told the major I was practically born in the saddle, and he believed me, but the fact is, I never threw my leg over a horse in my life. Val, I trust you to give me the facts on these cattle of yours. Whatever you tell me, that's what I'll tell the major."

"Well, they're all good animals, I wouldn't fib about it."

"No, I didn't think you would. Val, I brung something else along besides the canned goods, and I'd be grateful if you'd share it with me, just to kind of seal the deal."

"What is it?"

"They tell me all Aussies drink beer, the ladies too, is that right?"

"I'll take it if it's cold," Val admitted.

"That's what they told me about Aussies—they won't drink a beer that don't come with ice on the outside. Now, that's a tall order out this way with the heat and all, but guess what—I did it."

He went to the second sack and lifted it, untying the string around its neck. He came to Val with a smile on his face, the sack wide open. She looked inside.

"God, do you Yanks have ice?"

"The U.S. Army Air Force goes nowhere without it, Val. We're a class outfit."

He pulled a long-necked bottle of Swan lager from the chipped ice, its smooth dark surface beaded with moisture. Val felt something more than mere thirst rising in her throat. Brady produced a bottle opener from his pants like a magician conjuring a rabbit from a hat. His smile widened.

"You got glasses, Val?"

Brian had never been in such a huge vehicle. The truck cab was spacious and high up, much higher than Doug's Ford utility had been, and the engine howled a song of power. Brian wanted to ask the Yank if he wouldn't mind teaching him to drive it on the trip to Batchelor, but he was afraid to ask, since he had already been told he would be allowed into the belly of a Yank bomber when they arrived at the airstrip. Maybe on the drive back, when he and the Yank were better friends, he might ask to be placed behind the wheel. The Yank hadn't spoken a word to him since they started, and seemed to be in a crook mood about something. Brian didn't like to ask what the matter might be. He bounced up and down on the thickly padded seats and imagined himself sitting where the Yank was.

"Snake!" shouted Private Croker, and swerved the truck hard left.

Brian saw a long king snake undulating across the rutted track, then the Chevy's high, square hood hid it from view.

Croker uttered a whoop of satisfaction. "Got him!"

He steered back into the middle of the track. Brian looked into the rearview mirror and saw nothing but a red cloud of dust behind them. He hoped the snake had wriggled clear of the wheels. He saw no point in trying to kill a snake for any reason other than hunger, and the Yank certainly didn't seem hungry. It was a stupid thing to do, and Brian felt uncomfortable to be sitting beside someone capable of doing such a thing. He was not so sure now that he would be friendly enough with the Yank to ask for a turn behind the wheel on the way back.

"I hate snakes," Croker told him. "There's too many goddamn snakes around here, don't you think, huh?"

Brian was ashamed to find himself nodding his head. He should have shaken it and explained about not killing anything except to eat it and allow another creature, be it snake or goanna or kangaroo, to be born into the world to take the place of the one that had been eaten. A snake left uneaten was not the correct way to open holes for new things, since an uneaten thing left no hole; it was still there, of no use to the hunter who chose not to eat it, nor able to make room for a new snake. The Yank, Brian admitted to himself, was an idjit.

A loud bang came from the rear of the truck. "Fuck!" yelled Croker, and stood on the brakes. The Chevy slid to a halt and was blanketed for half a minute by pursuing dust.

"Blowout," said Croker. "Damn! It better be one of the outside wheels."

He climbed down from the cab, and Brian followed. They went to the four sets of double wheels at the rear of the truck. One of the inner tires had shredded around its circumference and hung from the rim like sun-dried meat.

"Those inside fuckers, they're a bitch. You know how to change a tire?"

"Yeah."

"Well, gimme a hand, then. Shit! This is the second time in a goddamn week."

Croker jacked up the truck with Brian's assistance, then took down the spare from its dusty perch under the chassis. He loosened and removed the nuts for the outer wheel and pulled it off. Brian rolled this away to lean it against a gum tree while Croker loosened the nuts on the inner wheel. He finally wrenched it free of the axle and thrust it behind him.

"Take this fucker away and gimme the spare!"

As Brian came toward him he saw something flash from the axle to the side of Croker's face. Croker screamed and fell back into the dust, his limbs thrashing with fear. The king snake had been tossed by the front wheel to the rear of the truck and had been able to wrap itself around an axle there despite its fractured spine. The snake was in pain, still terrified of the spinning thing that had stopped spinning, then been taken away. The living thing behind it was within striking distance, and so the king snake struck.

Its fangs were fastened so deeply in Croker's cheek he dragged it with him as he fell back, the snake loosening its hold on the axle to stay with the thing it meant to kill. Its poison sacs pumped themselves empty with the continuous pressure of fangs gripping hard into flesh, and its broken body flipped and jerked with Croker's thrashings across the ground to the edge of the track. Croker kept screaming as the snake accompanied him, its snout buried in his cheek. Croker felt as if a claw hammer had been slammed into his face and lodged there, but he knew it was a snake, the one he had tried to run over just minutes before, and the injustice of what had happened made him want to cry. He had already pissed his pants in sheer surprise, and expected to shit himself before too long.

The snake just wouldn't let go, and he was afraid to grab it and tear it free. The nigger was just standing there with his mouth open, doing nothing to help.

Croker felt his terror begin to wane, but could not understand why this should be so. The snake was still there, nuzzling him to death, but Croker was not so afraid of it now; in fact, he was sorry he had tried to run it over. The pain was receding, becoming a dull throb that matched his heartbeat, itself becoming louder as it slowed. Croker began to think he might be dying. He knew he wasn't moving anymore, but he couldn't remember when his thrashing and jerking had stopped. He could hear the cattle inside the truck lowing, but the sound came to him like the foghorn in Frisco the day they had sailed. He had been sure then that he wouldn't die in the war, and he supposed he hadn't, since no one had declared war on snakes. He wanted to laugh over it but could do no more than think about it. He couldn't do anything now but feel himself become smaller and smaller, as if he were falling backward into his own skull, his eye sockets like manholes filled with sunlight above him as he fell, until they were so far away in the darkness, those two little holes of sunlight, that they became one, and that one light was snuffed out, leaving Croker alone in the dark.

He waited until the Yank had stopped moving, then Brian grabbed the snake behind its head and prised its fangs from the cheek of the dead man. He was not sure what to do with it then; he didn't wish to eat it, not after so confusing an incident. The king snake would probably not live for long, not with the stiff kink in its back denoting a broken spine, but Brian didn't want to end its life himself, since it had been the Yank who began to do that with the most stupid of motives. The death of a snake, usually a simple equation of need and replacement, had been made complex, like clear running water unnecessarily muddied through mischief. He set the snake down a short distance away in the bush, and it tried to coil itself into a fighting knot but could not. The snake flipped itself over and over, its movements stiff and uncoordinated instead of beautifully sinuous. Finally Brian took a fallen branch and clubbed it to death rather than letting it go on moving in this unnatural way.

Now the snake and the man the snake had killed were both
dead. The bullocks were moving their feet restlessly in the
jacked-up truck. Brian supposed he'd better run back to
Redlands and tell the other Yank his mate was dead.

The first bottle had gone down Val's throat like foaming water,
bitingly cold and tangy. The sergeant sat opposite her at the
table. He opened a second bottle and poured more into their
glasses. The sack of tins and jars lay next to Val's elbow, its
neck widened to reveal the good things within, a swag bag of
loot, she thought, unable to keep her eyes from glancing at it
while she drank. Judy was already halfway through a melted
chocolate bar.

"Good health," said Brady, raising his glass.

"Cheers," Val responded, and drank deeply. She did not
actually like Brady, but he seemed to be a generous enough
man, sharing some of the Yanks' vaunted wealth with her, as
well as paying top quids for the meat. He deserved a little
friendliness and conversation, but she wouldn't let things go
beyond that. Val was not naive enough to think the sergeant
had brought her what he had solely out of concern for the
monotony of her diet. But he was a decent enough sort, she
supposed, and she was not worried about telling him where to
go if he started something.

"They say your husband's away someplace."

"He'll be home next week on leave," lied Val.

"It's a cruel thing, war, the way it separates folks."

"Are you married, Charlie?"

"No, not me, I was never that lucky of a guy. I'd like to be
someday. Can't think about that stuff while there's a war on.
How long's he been gone?"

"Too long," said Val, truthfully.

"Yeah, it's a shame, all right."

They drank again.

"You like living here, Val?"

"It's a bit rough, but it's home."

"No place like home."

Val was feeling the alcohol inside her now. She had drunk
the beers too quickly, but they had been so wonderfully cold;

chilled heaven in amber hues. Her throat was still a little sore from the iciness, and the beer was sliding down through her like a cool snake. She was genuinely grateful to the sergeant for having provided it.

"Thing that makes a home a real home, Val, it's the love that's there. That's what my mama told me, and she was a smart and loving woman, one of the best."

"Good for her."

"Smart and loving. Most guys, Val, they look at a woman and they see . . . well, they see the obvious. Me, I look deeper. I look for character. That's the thing. Most important part of a woman's body, it ain't what most guys think; it's the bit between the ears. I truly believe that. Nothing there, and there's nothing anyplace else worth having, that's how I see it, and I've been a disappointed man enough times to know the difference, Val."

"Unlucky in love."

"That's how you might put it, exactly. Unlucky in love, but still hopeful—that's more like the way I'd put it. Once in a long while a guy's lucky enough to bump into a lady that's special—not your ordinary female-type woman; something else. Special, like I said. That guy who bumped into her, he's lucky, and you know what, Val? The lady's lucky, too, if the guy's smart enough to see what it is he bumped into. Why? Because he knows what he bumped into is why, and she can expect to be treated right by that guy, because he's not looking for what the other guys might be, uh-uh, he wants more'n that by a mile. The deeper thing, that's what he wants, which is also what the lady needs, Val."

"Not this lady."

"Huh, Val?"

"This lady doesn't need anything deep, or shallow, either."

"No, no, I wasn't meaning you, Val. No, what I meant was, if a guy like me could meet with a gal like that, it'd be pretty fine, you know?"

"I hope you meet her."

"Not much chance around here, Val. One chance only, that's the way I got it figured. Only one lady with the extra thing around here."

"You don't mean me, I hope."

"I surely do mean you, lovely lady, and I mean what I say."

"Well, don't, all right? I'm married and pregnant, in case you didn't notice."

"That's fine, that's just fine, Val. Those things, they're nice things to be, but there's more to you on the inside than just that. Don't say there ain't another woman on the inside that's got her needs, don't tell me that, because I just won't believe it. I see that other woman behind your eyes, and I know."

"Look, thanks for the beer. Would you mind waiting outside now till your mate gets back?"

"Val, that'll take hours. You want me to stand out in that killer sun all day and get heatstroke? That what you want?"

"I want to hear you talk about the weather and the war and that's all."

"Aww, Val, I've gone and upset you, talking like I did. I apologise, I really do. You took it the wrong way, I swear. I wouldn't for the life of me wanna give offense to you. No, the problem with me is, I speak from the heart. That's always been my problem. I just can't sling the b.s. like your average guy. I have to say what I truly mean, and that's what gets me in trouble sometimes, like now. I'll talk about the weather, though, Val, if that's what you want. I can do that, sure."

"I just don't want any misunderstandings."

"Sure, I know what you're saying. Okay by me." Brady turned to look at Judy, who had chocolate smeared over her happy face. "You like that Hershey bar, kiddo?"

Judy nodded slowly. Brady laughed. "She get lonely out here for other kids?"

"No; she's never known anything different. Once she gets a brother or sister, she'll know what she's been missing."

"Yeah, I bet. You got a bathroom here, Val?"

"We take showers under the water tank in the Wet, but it's the Dry now, so the tank's low."

"No, I mean the can, you know?"

"Out the back. Follow your nose."

"Country living." He smiled, raising himself from the chair.

He left the house, and Val was aware that she felt better without him nearby. It had been no real trouble to dissuade him from romance, but she resented having had to do it. Soon he would be back, and he might be confident enough to start the whole silly thing over again. Val went to a tall wardrobe in the corner and took out Doug's .303. A full magazine was always kept ready in one of the drawers. Val pushed the magazine home and worked the bolt, placing a bullet in the chamber, then stood the rifle beside the wardrobe where Brady wouldn't be able to see it, assuming he returned to the same chair. Val would be able to reach it in just a few steps if she needed to.

"'Nother one," said Judy, reaching for the sack on the table.

"No, later. Don't be a greedy guts. Go outside and wash your face and hands."

"'Nothery?"

"No. Later on if you're good. Go on."

Judy went out to the tank. The big man was standing nearby, smoking a cigarette. He had brought all the lollies and probably had more. Judy went directly to him and looked at his face, willing him to understand her need without obliging her to use words, which she used sparingly, and only with her mum or Brian.

"Beat it, sweetheart, okay?"

Judy knew he was talking about sweet things. She looked at him some more, waiting for lollies to be produced from his pockets.

"Hey, take a hike."

The shooing motion he made with his hand sent Judy away. Brady watched her go back inside the house. He hadn't seen such a dump of a place since basic training in Georgia. Some of the white crackers and most of the niggers down there lived in places about as bad as this, but at least they were made of wood, not tin. Any woman who lived in a tin hut had no right to be turning down Charlie Brady.

Australia would have been taken by the Japs a long time ago if Uncle Sam hadn't poured men like himself into the fucking place, and trucks and planes. He hated it, hated the heat and flies and mosquitoes and the god-awful niggers, straight out of a Tarzan movie, most of them, with their spears and scars and seminakedness, and he didn't like the ones that dressed like white men, either. The kid who'd gone with Croker was a prime example of backward niggerdom. Brady had bribed Croker into taking him back to Batchelor for the afternoon by forgiving the ninety bucks Croker owed him from the poker game last week. Ninety was a lot to pay for a woman, but Brady wanted Val badly. She was a little scrawny and downtrodden-looking, but under the sweat and the faded dress there was as cute a piece of tail as he was likely to find in a few thousand miles. So he wanted her, and had tried his best approach, and been refused. She was no dummy, but that wasn't any excuse for turning him down, not after all the good stuff he'd given her. It was pretty much of an insult, really, taking everything into account.

He could hear the kid now, whining about something inside the house. If the kid hadn't been there, he might have been able to try a little strong-arm persuasion on Val, nothing rough, just a little reminder of where her obligation lay. She was too snooty for what she was; a bush widow, he'd heard women like this one called. It was just too bad. He had the whole afternoon to fill, longer than it would take Croker to deliver the steers and come back; that was what the nigger was for—wasting time at Batchelor, so he could take Val nice and slow several times, in the different ways he liked. She was some snooty bitch, all right, turning him down like that, after all he brought for her, paid for with his own money. It was a blow to his pride. He didn't want to have to lie to Croker on the homeward drive, didn't want to brag about nothing. He liked telling stories that were essentially real, but Val wasn't in the mood to give him anything. A real bitch.

She had met his type before; not bad-looking, in an overblown, meaty kind of way, and his hair was almost as thick as Doug's, but there was too much confidence placed in the slow drawl and the sleepy half-closed eyelids; bedroom eyes, Val supposed. It was a pose she could see through with ease, now that he had revealed himself. The sergeant was just a lovelorn fool with big ideas about himself and small ideas about Val; a typical bloke, in fact. There was nothing intrinsically American about his approach. She should have become suspicious the moment his mate drove off with Brian, certainly by the time he produced the beers. It was what Yanks in the gangster pictures called a setup, laughably obvious, with hindsight. Val was glad he seemed to be taking his time in the thunderbox. He was probably nursing wounded pride and wondering what to do with himself now, the silly bugger. She shouldn't have bothered loading the gun; he wasn't going to do anything stupid. He'd probably come back inside after a while and confess he had a wife and kids back home and show her their pictures.

Brady did return. He went to the sack on the table and took out some more of the lollies, then went back to the door. Val thought he had taken them for himself, to suck on while he waited for the truck to return, but he turned and waved the handful of boiled sweets at Judy, who ran toward him. He pitched everything outside, and Judy ran out to pick it all up. Val was furious, reminded by his action of someone throwing grain to chooks.

"She's had enough—"

Brady shut the door and dropped the latch.

"Lucky the lady who's had enough," he said. "And the guy. This guy hasn't had near enough. How about you, lady?"

"Get out. Open the door and get out."

"Come on, Val, just a little loving for a man a long way from home. Bet your hubby's doing the same thing somewhere, with some little brown girl."

"Get out!"

"No, no—now you listen to me just one minute. I don't hurt ladies, never have, just so long as they smooth out and do what's right. That's what I recommend here, honey, more smoothness, less shouting. No one'll ever know."

"You bastard . . ."

"Uh-oh, now we got the insults. Don't do that, Val. That won't change nothing. Just you smooth out and get over on the bed like I want, like you want deep down yourself, only you don't wanna admit it, do you? No one's watching, sweetie, not her outside, not anyone, so you be nice and we can get this done easy, with no harm to anyone. Just a little loving, that's all."

Val stood up from the table, fighting to control herself. She was afraid of him, the size and strength of him, and the mellow cajolery spilling from his mouth.

"You get on the bed first," she said, trying to sound resigned.

"No, sweetie, ladies first. Slip that hunka rag off, lemme

see them tits, all right? I know they're there, Val, so just you pop 'em out where I can see 'em, and all the rest, all the good stuff I been missing, okay? You do that for Charlie."

"All right . . ."

She moved away from the table, her hands inside the neckline of her dress, as if preparing to slip it off over her shoulders. She was almost within reach of the rifle propped beside the wardrobe. Brady's eyes were on her hands, his lips slightly parted. "That's it, baby, yeah . . . slide it off now, come on, hon . . ."

She darted for the gun and picked it up. It was heavy, too heavy for quick use, and she couldn't recall if she had already put a bullet up the spout or not . . . yes, she had, so she only had to aim and squeeze the trigger, but he was already sprinting around the table between them, intent on taking the gun from her before she could lift its heavy barrel. "Oh, you cunt . . . you fucking whore, you . . ." And he was on her, smashing her backward against the sheet-metal wall, his hands around the rifle, his breath in her face, angry spittle flying across her cheeks. "You would, would you, fuckin' little whorecunt . . . ? Do that to me, would ya, huh? Baby, you got lots to learn about Charlie, a whole bunch to learn, but I got the time if you got the snatch, you bet . . ."

He tore the rifle from Val's hands without real effort and stood back away from her. "Loaded, is she? You really wanted to plug ol' Charlie, huh? Let's just see here, honeybunch."

He aimed the rifle at the roof and pulled the trigger. The detonation of the cartridge in the breech was deafeningly loud inside the metal walls, and Val heard Judy give a little shriek of surprise outside. Brady stared at the wisp of smoke wafting from the barrel. "Jesus Christ . . . you really wanted to do me in." He laughed then. "You got some balls under that dress, Val, but I don't like it. I don't need no lady with balls right this minute—no, I don't. You would've pulled the goddamn trigger on me, wouldn't you, huh? Well, not anymore, uh-uh—now it's my turn to use my trigger. You can pull that one all you want, sweetheart."

He opened the door briefly and threw the .303 outside, then shut the door again.

"Judy . . . she might hurt herself with it. . . ."

"She won't touch the big bad gun while there's candy lay-

ing around, I guarantee it, and if I was you, I'd get in a coop-
erative mood real fast, so she don't hear no bad sounds coming from in here, understand? Understand, Val?"

"Yes . . . "

"Get that shitty dress off now, and I mean *right* now."

Val eased the fabric from her shoulders, shaking, breathing
through her mouth with fear. She had failed to stop him, had
made him angry, and now he would make her pay. It was in
his eyes, the narrowing of his sleepy lids, the way his tongue
passed slowly over his upper lip as he watched.

"Come on, come on . . . "

"Look, just go away. I won't let on to anyone what you
did—"

"Baby, I didn't *do* anything yet, so quit talking and get it all
off—come on now."

"No."

"What's that, sweetness? You don't tell Charlie Brady 'no,'
not if you wanna keep smiling, you don't. You move faster or
I'll change my mind about going easy on you, lady. You piss me
off some more, and I might just lay down heavy and hard on
your fat little belly there, know what I mean? You be nice and
do what I say, and I won't do that to you. You bend over and
put your sweet butt in the air, and there won't be no harm
done to whoever you got in there, understand? Get it off *now*!"

Val slid the dress from herself and let it fall around her
ankles.

"Oh, yeah . . . ," breathed Brady. "Too hot for panties, huh?
I know how you feel, babe. Hey, maybe you took 'em off for
me. That right, Val? Took 'em off when you heard the truck
coming? Hot and ready, huh? I like that, I like it that you did
that for me. Go on and get over to the bed and take a position,
butt high, okay?"

Val shuffled toward the bed, hands covering herself, watching him.

"Come on, don't string it out anymore. Time's come for
action, Val, so you do what I want and there won't be no problem, no problem for no one at all—"

The door opened. Brian came in with the rifle, working the
bolt, his face ashen with fury. He set the stock against his
shoulder and aimed at Brady's chest.

"Brian! No!"

"Hey now, fella . . . hey now, you just put that down, you hear. . . ."

"Brian!"

He lowered the barrel a few inches but kept his finger on the trigger.

"You get rooted, you Yank bugger! You get out!"

"Okay, okay, no need for you to get sore. I'm on my way. . . ."

Brian stood aside to let him pass, not allowing him within grabbing distance of the gun, still aimed at Brady's chest. Val dressed herself quickly and went to stand beside Brian. She saw that his skin was literally jumping with rage, his breath whistling through nostrils clenched tight.

"It's all right. He didn't do anything. Brian, give it to me."

She laid a hand over his on the rifle stock, and he released his grip reluctantly.

"It's all right. He's going to go away now."

"He better, Yank bugger. . . . Better go an see his mate!"

"I'm going. . . . Hey, no hard feelings, you guys. . . . This is dumb, you know?"

"Go an look at him!" Brian yelled. "You come here again, you're gunna get what he got! Go on! He's dead, your mate! Snake got him! Snake'll get you, you come aroun here! Garn! Bugger off!"

"He's . . . he's what?"

"Snake bit him! He's dead! You go fix the bloody wheel! Bugger! Garn!"

Brady turned and began jogging toward the Flying Fox and soon was gone.

Val leaned her shoulder against Brian. "Oh, Jesus . . . Brian, thank you."

"Bugger bastard! Fuck'm!"

"Yes, yes, he's gone now. Christ . . . "

"Better not come back."

"He won't. I know he won't."

Brian looked into her face. "Gulgulong, he put the snake there."

"What snake?"

"The one that bit the other fella. He put it there so I'd come back, so that bugger bastard Yank bugger couldn hurt you."

Brian saw now the reason for the snake's dying and was happy.

"He's really dead? You weren't making it up to make him go away?"

"Snakebit. Bloody big king snake. Gotta put the bloody wheel back on too, but. Bloody big job. Fuck'm, eh?"

"Yes."

They waited a week, but no one came to Redlands, inquiring after the events of that day. Val assumed Brady had changed the wheel and driven back to Batchelor with the bullocks and the dead man, and told them only about the snake. There was nothing to fear, no connection at all between what happened along the track and what happened at the house. Val thought several times of going to the American commander at Batchelor and making a formal complaint against the sergeant, then decided not to. Nothing would be accomplished by it. She did not want anyone else knowing what had occurred before Brian's return, did not want soldiers and airmen snickering over the sorry incident. It was better to remain silent.

Twelve days after Brady's last visit he came again, alone this time, on a motorcycle. He rode around the house three times, potshotting at it with his .45, then rode away, whooping and laughing, probably drunk. Val and Judy were inside, but none of the bullets came close. Brian had been approaching the house at the time of the attack and rode up, dismounting in a cloud of dust, to see what had happened.

"He's gone bonkers," Val said, looking down the track, where dust from the motorcycle's passing still lingered in the air.

"Bloody crazy fella," Brian agreed. "Boozed, eh?"

"I think so. It was too stupid a thing to do sober. What an idiot."

"Might come again, but. Get you next time. Might do."

"I doubt it. He just wanted to throw a scare into me. That type always has to have the last word."

Brian said nothing. He looked at Val's swelling abdomen without the least self-consciousness. Val had become used to his proprietary air concerning the baby inside her.

"Kiddie orright?"

"Yes, fine. I don't want to talk anymore about the idiot bugger, all right?"

"Yeah."

Batchelor was not so different from any of the other airfields gouged out of the Territorial bush. It was a long red gash among the gum trees, with lesser gashes leading off it to parking spaces for the P-40s and B-24s stationed there. Camouflage netting covered these parking spaces, and the mess hut and machine shop were daubed with grey-green splotches of paint. Batchelor was sometimes the object of Japanese bombing raids, but the damage was always quickly repaired by ground crews.

Sergeant Brady was in charge of one such crew. The Japs had laid down a stick of bombs that put three sizable craters in the southern end of the strip, and Brady's team had worked all day and into the night to fill in the craters and tamp them down firmly enough for the USAAF fighters and bombers to roll over without a hitch. The job was all done by eleven, finished off under a starry sky with a full moon that obviated any real need for arc lights to work by. Brady dismissed the crew and watched them take their equipment back to the tool shack.

He was restless. The little town beside the strip offered no opportunity for relief from the boredom that had begun to dominate his life. He wanted the war to be over and done with so he could go back home, where the bars stayed open late and the broads were willing and life was good. He'd keep on wearing the uniform for as long as he could, once he got back; the ladies went for it in a big way. He sat on a discarded fuel drum beside the strip and lit a cigarette, consoling himself for the way the war had gone and screwed up his life. A guy like himself should have been given a posting to Hawaii. A guy could have big-time fun in a place like that, with hula girls ready to do their bit for military morale. Northern Australia was a shithole. His best buddy had been killed by a snake. What kind of a way was that to die in defense of freedom? The bitch and the nigger with the cattle were the ones responsible.

Brady admitted that he hated them more than he hated any Jap.

Drawing on his cigarette, he stared across the strip at the nearest parking space. The big baby in there was almost invisible beneath its camouflage netting, despite the silvery wash of moonlight that made the strip itself stand out in a long red slash, as if a giant had bent down and licked all the trees off the earth in a straight line, or God maybe, since God was supposed to be on the side of the Allies, at least that's what the chaplain said every chance he got. Brady could just about make out the B-24's plastic nose bubble with the twin cannons poking out from it. Sometimes he wished he were air crew, so he could get behind the cannons and spit some lead. He slapped a mosquito from his neck.

"Eh, Yank."

He turned. A naked black woman was standing beneath the gum trees just a few yards away, moonlight shining on her breasts. She shook herself, making her body undulate. Brady flicked his cigarette stub away and stood up.

"How much?" he said, speaking quietly. He didn't want anyone else crashing the party he had begun to form in his thoughts.

"Ten bob."

"Okay."

He sauntered toward her. The lubra's face was indistinct, but Brady was not concerned with anything other than her breasts and the thrust of her round belly.

"Where at, huh? Got somewhere planned out, sugar?"

"Liddle bit this way."

She turned and walked into the bush. Brady was given a glimpse of her buttocks. He followed, watching the sinuous line of her backbone, the motion of her hips.

"How far?" he asked. "Come on, this is fine. You want ten bob?"

"Catch up!" she said over her shoulder, and began to run, but not fast, not so quickly Brady could not keep up.

"Come on now. . . . Hey, wait up, honey!"

And then she vanished, the faint sound of her bare feet suddenly gone, her shining skin licked by darkness. He stopped, listening for her, watching the silvered bush for movement of any kind. He guessed it was a game. Soon she'd call to him from someplace other than he expected, upping the price. He figured he'd go as high as a quid, just to give his long-standing boredom some relief. Fraternisation with the coons was off-limits, but in the dark of night, who the hell was to know?

"Sugar? Get back here, woman. You want fifteen bob? Okay, fifteen . . . "

A sound was coming swiftly toward him from the left, not the pad of feet against earth, a sound in the air itself—a shivering, swishing sound, as if something long and thin were vibrating as it rushed through space in his direction. The spear penetrated his rib cage, the vicious shovel nose of it ripping through flesh and cartilage, passing across the lower part of his lungs before it stopped. Brady stood like a wounded bull, uncomprehending. The sound was coming again, this time from behind, the same rapid whiffling in the air. The second spear entered his back, and he felt it touch the other one, already inside him, the merest sliding sensation of fire-hardened wood against wood, and then he knew what it was that he had stepped into, like a raw fool, but he could do nothing now and sank to his knees, infinitely sorry for himself and the pain just beginning to rise from within him, a terrible hurt no man should have borne. He hadn't taken a breath since the first spear ploughed into him, and found he could not do so now. He leaned forward and rested against the first spear. This made the pain worse, but it hardly mattered anymore. Brady could see dark figures detaching themselves from the night, approaching him: lithe shapes, thin as trees, eyes hidden under shaggy curls, feet whispering through the grass. He managed to raise his head in time to receive the nulla-nulla across his pate. Carved from heavy jarrah wood, it caved in his skull instantly.

They lifted the body, with the spears still lodged inside it, and carried it away, then began erasing all trace of the kill. They scooped up every speck and drop of blood with their long fingers and bore these away also, and passed branches of eucalyptus across the ground during their wordless retreat into darkness.

°　　°　　°

This time when Royce's jeep came roaring up to her door, Val did not run for the trees. She went out, with Judy at her heels, and wished him a good morning.

"Doing all right out here on your own, Mrs. Farrands?"

"Pretty good. I'm not on my own, though, not with Brian around, and as long as you're not going to try and run me off the place, you might as well call me Val."

"All right, Val. I suppose that makes me Royce." He took several postcards from the jeep and handed them to her. He had removed them from the Farrands' letter box, an Arnott's biscuit tin nailed to a gum tree near the junction of the Darwin highway and the Redlands track. "Took the liberty; thought I'd save you a long ride."

"Thanks."

She looked at the handwriting. "He's in Queensland again now," she said, glancing at the postmarks. "He was there before, then in New South Wales."

"Moving him around a lot, eh?"

Brian came out of his shed and walked slowly over to them.

"G'day, Brian. Working hard?"

"All the time."

"Good. Reason I came out here, Val, is because of those two Yanks, the two that bought beef from you."

"Oh, them. They haven't been back for more, I don't know why."

"You didn't hear what happened to them?"

"No, what?"

"Seems they were on their way back to the airstrip at Batchelor and had a blowout, and when they stopped to change the wheel, one of them got bitten by a snake and died on the spot."

"God, really?"

"And now the other one's gone missing."

"How do you mean?"

"Just that. Vanished. We've even had black trackers out looking for him, but they can't find any sign of him. Not often they can't find *something,* those blokes."

Val looked at Brian, who wore a distinct smirk on his face.

"He might've got drunk and wandered off into the bush," she suggested.

"If he had, the trackers would've found his trail."

"Well, I just don't know."

"Haven't seen him out this way since the last time they came for cattle, have you?"

"Wouldn't I tell you if I had?"

"I don't know, Val—would you?"

"Oh, I see. You think he's gone absent without leave and I've got him tucked away in my bed, do you?"

"No, no, I know you better than that, but the Yank brass out at Batchelor don't know you at all. You can see why they might think that's what's happened."

"Well, it hasn't."

Royce turned to Brian. "Know anything about this?"

"Nup."

"Haven't seen anyone roaming around the bush?"

"Nah."

"They said they wouldn't buy any more bullocks from you, Val. They're suspicious as hell."

"We can get along without their money."

"Bugger 'em," said Brian.

"If they're that suspicious, they should come out here themselves, not send you. They don't own you just because they gave you a jeep, do they?"

"That'll be enough of that. I'm a policeman, that's why I'm here. Missing persons are police business, and without that jeep I'd be walking the beat, so don't be so critical of them just because they're Yanks."

Val and Brian said nothing. Royce studied them both. He knew he was being lied to but was unsure of the exact nature of the lies.

"Well, keep your eyes peeled."

He got into his jeep and drove away.

"Brian, do you know anything about this?"

"Nah, nothin', dinkum I don't."

Like Royce, Val had her suspicions.

12

By late August, Val could no longer ride with comfort or safety, and Brian took over all stock duties. Val remained at the house, coping with the heat and her enforced inactivity as best she could. Judy was too small to be of help beyond obeying simple instructions to fetch and carry little things, and she often became bored by her mother's inclination to sit in the one comfortable chair for long periods.

Judy liked to put on her hat and go wandering. She was forbidden to venture far from the house, and had been given enough brief spankings in the past to restrict her longing for wider horizons.

Val, after one such punishment, had been exasperated enough to make a promise as well as deliver a lecture. "You know why you mustn't go too far from the house, don't you? I've told you over and over, haven't I?"

"Yes . . ."

"And what's the reason why you mustn't?"

"Might be los'."

"You might be lost, and I wouldn't want to lose you. If you got lost in the bush you might never find your way home again, and then you'd never see me or Brian or Daddy ever again."

This vision of desolation was too much for Judy to contemplate without tears, and when she saw that she might have gone too far, Val said, "If you're really good, and don't go wandering off, I'll take you to a place I know, a very special place. It's called Kukullumunnumantje, and it's somewhere near here in the bush. It's a secret place, Jude. I've only been there once myself. Remember all those times I took you on my back for walks in the bush? I was looking for that place."

"What is it?"

"Great big round stones all jumbled together like . . . old baldy men's heads."

Judy laughed at that. "When! When!"

"I don't know when. We'll just have to see how good you are at staying close to the house, all right?"

"I wanna go there . . . ," protested Judy. "Go *now!*"

"No, we can't, not for a while. I'm not sure where it is anymore, and you have to prove to me you can do what I told you. It's up to you."

"Bugger," said Judy, pushing out her bottom lip.

"Pardon me? Language like that won't get you there, little miss snotty."

"Bum."

"Bum to you too."

Judy gathered inner strength to commit her final folly, unsure if her mother was playing a game or not. "Sssssssshhhhhh . . . shit!"

"Charming," said Val. "Any more naughty words where those came from?"

Judy could not think of any, but was proud of those she had remembered. Val shook her head. Doug having left before Judy could speak more than a few words, and with Brian absent in the bush for much of the time, it was a mystery how Judy was learning bad language.

The incident with the American sergeant was receding from Val's thoughts. His disappearance from Batchelor was puzzling, and Val kept Doug's rifle loaded and handy in case Brady should stumble from the bush one day with vengeance on his mind. But he did not, and so began to fade as a player in the bad dreams that had come to her for a month or two. Her pregnancy was an inconvenience, made worse by Doug's absence. She had written to him with news of it and eventually received a postcard back, congratulating her and insisting on a boy this time.

Brian did what he could to keep her company, but Val wanted her husband with her now. A letter of two full pages had arrived in the biscuit tin a month before, addressed from Cairns, in northern Queensland, both sheets extensively ribboned and tattered by the military censor's scissors. What remained had hinted at an "interesting bunch of blokes up here." It was frustrating to get such a flimsy remnant; the first full letter he had written, and it arrived with nine tenths missing.

Val fell asleep one afternoon on the bed and dreamed of Blighty. The crocodile wore a top hat and stood on its hind legs, like something in a cartoon at the pictures, and bowed to her. "My compliments, madam," said Blighty, with the voice of an English gentleman. "They tell me our little one is shaping up nicely. Does he kick and bite? Does he scratch at your tummy with his little claws, hmmmm?"

Val sat bolt upright in an instant, sweat running from her brow, breath tight in her chest. Her womb was indeed under attack from tiny limbs, but it ceased the moment she was aware of it. Her head ached. Where had such an idiotic dream sprung from? Brian had said nothing for quite some time about her being the chosen mate of Gulgulong. She supposed it had something to do with the closeness of the birth.

Val placed her bare feet on the floor, still confused, her heartbeat slowing. The sound of birdsong came to her from outside, and the rasping of cicadas, and crowding behind these came the colossal silence of the bush. She looked at the floor, and at her feet. Val had always thought her toes were far too long, had been called Monkey Feet at school, but Doug had assured her there was nothing wrong with them, especially if she got tired of sleeping in a bed and decided to hang upside down from a branch like the flying foxes. She smiled, remembering.

Then the smile was gone. Where was Judy? Val could usually hear her talking or singing to herself outside, even if she was as far from the house as was allowed. Val hurried to the door and went outside.

"Judy! Juuuuuudeeeeeee . . . !"

There was no answering cry. She ran all the way around the house and the horse pens without catching sight of the child, then stopped and called her name again.

"Judy, if you're hiding from me, stop it! You'll get into trouble if you don't show yourself by the time I count three! One! Two! Three!" She waited, feeling slightly sick. "All right, you're in trouble now!" There was no guilty rush from cover, no half-smiling face pretending to be innocent of wrongdoing. Judy was not there, not where she should have been. Val felt panic take hold of her.

"Judy! You come here immediately! Judy . . . !"

Although it was the hottest part of the day, she had decided to explore. Mum had said the place was only a little way away, and that was as far as she intended to go, just a little way, to see if the baldy-headed stones were there. Judy could see for quite some distance through the widely separated trees, but there was no sign of the place with the funny name, so she went a little farther, beyond sight of the house, beyond the reach of sleeping Val.

A little farther on, and a little farther still. The place was not there, but it might be just a weeny bit farther, so Judy kept walking, expecting at any moment to see the stones, but they were never there, nor at the next place where she expected to find them, or the place after, and finally she began to think that Mum had been fibbing about the whole thing, or just telling a story, the way she sometimes did before Judy went to sleep. The place with the funny name wasn't really there at all, and she had gone and wasted all this time looking for it, and walked all that way from the house.

Judy turned, expecting to see the house, despite the distance she had covered. It was not there, but she knew that, unlike the baldy stones, the house was *some*where. All she had to do was go back the way she had come, and the house would be there, with Mum inside sleeping with her big fat tummy poking up in the air.

The first ten minutes of the return journey were pleasant, even if she was becoming a little thirsty by then. She would drink deeply from the special bucket Brian filled each morning from the tank and brought inside the house for drinking. The water would be warm and would taste of the bucket itself; Judy knew this because she had once licked its metal sides to see what it tasted like, and it had tasted like the water. The bucket occupied her thoughts, and only after more minutes had passed did she begin to wonder why it was that the house was still nowhere to be seen. She had been told many times that she must stay near the house because it was easy to become lost in the bush, where everything looked the same, no matter which way you faced.

Judy stood and asked herself what should be done. She had to get back home before Mum woke up, or she'd be in a lot of trouble for going off on her own as she had. Mum would yell at her and give her a smack across the backs of her legs. She had to make up her mind which direction she had come from. If she'd been walking in a straight line she would have been home again by now, so she must have walked funny and gone somewhere else. Which way was home?

One direction seemed every bit as likely as another to conceal the way back. It was impossible to choose, really. Judy settled the question by spinning in a circle with her eyes closed until she became dizzy. When finally she stopped, and allowed her head to clear, she walked in the direction her spinning had left her facing. Mum had once read her a story about a boy lost in an underground maze, who found his way out again because he was clever enough to leave a trail of thread to follow back. She should have got some from Mum's sewing box before leaving the familiar patch of open ground where the house stood. She couldn't even see the sandstone ridge behind it, because the trees were so tall and she was so short. It wasn't fair. It was so unfair it deserved tears, and so Judy stopped again and cried.

Nothing changed, even after all her tears were gone and there was an awful pounding in her head. And she needed to poo. Everything had gone wrong, and she would be in trouble when Mum found her. That was when Judy first admitted that she could not find her way home and would have to depend on being found by her mother. Now that responsibility for her rescue had been passed to bigger people, she felt a little better, but her poo wanted to come out a lot, so she went to the nearest tree and pulled down her underpants and pooed. There was nothing to wipe herself with, but she decided it didn't matter; soon Mum would come and find her and take her home, and she could finish inside the dunny as usual, with a few sheets of cut-up newspaper, which left black marks on her sweaty little hands and probably on her bottom too.

The poo didn't smell very nice, so Judy walked away from it, taking no particular direction. Direction didn't matter anymore, because Mum would be coming soon to find her and take her home. After a little while she felt tired and sat down beneath another tree, just like the tree she had pooed under. She went around to the other side of the tree, just to make sure it wasn't the same tree, but of course it wasn't; her nose would have told her if it was. She giggled and set her back against the trunk. Soon she would be found by Mum. It was silly to walk anymore, because that would mean Mum had to walk farther to find her. She would wait right where she was until Mum came through the trees with a bad mood all over her face and loud words coming out of her mouth. It wouldn't be nice, being found, because of the shouting and punishment that would follow, but it would be better than not being found.

She slept for a while, undisturbed by the dozen or more shots Val fired into the air to help guide Judy home and to summon Brian from his work with the cattle.

When she woke up, Judy found that nothing had changed. Mum was not standing over her. That made Judy feel afraid. She had not felt afraid since a long time ago when she had almost stepped on a long brown snake near the house. She had run away from the snake and hidden under Mum's big bed, but there was no bed to hide under here. Judy decided to run anyway, just in case there was a snake nearby. There had to be a reason why she was so afraid, and running seemed like a clever thing to do, just in case the danger was really there, whether she could see it or not.

When she had run until her chest hurt, Judy sat down on the ground and waited for her heart to stop galloping inside her so fast it hurt. She had come to a place with no trees, an open space with more trees growing on the other side, but between those trees and herself were lots and lots of termite mounds. Were these the same mounds Mum had shown her a long time ago, when she had been carried on Mum's back here and there through the bush? Or were they other mounds? They all looked the same, tall and knobbly and red; even the smallest was two times taller than Brian, who was taller than Mum, who was lots taller than Judy.

She walked toward them, her headache returning. If only she could have a drink of water everything would be so much better, but all of the water was somewhere else. The termite mounds were just as dry as dry could be, their red sides flaking off here and there, they were so dry, and the grass in between the mounds was dry too, and soon Judy stopped walking. She was among the mounds now. They stood all around her, red giants without arms or legs or heads, tall and silent and seemingly dead, although their hearts whispered with a million scurryings.

There seemed no reason to go anywhere else. At least among the termite mounds she could be sure she was not among the trees, which went on and on forever. There were lots more trees than mounds, so to stay where the mounds were was a good thing. The mounds were a *place*, but the trees were everywhere else that was *not* a place. Mum would find her easier here.

If only she could have had a drink of water.

The sun was falling down now, and that meant Mum would be looking.

A drink of water. And then another and another.

She lay down on the scorching earth, tired again, but it burned her skin, even through her dress, so she went to the nearest mound to lie down in its shade, where the earth was no warmer than herself, and she slept again, to dream of water.

And then it was dark. Judy opened her eyes to find herself in another place with termite mounds. These mounds were dark and threatening beneath the stars, looming over her like the animal-men Brian sometimes spoke of, the half-and-half people of the Dreamtime, when there was no difference between men and creatures and there was magic everywhere, good magic and bad, and the people living then made the people living now, or at least their grandfathers, by singing them alive, just as they sang alive the ground and the sky and the moon and sun and stars, all the trees and every bird that flew, and all the things that ran and hopped and crawled and spoke in a tongue that all other things could understand.

Judy was truly lost now, gone from the world of daylight into that of darkness, where all the things from time gone by

came back again, sung into being by the night. She felt them
all around her, invisible, moving like a gentle wind among the
termite mounds, rising up to touch the stars and falling down
again to feel the earth from which they came; all the nameless
and formless things born anew in scale and fur and wing and
claw, the entirety of living things present and past, here and
gone, their voiceless cries filling the air all around; their bodies, fantastical and ludicrous, strutting among the shapes of
what they had known eons ago, having called these things into
being and then called into being the singers who would continue the shaping of the world forever. The last of the animals
were tall and straight and slender, the children of night, dark
as darkness, their bodies filled with hidden sunlight, their
beaks and claws and fur and feathers stripped away so they
came in ultimate nakedness, to walk upright as the goanna
when he stands to search the horizon, clever as the bower
bird, which builds a special place for himself and his mate,
cunning as the crocodile that waits and waits and then
becomes teeth and thrashing tail with lesser things inside
itself. The final creatures were the singers of the songs that
could not end, or else the world would be taken away,
returned to the nonworld from which it had been sung as
many sunrises ago as there were birds in the air, fish in the
waters, animals passing across the land, and humming tiny
things. So long ago their coming, so brief their songs before
being passed on to new singers, who sang the songs to keep
the world beneath their feet until new feet could walk upon
the world, to sing again and again the never-ending songs.

She closed her eyes against them all, those things of night,
and wrapped herself in thoughts of the two people who cared
for her and for whom she cared—Mum and Brian—and that
third figure, growing paler with every day that came and
went—her daddy, whose name she had to think and think
before she could remember its sound: Doug, who was far
away for no reason that she could understand and whom she
was unable to forgive for his absence, since more tall people
would have meant less chance of her becoming lost, or at least
a better chance of being found. Mum had failed to do that on
her own, or even with Brian, and daylight was such a long way
away. If Daddy had been there to help, she would have been

found by now and been sleeping in her hammock with a tummy full of water. He should never have gone away and let her be lost the way he had. She would smack him on the backs of his legs when he came back, and make him say he was sorry for what he did. He had made her live among shadows she was fearful of, beneath stars that should have been kept from her by the tin roof she knew, but the roof was gone along with him, so she was alone with the shifting shadows that crept and curled and spoke to her of things she should not have been made to know. She thrust it all from her, threw a blanket over every thought, and fell asleep again, her ears deaf to the sound of distant rifle fire.

When it came again, the daylight was pale, without emphasis or direction. Judy saw the termite mounds standing around her like guardians, their redness less red than yesterday but becoming that colour even as she watched, with the sun coming up fully to strike them. They seemed for a few minutes then to glow, as if heated from within, then became their ordinary red selves. The faraway trees were alive with birds. Judy stood up and walked around for a little while, not knowing what to think about anything anymore. She squatted to pee, but only a tiny trickle came out. She walked some more, then stopped and tried to make herself cry, but no tears would come. Judy closed her eyes, telling herself Mum would be there when she opened them again. She kept them closed as long as she could, to give Mum enough time to reach her, then opened them to fresh disappointment; Mum had not come, and now Judy was beginning to believe Mum wouldn't ever come. She would have to walk around in the bush forever.

It was too horrible to think about, all that walking, with nothing to drink or eat. She was very, very hungry now and could not decide if she wanted to eat more than she wanted to drink, or the other way around. Either way, she hurt inside herself and decided not to walk at all. She went to the biggest mound and sat in its long shadow, as miserable as she could ever remember being. If Mum and Brian didn't come soon to take her home, she wouldn't ever be nice to them again. There was nothing to do but wait and think of food and water, and simply doing this made her tired again. By midmorning she was asleep.

A funny sound woke her up, a kind of coughing and snarling up in the sky, as if an animal were flying above her, clearing its throat. Judy got to her feet and looked for the thing making the sound in the sky, and saw it at last. She had seen planes before, way up high, making a steady buzzing noise, but this one was very low to the ground, coughing and coughing, with a long, thin tail of smoke coming out of it, a tail that stretched away farther than Judy could see.

The plane was sick, the whirly thing in front barely spinning, and it was clear the plane was going to come down and sit on the ground until it felt better. It was turning, leaning over on one wing, then it flew straight again, very close to the ground now. The coughing stopped, and the long black tail fell off, just as a lizard's tail will if held too hard. The plane was not going to stop in the air and then settle, like a bird; it was going to land running, but there was not enough room on the ground, with all the termite mounds spread everywhere, Judy could see that, and she watched with fascination as it came nearer and nearer, until it touched the top of a mound as it passed over, shattering it into an explosion of redness, and that made the plane slow down so much it couldn't go over the top of the next mound at all but slammed straight into it with an awful thump. The upper portion of the mound collapsed, and the plane slid a little way sideways around the heap of redness that a moment before had been so tall, then stopped. There was redness hanging in the air, already settling over the plane's broken wings in clods and lumps and fine dust.

Judy waited until everything was still and quiet, then went to the plane. It was pale green in colour, underneath all the dust that had settled on it, and the wings and sides had big red dots on them and lots of little black holes here and there. Termites dislodged from their towering home were scampering everywhere in their tens of thousands. A man was inside the plane; Judy could hear him groaning. She stood watching as the man attempted to lift himself out of the hole he sat in to fly the plane. She saw his gloves first, then the sleeve of his flying suit, and then his head, which was covered by a strange hat. The face beneath was covered with blood. Judy took several steps away from the plane. The man was groaning as he tried to lift himself out. She watched as he stood up inside the hole, then lifted out one of his legs, which made him scream, driving Judy farther back. The leg that hung outside the plane was even more bloody than the man's face. His upper body was lurching as he tried to lift himself across the edge of the hole to join the leg already outside, and all of a sudden he succeeded, falling out onto the wing and sliding down it to the ground, screaming all the way.

He landed with both legs in their heavy boots higher than his head, and was quiet for a little while. This encouraged Judy to come closer, until she stood just a few feet from him, at which time the man opened his eyes, making her jump. The eyes closed again, and Judy came closer still. The man had very smooth skin, like a lady, and Judy might have thought he was not a man at all, except for the thin moustache growing across his top lip. He was like a pretty lady wearing a moustache that wasn't real, just drawn there with a licked pencil. She wanted to touch the hair and see if it was real. The man might be a lady after all. Judy would have preferred to meet a lady rather than a man to ask for help, because Mum was a lady too. She came closer and reached out to touch the smooth face, avoiding those parts reddened by blood. The skin was wet and warm. She tugged at the moustache, pulling the flier's lip away from his teeth. His eyes opened again, and Judy jumped back.

Words came from his mouth, a strange gabbling sound, then the eyes and mouth closed again. Judy went a little way off, to think about what she had seen and to keep watching the man in case he should get up and be ready to show her the way home. The sun was at its highest, the air across the termite mound plain shimmering with heat. She had been gone for a whole day now. Mum would be cross with her for a long time for what she had done. It was almost enough to make Judy wish she wouldn't be found and taken home, but her hunger and thirst told her it was wiser to be found quickly and accept her punishment. She began falling asleep again, despite the awful pounding inside her head, which just wouldn't go away. The man on the plane's wing appeared to be sleeping. She would do what he did. He was a grownup, and his example should be followed.

A loud noise woke her. Judy felt her whole body hurting as her eyes opened. Her head was so painful she thought some-one must have come along and placed a big heavy hat on it that was far too tight and gone away again, but her fingers told her there was no hat on her head, just her matted hair. The effort to raise her arm had hurt her head even more. She looked over at the man on the wing and saw that he was some-where else now, lying flat on the ground, his arms flung out, something dark in one gloved hand. She crawled over to him, made curious by the changes that had occurred while she slept.

The thing in his hand was a little gun, and there was a hole in the side of the man's hat. Judy knew why he had put the hole there; it was to let out the pain he had in his head, the same kind of pain her own head was bursting with. He was not groaning now, so the pain must have gone. She crawled a little farther to find shade beneath the tilted wing, but the shade there was filled with scurrying termites, so Judy had to crawl all the way back to where she had started from.

She was halfway there when she stopped, unable to shift herself even another inch. Her head was trying to empty its pain through her mouth, but her mouth had swollen shut to keep the pain inside. She could feel her tongue all big and fat, blocking the pain. She knew then it was never going to go away, not unless her tongue dropped off. She had several times seen Brian cook a goanna in a fire, the whole animal simply thrown among the flames and covered with more branches. She knew how those goannas must have felt, sur-rounded by nothing but fire, lying on a bed of glowing coals, slowly cooking in their prisons of heat and skin. It was not right that she should be like a goanna that was going to be eaten, so Judy rolled sideways from her burning self into a cooler place that was much nicer, and fell asleep again.

Brian was no tracker; the men who had that ability were with Ranji's mob, somewhere to the south, too far away for him to contact. He had to find Judy himself. Val was in no condition to walk, let alone ride in pursuit of her daughter, and she knew it. Brian had ridden hard for the house when all the shots were fired, and found Val in a bad way, more agitated than he had ever seen her. She had a fresh horse ready for him, with canteens of water tied to the saddle, but she could give him no direction in which to begin searching. The ground, this late in the Dry, was hard as rock; anyone as small and light as Judy would leave virtually no trace upon it, but Brian said nothing of this to Val. He was an Aborigine, and all whitefellas assumed every Abo was able to track a bee through the air.

"I'll find her, no worries," he promised, and did find the beginnings of a trail over by the trees to the south of the house. He waved to Val and began following the tiny disturbances left by Judy's sandals, very worn sandals with no defined heel to leave a sharp impression·in the soil. He lost the trail within fifteen minutes and had to backtrack. The trail gave out again, and he dismounted, ashamed of himself for having failed twice. With his eyes closer to the ground, he fared better for an hour or so, then lost Judy's trail again over a stretch of particularly rocky ground. There wasn't the least indication that Judy had passed this way. It was as if she had sprouted wings and flown away. He smacked himself several times in the face for being no good, and then the true nature of the calamity came to him.

Brian had to squat on his heels to think about it. Judy's disappearance was not simply a matter of her having wandered off; it was the creation of the hole for Judy to go somewhere else, the same hole through which Boy b'long Gulgulong would enter the world. Even the best tracker in the Top End would not have been able to follow Judy's trail, because that trail no longer existed; it had been swept away by the spirit croc inside the body of Blighty, erased by his spirit tail, so that his son might be born. It was Judy's time to die, that was all.

Now that the truth had been revealed to him, Brian was not so ashamed of his feeble talent for tracking. It had all been arranged by the spirit world, where Gulgulong's boy was being prepared for the world of men. Val was fat with him, ready to set his body free of her belly. It could happen at any time, but before the boy could enter the world, his sister was obliged to depart. M'linga had told Brian not to speak of this to the mother, since a whitefella woman would not understand, and

Ranji had on several occasions repeated the warning, suspecting as he did that Brian was a talkfella who could not help but drop hints to Val concerning Pitjantjatjara affairs, which was blackfella business.

So now the time had come. It was saddening to think that he would never see little Judy again. He had learned to be fond of her and knew she had been fond of him. But she had to die. It was not his fault. The Pitjantjatjara half of him understood what was occurring, but the whitefella half of him knew what anguish Val must be feeling over Judy's vanishment into the spirit world, and that same part of him crawled with guilt over the lies he would have to fashion, the great and wonderful truth he would never be allowed to explain to Val, any more than he could have told her about the spearing of the Yank who had insulted Missus b'long Gulgulong. Brian was truly caught between worlds of black and white and must suffer the consequences of both.

He had no need to bother with any further searching, now that he knew why Judy was gone, but for Val's sake, and to hide his own complicity in the workings of the spirit croc, he would have to pretend that he had done his very best, and tell the lie with a face that betrayed no sign of the things Val must never know. He decided that he must go through the motions of a search, even though he knew there would be nothing to find, and so he mounted his horse again and began riding aimlessly among the trees, moving farther from the house all the time, uttering his loudest Cooooooo-*eeee!!!* every few minutes. He kept it up until sundown, then returned to the house.

Val was outside, waiting.

"Where is she!"

"Dunno. . . . I reckon I . . . I lost her trail."

"You couldn't see anything?"

"For a little bit, yeah, then . . . there was nothin'. . . ."

"Christ, Brian . . . Go out again! Take the gun! Fire it!"

"She won't hear nothin'. . . ."

"What the bloody hell's that supposed to mean! Are you saying she's dead?"

"Nah, only . . . she's asleep by now, I reckon."

"Bullshit! Why would she sleep when she's out there on her own, bloody terrified! Are you going to go out and try again, or do I have to do it myself? Oh, bugger it, I'll do it anyway. Saddle me a horse, and get a move on."

"Gunna hurt yourself an the baby, you go ridin'. . . ."

"Just get a horse ready!"

"Orright, orright. . . ."

They rode out together. Brian fired Doug's .303 into the air until all the ammunition was gone, and both Cooooooooo-*eeee*d themselves hoarse. Just before midnight, Val gave up the search until daylight and allowed Brian to guide her home.

Her pelvis ached, her back ached, her head seemed about to burst, and her skin was covered with mosquito bites. She fell onto her bed and felt the pain multiply. There was no chance of her sleeping, and having no other recourse, she began to pray. Never a religious woman, Val exhorted God to watch over her daughter. She made a bargain with God. If God saved Judy, Val would believe in him. If he did not, she would curse him forever. The one-sided nature of this arrangement gave her no satisfaction, and just before dawn she abandoned it, to fall asleep so deeply it required Brian's hand on her shoulder to waken her.

She could not rise. Her stomach felt like a balloon filled with hot water. She made Brian lift her from the mattress and assist her to the door, where she stood for several minutes, propped against the jamb, while Brian saddled two horses. She told him to get her into the saddle by any means possible, but had to abandon her plan to continue searching when a boost from Brian that raised her halfway up the side of her mare resulted in a horrendous pain inside her. She shouted to be let down again, and Brian supported her back to her bed.

"Go on, go out and look again," she told him. "I'll be all right, Brian, really, just go and look for her, please. . . ."

He went to the door.

"Brian!"

He turned. "Yeah?"

"Don't come back without her. You have to find her very soon."

"She'll be orright. I'll find her, promise I will."

The smile that accompanied these words felt like a fresh ritual scar carved into his face. He turned away and leapt onto his horse, taking up the reins of the second, so that he might ride them in turn for as long as it took to find Judy. He truly intended to bring her back with life inside her, because that was what Val, his whitefella mother, wanted. He would defy the tribe, dash M'linga's prophecy, and put himself in harm's way with Ranji, who would be quick to suggest punishment for Brian's misdeeds, his betrayal of the Pitjantjatjara and Gulgulong. The bone would be pointed at him, and he would have to rely on the whitefella side of his soul to resist its deadly influence. Just a piece of kangaroo bone, but once it was pointed by a kadaicha man in the direction of a wrong-doer, its magic became apparent. Brian knew of several men who had succumbed to the bone, simply wasted away and died, killed by the bone as surely as if they had been speared.

By the time he judged it was necessary to use the second horse, Brian was feeling quite differently about what he intended doing that day. If he rescued Judy from whatever the spirits had ordained should be her lot, he would throw a com-plex and still-developing incident—the birth of Gulgulong's human son—into disarray. The stars might fall if such a thing occurred. The moon might split in two and plummet to earth, killing the Pitjantjatjara and himself. The sun might reach out and turn the world to flaming cinders. She was only one little kid. Everything that turned upon her death was so much big-ger than Judy, so much bigger than Brian. He felt the weight of his role in the whole business resting across his shoulders like a fallen tree, a boulder, the entire sky from horizon to horizon pressing down on him, whispering into his reluctant ears of tribal obligation and the importance of his unique role in whatever transpired that day.

Brian dismounted and walked in a circle, moaning, beating his chest, in genuine torment. Every minute of delay meant a lessening of any chance to find Judy alive. Unless she had found water since wandering off, she was probably dead already, but not necessarily. He could still find her, if he wanted to. But there was no trail to follow, either because his eyes were simply not the best or because the spirit croc had swept the trail clean with his tail. Brian could not make up his mind what to believe, what to do.

Midmorning, while riding in no particular direction, in no particular hurry, his eyes focused within himself rather than on the ground, Brian heard a plane, its engine faltering badly, sputtering and cutting out completely for seconds at a time, then resuming its throaty rasp. He wished he were in a plane, one with a good engine, so he could look down at the area surrounding Redlands and spot Judy. But then he would have to go to her and save her. It was better that he was not in a plane, better that he had no real chance of finding her. That way the things that were meant to be would happen as intended, and he would have nothing to be ashamed of, at least while he was with his people. When he was with Val, however, it would be different. Every day would be a kind of lie, a denial of something that she might not have understood anyway, being a whitefella lady. M'linga might tell him to leave the house and go back to the tribe, once Boy b'long Gulgulong was born into the world. Then again, he might not. Brian shook at the thought of still being at the house when Doug came home. Could he hope to hide the truth from his own father? What would Doug do if he ever found out? It was every bit as tangled as mating snakes, and he despaired of ever knowing peace, whichever way things worked out.

Later, he heard a distant gunshot. It was not the sustained pit-*chow*! of a heavy rifle, the kind most often used in the Territory; it was more like the ka-*pit*! of a .22, or possibly a pistol. Very few men that Brian had seen carried pistols. Were there army blokes in the area? It had sounded too feeble to be a military pistol, certainly not one of the big Webley revolvers Australian officers carried, or a Yank's .45 automatic. It was a sound that did not belong, and Brian chose to see what manner of weapon had made it, even if his decision was nothing more than justification for abandoning still further his bogus attempt at finding Judy. He wanted distraction from that, if only for a little while.

Traveling in the general direction of the shot, Brian came to a broad plain with many termite mounds. He rode slowly among them, until he saw the wreckage of the Jap plane. Approaching this, he saw its pilot, dead on the ground, and, several yards from the dead man, Judy. He knew even before dismounting that she was dead also, a victim of thirst. The Jap, covered in his own blood from serious wounds, had spared himself further agony with a shot to the head. Brian picked up the weapon and tucked it into his saddlebag. He did not want to touch Judy, but he must, to be sure Gulgulong's intentions had been carried out by the fierce sun, the burning sky.

She lay on her side, utterly still, and had never seemed smaller, more defenseless than this. Her body was not Judy, not the girl he had carried on his shoulders, bouncing her to make her scream at the mock danger of falling, then both of them laughing together when he pretended to collapse, allowing her to scramble free of his hands around her skinny ankles. This was not her. That girl was gone. Her old self was discarded now, left behind like a worn-out snakeskin. He picked her up, tears starting from his eyes. She weighed nothing, because she was not there. He had done this to her, and he had not. It was his fault she was dead. It was not his fault. Her death had served a greater thing. Her death was no business of the Pitjantjatjara. He was responsible, for not having tried hard enough to find her. He had done what was expected of him, and would be praised for it. She was dead, and a small part of Brian was dead also. He carried her to the horses.

Val knew even before he rode away what would happen to her in his absence. Even as the sound of hooves receded, her waters broke, flooding the bed. She would have to do everything herself. Doug had fetched a bush nurse for Judy's birth, and Val could still remember the instructions, the procedures to follow. The mattress was going to be a bloody mess; she would have to wash it and stand it outside in the sunlight for days afterward—outside, where Brian was searching for Judy. She tried turning her mind back inside the house, to herself and the baby that was coming, but even as her contractions began, Val's thoughts were elsewhere, sometimes with Judy, sometimes with Brian, and, as her discomfort turned to pain while the morning wore on, with Doug, wherever he might be. Val bore down on herself and began to push her baby into the world.

M'linga and Ranji and some others were waiting near the house when Brian returned. Somehow they had known and had come to the special place. He was not surprised to see them there, squatting beneath the trees. They rose and came to him as he dismounted and slid the body of Judy from the saddle. Ranji looked closely at the girl and spoke a few words to M'linga, whose eyes, hidden behind cataracts, stared at nothing.

Brian could hear the sound of a squawling baby inside the house, and felt additional guilt for having been somewhere else when Val needed him most. He didn't want to be the one to go in and tell her Judy was dead, but he had to. M'linga and Ranji went back to sit beneath the trees, waiting for Brian to do what he must. They wanted to see Boy b'long Gulgulong, but they could not simply walk into the house to do so. Brian would have to be the one to go in with the dead child and, later on, come out again with a living baby, if its mother could not rise.

The house was filled with the smells of birth. Brian set Judy down in her hammock, then turned to Val, busy nursing the newborn. She was watching his face, waiting for a sign that the limp little figure he had brought inside was merely unconscious. Brian hung his head and began to cry. Val turned back to her baby. She would not allow herself to grieve, not now; maybe at some other time, when she was better able to see everything that had happened in all its detail. Her milk flowed into her son. She would call him Wilfred Timothy, because she liked those names. Wilf, he would be called by most. He would have no sister now. He would be on his own, as Judy had been, but he would never be out of Val's sight, not for a minute, never, never, never.

"Boil a knife, Brian," she told him, still gazing at the feeding baby. Wilf was still attached to the afterbirth by his umbilical cord. Brian added kindling to the stove and slowly brought water in the pot there to a bubbling fury, then dropped into it the sharpest knife in the house—the blade used to castrate bull calves. When the knife had boiled for several minutes, he lifted the pot and took it outside to tip the water away. M'linga's mob watched him from the trees. Brian waited for the knife handle to cool, still inside the pot, then went back indoors and offered the pot to Val.

"Set it down," she said, "and wash your hands."

Brian was the one who picked up the knife to cut the cord. M'linga would be happy to hear that black hands had come close to the baby this soon.

When the job was done, Brian asked her, "Want me to . . . y'know . . . clean up?"

She nodded. He slid the spattered sheets from beneath her and bundled them around the afterbirth, then took this outside. M'linga rose and came forward to speak with Brian.

They went to Blighty's Pond, just the two of them, and set the afterbirth down on the bank, free of the bloody sheets. M'linga began a wailing chant. Soon the surface of the water was broken by the monstrous bulk of Gulgulong. Brian felt the hairs on his neck begin to stiffen, but he could neither turn his eyes away nor command his legs to run. The crocodile waded ashore and went directly to the meal set down for it. The afterbirth was snatched up without hesitation and taken to the water. Brian watched the crocodile sink beneath its dark surface. He was shaking by then, from his shoulders to his knees.

M'linga abruptly brought his chanting to a close and told Brian to lead the way back to the house where Boy b'long Gulgulong had come into the world. Tonight a fire would be built, a kangaroo roasted and feasted on in celebration. The click-sticks and the didgeridoo would sound, and Missus b'long Gulgulong would come outside with the one they all wished to see, and show him to them by firelight.

PART THREE

13

KEITH RAMSEY SUPERVISED THE LOADING of Q team's equipment onto a tugboat of the Royal Australian Navy. It was an ugly vessel, but a steady platform for transferal of the equipment to a submarine waiting more than a hundred miles offshore for the scheduled rendezvous at 2100 hours the following day. The men loading Q team's boxes and bales on the Townsville docks that afternoon knew nothing of their contents or the mission these would serve. The security precautions ordered by Ramsey's CO were necessary, given the risks involved. Ramsey was directly responsible for the safe loading and transfer of everything his men would require. The submarine awaiting Q team was British, but the entire operation had been conceived by Australians and would be carried out by them.

The team was a mixed bag, as Ramsey was inclined to call them, drawn from different divisions of the army. They had been trained in jungle warfare for six months at a secret location near Cairns, and tonight would see them embark on their first mission behind Japanese lines. Ramsey could not deny he was excited at the prospect. Their expansion had been halted since late 1942, but the Japanese were entrenched across the southwestern Pacific and would have to be rooted out piecemeal before the war could be won. Q team would make its own unique contribution to that process. Just four men, Ramsey included, but they would make a difference, he was sure of it.

Ramsey likened Q team's proposed mission to the nibbling of four mice at one small corner of a bag at the bottom of a million stacked bags of rice; when that first bag spilled its contents through the hole opened up by Ramsey's mice, the bags on top would begin to sag, and the bags atop those would do the same, until every bag fell. He had considered requesting that the mission be designated Operation Mousetrap, then realised that this would not bode well for his mice, and so had suggested instead that it be called Operation Ricebag. His superiors had not approved, and so the mission was simply named Greenfly. Corporal Farrands, whose wit sometimes was appreciated and sometimes was not, had taken to calling it Aphid, or Thrip, until requested not to.

In so small a team it was important, Ramsey knew, for each man to get along with the other three, and Doug Farrands had proved himself capable of doing that during his training. His name had been selected from AIF files in a search for men with an outdoor background broader than that of the average weekend camper. Doug's designation as a Northern Territorian was noted, and his experience as a seagoing member of the Nackeroos had piqued the interest of the file-searchers. The official explanation of his dismissal from the NAOU intrigued them even further; Alpha (for Alphabet) Force had need of men with firsthand experience in the death of another human. Alpha's originators considered this type of fellow a prime candidate for their very special needs. Military protocol, square-bashing, and the commonly accepted norms of army life were not for Alpha Force, and so Doug Farrands had been taken from a barracks in New South Wales for immediate transfer to Queensland, first to Townsville, and then farther north to the training camp outside Cairns. He had proved a willing apprentice to the informal art of war by stealth.

There was also an M team, and teams lettered N, O, and P, but Keith Ramsey was never made privy to whatever assignments they had been given, in keeping with the covert nature of their training. The other two members of his own team were Athol Harris and Trevor Costigan, both young. Athol was the radio specialist and Trevor the explosives expert, although every Q member could perform the appointed tasks of any other, to maintain viability in the field should someone be killed. Doug's own specialty was the crossbow, a weapon he thought had vanished from the hardware of war hundreds of years ago. He was the oldest Q of all, three years Ramsey's senior, but he appeared to have the necessary stamina for the work ahead of them. Ramsey was designated as team leader. The mice had worked together for half a year and now were about to be sent out to play.

The tugboat sailed at 0600 hours, its captain allowing plenty of time for negotiation of the Great Barrier Reef stretching along the Queensland coast. The submarine was lying at the bottom of the Flinders Passage, beyond the reef, and would surface after sundown to take aboard Q team. As it chugged slowly to the east, the tugboat altered course many times to avoid coral, and its passengers peered down into the beautiful and deadly waters.

"Shark!"

Trevor pointed straight down. A slim grey torpedo seemed to hover in air below the boat, then lazily it flicked its tail and passed from sight beneath the hull. Trevor had a fear of sharks he had managed to make others believe was a fascination. He very much wanted to be a commando rather than an ordinary soldier, and had stated to the men who interviewed him for Alpha Force that he would not mind in the least having to swim through waters thick with shark, any more than he would be unable to cope with living in mosquito-infested jungle for weeks on end. While Q team trained among the rain forests of the Atherton Tableland behind Cairns, and practiced using their inflatable rubber rafts among the coral reefs offshore, Trevor had seen more mosquitoes than sharks and was aware that his fear had not abated at all.

"Water's clear as glass," he said.

Doug nodded. He knew Trevor was afraid of sharks. It was not anything to be ashamed of, in Doug's opinion, but he never once made Trevor aware that he knew. An explosives expert should be kept as calm as possible, Doug reasoned, and not teased about something that was perfectly understandable.

Athol Harris, standing on Doug's other side, was the one he would have preferred to be the explosives handler. Large and a trifle slow in his movements, Athol seemed never to become perturbed by anything produced by man or nature, and could send messages in Morse code while hanging upside down in a tree. Doug had seen him do this for a dare; of course, the transceiver was safely wedged into a fork of the tree; Athol would never submit his radio to any kind of risk if it was avoidable. Their radio would be Q team's lifeline.

The tug meandered east through reef passages that sometimes were narrow, their margins close to the surface and near to the hull, and sometimes broad and deep enough to be invisible. It was not until late in the afternoon that the final corals of the continental shelf were passed and the captain was able to increase his vessel's rate of knots. The Flinders Passage lay ahead, with its waiting submarine.

The members of Q team played cards or watched sunlight on the water, their thoughts elsewhere. Any man who went up on deck to be alone was left that way until he cared to return, and all four men were alone at least once through the day. As the sun began lowering toward the horizon behind them, Q team gathered together for a final game of cribbage. Doug quickly lost four pounds to Athol, who played as if he were seated at his own kitchen table back home in Melbourne.

The rendezvous point was reached in darkness. The tug's diesels were shut down and all hands ordered to watch for the submarine. Somewhere beyond their vision, there undoubtedly was a periscope, watching them, sneaking silently closer. Keith Ramsey had heard that British sub commanders liked to surprise their rendezvous pickups by appearing as if by magic, as close to a vessel as possible. As 2100 hours approached, he scanned the shining waters around the tug, anxious to be the first to spot the submarine.

"There she is."

It was Doug Farrands who saw it, a sudden upwelling of surface water that quickly began pouring from the shape rising beneath it. The conning tower rose like a small metal building, then the bulk of the submarine, the length of two cricket pitches. Its steel flanks glistened in the moonlight as hatches were quietly opened, the merest suggestion of red light emerging from the interior. Then the decks of both vessels were aswarm with seamen manoeuvering the equipment for Greenfly from one to the other, by way of a small crane on the tug's afterdeck. Q team went over to the submarine, dangling from the same hook. Doug could hear barnacles on the tug's hull scraping against the black sides of the sub as he was swung over, chest-to-chest with Trevor. They were escorted below before the hook was returned for Keith and Athol. The transfer of men and equipment was accomplished in nine minutes. The submarine's hatches were closed and locked, the tanks were blown, and HMS *Bangalore* sank from view. The tug's diesels were started, its course set for Townsville.

When his men were crammed into the tiny space made available for them in the aft torpedo room, Keith surprised them with mail. He had been holding several letters for each man over the last few days, thinking that a letter from home, once they were aboard the submarine and truly on their way, would provide a tremendous uplift of spirits. It would be a long time until they next received mail of any kind.

"Thanks, postie," Doug said, accepting two letters.

Keith allowed the lack of respect for his rank to go by without reprimand. It had been impressed upon him, during his own training as a team leader, that occasional informality between an enlisted man and an officer should be permitted to pass, since it fostered a sense of togetherness that sometimes was not present among conventional forces.

"Tuppence to pay," said Keith. "Tell your wife to put the correct postage on in future, Corporal."

"Right-oh."

Doug took his letters and attempted to read them amid the muted din of the submarine's engines. Athol and Trevor were similarly occupied.

The first letter was dated seven weeks earlier.

> *Dear Doug,*
>
> *I'm as big as a house and will be ready to lose a lot of weight around the end of August. I think it's going to be a boy this time because he kicks a lot more than Judy ever did, if that means anything. I can't wait.*
>
> *You'll never guess what, Mr. Cattle Station Owner, but we just sold four bullocks to the Americans down at Batchelor so they can have fresh meat. They paid ten pounds each. They only took four and then some-*

thing went wrong with the arrangement. One of the Americans who came to pick up the bullocks was killed by a snake and the other one went bush after that, so I think the Yanks are superstitious about buying any more meat from us. Oh well, it was good money while it lasted.

They gave us some extra food as well as cash, including lollies for Judy. Her eyes got so big looking at them. Now I'll have to make her clean her teeth much more carefully. I don't know what I'd do if she needed a dentist now. She asks when Daddy is going to be back, and I have to say I don't know. She thinks that the planes we see sometimes have got you inside them, and she wants them to come down and land. We still go for long walks together, looking for Shangri-la, ha, ha, but no luck. Brian says it isn't there, but he's fibbing and he knows I know.

One sheet of paper, that's all I can spare. It got filled up quickly, didn't it? We all miss you and can't wait till you come home. I love you, my husband.

Val

"My missus just had a baby," said Athol. "It's a girl, but she wants to call it Rebecca Anastasia. Bloody hell, what's wrong with something ordinary, I'd like to know."

"My missus has got one on the way too," Doug said. "She reckons it'll be a boy. She better not want to call him Marmaduke Sebastian or somethin' poofterish like that."

Trevor said, "My mum thinks the government should let her paint the house and not keep all the paint for itself. You'd think she was the one going up the ladder and not the old man. I'll bet he wants the government to keep every can of paint it can get hold of."

Doug looked at his second letter. The postmark was more recent, less than a week old, and it bore the letterhead of the Territorial Police, which probably explained its speedy delivery. Royce Curran's name was on the back of the envelope. Doug began to worry that Brian had done something stupid and got himself into trouble.

Dear Doug,

I asked Brian when was the last time your wife wrote you a letter, and it was a long time ago, with nothing about what happened here. It looks like she isn't in any shape to be writing about it, not for a while yet I'd say, so I have taken the liberty to do so for her, Brian not being a writer.

Doug, there has been a tragedy here. Your daughter Judy got lost in the bush and was missing for twenty-four hours before Brian could find her, but he was too late I'm afraid to say. She was found where the termite mounds are, about four miles south of your place. Brian took me out there afterwards, and there is a Jap plane that crashed there, but that isn't what took poor Judy, Brian said, even if he found her right next to it and the Jap pilot, dead by suicide. It was the heat and her having no water that did it. I've known cases where adults died in a single afternoon out in the bush in Dry season. There is no way of being certain just when she died. Doug, I'm sorry to be the one telling you this awful news. Judy has been buried just a little way from the house, under the trees.

You have got a son now, Doug, a fine-looking boy, Wilfred, very healthy and with you written all over him. I suppose it's a blessing that he came along when he did, to balance things out, if you take my meaning. Your wife is very involved in looking after him, which is probably a good thing, being distracted that way and taking her mind off the other. I won't say she's apples by any means, but she does seem to be coping all right with the tragedy, and Brian is doing everything he can to take responsibility for Redlands off her shoulders. That's a good boy you've got there, Doug.

My one worry about Brian is he's got a lot of his old bunch of mates roaming around the place, Ranji's mob. Ranji is a strange one, a troublemaker sometimes, but not for some years now, and his old man M'linga is there too, gone blind now since the last time I saw him back in 1934 I think it was. I asked Val if she wanted me to send them all away but she said no, they aren't doing any harm. I asked if they were bludging food from her and she said it's the opposite, with them supplying a lot of grub, kangaroo and wallaby meat mostly, so they're all right where they are. It's her decision.

Doug, I can't say how sorry I am about what happened. You never think it'll happen to anyone you know, but it does, and it makes you wonder. But there is one thing, Doug, and that is Val blames herself for Judy wandering off the way she did when her mum was asleep. I told her a woman in her condition with the temperature what it is, she wasn't doing anything wrong, wasn't neglecting to be a mother. But she still feels badly about it, which is understandable I suppose. You might write to her and tell her it wasn't her fault, Doug. A letter from you would mean a lot, much more than anything I can say.

Again, I regret being the one to bring this news to you, but it had to be someone.

Yours sincerely,
Royce Curran

Doug reread the letter, then folded it and returned it to the envelope.

"How's things back home, Doug?" Athol asked.

"Not bad. Me missus sold some bullocks to the Yanks, made a bit a money."

"That's good. They get paid too much anyway, the Yanks. Take a bit off them before they spend it all on beer and prossies, that's the way."

Doug put both his letters inside his shirt. He knew he would read them many times before being able to discuss their contents with anyone. A steady vibration ran through the steel hull behind his back. The submarine was running north-northwest, following the Barrier Reef. It would turn west and pass through the Torres Straits, separating Australia from New Guinea, then cross the Arafura Sea, above the Territory, where Doug had once gone pearling. It would pass within a few hundred miles of Redlands, where his daughter lay buried and his new son took milk from his wife, and it would keep going west before resuming its north-northwest course toward the place Q team had trained for.

Dombi lies in the Banda Sea. It is thirteen miles long by eleven miles across and nowhere rises more than fifty feet above sea level. It is unremarkable in appearance, but in 1943 Dombi was considered a place of considerable strategic importance. In 1922 it was discovered to contain, deep below its inauspicious surface, possibly the world's richest concentration of bauxite. The British company Bandax established and operated a mining complex there soon after, and a garrison of British troops was stationed there in 1940, as war in the Pacific became more probable. These troops were overwhelmed in April of 1942, and Dombi became one of the most important prizes taken in all the territory occupied by the Japanese.

At the very centre of the island was a prison camp containing over four hundred Australians, captured during the ill-fated Timor and New Guinea campaigns, and an equal number of English servicemen, captured in Singapore, then transported to Dombi. These prisoners worked alongside the Malays imported by the British prior to the war, to perform the more arduous tasks underground, in the heart of the bauxite mines. The Malays had been told by their new masters that they would no longer be exploited by the white race, but the conditions of their working lives had not improved. Their wage, minuscule under the British, had since been halved, and the amount of food made available to them had been substantially reduced because of the massive numbers of Japanese troops now stationed on the island.

The prison camp had been erected around the original mining complex built by the British. The mines were within range of Allied bombers flying from the Northern Territory, but any damage inflicted on the buildings and pit-head operating gear would also have caused significant loss of life among the prison camp population. A narrow-gauge railway line connected the mine with a natural harbour at the southern end of the island, where the original loading wharf, stretching out to deeper water, conveyed raw bauxite for loading onto freighters that transported it to the smelters and foundries and aeroplane factories of Japan. The wharf was also manned by Allied prisoners and so was able to operate during daylight hours without the threat of bombardment. There had been two night raids with heavy bombers from Darwin, but damage to the wharf had been minimal, since cloud cover had spoilt the advantage of the full moon on both occasions. The railway line linking the mine with the wharf was an easy target and could be bombed without fear of harming Allied prisoners, but the harm done to it was easily repaired, its single track never being out of operating order for more than half a day.

The Japanese ran the mine and harbour with impunity, knowing that the thing which made it possible to operate Dombi cheaply—an endless supply of slave labour—was the very same thing that protected it from harm. Only a full-scale invasion could have retaken Dombi, and the Japanese troops on the island, some four thousand strong, were capable of mounting a formidable defense. The sole recourse available to Allied forces was submarine attacks on the bauxite-laden freighters after they had left the harbour and begun their three-thousand-mile journey to Japan. Sometimes these succeeded, and sometimes they did not, the bauxite convoys being protected by swift warships equipped for antisubmarine warfare.

The Dombi Situation, as the conflict between open warfare and the humanitarian impulse came to be called, was a thorn long overdue for extraction, and Q team was to be the extractor.

On a moonless night, HMS *Bangalore* came to periscope depth a mile from the eastern shore of Dombi. Through his night-vision lens, the submarine's commander watched a fifty-foot gunboat pass by at a distance of less than a hundred yards. Four of these vessels, equipped with antiaircraft guns and depth charges, guarded the island's quadrants twenty-four hours a day, passing back and forth through their allotted arcs of patrol. Once the gunboat was out of sight, the sound of its throbbing engines receding, the operation began. The submarine rose until its decks were clear of the water, and its for'ard hatches were quietly opened. Q team's rubber rafts were launched within minutes, and the four men began paddling hard to escape the submarine's powerful suction as it submerged, swallowed by darkness behind them.

Dombi was encircled by a series of reefs, virtually the only opening for shipping being the artificial channel created by Bandax in 1924, when a series of carefully positioned underwater explosions had blasted a way through to the harbour. Since all shipping, in and out, was obliged to pass through this channel, it was patrolled with particular intensity, to prevent Allied submarines from lurking in the area, conveniently close to their prey. An assault by frogmen via the channel would have been suicidal and would never have done more than cripple some of the freighters at the docks. It was of greater strategic importance to cripple the mine itself and halt the production of bauxite. Q team had studied plans of the mine provided by the London office of Bandax and knew precisely where to place their charges underground for maximum effect.

Twice, while passing across the reefs, Doug felt the tip of his paddle strike coral. The tide was already turning, the water level around the reefs dropping. The sub had released them almost three hours late, owing to intensified patrols by the gunboats, but there was still time to reach the shore. He could hear breaking surf ahead in the darkness and smell the odours of land, welcome after the sweat-and-oil stench of the submarine.

The two rafts grounded softly onto sand and were dragged up the beach. The falling tide meant that there was a broader stretch of sand to cross before the jungle could give Q team cover, and disturbances left in the sand by their boots and rafts would remain visible until well after daybreak, instead of being erased by the rising tide as planned. It was not a good beginning to the operation.

Once the rafts had been deflated and buried, there was little time left before dawn, and many miles between their landfall and Q team's first objective. They began walking through the jungle in single file, finding a variety of narrow pathways to follow beneath the canopy of trees. "Wild-pig runs," said Doug, "same as back home in the Territory."

"Any chance the natives have set traps along them?" Keith asked.

"Pigs are probly all gone by now, with all those extra Jap mouths to feed around here, but any bloke up front that falls in a hole and gets a stake through his guts can call me wrong, I won't mind."

"Very bloody funny," said Athol, in the lead.

Trevor asked, "How far now?"

"At least four miles," Keith told him. "Close enough to be there by sunrise, with a bit of luck. These pig runs are a blessing."

As he walked, Doug felt his thoughts slipping away. He had done a good job of hiding from Keith and the rest the fact of his daughter's death, even going so far as to destroy the letter from Royce Curran so that it might not fall accidentally into the hands of Q team. He told himself it would serve no purpose to let them know; they might worry that Doug was unable to perform his tasks in Operation Greenfly, and there was no need to introduce that kind of doubt into a situation already balanced by its very nature along a razor's edge. He could do what he had been trained to do, and cope silently with the weight in his heart. He had not allowed a single tear to fall since he'd read the letter, a submarine being without privacy, and the sudden pain that had cut through him on learning of Judy's death was already passing, becoming a burden of grief that simply had to be borne, now and forever. Doug had made jokes and kept a smile on his face for the sake of what Q team had to accomplish. It was nobody's business but his own.

But he could not keep his mind from picturing Judy at odd moments: peering at him from behind a bulkhead, standing among the clutter of the submarine's interior, and, now, stepping from behind the jungle growth to watch him passing quietly by. He knew she was not there, knew also that he was not suffering hallucinations; it was a way of reminding himself of her existence, sliding his memory of her face and form into these inappropriate surroundings. He could not ignore her death, nor could he truly accept it; she existed still as a part of his mind, he supposed, and as an entity living there, she must be allowed to come and go as she pleased. He just hoped she would keep her head down if bullets began flying.

The Malays had been permitted by the Japanese to remain in their own accommodations, separate from the POW camp built in the immediate vicinity of the mine. Their quarters consisted of traditional bamboo huts for the most part, but their kampong had been surrounded by a tall fence of barbed wire to prevent any Malay from venturing out at night to contact an Allied unit that might have found its way ashore, as Q team had. Less than six months before, five British commandos had been caught and executed on Dombi as a result of betrayal by a Malay purporting to be anti-Japanese.

The Malay, Anwar Hamzah, had been made foreman over all his countrymen as a reward for his act. Q team knew who he was and had been given permission to assassinate him if possible, but that option was to be exercised only following a successful completion of the team's prime task—destruction of the mine's central shaft.

Alpha Force was also aware that there were Malays who did not welcome the arrival of the Japanese. One such was Baginda Perak, formerly employed by Bandax as assistant to the wireless operator. When the Japanese invaded Dombi, they had taken all radio equipment at the mine and smashed it beyond repair, but before this occurred, Baginda Perak had surreptitiously looted the stores and hidden away sufficient spare parts to assemble a second transceiver, albeit with a much reduced range of operation. His transmissions traveled barely twenty miles from shore and were not heard until some time after the first attempt to stop the shipment of bauxite from Dombi had been betrayed by Anwar Hamzah.

Q team could not be absolutely sure that Baginda Perak was not also a traitor, but a former Bandax employee, who had been on leave from Dombi at the time of the invasion, testified to representatives of Alpha Force that Baginda was "a very decent little chap, very go-ahead. Half-Chinese, you see, so that explains it, the brains, you know, and the ambition. Absolutely hates the Nips, Baginda does. His mother's people back in China were wiped out by them, or so I was told. Oh, yes, I should say he's reliable, all right." Operation Greenfly rested almost entirely upon the truth of this opinion.

Constantly shifting the location of his radio, Baginda Perak had several times made contact with British submarines and had transmitted instructions on how he might be contacted by the next team of commandos to try their luck on Dombi. Q team was on its way to fulfill the first of Baginda's directions.

The wild-pig run became a jungle path worn by sandals and was easier to follow as the sky brightened. Keith forced the pace as the light of dawn began creeping overhead. The place they had to reach was close to the Malay kampong, and the Malays were known to rise early, their work at the mine beginning before the sun was more than ten degrees above the horizon.

"Wait on—I think we just passed it."

Ahead of them along the path, they could hear barking dogs and the general early-morning sounds of a stirring kampong. Keith turned and went back about fifteen yards, to a place where the path branched into two. At the junction of the path a banyan tree grew. Around the lowest branch was a garland of dried flowers. "Get them," said Keith, and Doug, unburdened by either radio or explosives, was the one who stripped the garland from the branch. When Baginda Perak walked by that morning on his way to the mine, he would take note of the missing flowers and know that uninvited guests were at large on Dombi.

"Right. The other place is"—Keith consulted his compass, and pointed into the jungle—"that way. Quiet as you can, everyone."

Q team slipped into the shadows beside the path and began heading toward the rendezvous point assigned by Baginda. Doug dropped the flowers as he pushed his way through tangled undergrowth that snatched at his weapons. A machete would have been useful in clearing a way through, but slashing at the jungle would leave a trail the Japanese might be able to follow. Q team pushed aside every frond and branch and avoided stepping in any earth moist enough to sustain a bootprint.

It required less than an hour to reach the place, Keith pausing often to check his compass reading. In a small clearing stood a rusting metal tripod, seven or so feet tall, above a metal tube that entered the ground vertically. The neck of the tube had been sealed with cement. This was the location of a rock sample bore drilled by Bandax engineers in the 1920s to ascertain the best site to begin opening the ground for mining.

"Bang on the nose," Trevor said. "Good navigating."

"Once a boy scout," said Keith, "always a boy scout."

Athol slid the heavy transceiver from his shoulders and sat down with a stage groan. "Bloody hell, why don't they make a radio that's smaller?"

"Garn, you need the exercise, mate," Doug told him.

"All right for you to talk," Athol said. "All you've got to carry around is your popgun and your William Tell apple-shooting kit." He meant Doug's Thompson machine gun and his crossbow.

"Well, it's a law a nature, Athol. Some blokes are worker ants and some blokes are soldier ants."

"You don't have a killing bone in your body."

"Won't know till some Jap finds out for us, eh?"

"No arguments, you two," Keith said. "Everyone find a spot just out of the clearing. Stay under cover, and don't smoke. Don't talk except in a whisper, and only if it's absolutely necessary. Keep your weapons handy."

"Do we put on our camouflage?" Trevor asked.

"Might as well."

They began applying green greasepaint to their faces.

"You look gorgeous, Hilda," Athol told Doug.

"Thanks, Gertrude; you're lookin' real kissable yourself, you old tart."

"You always were a jealous cow."

"That's enough," Keith ordered. "No more talking."

They settled down beneath the jungle foliage to wait for nightfall, when Baginda Perak would come. The air began humming with insects as the sun rose higher. Doug slapped at his neck. It would be a long day, and he knew he would not be able to resist filling the empty time with thoughts of Redlands, and of Val with the boy whose face Doug had not seen, and of Brian. And he would see Judy standing among the jungle vines, watching him remember her.

14

ENGLISHMEN . . . ! HSSSSSS! ENGLISHMEN . . . !" The words came to Doug like the rubbing of leaves, softly insistent. He awoke from shallow dreams. A six-inch centipede was ambling across his forearm. He watched it drop onto the earth from his wrist.

"Englishmen! You are here . . . ?"

Doug waited for someone else to answer; he wasn't going to be the one to raise his head and hope the voice wasn't a trap. Taking the initiative was Keith's job. He felt secure where he was, the air around him turning swiftly to purple in the twilight.

"Englishmen! Come out now, please!"

"Stop calling us bloody Englishmen," said Athol, from the clearing's far side.

"That's enough." Keith's voice. "All right, everyone, it's him."

Q team emerged from their positions of hiding. Doug was the last one out. A slender man in baggy pants and a sleeveless shirt stood by the Bandax bore head. It was already too dark to make out anything other than his high cheekbones and delicate jawline, and a shock of dark hair held back from his brow with a cloth tied around his head. "I am Baginda Perak. You are Englishmen."

"We're bloody not," insisted Athol.

"We're Australian," Keith explained.

"Ahh, Australian. Come with me now, please."

"Wait a minute. Where exactly are we going?"

"Malay kampong. There is a way inside. I have made it

myself. Very safe. No one will see. You must kill Anwar Hamzah. He is a traitor."

"Yes, yes, but first we need to take care of the mine, do you understand?"

"Of course, but I will show you the house of Anwar Hamzah; then you will know where to kill him later."

"We want to see the mine first. Can you show us a way into the Allied prisoners' compound?"

"Yes, also very easy, but not so easy as kampong. You must know the house of Anwar Hamzah. He likes Japanese more than Englishmen. Please, first we go there, just to see."

"Very well, but we won't kill him until later, is that clear?"

"Yes, thank you. Tonight you will blow up the mine?"

"No; first we have to talk with the highest officer in the prison camp. Can you take us to him?"

"Easy to do this. Follow near to me, very quiet."

Baginda made a hurrying motion with his arm, then turned and walked into the jungle.

"Leave the radio and the explosives here," Keith ordered. "Fall in, single file."

They followed the Malay for far less time than it had taken them to reach their hiding place; Baginda presumably knew of shortcuts through the jungle, even though they did not once use any kind of path, not even a pig run. Full darkness had descended long before they stood beside a fence of thick bamboo poles and barbed wire. It was clear at a glance, despite the gloom, that the fence served as a psychological rather than an actual barrier to flight from the kampong; its five strands of wire were separated by several feet, and the lowest strand allowed any lean person to wriggle beneath it without difficulty. Beyond the fence were a dozen or more long bamboo huts roofed with atap leaves.

"Seven hundred man live here, Malay man, all who work for the Japanese. Not all think this is good, like myself."

Baginda pointed to a dwelling smaller than most, just a few yards from them, where the fence created a right-angled corner. A dim glow could be seen behind a split-bamboo window blind. "That is the house of the traitor. Remember where. Anwar Hamzah has no one with him, just one servant. The Japanese have given him this for his reward, when he betrayed

the Englishmen who came before you. Now he is big boss in
the mine, but he does no work. Every day he walks home at
noon to eat food, all made for him, then he sleeps, then goes
back to the mine for just a short time, then home again. Every
day he does this. You must kill him on the path, when he is
alone. He is a man with a beard and a fat belly."

"Everybody got the place firmly in his mind?" Keith asked.

"Yes," said Trevor. Doug could hear the nervous quaver in
his voice.

"Carved in stone," said Athol. "Can we go to the bloody
mine now?"

"Yes, the mine. I will take you there."

Baginda led them along the wire fence a short distance,
then entered the jungle again, emerging minutes later where
the two paths forked at the banyan tree. "I see there are no
flowers today, my heart is in my teeth with joy," said Baginda.
"This path all men take to do work. Follow very quiet, please."

"Are there likely to be Jap night patrols?" Keith asked.

"Sometime yes, tonight no. When you have seen the mine,
I will show you my radio. I have built it with my hands from
spare parts. The Japanese, they do not know. They think only
an Englishman could do this, to make a radio from pieces."

"It isn't necessary to show us that. We have our own radio.
We're interested only in the mine."

"Yes, the mine, it must blow up. There is only one time you
can do this without killing many men. When the sun is down,
then work is finished, and all men go away. Air pumps are left
on for one hour to take much dust from air in the mine, then
the air is clear again, and the pump is shut off until the sun is
coming up. In the night you must blow up the mine, when
there is no one under the ground."

"Fair enough. Please, less talk, until we know there are no
Japs around."

"Yes," agreed Baginda. "Shhhhhhhhh . . . ," he advised the
men following.

"Bloody hell . . . ," breathed Athol.

The mine path was less than a quarter-mile long, opening
suddenly onto a vast clearing in the jungle. Doug saw the
familiar layout he had memorised from aerial photographs and
Bandax maps.

There were two main buildings, both several storeys high, both clad in corrugated-iron sheets. The first contained the crushing mills, where the ore drawn up from the mine was pulverised, and the second, connected to the first by an endless beltway under a long corrugated-iron roof, was the loading facility, into which the narrow-gauge railway ran, to receive load after load of crushed bauxite for delivery across seven miles of jungle to the harbour and the wharf facilities.

Towering above these structures was the pit head, containing under its sloping roof the mighty wheels and steel cables that sent men down into the earth and drew up iron hoppers laden with ore. There were large office buildings and equipment sheds and a locomotive turntable in the adjacent railyards, and interspersed among these were many dozens of bamboo huts. These were the quarters of the English and Australian prisoners, and not a single light shone from any window. Around the compound stretched a high fence of barbed wire, with sentry boxes at regular intervals along its length.

"Over there," Baginda whispered, gesturing beyond the mining complex and POW hutments, "is Japanese soldier place to live. Many, many place. More Japanese here than Malay and Englishman and Australian."

Doug had seen the wide-angle aerial reconnaissance photos depicting the Jap presence on the far side of the mine. It had been difficult at first to believe that the few darker dots here and there represented the entrances to a warren of tunnels the Japanese had dug deep underground to house their troops, away from possible harm from the B-24s and B-17s stationed around Darwin. They lived like rodents under the earth, thousands of them, awaiting the day when the tide of war should change and they would have to defend Dombi against invasion by Allied forces. There were antiaircraft emplacements by the score, all netted with camouflage, and footpaths intertwining among the various innocuous openings to the subterranean city. Doug could not imagine living in such a place and had been unable to decide if the Japanese, clearly capable of it, were animals or supermen.

"Now we meet English major," said Baginda, his voice barely audible.

"You have a way to get inside?"

"Of course, many ways. The fence is nothing. The ocean is the true fence."

"Will the major know we're coming?"

"He knows. I have left a sign today, like the flowers you took, so he will know and wait for you now."

Q team followed Baginda Perak along a path running roughly parallel with the fence but separated from it by thick jungle. Doug heard a sentry cough and spit as they passed. Five minutes later, at the southeastern corner of the compound, they approached a wall of corrugated iron at least sixty feet high, without a single window. "Equipment shed," Baginda explained. The barbed-wire fence ended where the wall began; the outer wall of the shed was in effect a continuation of the wire. "Inside is concrete floor," said Baginda. "Japanese think no one will dig under it. Ha! No need."

He produced a set of keys from his pants and jingled them softly, pointing with them to a narrow metal door set in the back wall of the shed. "Also think they have only keys. Too bad for them, I take spare keys."

For all of the team to go inside would have been folly, Keith decided. He still was unsure about Baginda Perak's loyalties, and the shed would be a perfect place to spring a trap. "Athol, Trevor, find a spot nearby and wait under cover. If we don't come out in an hour, go ahead with plan B."

"Right," said Athol.

There was no plan B. Doug watched his companions walk back into the jungle.

"Open it," Keith said.

Baginda inserted separate keys into the door's two locks. "You first," Keith told Baginda as the door swung open. The three men passed through, and the door was closed again behind them. "Must lock," said Baginda, working the keys. "If Japanese come by outside and find this door not locked, look very bad, very suspicious, all lights come on, so we lock."

Looking around the interior of the shed, Doug felt, rather than saw, the vast space contained by its walls and could smell the machinery and metal parts kept there. As his eyes adjusted to the gloom, he began to make out darker blocks of darkness.

"Come," Baginda ordered, and began moving away.

Doug slipped off his Thompson's safety catch as Baginda weaved among the high metal shelves and piles of mining equipment. They came eventually to another door, and Baginda attended to the locks as before. On the door's far side was the camp, its atap-leaf rooves shining grey beneath the moon, every hut's overhanging eaves producing deep shadow.

"Come. Be close behind."

Baginda slid among the narrow avenues of darkness between huts, never allowing moonlight to touch him. Doug smelt the odour of unwashed men wafting from the huts as he passed, and the stench of an open latrine trench. Baginda stopped often, whenever a groan or a cough came from the nearest window or doorway, then proceeded deeper into the camp, Keith and Doug at his heels.

"There, that is the major's hut. He is waiting. I will stay here." Baginda leaned closer to Keith and whispered, "The major does not know my face. I want no one to know, so Japanese can never be told my face. Only you know. Better that way for me. You go inside, I will wait."

Keith lifted aside the shabby piece of cloth that served as a door, and stepped into the hut. "Major Birnham?"

"Reese-Birnham," came a voice from the darkness.

Doug slipped into the hut behind Keith. Two figures could be dimly made out, the first seated behind a table, the other standing behind him.

"Identify yourself," said the same voice. Doug had never heard anyone so English-sounding. The words were crisp and high-pitched, the tone that of someone used to command.

"Captain Keith Ramsey, Australian Army, Alpha Force."

"Alpha Force? That's a new one. Cloak-and-dagger boys, eh?"

"Yes, sir, you might call us that."

"We'll have a light, if you please, Lieutenant," said the major.

The standing figure struck a match and applied it to an oil lamp on the bamboo table. The interior of the hut glowed softly. Major Reese-Birnham was a gaunt man of around fifty, Doug guessed. His uniform was patched and stained but still bore the markings of his rank. His moustache was neatly clipped, his gaze direct. Despite the circumstances, he exuded an aura of strength and authority.

But it was the lamplighter Doug found himself staring at. He had lost at least twenty pounds of weight, but it was Clive. Doug assumed Clive had not recognised him because of the feeble light from the lamp and his green camouflage face paint.

"I assume you're here to carry on where the other chaps left off."

"Yes, sir, we are. Our orders are to destroy the main shaft with plastic explosives."

"The last lot of johnnies tried to demolish the wharf. I suppose you know what happened to them."

"Caught and executed by the Japs, sir."

"Yes. Our free agent on Dombi told you?"

"He contacted one of our sub patrols by radio."

"Mysterious fellow. We don't even know who he is, do we, Lieutenant?"

"No, sir," said Clive. "We just follow the signals he sends us."

"A rag tied to a certain section of wire along the fence, that sort of thing," explained the major. "He must be one of the Malays."

Keith cleared his throat. "I'd rather not say. The last lot were betrayed by a Malay who likes the Japs. This time everything has to be on a need-to-know basis. Those are my instructions, sir."

"I suppose you have a plan all worked out in advance."

"Yes, sir. It won't involve any of your people, just us."

"And how many of you are there?"

"Four, sir."

"Not a large number."

"We've been told to handle everything ourselves, along with the outside agent."

"Who shall remain nameless."

"Yes, sir. I think it's better that way. He insists on it himself."

"G'day, Clive . . . "

Three faces turned toward Doug, who took several steps forward, grinning.

Clive's jaw dropped. "Good Christ . . . Doug!"

The major said, "You know this man, Lieutenant?"

"Yes . . . my God, who'd have believed it. . . ."

"Showed up like a bad penny, eh, Clive?"

Keith said, "What's all this about, Doug?"

"Mate a mine from the Territory. I'm married to his cousin."

"How are you, Doug?" Clive came out from behind the table, and an intense round of handshaking took place.

"I'm fine, mate, and so's Val. Just had another kid, a boy this time."

"Bloody marvelous!"

"Lieutenant." Reese-Birnham's voice turned Clive back to the table.

"Sir?"

"I'm happy that you've been reunited with your friend, but there are other matters in need of our attention."

"Yes, sir."

Doug gave Clive a slap on the shoulder as they separated.

The major watched a large moth dashing itself against the lamp wick. "Now then, Captain Ramsey, I have something to tell you that may save you from harm. This is privileged information, known only to myself and the Nips. Here it is, in a nutshell: the bauxite deposits on Dombi are just about finished. Another few months or half a year of operation, that's all, and the entire place will have to be shut down for lack of ore."

"Sir, are you sure? I was given access to a lot of material provided by the mining company, and there was no mention of anything like that. The bauxite deposits are supposed to last well into the next century."

"Bandax is a company like any other, Captain; they tend to exaggerate their assets for the sake of their stockholders. They've made plenty of cash out of this place, but now the bottom of the barrel has almost been reached. It's ironic, really, the way you fellows have been trying to blow the place up when it's practically worthless."

"I wouldn't call six more months of ore production worthless to the Japs, sir."

"It's all relative, of course, but even if the mine produces for that long, how greatly is that going to help the Japanese war effort, do you think? They'll use the stuff to make more aircraft aluminium, but just how many aircraft? They can't possibly compete with the tremendous industrial might of the Americans. No, it's just a matter of time before the tide turns against the Nips. Blowing up the mine won't make more than a handful of difference, I assure you."

"You may be right, Major, but our orders are to destroy the main shaft and halt production permanently."

"Given the state of ignorance your commanding officers are working under, I don't blame them for telling you to do exactly that. But now that I've explained to you the true nature of the circumstances here, I'm sure you could see your way to reconsidering. You have a radio transmitter, I presume, or your free agent does? Convey the facts to whoever is listening, and see if they don't rescind your orders."

"I don't need to do that, Major. I've been given full authority to do as I see fit on this mission, and for my money, stopping the Japs from mining, even if it's only for another six months, is worth the risk."

"I see. If you proceed with your plan, there'll be repercussions among the prisoners here. Have you considered that? Last time, the Japanese were content to execute the raiding party, but a warning was given to me by Colonel Yoshishito, the camp commander, that any further attacks on the mine would result in retaliation against my own men. You can understand my reluctance to endorse this plan of yours, Captain."

"I can understand it, sir, but I can't help it. I have orders to carry out."

"Against my wishes."

"Yes, sir. I'm sorry."

"Not as sorry as the prisoners who are going to suffer for what you've done."

"Nothing much I can do, sir."

"You can do as I've suggested, Captain."

"It's not what we were sent here for."

"But you'll consider it, surely. Just take some time to think it over."

Keith felt himself succumbing to the major's voice, its innate power to command.

"Sir, I . . . I was told to make the decisions myself and

maintain radio silence until we're ready to be picked up by submarine."

"But these are exceptional circumstances you find yourself in, are they not? Use your radio, explain what you've found here."

"Those are not my orders. . . ."

Keith felt himself becoming flustered. He was losing the argument. "I want to speak with the ranking Australian officer in camp," he said.

"Unfortunately, that's you, Captain. None of the Australians here rank higher than sergeant, I'm afraid. There were a couple of lieutenants, I believe, but that was last year. Beriberi, wasn't it, Lieutenant, or was it some kind of fever?"

"Heart failure for one of them, sir," said Clive, "and I believe the other one had a fatal accident in the mine. There's a medical officer left, though, sir, a captain, I think. . . ."

The major ignored this. "Sorry we can't oblige you, Ramsey," he said.

Doug stepped up beside him and spoke directly to the major.

"We're gunna blow it up," Doug said.

"Hold your tongue, Corporal. Captain, does this fellow often talk over you?"

Before Keith could respond, Doug said, "We got told to do something, and we're gunna do it."

"You'll obey the orders of a superior officer! That's what you'll do!"

"We're not in your army, we're in ours, and we got told by our blokes to blow this mine up, so we will, all right?"

The major glared at Doug, unable for the moment to respond to such outright lack of respect. Keith wished himself elsewhere. He watched the moth fall onto the table, its wings alight, long brown body thrashing.

"The chain of command, Corporal," said the major, his lips barely moving, "extends throughout your forces and ours. I am the ranking officer present, and as such, I expect my orders to be carried out, regardless. When the war is over, I fully intend to have you court-martialed." He turned his gaze on Keith. "Have you considered what going against my express wishes might entail? I warn you, I know men in the highest of places."

Clive said, "Sir, it might be best if we all began from scratch, as it were. Captain Ramsey was obviously not prepared to about-face on a mission of this importance. Might I suggest we wait twenty-four hours and allow the captain to reconsider?"

"We don't need it, Clive," Doug said. "Thanks anyway, mate."

"Address your remarks to me," the major told him. "My junior officers do not speak on my behalf."

"Nor do my men," said Keith. He resented the major's attempt to usurp the authority that had been granted him for the duration of Operation Greenfly. At the same time, Keith wondered if the twenty-four hours suggested by Doug's friend was not perhaps a good idea. "But when one of them offers a solution I think has merit, I listen."

"So glad to hear it," said Reese-Birnham. The smile accompanying the words was like a death rictus. "Well?"

"Twenty-four hours," said Keith.

"And you'll contact your submarine?"

"I'll consider my options."

"I suppose we should be grateful, eh, Lieutenant?"

"Yes, sir," Clive said. Doug could tell Clive was embarrassed by the confrontation. He wanted to take him aside and talk of personal things.

"Got a minute, Clive?"

Clive looked at the major, whose smile widened. Doug was reminded of a crocodile's grin. "Certainly; you two must have plenty to reminisce about, I'm sure. Use the next room, Lieutenant. You have five minutes. The captain and I can continue our own discussion in the meantime."

Clive led Doug through to another room of bamboo and atap leaves. He lit a lamp there, and Doug looked around. Two thin palliasses lay on the floor. Doug supposed the major was the kind who wanted a servant right next to him, to answer the least need. He felt sorry for Clive, living alongside Major Reese-Birnham and having to obey his orders.

"Jesus, Clive, you coulda knocked me down with a feather when I saw it was you. I wasn't sure at first . . . I mean, you've got a bit thin in the chops, I reckon."

"The Japs give us just enough to eat and no more. Is Val all right? God, it seems like years. . . ."

"It *has* been years. The bastards got you at Singapore, eh?"

"All of us, practically. We've been on Dombi almost a year

now. Well, the major's been here longer than that, actually. Listen, Doug, don't be too hard on him." Clive lowered his voice. "He's the one who was in charge of the battalion stationed here when the Japs invaded. He lost half his men, then surrendered, and . . . well, I think it haunts him, the way he lost the island. He doesn't talk about it, of course, but I can tell. Don't fly in his face if you can possibly help it, Doug. He's an awfully proud man, and he doesn't even have his military reputation intact anymore."

"Is it bullshit about the bauxite runnin' out?"

"I don't know. It's the first I've heard about it. I'm the major's adjutant, but I'm not his confidant. He talks to Yoshishito quite a bit, just the two of them, so he could have been told. I can't say, really, but why would he tell you such a thing if it wasn't true?"

"Dunno. How's your health?"

"Better than most. Bit of malaria that flares up now and again, but conditions here are better than Singapore. Most of my chaps were left behind in Changi prison. God, that's something the Japs are going to pay for when this is over. I can't tell you . . . it's a hellhole. This place is a hotel by comparison. Yoshishito seems to be a fairly civilised type, for a Jap; at least he doesn't impose cruelty for its own sake."

"What about the blokes that got caught tryin' to blow up the wharf?"

"If it were me, I would have simply added them to the prisoners, but the Japs have a different code, Doug. To them, sabotage is a crime that deserves . . . beheading. I'm not making excuses for them, mind."

"So you reckon we should call the whole thing off?"

"I really couldn't offer an opinion, Doug. That's between yourself and the captain. He seems an intelligent sort."

"He's a good bloke, and I don't like to see a ratbag like the major try to walk all over him, that's all. No reflection on you, Clive."

"A new baby, you said. That's wonderful. And how about . . . I'm sorry, I can't recall her name for the moment—too much excitement and not enough food, I expect. . . . Judy! How's Judy?"

Clive watched Doug's face cloud over. "Gone," he said.

"Gone? You mean south, out of danger?"

"She's dead. Got lost in the bush. Brian found her, but she was gone."

"Oh, God, I'm sorry, Doug. . . ."

"One a those things. Turn around once, somebody's gone."

"And Val, is she . . . you know . . . coping with it all right?"

"Couldn't tell you, mate. It all happened while I was away trainin' with the Alpha Force mob. Got a letter about it from someone else; that's how I know."

"Christ . . . I don't know what to say."

"No need to say anythin'. I'm the same way meself about it."

Keith came through from the first room. "We're going," he said, and turned away.

Doug held out his hand to Clive. "See you in twenty-four hours, probly."

"Yes. I'm sure we can work out some kind of compromise."

Doug went back to the first room. Keith was already passing through the cloth door to the camp outside. Doug glanced at the major, then joined him.

Clive entered the room slowly. The major was staring at the cloth the Australians had brushed aside. "Do you know, Lieutenant, neither one of them saluted me even once. I overlooked it the first time, no light in the room and all that, but they could have saluted before leaving. What kind of slovenly wretches are these chaps?"

"Well, the Aussies tend to be a bit rough and ready, sir."

"Indeed. I doubt that they're ready for me. You actually permitted your cousin to marry that fellow?"

"Doug's a wild colonial, sir, from the Outback. He's got all the heart inside him you could want in a soldier."

"I would have thought the operative organ in his case was his mouth. I'm prepared to be lenient, of course. You probably understand these fellows better than me."

"Just give them time to think about it, sir."

"That was my own proposal, Lieutenant."

Baginda guided Q team back to the Bandax bore marker in the jungle. Keith explained the gist of the meeting with Major Reese-Birnham.

Athol said, "Why the hell would a Jap officer tell a British officer the mine's running out of bauxite? That's bloody important information, wouldn't you say? The Japs'd want to keep something like that a secret as long as possible, wouldn't they?"

"Doesn't smell right," agreed Trevor.

"He's worried about reprisals, like he said," offered Doug.

"You mean he's prepared to help the Japs keep mining, just so the camp avoids punishment?"

"Probly makes sense from his way a lookin' at it."

"That's bloody treason," Athol said. "He can't do that, can he?"

"He'll do what he wants, regardless," said Keith. "Doug, what's your best guess on this bloke?"

"Clive told me Reese-Birnham's the one that surrendered Dombi and the mine to the Japs. Probly got a guilty conscience about it and wants to keep things nice and steady, not rock the boat and get the Japs all hot and bothered. You can understand it, sort of, but I wouldn't trust the bastard."

"I agree. We'll go ahead as planned, without consulting the major." He turned to Baginda. "How soon can you get us into the main shaft?"

"Tomorrow night, why not. The work is finished when the sun goes down. When all workers come up, then I will take you into the mine."

Baginda Perak went back to the kampong, and Q team settled down again for a restless night's sleep in the jungle.

15

RATHER THAN SPEND ALL DAY as he did the day before, Doug asked for and received permission from Keith to spy on the Malay responsible for betraying the first commando raid to the Japanese. If Doug was to kill this man, he argued, he'd better be sure he had the right bloke in his sights. Keith agreed, and Doug worked his way back through the jungle until he reached the path leading from the kampong to the mine. Then he waited for Anwar Hamzah to come home for his midday meal.

At a little after noon, he heard someone approaching and shifted some undergrowth from in front of his face to peer along the path. A short man, bearded and potbellied as Baginda had described, was ambling toward him. When he had passed, Doug hurried around to the side of the kampong nearest to Anwar Hamzah's hut and climbed a tall tree there, to see if he could aim his crossbow through the window and to ascertain that the man he had seen on the path was the same one who lived in the hut Baginda had said was the traitor's.

Doug heard shouting inside, then saw a small Malay run past the window, followed by the potbellied man he had seen ten minutes earlier. So it was indeed Anwar Hamzah, and he seemed to be displeased with his servant, for some reason. Doug listened and heard slapping sounds, followed by wailing. Anwar Hamzah clearly was an intolerant master. Doug wondered how it would feel to send a crossbow bolt through his heart. He deserved it, for what he had done. It would be a tricky killing to perform, with every Jap on the island running around looking for Q team. Anwar Hamzah just might escape what was owed him, unless Doug could get back to the kampong immediately prior to the mine explosions, which would be set off by timing devices to allow Q team plenty of time for their escape. Killing ahead of time would be easier, but then the Japs would be alerted to the presence on Dombi of Allied commandos. Destroying the mine was more important than killing one man.

Doug wondered also if the reprisals against prisoners predicted by Reese-Birnham would take place as a result of Q team's efforts. Would Clive be among the ones singled out for punishment? It made Doug squirm to think that, having found Clive again after all this time, he should be responsible for bringing harm down on his best mate. It was an intolerable situation to face, but again, the mine's destruction was more important than the fate of one man. There might be a way to accomplish Clive's rescue, though, if Keith gave his permission. Doug began planning.

Baginda returned to the bore marker in the jungle at dusk, and Keith included him in the final briefing.

"The operation proceeds as follows: Baginda leads us inside the camp again. We leave the radio outside, since it won't be needed until after, and all of us will go inside. Doug'll use the crossbow to take care of any guards or sentries between us and the pit-head building. Once we're there, Doug stays outside to warn us of any Japs approaching. The rest of us will shimmy down the main shaft's lift cables a little way and lay our charges against the walls, then set the timers for detonation just before dawn. Baginda leads us out again, we pick up the radio and head for the same beach we came in on. Athol gives the signal at the prearranged time, we inflate the rafts and paddle like mad for the sub, which with any luck will be exactly where it's supposed to be, waiting for us. By the time the mine shaft collapses, we'll be under the waves and heading for home."

"But Anwar Hamzah will still be alive," protested Baginda.

"Yes, well, we can't afford to make a detour back here and hope to kill him without anyone seeing it happen. It's just too risky. Taking care of him was always a secondary consideration."

"But he should die!"

"I agree, but he won't, not this time."

"You told me he would die."

"And I was wrong to do so. I should have said it was a possibility, that's all."

"Then I will not help you."

Baginda folded his arms across his narrow chest.

"Little bugger," breathed Athol.

"You've got to," said Trevor, sounding panicked.

"No, I will not. Anwar Hamzah betrayed your countrymen to the Japanese. He must be killed."

"He betrayed Englishmen," Athol said, "not Aussies."

"It just isn't possible," Keith insisted. "Are you willing to throw the whole mission away just because of one man?"

"He is a dog," said Baginda. "He should die, to show others they must not help the Japanese."

"No," said Keith. "I won't risk the safety of my men just for that. There'll be little enough time for us all to get clear before the explosion. We simply can't squeeze in an assassination. I'm sorry. Will you help us or not?"

"He should die," said Baginda, but his voice was less insistent.

"Tell you what," said Doug. "How 'bout we take Baginda with us on the sub, for services rendered. No more Japs to work for, and I bet there'll be a tidy bit a cash for him as well, because a the way he helped us out."

There was a brief silence, then Keith said, "Very well. Baginda?"

"I . . . I will come with you, to the mine and then the submarine."

"Good. Then everything's settled."

"If we're takin' him," said Doug, "how 'bout takin' along me mate Clive?"

"Absolutely not. Don't start arguing with me about it, Doug. We can't afford to go anywhere near Major Reese-Birnham's hut, or the operation will be jeopardised. By us staying away, he'll assume we're waiting for fresh orders, and that's what I want him thinking right up until the blast wakes him up tomorrow morning."

"I bet I could sneak in and get Clive out without the major wakin' up."

"No; I mean it, Doug. He probably wouldn't come anyway, out of sheer loyalty. He's the major's adjutant. You can't expect him to simply walk out, even if he's a mate of yours and you're married to his cousin. It won't work. The subject is closed. Does anyone else want to say anything?"

No one did.

"Then let's get started."

Q team followed Baginda Perak as they had twenty-four hours earlier, past the Malay kampong, then on to the equipment shed in the corner of the POW camp and mining complex. Athol set his radio down in the jungle, and Baginda used his stolen keys to allow all five inside the building. They passed through to the compound, and Baginda led the way between the prison huts. Once, while passing a doorway, someone inside a hut challenged them with a "Who'zat?" but they hurried by without arousing any further noise. Ten minutes after entering the camp, they were near the towering metal structure that housed the entrance to the main shaft. They studied it from behind the nearest hut.

"Where are the sentries?" Trevor whispered.

There was not a single Japanese to be seen.

"Confident buggers, aren't they?" said Doug.

"All right, it's our lucky night," Keith said.

"I don't bloody like it," Athol said.

"Too easy for you, mate?" Doug asked.

"I will unlock door," whispered Baginda. "Wait."

He ran silently across the bare ground separating the huts from the building. A faint jingling was heard as he opened a small door beside the much larger sliding doors through which workers poured in the morning and evening. When the door had been opened, he waved, and Q team went across in twos to the doorway.

"Right," said Keith. "Baginda, you stay outside with Doug and keep watch. Doug, if you start wandering in the direction of your Pommie pal, you'll be court-martialed. Understood?"

"Yeah."

Athol, Trevor, and Keith disappeared inside the building.

"Not enough cover here," Doug said. "Let's get back behind the huts."

They returned to the shadows.

Baginda said, "If you wish to get your friend, who am I to stop you? Your friend, he will die here one day. You take him away with you. Why should I come with you and not him also? The captain, he will have no choice to send him back—there will be no time. You go now if you wish, while they work, but be quick."

Doug thrust the loaded and cocked crossbow at him. "Here, shoot any Japs that come strolling by. Just aim it like a rifle and press the trigger."

"You remember the way?"

"Pretty well . . . "

"Then hurry."

Doug began working his way toward the place he remembered as being the location of Reese-Birnham's hut, sliding from shadow to shadow beneath the overhanging atap-leaf rooves. One hut resembled another beneath a moon obscured by clouds, and within minutes he became lost. There was not a single light anywhere in the camp, and the one thing tall enough to act as a locator—the mine shaft building—could not be seen from the narrow corridors between the prisoners' huts.

"Shit . . . "

He decided to hunt for the major's hut for another ten minutes, then try to rejoin Baginda at the shaft, if he could locate it again. If Clive hadn't been found and persuaded to come along within those ten minutes, Doug would simply not tell Keith he had deserted his post. He doubted that Baginda would say anything to betray him.

The sudden eruption of gunfire was muffled, and Doug knew immediately it had come from inside the shaft building. His first thought was that Baginda had encouraged him to go looking for Clive in order to allow the Japs access to the building.

"Bastard!"

His next thought was for his own survival. He must not be captured. But Baginda was in possession of the keys that would have given him an exit through the equipment shed. He was trapped within the camp itself, unless he attempted to wriggle under the wire, but he was not even sure in which direction the fences lay, and there were machine gun towers covering every approach. . . . Suddenly there were lights filling the camp perimeter with brilliance, and sirens began howling.

"Shit . . ."

He was stuck between huts, a machine gun in his hands, all hopes of escape dwindling by the second. Doug turned in a circle, as if expecting a magical doorway to open behind him, offering a way out. He could see the huts a little better now, thanks to the fence lighting, but that only made him a more obvious target for the Japs when they came hunting, as they surely would when Baginda sent them after him. He felt panic crowding up into his throat. There was nowhere to run, no chance of slipping by the troops that soon would come swarming through the camp.

"In here, mate."

Doug spun around. An arm was beckoning from the doorway of a hut.

"Move your arse!"

Doug ran inside the hut.

"Where the fuck did you come from?" said a voice beside him in the semidarkness. The accent was distinctly Australian. Doug could see a bushy-headed silhouette and could smell the man's unwashed stench.

"Australian Army . . . special demolition team . . ."

"Sounds like you buggered it up, sport. Any more of you out there?"

"Three . . . I reckon they're already captured. . . ."

"You need a nice rathole to hide in then, don't you?"

"I bloody do. Got one handy?"

"Who's this bastard?" came a voice from deeper inside the hut.

"Aussie commando. Gotta hide him before the Japs get moving."

"Yeah? Where?" came another voice.

"I know," said the first voice. "Put him in the infirmary hut. Jack Donnelly died just before sundown. They're gunna bury him tommorer mornin', but this bloke could take his place, eh?"

"Whatta we do with Jack, then?" asked the bushy-headed man at Doug's side.

"Bury him tonight, along with this bloke's uniform and gun. Can't hide a bloody tommy gun in here, mate; that's gunna have to go."

"We can't just start diggin' a hole while there's Japs runnin' everywhere."

"Put Jack and everythin' else in the latrine trench. It'll all sink into the shit."

"Jesus, mate, that's a bit rough on Jacko."

"He wasn't religious. Better make it snappy, or this bloke's gunna be dead meat."

"Anyone think of anythin' else?"

There was silence in the hut. The sirens were still howling.

"Right-oh, mate. Foller me."

Doug was yanked outside again and ran behind the bushy-headed man through the winding maze between the huts. There had been no more gunfire since the original burst. Doug felt sick at heart. If he had stayed where he was, Baginda would not have had the chance to betray them. It was Doug's fault, yet he was the only one still free, maybe the only one still alive. Doug was incapable of decision. He was disoriented, confused, guilt-ridden. If the prisoners could not save him now, he knew he would not be able to save himself. He placed his trust in his countrymen and did as he was told.

"In here."

He was shoved inside a long hut and immediately confronted by several men.

"What's all this?" demanded one.

"Aussie commando. Japs've got his mates. Jack Donnelly still in here?"

"What's he got to do with it?"

"Strip his clothes off and shove him in the latrine trench. This bloke's takin' his place, all right?" The bushy-headed man said to Doug, "Get outa that uniform and hand over the tommy."

Doug began taking his clothes off. More men, awakened by the disturbance among them and the sirens outside, were crowding around, the situation being explained to them in whispers. Soon Doug stood naked, and two men carried a similarly naked dead man past him and out the door. Doug's uniform and gun were in the care of a third man accompanying them. A pile of rags was placed in Doug's hands.

"Get dressed," he was told. They were the dead man's clothes.

He put them on, a sleeveless shirt and a pair of baggy

shorts, rank with the odours of sweat and what Doug soon would learn to identify as bauxite dust, and another stench. "Sorry about the smell," said the man who handed him the rags. "Jack died of gangrene, among other things. Is that camouflage paint on your face? I can't see you properly."

"Yeah."

"Come over here."

Doug was led to a bucket of water. "Scrub it off, all of it. One trace of that stuff, and you might as well be wearing a sign around your neck."

Doug dipped his face into the bucket and began scrubbing.

"I'm Ted Moffet, medical officer."

"Doug Farrands."

"Mind telling me what your mission was?"

"Blow up the main shaft, bugger the whole mine."

"Pretty ambitious."

"The bloody Malay with us musta tipped off the Japs."

"Bad luck."

"Bad luck my arse. I'll get the little bastard for it."

"You need to think more about keeping your head down. You're a very sick man, that's why you're here in the infirmary, right? As a matter of fact, I think you're about to undergo a miraculous recovery and be returned to Jack Donnelly's hut, before the Japs start combing through the place. Better get started right now. Got all that paint off?"

"I think so."

A match was struck before Doug's face, blinding him.

"Good job," said Moffet, blowing out the match. "Come on."

Again Doug was led among the huts. The sound of Japanese shouting could be heard, but it did not seem to be close by. The men who had taken away the dead man passed Doug and Moffet, and words were hurriedly exchanged.

"Get rid of him all right?" Moffet asked.

"Yeah. Had to poke him under with bamboo poles, though, and the uniform. The tommy gun went straight down."

"You're sure there's no sign of anything above the surface?"

"We struck a coupla matches. Couldn't see Jacko at all, or anythin' else. The Japs won't find any of it."

"Take Doug on to Jack's hut and explain things to the others, will you?"

"Right-oh. Come on, mate."

"Thanks," Doug said to Moffet, as he began moving away.

"Thank me if it works. It hasn't yet."

Several more minutes of weaving among the huts brought Doug and his guide to a hut like any other. Every man inside had been awakened by the sirens, and the bushy-headed man had to explain twice to the dozen or so men there what it was that Doug's presence required of them.

"Right," said someone. "Leave it to us. Over here, mate. You better piss off quick, Reg, if you don't wanna get caught."

"Keep your nerve, mate," advised the man who had brought Doug there, then he was gone. The sounds of the Japanese were closer now.

"This is your bunk. Get in it and don't make a move until the Japs come in and start screaming. The rest of you, back to bed."

"Yes, nurse," said a voice in the darkness.

"No funny buggers."

Doug lay down on a creaking platform of bamboo several inches from the ground.

"Comfortable, mate?" asked a voice to his left.

"Not a lot."

"Bloody hotel, this. Had to sleep on the ground, the last place we were at."

"Shut up, both of you."

The sound of running feet came through the open door, then an electric torch was shone inside the hut. Doug felt his entire body jump as the beam swept over him.

"All man get up!" screeched the Japanese behind the torch.

The prisoners eased themselves from their bunks.

"All man go tenko now!"

They began filing out of the hut. Doug made sure he was not the last one through the doorway. The prisoners from all the adjacent huts had also been ordered outside and were filing in an orderly fashion in the same direction.

"What's *tenko* mean, mate?" Doug asked the man beside him.

"Roll call. They're checkin' up on the numbers, probly go through all the huts while we're standin' around. Just do what everyone else does, and you'll blend in like one more dag on a sheep's bum."

The pathways opened onto a broad parade ground. Doug followed the men from Jack Donnelly's hut and stood to attention with them. There were electric lights at the parade ground's four corners, and Doug could see his fellow Australians properly for the first time. Most were in need of a haircut and shave, and all were skinnier than himself. He buttoned the filthy shirt he wore, to hide the layer of muscle and fat on his chest and belly, and ran his hand through his hair several times to give it a tangled appearance. He had not shaved since leaving the submarine, forty-eight hours before, so his appearance was not conspicuously neat, and he already smelled as bad as the rest.

As the minutes passed, Doug became aware that a body of men numbering more or less the same as the group he stood among had assembled on the opposite side of the parade ground. "Who's that lot?" he whispered to the man beside him.

"Poms," came the succinct reply. "That's their side a the camp. Poms work on the wharf and railway; us bastards go down in the fuckin' mine."

"Japs hate us more'n they do the Poms?"

"Not bloody likely. Bloke called Reese-Birnham runs this place, mate, not the Japs; they're just the bloody jailers. It's his majesty the major that doesn't like us."

"Why not?"

"Our blood's not blue enough for that bastard."

"And our noses aren't fuckin' brown enough," said the man on Doug's other side.

"There's three bunches of blokes in this place," explained the first man, talking through the side of his mouth. "Japs and Poms and us Diggers."

"It's us against the other bloody two," said the second man.

"Sounds a bit crook," Doug said.

"You're bloody right it's crook. You'll get used to it before long."

"I won't be stayin' around, mate."

"Fuck off. Nobody gets away from Dombi."

"Here we go," said the second man. "No luck with the search, so it's bloody tenko twice over, I bet."

Two men were mounting a low wooden platform at one

end of the parade ground. One was a small Japanese wearing the polished knee boots of an officer; the other was Major Reese-Birnham. The low murmurings that had been sweeping back and forth among both groups of prisoners died away. Doug winced as a sudden burst of static screeched from loudspeakers mounted atop the light poles.

"English mans, Australia mans, all listen now," came a voice from the speakers. Doug could see a microphone in front of the Japanese officer's face. "All listen, verrer important you listen to me." The voice was as small as the man, despite its electrical magnification. "Verrer bad thing has happen tonight here. Four man has come to do bad harm to you. Try to hurt mine, stop you to do what we wish. That is bad for you. So I say, make this man, one man we do not take, make him come out now. If you do not, that is verrer bad. You hide this man, you make bad more bad. I say to you, give to me this man if he hides with you. Better for you this way. You do not give him to me, I think more bad for all man in camp. So you listen now to Major Ris-Birm."

The major stepped up to the microphone.

"You chaps have probably worked it out by now," he said. "There's been an attempted sabotage raid on the mine, and it didn't work. I won't repeat what Colonel Yoshishito has said to you. Instead I'll address my remarks to the individual himself, if he can hear me, which I'm sure he can. I have only one message to convey: Give yourself up. Give yourself up now, wherever you are, or there will be repercussions for every man assembled here. Your companions have been caught, and you must surrender voluntarily to spare them what will surely follow if you do not. I'm sure you understand my meaning. Your mission here has failed. There remains nothing left for you to do, other than to ensure the continued good health of your companions and every other prisoner. There is no shame in a surrender that is in any case inevitable. By saving time, you save us all unnecessary discomfort. I urge you to step forward now."

Doug felt a quivering in his legs and was surprised to find that he wanted to do as the major asked. He had caused the failure of Operation Greenfly and should own up to it. Keith and Athol and Trevor would be spared the torture Reese-Birnham and Yoshishito had hinted at. Doug wanted to do as he had been told, but his legs, already willing to admit their guilt, could do no more than tremble, and support him where he stood. There were whisperings that ran back and forth across the parade ground, like a soft wind among trees, and many British heads turned this way and that, searching for the man they had been told of. Among the Australians, every head faced to the front. The public-address system hummed its electrical song, emptied of words.

The colonel and the major left the platform and held a brief discussion with single representatives of the British and Australian forces. These men went to their respective ranks and issued the command for roll call.

"I bloody knew it," said the man on Doug's right.

"Got your new name straight?" the other man asked.

"Jack Donnelly."

"Don't you forget it, or we're all dead."

Tenko progressed slowly. When Donnelly's name was bellowed out by the sergeant reading the roll, Doug answered promptly with a nervous "Present!" and the roll call ran on past him to the rest of the men.

The results of tenko having proved that all prisoners were in attendance, the next step was to count them. This was done, the tallies being taken to the colonel and the major, both of whom appeared to be dissatisfied by the results. The ranking officer on either side then passed along the lines of men, with a Japanese soldier at his side, equipped with a torch which was shone for several seconds onto the face of each prisoner. The ranking officer for the Australians was Ted Moffet, and Doug recalled Clive having mentioned him the night before as the sole surviving Aussie officer, only to have been ignored by Reese-Birnham.

When the beam of light finally fell upon Doug, he squinted his eyes against its brilliance and held his breath, and so missed the absolute lack of reaction that kept Moffet's face as inscrutable as a plaster mould. When the light had gone on to several more men along the row, Doug allowed himself to breathe again. He was being protected. No one on that side of the parade ground would give him up, and among the British on the other side, only Clive, and possibly the major, could identify him.

Reese-Birnham went back to the microphone. Yoshishito was already walking away in the direction of the office building that served as the Japanese officers' quarters.

"Very well," said the major. "If reason and unselfishness cannot win the day, then other means must be employed. I am prepared to meet with any man in camp, at any time, to discuss this matter."

"Wants us to turn bloody informer," spat the man on Doug's left. "Pommie bastard," he said, crooning the phrase softly, as if having honed it to suit his mood many times over, until the words spilled from him as naturally as breathing. "Fuckin' Pommie bastard cunt. Upper bloody crust of a Sandhurst bastard. Jap bumlick bastard bugger."

"He's all a that," said a voice behind Doug. "You watch out, mate. He'll have you by the balls if he can grab 'em, just to keep it sweet between him and Yoshy-shitto."

Both sides of the parade ground were dismissed and began filing back to their separate compounds. Now that Doug was a little better oriented, he could see that the camp, for all its apparent higgledy-piggledy appearance, was in fact two camps, without benefit of a fence between them. It had not occurred to him until then that the two nationalities might be housed at a distance from each other. This would make it difficult for him to see Clive again. Of course, it might be best to stay clear of Clive and so avoid implicating him in anything. It was bad enough that Reese-Birnham already knew they were acquainted. He should have kept his mouth shut the night before, when Clive clearly had not recognised him beneath his camouflage paint, but it was too late now to regret having revealed himself.

Lying on the dead man's bunk, Doug felt panic begin creeping through him again, and was kept from being overwhelmed by it only through the insistence of the men around him to know everything he knew about the war's progress. They were cheered when Doug told them the Yanks had managed to recapture Guadalcanal and the Japs had lost a large naval force in the Bismarck Sea. "You beauty," someone said, when he told them of the increasingly heavy bombing raids against Germany.

"Reckon we've got a chance still?" he was asked.

The question was an abstraction to Doug, concerned at that moment with his private hell. He could sense the expectation around him; they wanted confirmation that their suffering would eventually have been endured for something, for the possibility of rescue or escape, and ultimately for victory.

"Too right," he said, tears squeezing from his eyes, his face hidden by darkness. "Too bloody right we have, mates. What happened tonight's a real bugger, no two ways about it, but it's a drop in the bucket. We won't be here forever, not us. Fuck the Japs."

"Amen to that, mate."

"Can we get a bit a bloody shut-eye now, you yakkin' buggers?"

The hut soon became quiet, each man thinking of his own torment and of the stranger hiding among them, shifting restlessly on his unaccustomed bed. The night would pass slowly, as every night did. Four men had attempted to hit the Japs where it hurt and had failed, but one of them was still free, with a slender chance at remaining that way, because a dead man had been dropped without ceremony into a latrine trench and poked down beneath the shit. It was a world of madness and sacrifice, and the greatest battle, for most of the men around Doug, was against futility and despair. Doug, for all that he represented a bungled mission, was from the outside world they remembered; he was one of them, as they once had been, and now he lay among them, an unlikely angel fallen into their stinking pit. From his presence, they drew what they could.

At sunrise, all prisoners were assembled again on the parade ground. Doug was told that this was the usual routine but the appearance of Major Reese-Birnham and Colonel Yoshishito on the platform was not. The Japanese commander spoke first.

"Now is made worse, what you one Australia man has done. Your Australia friends, they have suffered much. You do this to them still. Now you must come forward so their suffer will stop. You hurt them now as I speak to you. Hear what I tell to you, Australia man. You are here, I know. More time is waste while you do nothing. Your friends, they hurt more. You must not hurt them more."

Yoshishito stepped aside, allowing Reese-Birnham access to the microphone.

"It's simple enough, Corporal Farrands. Either you give yourself up or the other three will suffer the consequences. They've already suffered quite enough, believe me. You have one minute to present yourself, beginning now."

The man beside Doug whispered, "That your name, mate?"

"Yeah."

"No it fuckin' isn't; it's Jack Donnelly, you stupid prick."

"Sorry."

The minute passed slowly. Reese-Birnham spoke to an officer standing beside the platform, and that officer began walking toward the Australian ranks. He was quite close before Doug recognised Clive. He felt his stomach lurch; it was another identification inspection, and the major was determined to use every means at his disposal to ferret out the missing man. Doug was surprised to find himself wondering if Clive would point him out or pass him by. How could he doubt that Clive would do the right thing by him? Doug reminded himself that he was not yet sure that Q team had been best served by himself, and as Clive worked his way along the ranks, sweat began oozing from Doug's brow. Q team probably had already been tortured to extract information from them. It was his fault they had been captured. If Clive was to touch his shoulder and say, "This is the man," it would serve him right. It would be rough justice, and he would not be able to blame Clive for it at all. It was a toss-up. Capture would offer relief of a kind, and evasion would bring him nothing but a greater sense of guilt. Clive might even get into trouble himself if he failed to identify Doug.

Now Clive was just a few men away. Doug focused his eyes on the far side of the parade ground and held his breath. Clive paused before him for not one second longer than he had paused before every other man, and then was gone from Doug's sight, the sound of his boots passing down the line. Doug breathed out, then inhaled deeply. Safe. He could begin suffering again.

Clive returned to the platform for an inaudible conversation with the major, who returned to the microphone. "Very well. I declare to every man present that what follows has been argued against by me for most of the night." He turned to the little Japanese beside him. "I ask you once again, Colonel Yoshishito, to reconsider."

Yoshishito did not look at the major. Reese-Birnham stepped back from the microphone. Several minutes passed, then Keith Ramsey, Athol Harris, and Trevor Costigan were led out to the middle of the parade ground by three Japanese soldiers and an officer wearing a samurai sword. They were made to kneel. An undercurrent of murmuring began running through the prisoners. Doug could see blood and bruises on all three men. Trevor was crying.

"Jesus . . . ," Doug said.

"Don't you fuckin' move, mate," the man beside him warned. "This'd happen anyway, even if you gave yourself up. This way they only get three of you, the bastards."

The officer unsheathed his sword. The men of Q team had their heads pushed forward by the soldiers, baring their necks. The officer raised his sword above Athol and brought it swiftly down. Athol's head seemed to leap from his body, and blood gouted from the stump of his neck. His body collapsed slowly sideways. The officer stepped back to avoid its touching his boots. He went to Trevor, whose cries were heard across the parade ground, and beheaded him with equal precision. Doug felt himself beginning to experience the first wave of nausea and fought to control himself. He closed his eyes, but what he had already seen came crowding into his head. He stared instead at the shoulder of the man standing in front of him. He heard Keith's head strike the ground but did not see it roll to a stop. He could literally smell blood in the air. Tears were trickling from his eyes by then, and he had to chew his lips to keep from making any sound. He heard an Australian and an English sergeant dismiss the prisoners and turned away with the rest.

"Listen," said his self-appointed custodian, "you better try and get some breakfast down you, because you won't see food again till you knock off work late this afternoon. It's hard yakka down the mine, so eat what they give you, and don't think about what just happened."

Doug nodded dumbly, convinced he could willingly avoid food for a week.

Breakfast consisted of a bowl of rice with several finger-sized portions of tough chicken, and watery tea. Doug forced it all past his throat, badgered by the Australian who seemed to have made him his protégé. "That's it, Jack, every stingy morsel. This is a bloody banquet compared to the tucker in other places I been."

Doug was aware of sympathetic looks directed at him while he ate. None of these men was aware he had deserted his position as guard over the mine shaft. They would spit on him if they knew. He kept his eyes lowered and scooped the rice into his mouth with his fingers, pushing away all thought of the beheadings. He could not even feel gratitude toward Clive for having refused to betray him.

Breakfast was done with in just ten minutes. Doug followed the rest of the Australians toward the scene of his crime against Q team and walked across to the shaft housing through the wide double doors. Inside, he was vaguely aware of massive machinery, the air pumps and lift engines, and the huge spoked wheels whirring above. There were two lift cages. Into one filed the Australians; into the other went Malays, entering the building from another set of huge sliding doors. Doug was jostled into a cage, saw the wire-mesh door slammed shut, and then plummeted into darkness. I'm goin' to hell, he thought, and smiled bitterly.

The work assigned to him was simple. Ore mined from the rock face of the various side tunnels was transported in tiny railway carts back to the main shaft for raising to the surface. Two men pushed each cart, their way along the narrow tunnels illuminated by light bulbs at intervals of ten yards or so. The air was thick with bauxite dust that clogged the lungs and eyes. Speech was superfluous. Doug and his partner, an undernourished man with a straggly beard, worked virtually without a pause, pushing empty carts one way, full carts in the other direction. Only once, when there was a lull of several minutes while fresh ore was brought from the mine face on a separate set of tracks to the changeover point where Doug and his partner stood waiting, did the man speak, his face a dusty mask.

"Bloody Victorian system," he said. "They did it like this a hundred years ago, you know."

Doug nodded. The man continued: "The upper levels have got ore conveyor belts, set up before the war, you know. The deeper you go in here, the more primitive it gets. Manpower, that's what they use down here. Really ineffective. Bloody stupid, in fact, but the Japs aren't interested in getting the fullest production they possibly can. They're supposed to be incredibly efficient, the Japs, but they're not. I've seen it. They just muddle along, using men like pit ponies. Bloody stupid. They should use bloody conveyor belts down here. Can't get hold of any, I suppose. Wartime rationing's a bugger, isn't it." He laughed at his own joke, then held out a stick-thin arm. "Name's Tyson, Wally Tyson."

"Doug . . . Jack Donnelly."

"Ahh, yes. Jack, of course. Awful bloody thing up there. Not your fault, though."

Doug looked away. Wally Tyson coughed for a moment, then said, "It's that major, that Reese-Birnham. Hand in glove with the Japs from the beginning. Anything to keep things working smoothly, that's him. Too bloody accommodating for his own good, that bloke. For *our* good, I should say. Keeps all the Poms working on the loading wharf down at the harbour, did you know?"

"Yeah, someone told me that."

"Rank favoritism. We're only colonials, so down into the mine with us, along with the Malay boongs. The Poms are up there getting a bloody suntan, and we're down here getting lung disease. That's prejudice. I'd like to clock that bastard. Doesn't do any work himself, just sits under Yoshy-shitto's chair and licks his bum all day. Good way to win the war, eh?"

"Bloody good."

"Here we go again."

Another cart came through from the mining face, its tracks on a higher level than those worked by Doug and Tyson. The men in charge of the cart released a catch and tipped their ore into the other cart below, showering Doug and his partner for the fifteenth time with dust and fine debris. They began pushing their newly laden cart almost immediately to escape the cloud that would hang in the air behind them almost as long as it took to reach the shaft, dump their ore into the hoppers there, and return for their sixteenth load.

By the time a whistle sounded shrilly throughout the mine, Doug had found that hard work, relentlessly performed, was so numbing a task that his mind could not for long hold on to thoughts of Q team and Clive. No matter how often he might attempt to summon them before his eyes, the back of the ore cart would block these things from sight. Physical exertion, at least for the duration of that first day, was what he required to ease himself from under the mountain of guilt he had accumulated.

Rising toward the twilight in the lift cage, he felt a little of his former self return. While it had probably been a shamefully brief period of mourning for his lost integrity, Doug did not regret its passing. The dead would remain dead, however he felt. The living, himself included, were more deserving of his attention now. He reminded himself of this when he saw that the heads of Q team had been mounted on top of the camp's main gate.

16

It was felt by the rest of the Australians, when Doug failed to engage in conversation for more than a few words, that he was suffering still from the shock of witnessing a triple beheading in which he was involved on a personal level. They assumed he was lost in some kind of fog, part guilt and part gratitude, but it was not an unmanly place for him to occupy, at least for the present, and so they left him alone.

The Japanese apparently were still convinced the fourth member of Q team lingered within the camp's perimeter. There were two more sudden searches of every hut during the next three days, and tenko was conducted with unusual exactitude, every name on the rolls being accounted for, and every man present on the parade ground counted twice over.

Underground, Doug kept a careful watch on every Malay he passed in the mine. They worked on the upper tunnels, Wally Tyson told him, because the Japanese still chose to believe that their much-publicised Greater East Asia Co-Prosperity Sphere was at work on Dombi. The Malays were paid a few pennies a day and given the easier work associated with mechanisation in the mine's upper levels, where the conveyor belts ran and there were electric lights every five yards, instead of ten. But some Malays were sent to the lower levels to work with the prisoners, usually when an Australian collapsed and had to be taken up to the surface.

The air in the mine was laden with moisture that the air lines and pumps could not cope with. Every man became drenched in sweat and soon was covered in bauxite dust. The water supply—buckets placed at intervals along the tunnels—was often inadequately replenished, and men would faint from dehydra-

tion as often as they would from exhaustion. When this happened, a Malay sometimes was brought down to replace him,
and every time he glimpsed the slender form of a native, Doug
peered at the face, attempting to see the features beneath the
dust accumulated there. He was searching for Baginda Perak.

He still believed it was the Malay who had taken advantage
of Doug's stupidity and let the Japs into the shaft building
within minutes of Q team's arrival there. Doug could not see
how else the mission might have been betrayed so swiftly.
Doug very much wanted to kill Baginda, if it was at all possible.
But if it was Baginda who had done this, why would he still be
working in the mine, Doug asked himself. The Japs would have
rewarded him for his work as they had Anwar Hamzah, by lessening his workload and placing him in a position of authority.

The Japanese seldom came belowground, Doug noticed;
instead they kept a careful tally of the ore produced each day,
and if the allotted quota had not been met at the end of each
day, one or more men were selected at random from the exit-
ing Australians and beaten with bamboo canes. It was a cruelly
effective discipline; Doug saw only one man beaten in this
manner during his first week, and two during the second
week. The miners, obliged to be self-regulating, usually paired
stronger men with weak, to facilitate production. That was
how the Australians worked, and Wally Tyson assured Doug
that the Malays had pretty much the same system.

If Baginda Perak was in the mine, then he had not done
the thing Doug believed him guilty of. Doug searched for his
face, he supposed, in order to prove his own theory wrong. As
time passed and Baginda did not appear, Doug took to loitering around the lift cages after he had come up in the evening,
to scrutinise the Malays as they left the mine. He watched
them moving in dusty droves toward their own exit and
scanned their faces, and still Baginda was not among them.
The unproductive nature of his scheme became frustrating,
especially when his loitering and watching meant he arrived
late at the Australian mess hut and was served the leftovers of
rice and chicken, if any remained.

There seemed little point in continuing the exercise, given
its illogicality and the missed meals it engendered. Baginda
Perak was somewhere else, probably in the offices above-

ground, enjoying the perquisites of betrayal. Doug still had not visited the three new graves in the prisoners' cemetery and had promised himself he would not do so until he had set himself free of guilt over their deaths.

Doug knew he needed to concentrate on a far more appealing task than revenge, albeit no less difficult to bring about: he wanted to talk with Clive. He had not told a single Australian that his best mate was adjutant to the major, had never hinted that the English officer who perused the Australian ranks before the execution of Q team was that man. To reveal his connection with Clive would have cast him under suspicion, given the general level of hatred for the English on Doug's side of the camp. He would have to make contact by means so subtle that his own countrymen would not be made aware of the relationship.

Following the evening meal, prisoners were left to their own devices until the whistle blasts of lights-out sounded, an hour or so later, at which time the dim glow of oil lamps was extinguished. Doug began using this free time to study the unmarked boundary between the camp's two sets of prisoners. There was a distinct no-man's-land separating the nationalities, a strip of earth no more than ten yards wide, where no one ventured. It was not a ruler-straight division, since the huts on either side were not laid out to any draughtsman's plan; it was a crooked scar of emptiness, and it was infringed upon only by accident. This was the place Doug must somehow negotiate to find Clive, but it could not be crossed during daylight. He would have to visit Clive and the major's hut by night.

An alarm clock would have made it easier to carry out his plan, but there was no such thing in the entire camp, nor did anyone but the major wear a wristwatch; Doug's own watch had gone into the latrine trench along with the tommy gun and Jack Donnelly's corpse. Doug would simply have to try and rouse himself from sleep during the night and set off in search of the right hut on the Pommie side of camp. He was accustomed to waking often during the night, because of the uncomfortable bunk he slept on, but these brief periods of wakefulness were subsumed by his overall weariness after ten hours of working in the mine, and he would quickly drift back into uneasy sleep. To accomplish his purpose, he would have to waken himself fully. He felt some excitement at the prospect of following through with a plan he had conceived himself, and on the chosen night had difficulty falling asleep at all.

Anwar Hamzah was restless. He had eaten far too much for his evening meal, despite the abominable cooking of his servant, and now was paying the price; his chest was gripped by a demon's fist, and the demon would not let go. Anwar Hamzah was obliged to get up and walk around his hut by the light of the moon lancing through his windows. He had awakened his useless and wicked servant by kicking him in the rump several times, until the fellow had fled whimpering into the night, so now he was alone with the demon inside him. He drank water from the bucket his loathsome servant filled each day, but it did no good; the demon must have been consuming the liquid as it went down, and laughing over Anwar Hamzah's undeserved pain. He would beat his cringing and unmanly servant with great joy in the morning, by which time the son of a dog would have brought his unworthy carcass back to his master's hut to receive the punishment that was so rightfully due. The prospect of repaying so terrible a cook was cheering, but it did nothing to lessen the demon's hold on Anwar Hamzah's heart.

A sound came from outside. He turned to the doorway, expecting to see there the silhouette of his contrite servant, but the figure entering the hut was unfamiliar. Anwar Hamzah was puzzled also by the strange instrument held in the hands of the intruder, and had begun to open his mouth to demand that the fellow announce his name and business at this late hour, when the instrument uttered a sharp sound, like a truncated harp string, and he found he could not ask a single word. The demon had reached out from his heart and torn a hole in his chest; nothing else could explain the terrible agony he felt there. Raising his hand, Anwar Hamzah found one of the demon's hard claws sticking straight out from his skin. As he collapsed to his fleshy knees, he understood that the demon he had thought was inside his chest was in fact the figure before him, and that the demon had come to take away his life. Anwar Hamzah wondered why.

°   °   °

When he stepped outside his hut near midnight, to judge by the moon's height above the camp, Doug took himself in the direction of the latrine trench, in case anyone might be watching him. He walked past the open and stinking grave of the man whose identity he had assumed, and continued on in the direction of the English huts, keeping to the shadows, moving slowly, pausing often to match what he saw with the blurred memories of his first venture into that part of the camp.

Eventually he saw what he was fairly sure was the hut he and Keith had entered. He studied it until he was certain, and then went to the window of the room to the left, where the palliasses had been.

"Clive . . . ," he whispered into the darkness inside.

There was no response. Doug could hear breathing but was unable to tell if it was produced by one or two people.

"Clive . . . Hey, Clive, you there, mate . . . ?"

He heard someone stir and hoped it was not the major. Doug backed away from the window and hid himself in shadow in case he had awakened the wrong man.

"Who is it? Who's there . . . ?"

"Me, Clive. Dougo."

"Doug . . . ! Wait there a minute."

Clive joined him outside the hut, and they wrung each other's hands.

"Christ, Doug, I was wondering how to reach you, but there wasn't any way I could ask after you over there among the Aussies without giving the game away. How on earth are you managing to hide? The Japs keep a careful tally of how many there are in camp."

"I took a dead man's place. He got buried on the sly, and now I'm him; simple as that. Took over his bed, do the work he did in the mine."

"That's marvelous, the perfect cover for you, hidden right under their noses."

"Thanks for not dobbin' me in that day."

"God, what followed . . . "

"They'll pay for it. Heard anything about a little Malay bloke called Baginda? He's the one let the Japs get Keith and the rest when I . . . when I went lookin' for you, like an idiot."

"Looking for me? What for?"

"I wanted to try and get you to make a run for the pickup sub with us."

"Did you have permission?"

"Nah, never bothered. Thing is, I couldn't find the bloody hut, then the fireworks started. If I'd stayed where I was sposed to be, I mighta taken a few Japs with me. We might all have got away. I fucked it up, Clive, no bullshit."

"But you said it was this Baginda fellow."

"Yeah, but it was still my fault. I'll get Baginda, though, somehow. Did the major say anythin' to you about a traitor the Japs've rewarded for what happened?"

"No, nothing. He thinks you're still on the loose, by the way, and so do the Japs."

"Eh?"

"This evening—can't be more than a few hours ago now— someone shot a Malay called Anwar Hamzah through the chest with a crossbow bolt. He's the one who sold out the British team six months ago. His servant came running up to the camp gate screaming blue murder. Yoshishito sent for the major and had a flaming row with him about it. He's only just gone back to sleep. You're lucky it wasn't him you woke up."

"A crossbow bolt?"

"Naturally the major and myself remembered the crossbow you had over your shoulder when you came to see him. I thought myself it must have been you who did it."

"Not me, mate. I gave the bloody thing to Baginda and told him to watch out for Japs while I went lookin' for you. . . ."

Doug and Clive looked at each other, sharing the same thought.

"He didn't betray you, Doug; he must have simply run off when he heard shooting."

"Bloody hell . . . and then does what was supposed to be something handled by yours truly, if we had the time, which we didn't . . . Baginda, you little ripper! I had him all wrong, Clive, looks like!"

"But that means the Japs were already waiting for you and the rest, doesn't it? I mean, the Japs don't patrol the camp at night. Why were they there to catch your demolition team, if this Baginda wasn't the one who let you down?"

"Someone else did it, told the Japs we were comin', that's what happened."

"But the only ones who knew were myself and . . . "

"And the major. Reckon he'd do it?"

"That's absurd. Why would he betray Allied forces to the Japs?"

"Like he said, to keep the Japs from takin' it out on you blokes, if we had've gone ahead and blown the mine."

"It doesn't make sense. No Allied officer would do such a thing. It's not possible."

"He was dead set against us doin' what we came to do, remember."

"Yes, but . . . it's quite a jump from attempting to dissuade you from the job and actually telling the Japs about it. No, no—I can't accept it, Doug. He's not that type at all. I'm not saying he's perfect, but something like that . . . absolutely not."

"Sure?"

"Yes, quite sure. It had to have been someone else."

"There's only you, mate."

"That isn't the least bit funny."

"It was him. He doesn't like Aussies."

"Oh, really, Doug . . . you're trying to shoehorn him into the role of villain, and it's utterly absurd. Something like that would be treachery of the worst sort. Whatever his faults, Reese-Birnham's a gentleman, and I mean that in the old-fashioned sense of the word. His type simply isn't capable of . . . what you're suggesting."

"If you say so, Clive. Listen, if Baginda's on the loose and he's still on our side, it means he's probly got hold of our radio—"

"No, the Japs found that. They've destroyed it."

"Bugger. Wait on, he's got his own radio, he told us; bit of a ramshackle piece a shit, but it transmits. He's probly told our sub what happened. They were sposed to come and get us after we set the charges in the mine."

"Well, they won't have hung around when it didn't happen."

"Nah, spose not."

"You shouldn't have come looking for me that night, Doug."

"I know."

"This place . . . it isn't so bad, not as bad as some places. I can stand it, you know, along with all the rest of the fellows here."

"Haven't seen any Poms down the mine, Clive. You might

think different if your bloody major sent some a you blokes down there."

"It's something I . . . I don't approve of, frankly, but he won't hear of sending our lot underground. I admit, it's not right."

"You bet it isn't. A commandin' officer who'd do that to Aussies, he wouldn't lose any sleep over turnin' in a few of us to the Japs."

"No!"

"Willin' to put a fiver on it, Clive?"

"I don't have a fiver, and neither do you. I don't want to hear any more about this idea you've got stuck in your head, Doug. It's simply wrong."

"Might be, might not be. Just thought a somethin': Baginda never wanted the major to see his face. Reckon he had his own suspicions?"

"Surely he would have shared them with you."

"Not really. So far as he was concerned, the important thing was to take care a this Anwar Hamzah bloke."

"You're grasping at straws, Doug. If I can't convince you you're wrong, I think I'd prefer to end the conversation for now, if you don't mind."

"Fine by me, mate. Listen, I'll sneak over and have another chat with you sometime or other, all right?"

"Yes, please do."

"But you can't tell the major anythin'. I don't trust him, Clive, I don't care what you say. So mum's the word—fair enough?"

"You have to . . . you must take care, Doug."

"Too right. You do the same."

"Yes . . ."

Doug began backing away, returning to deeper shadows. Clive watched him until Doug was a shadow himself and then was gone altogether. He went inside the hut and lay down on his palliasse, six feet from that of the major, whose light snoring indicated to Clive that he was deeply asleep. By close association over a sustained period, Clive had come to understand the major's sleeping state by the sounds it produced, but he could not have claimed to understand the workings of Reese-Birnham's mind while awake.

Clive had studied the man in considerable detail, since it was his intention, if he survived the war, to write a book based loosely on the major. The book's theme would be the intellectual and moral quandary the man faced each day as symbol of a force that had been conquered on the very soil he now held some dominion over, but only at the whim of the conquerors. The major was an interesting character, and Clive resented Doug's outrageous reinterpretation of the fairly complete picture Clive had formed of Reese-Birnham. Doug was an angry man, a guilty man, in much the same way the major was, since both felt responsible for having allowed their countrymen to fall into the hands of the Japanese. But there the comparison ended. The major was definitely not the ludicrous figure Doug wished to see. No Englishman would behave in that fashion, even toward allies he felt were his inferiors.

Clive settled himself on his palliasse and closed his eyes, but no matter how much he attempted to find sleep again, he kept seeing Doug, the shadow that came in the night, bearing bad dreams and unthinkable thoughts.

At tenko the following morning, the prisoners were counted twice, even the English, before being sent off to work. A whisper was passed from man to man that "the Japs are gettin' their balls in a fuckin' knot" over some unnamed incident that had occurred the night before. "Swarmin' all over the bloody island they are—lookin' for you again, I expect, mate," Doug was told.

"Good luck to 'em."

"Know anythin' the rest of us don't, Jacko?"

"Nah."

"You'd be expected to share and share alike, y'know. A bloke that gets his bum pulled outa the wringer just in time, he owes the blokes that done it a favour, I reckon."

"That'd be about right."

"Just so's you know."

"I'll keep me eyes open."

Doug worked alongside Tyson, who kept looking at him sideways, until Doug asked, "Well?"

"Just wondering if you knew what's got the Japs all stirred up this time. Haven't got more of your commando mates stuck out in the jungle making mischief, have you?"

Doug ignored him.

At evening tenko, a small figure was led onto the parade ground. Doug recognised Baginda Perak, supported between two Japanese soldiers. His naked feet dragged in the dust; his head and torso were extensively bloodied. Around his neck, like an albatross, hung Doug's military-issue crossbow.

Colonel Yoshishito tapped the microphone to be sure it was working.

"You see now Malay traitor man. This one work for Australia mans losing head. All head now on gate. Two more head join them soon. This man, one other man. Major Ris-Birm explain now to you."

The major stood at the microphone, hands clasped behind his back. Doug felt a powerful hatred for him as he watched and listened.

"This chap, this Malay, has a weapon issued by our side. He hasn't told how he got it, says he found it in the jungle, but Colonel Yoshishito does not believe him, and frankly, nor do I. The man the colonel is after is among us. He is present here tonight. This Malay chap had the weapon hidden in the roof of his hut. The one the colonel wishes to find is not out there in the jungle, although that is what he wants everyone to think. No, he's here, watching me speak. I have this to say to that man. Three of your fellow Australians are dead, and this Malay will also die if you do not give yourself up. Having watched the first three die, I don't expect you'll reveal yourself for a Malay, but understand this: tomorrow morning, so the colonel has told me—and I believe him—two prisoners chosen at random will be executed. This will certainly happen. I say to you: Corporal Douglas Farrands, reveal yourself! The colonel has said he will not kill you. Again, I believe him. Most of you men have been in other camps, places far worse than this. The colonel has said to me that if he does not see the face of the man who has caused all of this unnecessary death, Dombi camp will become as those other camps are. Two prisoners every day will die, until Corporal Farrands gives himself up."

"Aussies or Pommies!" yelled a voice from among the Australians.

"The choice was Colonel Yoshishito's," the major replied. "I regret to tell you that given the nationality of the fugitive, the two men per day will be selected from the Australian ranks."

"Bastard!" called the same voice, and the rest of the Australians joined in, their rage directed in equal measure at the colonel and the major.

Doug felt something inside him fall into place, like the tumblers of a heavy lock. He began pushing his way through the lines of men that separated him from the parade ground's open space. The yelling and jeering stopped as the Australians became aware that he had revealed himself.

Doug went to the microphone platform and stood before it.

"Thank you," said the major.

"Any day," said Doug.

The prisoners were dismissed, the English displaying less reluctance to leave the parade ground than the Australians, who had to be persuaded to begin moving by shouting, shoving Japanese guards.

Doug was marched to the mine's administration offices and forced to sit on a chair in what appeared to be Yoshishito's room. A large Japanese flag was tacked onto the wall behind a large metal desk, probably the property of the mine's manager until the Japanese invasion.

Baginda was brought in several minutes later and set roughly down on another chair. The colonel and the major entered together. Yoshishito seemed even smaller than he had on the parade ground platform. His figure was slim, his face handsome and shaved to perfection even at that late hour. His uniform was immaculate, without the least sweat stain, his black hair as sleekly oiled as a penguin's wing. The colonel sat behind his desk. The major stood to one side of the room. There were two guards each behind Doug and Baginda.

Colonel Yoshishito lit a cigarette and studied Doug while he smoked half of it.

"You are interesting man," he said.

Doug looked at the floor. He fully expected to be tortured, then executed. He tried to summon Val's face before him, and Judy's and Brian's, but could do no more than recall their names. He supposed it was because he was so scared of what was about to happen that his mind refused to function as it should.

"This Malay man, he has been your friend?"

Doug heard the question but could not respond. A rifle butt between his shoulder blades knocked him from the chair. He was ashamed to be on the floor and so got up to sit in the chair again. The question was repeated. Before Doug could think of opening his mouth, Baginda said, "Yes, I am his friend."

Yoshishito nodded, watching them both through a haze of cigarette smoke. He picked up a bunch of keys from the desk. Doug recognised them as Baginda's stolen set. Yoshishito swung them back and forth, then let them fall.

"Today is my birthday," he said.

Doug thought at first it was some kind of Oriental joke, but the smile on the colonel's face appeared to be genuine. "Birthday is better when no trouble comes. Today there is much trouble. You have done this." He scowled at Doug and Baginda, then smiled again. "But I am generous man. So old, must be generous." Doug felt himself begin to drift. The words were without meaning. Soon he would be dead. He almost wished it would happen instantly, so he would not have to wait and endure more pain than he knew he could withstand. It was better to be dead than to be humiliated for no purpose.

"And so," the colonel continued, "one man only will die. You."

Doug looked up, expecting that he was to be the one, but the colonel's finger was aimed at Baginda. The finger moved on until it pointed to Doug. "And you will kill him."

"Why?" Doug asked, his voice not much more than a whisper; fear had closed off his throat like an unwanted room.

"Because I say to you it is my birthday."

Doug looked at the floor again, unwilling to understand.

"Colonel," said Reese-Birnham, "surely this is not necessary."

"Then two will die. You choose, please, which."

"I . . . I don't think I follow you, Colonel."

"You choose. One die or two. You choose now."

"One," said the major, his voice softer than Doug had heard it before.

"Australia man, stand up," commanded Yoshishito.

Doug stood. The colonel took an automatic pistol from his belt, worked the slide to place a round in the chamber, then removed the magazine, so only one shot could be fired. He placed the pistol on the desk. "You take it. You shoot him," he said, pointing at Baginda.

Doug picked up the pistol. The guards leveled their rifles at him, to ensure that he did not shoot at the colonel.

"You turn," Yoshishito directed. Doug turned to the Malay.

Baginda's eyes went from the pistol to Doug's face. He nodded, then closed his eyes. Doug understood that he had been given permission to kill by his intended victim. He raised the pistol and aimed at Baginda's forehead, but could not pull the trigger.

"Shoot," he was told by Yoshishito, but he could not do it.

The colonel came from behind his desk and took the pistol from Doug. Without the least hesitation, he shot Baginda Perak in the chest. Baginda fell to the floor and soon was still. Doug tried to look elsewhere but could not.

Colonel Yoshishito returned to his desk and inserted the pistol's magazine, worked the slide, then removed the magazine again. "Australia man, no courage. One more chance. You take." He thrust the pistol across his desk. "You pick up, yes!"

Doug again picked up the pistol.

"Now put bullet in own head," the colonel ordered him. "No courage to kill Malay man, now see if you have courage to kill you. No kill you, hurt you verrer bad. Better you kill you now. Over quick. You kill you now."

Doug placed the muzzle against his temple.

"Colonel," said Reese-Birnham, "this is not what you said you would do. You said if he gave himself up he would not be executed."

"No executed." The colonel smiled. "Soo-cide," he explained, the smile widening.

"This is not what you told me would happen—"

"Be silent! Australia man has no courage! He does not deserve to die with honour! This way I give chance to die with honour. You shoot you now!"

Doug turned to Reese-Birnham. "You told the Japs, didn't you?" he croaked.

"I did no such thing."

"They were waitin' for us. You told 'em we were comin', didn't you?"

"That is a ridiculous accusation. Don't lose your nerve now, Farrands. I'm sure if you tell the colonel more about the operation, he may very well change his mind and allow you to live."

Doug faced the colonel. "Is that right?" The gun was still held to his own temple.

The colonel nodded. "If you wish to talk more, no need to shoot you."

Doug suddenly aimed the pistol at Reese-Birnham and pulled the trigger. The hammer fell against an empty chamber. Doug squeezed the trigger several times more. The major's mouth had fallen open in surprise. Colonel Yoshishito began to laugh. The guards had not made any move to prevent Doug from shooting the major, and now they, too, began laughing.

The colonel held up a bullet in his fingers. "Slay of hand," he said. "Verrer quick slay of hand. No one see, only Japanese. Australia man, English man too slow, they no see. Verrer good joke."

The major turned and left the room. Doug placed the pistol on the colonel's desk.

Yoshishito finished laughing. He studied Doug for some time, taking another cigarette from his gold case and lighting it with a gold Dunhill lighter.

"You do not like Major Ris-Birm."

"I love him like a brother."

"No brother. Australia mans, English mans, I see sometime, they do not like. Fight sometime. Keep them together, they fight. Why?"

"We don't like the way they part their hair."

"English people, they own your country."

"They bloody don't; they only think they do."

"I say to Major Ris-Birm, You run camp, make all more easy for me. You run camp like English man. He put Australia mans in mine, English mans load ship. I say to him why. He say to me better this way. I say why better. Ris-Birm say Australia man more better do donkey work. I say to you, you agree?"

"The major's the donkey."

The colonel laughed briefly.

"Why you do not kill Malay man?"

"He didn't deserve to die. The major does."

"You say to me, Ris-Birm tells me you come to blow up mine?"

"If he didn't tell you, who did?"

"Litter bird tell me," said the colonel, making flying motions with the hand that held his cigarette. "Verrer litter

bird sing in ear, say bad Australia mans come, must be ready
to make welcome."

He offered the pack of cigarettes to Doug. "You wish to
smoke?"

"No."

"I say this to you. One thing more you do. Make me know
you have courage, I make you leader Australia mans. No more
Major Ris-Birm. Only English mans for him. All Australia
mans, they take order from you, you take order from me. I
make you major, like Ris-Birm."

"I wouldn't want to be an officer."

"But you wish to be leader of Australia mans?"

"Yeah, all right, if we can swap jobs, us and the Poms."

"Sawop?"

"They work in the mine, and we load the ships."

The colonel stubbed out his cigarette.

"Verrer well, when you do one thing more."

"What thing?"

Morning tenko found Doug already standing at the centre of
the parade ground. He had been placed there just minutes
before sunrise. As the sky brightened, he could see before him
on the earth the brownish bloodstains created by the beheadings of Q team. The prisoners began assembling as usual.

"Good on you, Dougo!" called a voice from the Australian
ranks.

"You beauty, mate!"

A Japanese soldier marched up to Doug and handed him
Baginda's head. Doug took it and held it away from himself.
The back of Baginda's head was toward his face until the soldier took the head from his hands and turned it around before
returning it to Doug. He would have to stare at Baginda's face
all day without once allowing his arms to fall. This was the task
assigned him by Colonel Yoshishito. The head weighed at
least six or seven pounds, by Doug's estimation, but he knew
that before long it would weigh a ton.

When roll call was over and the prisoners began filing from
the parade ground to begin working, Reese-Birnham said to
Clive, "You're relieved of your duties for today, Lieutenant.

Stay here and keep a watch on your friend. Report to me if something happens. Looks like some kind of endurance test, wouldn't you say?"

"Yes, sir. Yoshishito didn't explain it to you?"

Clive was puzzled by the major's behaviour since his return from Yoshishito's quarters the night before. Usually willing to discuss anything that had passed between them, this time he had said nothing and had become angry over the questions Clive asked concerning Doug.

"No, not a word. Queer blighter, as you know. Wouldn't surprise me if the corporal's life depended on his holding that little package till nightfall. Looks a bit like Hamlet with Yorick's skull, don't you think?"

"Not really, sir."

"No, suppose not. Can't imagine Farrands asking himself philosophical riddles."

"Am I permitted to approach him, sir?"

"Absolutely not. The Nips would probably put a bullet in the both of you. No, this is some kind of medieval Bushido nonsense to tickle Yoshishito's idea of . . . courage, or some such thing. Keep me informed, Lieutenant, but do nothing else. Understood?"

"Yes, sir."

The major walked away. Clive stood in the nearest shade and watched Doug staring into the dead gaze of Baginda.

By midmorning, Doug was more intimately acquainted with the lines and pores of Baginda's face than any wife could be. The eyelids were partially opened, his eyes looking back at Doug, whose fingers cradled the head along its jawline and beneath the shapely ears. Blood still dripped on occasion from the severed neck, to land eighteen inches from the shabby toes of Doug's boots. The head was already assuming the weight of a cannonball, and Doug could feel the jumping of his muscles as they fought to keep his arms extended horizontally. It helped a little to imagine that a special wooden brace had been fitted to his waist, with supporting arms set at forty-five degrees to meet his wrists. He could actually feel the brace touching his waist and wrists, and the weight of Baginda Perak's head sometimes seemed to become lighter as a result.

He was given no water. The sun stood above his head, casting his features into deep shadow beneath the shapeless brim of his Digger's hat. Every atom of his body made its presence and its suffering known to Doug's brain, itself stewing in the cauldron of his skull. He had abandoned the wooden brace and become a statue of the kind he had seen in magazines, life-sized muscular figures holding conch shells from which spouted cooling fountains of water in green city parks. For minutes at a time he could hear the hissing of the nozzles, feel the spray settling on his burning forearms and shoulders, seeping down into his boots to quench the sizzling along his soles.

He was a statue, and he knew he had a name, some foreign-sounding name that had been told to him long ago, a fairy-story name that eluded him. There had been a man in the story, a young bloke from somewhere or other a long time ago, thousands of years, and he had cut off someone's head for a reason that Doug could not recall, but he knew the reason must have been a good one, because the decapitator was the hero of the yarn. So now Doug was that man, with the head held before him, and after a while Doug remembered that the head in the story had the power to turn to stone anyone who looked at it, and that became the source of his strength, since he had done nothing since daybreak but stare at the head with the power to turn men to stone. Stone arms were what he needed to keep from letting the terrible head fall. If the head was to fall, Doug would lose everything he had gambled on winning, so he had become a stone statue to ensure that that did not happen.

He heard the sounds of the mine: the distant rumbling from the cable wheels at the main shaft; the humming of the endless belts; the thump-thump-thump of the ore crushers, and sometimes the reedy whistle of the locomotive that ran back and forth all day between the mine and the harbour with its carloads of pulverised bauxite. Everything around him was proceeding as it should, without regard for his suffering. The significance of his stand on the parade ground existed, for the moment, solely inside Doug's head, and perhaps inside the head of Colonel Yoshishito. It was a game of chess without movement, with one of its participants wholly absent.

Sometimes his eyes wandered from those of Baginda, and Doug looked at the empty parade ground. Waves of heat danced across the naked earth, distorting the huts beyond, and once in a while a willy-willy would spin across the ground, twirling itself almost immediately into dusty nothingness as he watched. The willy-willies were just the same as the ones back home in the Territory, which began their gyrating as soon as the Wet ended and the earth dried out enough to loosen up the red dust. The willy-willies in this place were also red, from the bauxite dust, but he preferred the ones back home. If he didn't drop the head he might not die; and if he didn't die, he might one day be able to go home again. But that line of thought was quickly erased; there existed no future beyond sundown. His world of stillness and pain would cease to exist at sundown, and all Doug had to do was hold the head before him at arms' length until then. With sundown would come his reprieve. He must hold the head. Remain a statue until sundown. Beat the Jap colonel. Above all, beat the English major.

Doug was aware of the man watching him from one side of the parade ground: the English side. He thought it might be Clive, but the figure seemed not to move at all, and Doug couldn't imagine Clive not coming over for a chinwag and an offer to hold the head for a while. Clive wouldn't understand about being a statue, or what it meant to remain one until the sun settled below the horizon. Of course, Clive was an Englishman and so would not be pleased by the results of Doug's efforts to turn the camp system upside down. It would be best if the watching figure wasn't Clive at all but some other Pom, whom Doug could despise wholeheartedly. Hatred lent him strength. Doug wished the major would come and stand before him. That would turn his arms to granite for the rest of the war. He was amazed that he had stood for so long already without allowing the head to drop more than an inch or so. He was truly a man of stone, and would remain one until there was no more light in the sky. A stone man under a fountain of cooling water.

There were Japs too. They came in ones and twos to stare at him from the edge of the parade ground, but none approached him. He supposed they were reporting to Yoshishito, but the colonel himself did not appear. The Englishman who might have been Clive was probably the major's man, waiting to see what would happen. They would all be disappointed if they expected him to drop the head. He wasn't going to drop anything. The head was a part of him now, joined to his hands; inseparable. The Japs and the Englishman could hang around and stare at him as much as they pleased, but nothing would happen before sundown, when the world would be changed.

In the early afternoon, Doug realised he could no longer imagine the cooling hiss of fountain waters or feel their trickling upon his skin. His tongue would not turn to stone but insisted on becoming leather instead. It began to swell inside his mouth, rasping against his stone teeth, attempting to poke itself out into the daylight. He knew if the tip ever pushed its way past his lips he would not be a statue anymore; statues did not have their tongues poking out. Doug had to keep his creeping, expanding tongue inside his mouth. He did not think of water now. Water had become an unknown thing. Baginda told him it was best to forget water. Baginda was on Doug's side, willing him to remain a statue. His lips did not move, but he spoke to Doug, sometimes with his own voice, sometimes with Clive's, offering encouragement for the bargain that had been struck with Yoshishito, and condemnation of Major Reese-Birnham, the traitor.

In the afternoon a monsoonal rain descended, but Doug could catch none of it without tipping back his head. He watched the drops running from the brim of his hat and wished he had the tongue of a frog, long enough to dart out and snatch a few morsels of moisture as they passed his face, a dripping curtain of enticement. But he would not move. The huts disappeared sometimes behind curtains of rain, and Baginda's hair hung like seaweed from his scalp. Doug felt water invade his boots through leaking seams. Soon the rain passed by, and the parade ground began to steam, and then the ankle-high mist was gone, burned away by the returning sun. It had been a momentary reprieve, but now it was over.

When the sun came into view beneath the brim of his hat, and the day was three-quarters done, Doug tried to ignore the pain extending along both arms and across his shoulders by recalling the house at Redlands. Its occupants were too shadowy to bring to mind, but the house itself, a thing of metal and reflected heat, was perfectly clear, as if it stood on the far side of the parade ground, rooted in redness, its galvanised-iron roof twisting in the turbulent air of the Dry. Doug could not recall if the Territory was currently in the grip of the Wet or the Dry. He could not be sure how long he had been on Dombi. Was it just a few weeks, or had he been there for much longer? Baginda told him time was not to be trusted in any case, since it all belonged to God, who could shape it as he pleased. Doug said he didn't see what it had to do with God, but Baginda would not respond.

The parade ground often would tilt to one side, as if trying to tip him over, but Doug always told it to stop, and the ground did as it was told before he could lose his balance and fall. Doug tried counting to ten several times and was surprised to find that he could not. Somewhere between six and eight, the numbers lost reality, began blurring into the God-time Baginda had spoken of, and Doug eventually gave up. He could not be sure how many attempts to count to ten had been abandoned by then, and did not care. The muscles of his arms and back were screaming, and rods of white-hot metal had been inserted into his legs to keep them straight. He could not imagine what it might feel like to bend his knees. The rods of metal had replaced his knees, in any case. A statue had no need to flex itself and would in all likelihood break apart if it tried to do so. Absolute rigidity was the order of the day. He had given the order himself. He would not accept orders from anyone else, although he would give serious consideration to anything suggested by Clive. If Clive told him to drop the head, though, he would ignore Clive. Clive was a Pom, after all, and so was the major. Doug would do nothing to suit the Poms, not if he had to stand there until the moon went through all its phases a million times and the sun began to cool. That was the reason, the justification for his pain, and he would live in that world of pain for as long as it took to undo all of it.

The light was burning directly into his eyes now, shadows alongside the parade ground lengthening. Doug had to stand with his eyes closed against the brightness. Each time he opened them, he saw that the sun had lowered itself a little closer toward the rooves of the huts on the western side. Soon shadows would crawl across the ground toward him like fawning dogs and creep up his legs, his body, his arms and their burden, and finally they would cover his face. He could see the shadows approaching now. His torment was almost over. He was smiling just a little, like Baginda. His legs were cooling. His arms were covered by shade, then his face, and he was a statue still.

o   o   o

The prisoners began assembling for evening tenko. Clive had been watching Doug all day and was astounded that he had stood as he did without moving. It had been a superhuman effort, and when Major Reese-Birnham appeared at Clive's side and said breezily, "Still at it, I see," Clive felt a sudden revulsion for his superior officer.

"It's been absolutely remarkable. He hasn't moved a muscle since sunup."

"And for what, I should like to know. Perhaps the colonel is about to tell us."

Yoshishito was mounting the steps to the microphone platform, and Reese-Birnham joined him there. Clive turned to watch Doug, still with the severed head at arms' length. The public-address speakers crackled.

"See this man before you," said Yoshishito. "Has been this way all day, Australia man. Not move. This man now make leader all Australia mans, whole camp."

There were whistles and cheers from the Australian ranks. Clive turned to see the effect Yoshishito's announcement had on the major. Reese-Birnham's expression was made indistinct by the approaching dusk, but Clive could tell, by close association with him, that the man had been struck a blow.

Yoshishito went on. "This man now leader you," he said, facing the Australians. "Major Ris-Birm now leader English mans only. Also new order now. English mans go down mine. Australia mans load ship."

The Australian response was immediate.

"You fuckin' beauty, Dougo, mate!"

"About fuckin' time!"

"Fuckin' Pommies! Try a bit a fuckin' work for fuckin' once!"

The English ranks began booing. Reese-Birnham went to the microphone as Yoshishito stepped back from it. The major held up his hand for silence.

"Now then, let's have none of that. It must be said, in all fairness . . . "

He paused. Clive watched him. The booing died away.

"In all fairness," the major continued, "it must be said that there may have been . . . a lack of balance in the apportioning of the various types of work we must do here—"

"Too fuckin' right there has!"

"—and perhaps it's best that this inequity be . . . redressed, as it were."

Clive felt himself caught between powerfully conflicting currents. As an English officer and adjutant to the major, he was distressed over the sudden changes Yoshishito had ordered; but as a friend of Doug's, and as a man of conscience, he saw that justice, if such an abstract notion could truly be found within the confines of a prison camp, was at last being served. Reese-Birnham's obvious distaste for the Australians had been allowed to manifest itself fully under the delegation of authority allowed by Yoshishito, who had himself been less than impressed—until now—by the men from Australia.

Clive could well imagine the effect Doug's act of immobile resolution had had on the colonel. The Japanese admired bravery above all. Every prisoner, because he had not committed suicide rather than face capture and humiliation by his enemies, was considered less than human, fit for nothing but slave labour. Doug's eventual surrender had not impressed Yoshishito at all, even though Doug had done it to spare the taking of further life. It had been the act of standing for a full day beneath an unrelenting sun, gazing at the Malay's head, that had turned the colonel's scorn to something like admiration. It made no moral sense whatsoever, but Clive had long since accepted that the Japanese were as unlike Europeans as H. G. Wells's Martians. The commonly accepted norms of human behaviour meant nothing to them. It had been Doug's physical toughness, nothing more, that had given an Australian corporal so powerful a victory over the English major he so clearly disliked. Despite himself, Clive was pleased.

Reese-Birnham had paused again, for much longer this time, and the English ranks were becoming restless. The major was their spokesman, their voice in captivity on Dombi, and an Aussie somehow had made him look like a complete chump. Most of the enlisted men had no more love for Reese-Birnham than the Australians did; they were working-class men who had been drawn into the war for the safety and protection of the British Empire and the world at large. Their senior officers came from another world, a place of privilege and wealth no Tommy could aspire to. The major was a toffee-nosed git who had managed to lose Dombi to the Japs without having put up much of a fight. The empire's greatest source of bauxite was intact and being operated by the Allies for the benefit of Japan. It wasn't right. The major had done it, surrendered the freedom of his men, without consulting more than a handful of his officers. The rank and file did not love him, but he was their leader, for right or wrong, and that meant they shared in his shame, his sudden and inexplicable fall from the strong right hand of Yoshishito. The Tommies looked across the parade ground at the exultant Aussies and felt emotions they had, until that moment, reserved exclusively for the Japs.

"And so . . . the situation being what it is . . . I ask that all of you accept, for the time being—"

"For fuckin' ever, you bastard!"

"—that the . . . the situation here has altered somewhat—"

"Fuckin' oath it has!"

"—and we must follow suit, as it were."

He stepped away from the microphone. Bawling sergeants ordered the prisoners to dismiss and disperse in the direction of the mess huts for their evening meal. Clive could not quite accept that the man who had, until mere minutes before, exercised such complete control over both sides of the camp was now a pathetic figure. The major's head was held high, as usual, but it was not out of pride; Reese-Birnham thrust his chin out to deny what had occurred. His fall had been as swift as that of Milton's Lucifer, cast down from Heaven. The reasons, from Clive's admittedly restricted and subjective point of view, were not dissimilar. The major was coming down the platform steps, his lips compressed. Clive put himself in step with him, but for the first time since his assignment as adjutant to the man, Clive felt that his every footfall need not strike the ground a fraction of a second behind Reese-Birnham's and six inches behind.

Clive turned once before leaving the vicinity of the parade ground, in time to see Doug being swamped by Australians.

Even as he fell to the ground, convinced at last that he had won, Doug could not release the head of Baginda, nor straighten his arms and legs. He toppled sideways under the friendly assault of his countrymen and met the earth like an overturned idol, unsure of the words spraying around him, but certain of their meaning.

17

CLIVE COULD PINPOINT EVENING tenko on the sixteenth of October, 1943, as the moment of Reese-Birnham's eclipse and eventual demise. Everything after that date was different. Clive had never been made fully aware of the relationship that existed between Colonel Yoshishito and the major, but he knew that whatever its nature, it had been terminated on the sixteenth. Reese-Birnham was no longer called to Yoshishito's quarters in the Bandax administration building at odd hours of the day and night. He was not invited to speak over the public-address system at morning or evening tenko, apart from a brief speech shortly after dawn on the seventeenth, in which he stated that those Englishmen with particular knowledge of certain loading operations would remain on hand to teach the Australians their kind of expertise, and those Australians in charge of the mining operation underground would reciprocate.

That speech was known thereafter as the Changing of the Guard. Doug was not present on the platform when it was made and did not make himself available for speeches or scrutiny on any subsequent occasion. It seemed that he had no wish to step into the shoes of the major, not because he was unsure he could fill them, but because he could see no reason why his army clodhoppers should be present on a platform alongside the polished boots of Colonel Yoshishito. Doug Farrands was a custodian in absentia, a leader who ignored the shabby trappings available to him. The major understood none of this and asked for no explanation from Clive, the only Englishman in camp who could have told him why it was that having been allowed only half a throne, the major sat on it alone. Clive could have told the major that Doug was not interested in sharing anything with anyone unless he could share it with everyone. He was a natural-born unseater of kings, and a throne to him, as a Territorian, was useful only as kindling. Clive would have enjoyed explaining this to Reese-Birnham, but he was not asked.

The lack of communication between nationalities became acute, once their working roles had been transferred. Doug simply informed the Australians to do the work the Japs required of them, while he tried to work out a plan whereby one of the freighters that entered the harbour to take on baux-ite could be commandeered and used for a mass escape. Doug made it clear he would not share such a plan, if one was ever devised, with Reese-Birnham, though he would accept as ambassador for the British prisoners a lieutenant by the name of Clive Bagnall; but this man would be kept in the dark until the plan was prepared. Doug would take Englishmen along with him if he possibly could, but if the only options were to escape with nobody but Australians or not escape at all, he was quite prepared to leave every Briton behind, with one exception.

"What's so special about that one, Doug?" he was asked.

"I'm married to his cousin."

"Garn, you never married a Pom, didja?"

"She's an Aussie, no worries, and Clive's a real decent bas-tard. He's the one bloke over there I'd trust, even if he's Major Rusty-Bumhole's adjutant. He's all right, Clive is, and he's comin' with us."

But no plan was born that did not involve risks beyond acceptance. The wharf that now was manned exclusively by Australians did not offer any reasonable avenue of escape. Japanese guards were thick along its length, overseeing the never-ending line of men who conveyed pulverised bauxite from the train that had brought it to the harbour from the mine, to be unloaded and conveyed along the wharf for dis-persement in a steady stream of particles and dust into the cavernous hold of whichever vessel was waiting there. The entire process had been automated, prior to the first bombing raids on the harbour, the raw material transported via endless belts from train to ship, but those devices were gone, reduced to twisted metal that still could be seen protruding from the water. Now the bauxite was carried in woven baskets, coolie style, along the wharf and up the gangplanks, along the decks to the yawning open hatches, and tossed into the darkness waiting below. It was an endeavour akin to filling a bathtub with soil by means of a single thimble; but there were hundreds of thimbles to do the work on Dombi, and they scuttled back and forth like ants, their loads similarly disproportionate to their own size. It was hard work, ceaseless work, but it was conducted in the open air, and the Australians did not complain.

Doug was surprised to learn that no physical labour was expected of him. The privileges of power, always reserved for those who wanted such things, were now bestowed upon him, willing or not. He was made uncomfortable by such ease as the new system allowed him, and had to be persuaded by the medical officer, Ted Moffet, to accept his newfound status as leader of Dombi's contingent from Down Under. "The Pope doesn't have to pour himself a glass of wine, Doug, someone does it for him, and wipes up the drops if he spills it."

"I'm not the bloody Pope."

"Around here you are, and there's nothing you can do to change it. Popes have to die first, Doug, and that tends to mess things up. A long-lived Pope, that's what the people want, generally speaking."

"Just so long as it's understood that I'm thinkin' up ways to get away from here, not just sittin' on me bum."

"Doug, the Pope makes policy for the church, so to speak, and it's expected of him that he use the mind that God gave him."

"You a Catholic, Ted?"

"As a matter of fact, yes. I gather you're not."

"Wouldn't know which end of a Bible to blow, mate."

Ted Moffet was a captain, but he knew better than to point out to Doug Farrands the error of his military ways. Doug was the pope of Dombi, after all, and there was a higher authority than that of the Australian Army whose service Doug seemed to be in, although he gave every indication of being unaware. Moffet, like others before him, found Doug a fascinating study in primitive or unsophisticated psychology. In any other place than this he would have been a ditchdigger, but on Dombi, as a prisoner of Nippon, Doug Farrands had about him the elusive quality of inspiration. He was able, without actually trying, to give hope of salvation to others. It was a gift from God, Moffet saw, even if Doug did not.

"Strategy requires cardinals, Doug. We don't have too many."

"Meaning what?"

"Meaning that this relative of yours, Clive Bagnall, needs to be brought into whatever it is we eventually plan."

"I've thought a that. Clive's a smart bloke, but if we go gettin' him involved too soon, he's liable to cop a hidin' from the rest a the Poms. He needs to keep his head down till the last minute. That'd be better for Clive."

"Even so, he should be contacted."

"No."

"Doug, this rift between us and the English has got to be narrowed. It's the Japs who're our enemy, not each other."

"I've got nothin' against Poms, just the major."

"Then he won't be included, but Clive should be."

"Not unless we can work out a way to do it that won't get him buggered."

"What would you say to approaching Yoshishito with a request for more medical supplies, for us and the English? It'd be a legitimate request. My medical equipment consists of half a bottle of Dettol for sterilizing and a handful of instruments I wouldn't care to peel potatoes with. We need quinine, sulphanilamide, sulphapyradine, Atebrine, and a half-dozen more. We need syringes and bandages, and we need more meat in our diet. Asians might be able to work on rice and chicken, but we can't. Tell Yoshishito our work production would improve if we were fed properly."

"That's a lot to tell a bloke who likes choppin' off heads."

"For anyone else, yes, it'd be too risky, but he admires you."

"He's already done me a big favour, puttin' us all on the wharf."

"The thing is, it wouldn't be just you doing the asking. There'd be someone speaking for the English as well, and since the major seems to have fallen from grace, I thought your friend Clive might be perfect for the job. After you've spoken with Yoshishito, you and Clive can go somewhere private and discuss whatever you please."

"Sounds all right. I'll give it a burl if Clive wants to."

"Let me arrange it. If you walked into the English side of camp, there might be fireworks."

"I am the commanding officer, and if petitions are presented to Colonel Yoshishito on behalf of the prisoners, I shall be the one to make them."

Moffet was in Reese-Birnham's hut, and the major would not hear of Clive representing him. Clive had stood to one side while Moffet explained the plan the major refused to sanction.

"Perhaps you'd like to go with Doug, sir," Clive suggested, "since you represent us and he represents the Australians. Having the two leaders together might be the way to go about it."

Clive knew the major would not accept any arrangement that equated Doug's authority with his own. Reese-Birnham glared at him.

"Your advice will be asked for when and if it is required, Lieutenant."

"Yes, sir."

Moffet, fully aware of Clive's ploy, said nothing.

The major spoke after a half minute of silence. "I shall go to Yoshishito myself, on my own," he announced. "You have a list of the supplies you need, Captain?"

"I do, sir," said Moffet, "but I won't give it to you."

"I beg your pardon?"

"As the camp's commanding officer, you've had more than a year in which to make a request like this. To my knowledge, you haven't done so."

"That is not true! I've approached the colonel on several occasions and been told every time that the Japanese themselves require whatever food and medical supplies reach Dombi. You do know there's a virtual submarine blockade around the island, I take it?"

"Yes, sir, I know that. The point is, if Yoshishito hasn't given you what you wanted in the past, he's not likely to give you anything now, whereas Doug Farrands seems to have made some kind of impression on him. The man may respond to a new voice."

"Absolutely not. I forbid any such attempt."

Moffet and Clive exchanged the briefest of glances.

Clive said, "It's worth a shot, sir. I'll back out of the arrangement if you'd prefer. We can let Doug do the talking on his own. He's quite a talker, given half a chance."

"I have said no."

Moffet began to see why Doug hated the major. This was the closest Moffet had been to Reese-Birnham since his arrival on Dombi more than a year before, and the longest conversation with the man he had been a party to. Reese-Birnham was known to have made perfunctory visits to the English infirmary, but never to that of the Australians. He was a man, Moffet now saw, who did not like to mingle with other men. The major was an ivory-tower type, and if men far below his perch were in need of his help, the major was likely to shift his gaze to the clouds above and ignore events he felt were beneath his interest.

"You have said no." Moffet repeated the major's words, his voice flat.

"I have. Good day to you, Captain."

"And a very good day to you too, sir."

Moffet saluted and left the hut. He half expected that Clive Bagnall might follow, but that would have been foolish, if Clive truly wished to disobey the major. Stealth and subterfuge would achieve more than confrontation in this instance.

Doug and Ted Moffet waited after lights-out at the edge of no-man's-land. They did not wait for long. "Here he is."

Clive approached from the English side, and hands were shaken when he reached them. "You fellows must be mind readers. I was wondering how the hell I'd find your hut, Doug."

"Woulda been easy, mate. Mine's the one with the Free Beer sign outside."

"Naturally."

They began walking toward the Australian infirmary.

Ted Moffet said, "Doug's suggested that the three of us present ourselves at Yoshishito's door first thing tomorrow morning. Can you get away?"

"Of course," said Clive. "The major will squawk when he sees I'm gone, but that can be handled later. Umm, I have a feeling that a petition for medical supplies isn't the whole purpose to this little exercise."

"Told you he was brainy," Doug said to Moffet. "Clive, the chances of a bastard like Yoshishito givin' us stuff like medical supplies is practically nothin'. We'll ask for it, yeah, but what we really wanted to see you about is cookin' up a plan to get away from Dombi by ship."

"A Jap ship?"

"Nothin' else available. We'd fill one a their freighters with prisoners instead a bauxite and make a run for it."

"No details worked out as yet," offered Moffet.

"We thought you'd like to have a crack at thinkin' up a plan," said Doug.

"And you don't want the major to know of it, I presume."

"He finds out, and it gets whispered in Yoshishito's earhole."

"You don't know that."

"I couldn't prove it in court, but I know it. The major gets told nothin'."

"We need to have your agreement on that," Moffet suggested.

"Very well, you have it, but I do think you're exaggerating the major's faults, Doug."

"No I'm not."

"Well, I won't argue. The plan's the thing to concentrate on. I suppose you're both aware that what you've told me so far sounds like something from a boys' adventure story."

"The hard part," Doug admitted, "is gettin' hundreds a blokes aboard a ship. Once we're outa the harbour it's not so bad. The Japs've only got their patrol boats to throw at us, and they're equipped for sinkin' subs, not freighters. The closest Jap airfield's four or five hundred miles away, so they'd have a hard time sendin' planes after us. Once we got movin', we could head south for Aussie. I reckon we'd have a fifty-fifty chance a gettin' there."

"If you can overcome the hard part."

"That's it."

"Doug, there are seven miles between the camp and the harbour. How are you going to move all those men? Use the train that takes the wharf crews down there and back?"

"Too noisy. Everyone's gunna have to walk along the railway line."

"You've got that far with the plan."

"We know it sounds preposterous," Moffet said, "but the mere fact that it's so absurd is the thing that makes us think we might be able to pull it off. You know yourself the Japs are incredibly slack. There isn't a single Jap inside the camp, day or night."

"But there are guards along the wire."

"We sneak out along the railway line, there's only a couple of 'em," said Doug.

"Assuming they can be disposed of silently, and the entire camp empties itself at a jog; assuming every man reaches the harbour while it's still dark—what then? How do you guarantee there'll be a ship waiting, with an empty hold?"

"We make that arrangement first," said Moffet, "and empty the camp at a moment's notice. We know from one day to the next what ships are there and their current state. We're the ones who unload the Japs' supplies. Once a ship's been emptied, it takes on bauxite. We seize that ship while it's empty."

"And do you know where every guard is located along the harbour and the wharf at night? They'd all have to be silenced before you could load a vessel with men and get it under way."

"Someone needs to sneak out and get all that information beforehand," said Moffet. "We know it's a big order."

"Bit of an understatement," said Clive.

Doug stopped walking. "I don't like it here," he said. "I don't like workin' for the Japs. Everyone keeps tellin' me this place is a bloody paradise compared to other camps, and maybe it is, but I've never been in any a those other camps, and this one gives me the shits. If we just hang around and do what the Japs tell us, we're no better than fuckin' Reese-Birnham. He's all for a quiet life, that bloke. We're all supposed to be soldiers, not miners and wharfies."

"But this plan . . . it's not possible that it could succeed, Doug."

"Says who?"

"Me, for one. It's simply too . . . audacious."

"Jeez, Clive, come on, mate. You've been hangin' around the major too long. Know what he wants? He wants to live to see the end a the war, that's all. By then he'll probly be ready to get his pension. He doesn't want any trouble, and he doesn't want anyone else stirrin' it up, either."

"Assuming that's true, is it so bad? He knows that if we attempt anything that gets the Japs annoyed, there'll be trouble, possibly out of all proportion to whatever it is that stirs things up. The Japs are cruel buggers when it comes to punishment, Doug. You haven't seen anything here. Beheadings are civilised behaviour by comparison with some of the stunts they're capable of pulling."

"So you don't want any part of it, eh?"

"I . . . I'll be frank with you both. I'm torn between maintaining the conditions here, bad though they sometimes are, and throwing in my hand to do . . . something that'll tell the Japs we're not docile sheep. That's how they see us, I know."

"Can we take this for a vote of confidence?" Moffet asked.

Clive hesitated before saying, "Very well, if the details can be worked out. It's still an outrageous plan, but then why follow any plan that's merely ordinary."

"So we've got the beginnings of something," said Moffet. "We want this to be shared with the English when the time is right."

"We've got some very able chaps who might be helpful. They've been on the wharves a lot longer than your lot."

"But don't tell the major," Doug said. "I mean it."

"I know you do."

Moffet said, "I think we understand each other, but before any grand plans are hatched, we need to ask Yoshishito for the stuff we need. On the night we pull this trick off, I don't want any sick cases slowing us down. If we escape, we *all* escape. Anyone left behind would be massacred."

"Tomorrow," said Doug. "All right with you, Clive?"

"Certainly."

Clive felt a shiver pass across his shoulders. He could not tell if it was prompted by excitement or apprehension or naked fear—or all three.

°   °   °

Colonel Yoshishito sipped tea while he listened to the petition presented by the three prisoners. He was only mildly surprised that Major Ris-Birm was not present. The major had lost much face when the Australian soldier toppled him. Yoshishito had been very amused by this. His task of maintaining bauxite production for the greater glory of the Emperor, although important, was without honour. The colonel was bored. He had once thought that he would be given the chance to defeat entire armies, but that dream had faded. He had not even taken part in the invasion of Dombi, had simply been installed as caretaker of the island and its industry. He was not in command of the thousands of troops stationed there. He was charged with unloading and delivering all supplies that arrived by ship and filling up those same ships with bauxite. It was not a task that would cause his name to ring through the corridors of history for all time. And so the colonel amused himself from time to time with his prisoners.

He did not have them beaten by guards for trivial infractions of camp rules. The camp rules were the business of the prisoners' own officers. Yoshishito did not believe that brutality for its own sake was necessary for the continued efficiency of the mining operation. He knew, through having read works by Western authors, that the white races were sentimental and would respond better to a full belly than to sticks and whips. Yoshishito held in some scorn the Japanese he was obliged to work with, simpleminded peasants for the most part, who would have enjoyed tormenting the prisoners if he allowed it. He had once heard of a saying, much quoted by those Englishmen who had lived in the East: Softly, softly, catchee monkey. Every man beneath Yoshishito, be he Japanese or English or Australian, was a monkey of some kind.

Three monkeys stood before him now: the tame monkey that usually stood beside Major Ris-Birm; a monkey who called himself a doctor; and the only truly interesting monkey in the camp—the one who had become carved from wood for an entire day. This one did the most talking, even though talking was not a thing he did well. The colonel listened but was not moved by their request. He did not wish to refuse, since that would have made him appear heartless and cruel, which he was not, but he had no intention of giving to mere monkeys any of the precious medicines that lately had become so difficult to obtain. All medicines were for Nippon men. The monkeys would have to content themselves with what the colonel considered to be a generous ration of food. It was a shame the biggest monkey, the English major, was not there to beg, but he had no more face to lose. The major was a very low monkey indeed now.

Yoshishito set down his empty teacup and took a cigarette from his gold case. Lighting it carefully, he surveyed the three unwise monkeys before him.

"I will give to you what I can give," he said. It was a reasonable answer, a polite way of denying them the things they wanted, an answer not so subtle it could not be understood, even by monkeys.

The doctor monkey said, "Thank you," and the English monkey inclined his head a little, in the stilted English monkey way, but the Australia monkey said, "When do we get it?"

The colonel tapped ash from his cigarette. It was a Malayan cigarette, unworthy of being placed inside his gold case, but there was nothing else available. The Australia monkey had not understood. He was a monkey of strength and will, but he was not a clever monkey. A clever monkey would have known he had been refused, would have bowed, and expressed thanks for having been given the opportunity to be refused, and accepted the refusal. Not so the Australia monkey.

"We've got sick men," he said, as if this should be a matter of any concern to the colonel, who smoked further, then said, "Feed them. You have much food."

"But not the right kind," said the doctor monkey. "We must have more red meat."

The colonel allowed himself to laugh. The thought of feeding red meat to prisoner monkeys was simply laughable. They were coolie monkeys and would eat coolie food.

"I will give to you what I can give," he said again. The monkeys were boring him by their presence and their inability to understand the concept of social correctness. He had given them his answer, and they should now depart. He had given them a large enough cage in which to perform their simple monkey tasks, and to their cage they should return.

They began backing away from him. They had understood. He watched them leave. The colonel was disappointed that the interesting Australia monkey had not done something spectacular to amuse him. Perhaps he was not so interesting after all.

The colonel rose from his floor mat and went to his desk. He took from a locked drawer a magazine he had discovered hidden in a filing cabinet when he assumed custody of the mine's administration building. The magazine was filled with pictures of Western women with impossibly large breasts and foolish smiles, who offered their flesh to anyone who cared to look. They were obviously prostitutes, with none of the silken charm and wordless deference a geisha would use to excite a man. White women of this type were also monkeys, baring their behinds, enticing male monkeys to mount them. They were despicable whores, beneath contempt.

He threw the magazine from him, as he had thrown it many times before. When he had lit and finished another cigarette, he would retrieve the magazine from the corner of the room and place it back in the locked drawer. The magazine was a permanent fixture in the drawer, along with a very thick book published in 1937. The colonel often turned to a particular page of the thick book, read the entry there, and smiled. His success as commander of the Dombi camp was based almost entirely upon the few dozen lines of small script that began with the words: REESE-BIRNHAM.

Clive separated from Ted Moffet and Doug and returned to the major's hut. He only half expected that the major would be gone; it had been Reese-Birnham's habit to inspect whatever it was his men were doing, up until the time Doug turned everything around. The major was perfectly happy to watch over the unloading and loading of ships, but he would not descend the mine, now that the English prisoners were engaged underground. He had attempted it once, had ridden to the bottom of the shaft with Clive, then come straight up again, his face slick with sweat. "Hellish . . . ," he had gasped, and hurried toward the light of day beyond the doors. Since then, confined by his claustrophobia to the surface world now run by Australians, he spent most of his time doing nothing, isolated in his hut, and he insisted that Clive keep him company for much of that time. The major had been visiting the latrine when Clive left to attend the meeting with Yoshishito, but he was in the hut when Clive returned.

"Et tu, Brute?" he said, as Clive entered.

"Pardon me, sir?"

"Is there a plot as yet, or is it just a piddling little plan? You can tell me, you know."

"I don't know what you mean, sir."

"You don't lie at all well. I saw you and those two Australians walking up to the admin building. Only one reason to go there, wouldn't you say?"

"We went to ask Yoshishito for more medical supplies."

"The very thing I forbade."

"Yes."

"You'll face a court-martial for this."

"I feel we did the right thing."

"Oh, you do, do you? Begging from the Japs isn't a wise course of action. They despise us all, you know, and begging just makes them think we're lower than dirt. You shouldn't have disobeyed my explicit order, Lieutenant."

"Perhaps not, but I did so anyway."

"And the colonel told you he'd give you what you want, I suppose."

"He did."

"And you believed him."

"I await the outcome of the interview with interest, sir."

"You bloody fool, Clive. You can't trust the word of a Jap, not ever. Nothing will come of this, nothing good, at any rate."

Clive said nothing. The major studied him.

"So now your allegiance lies with your kangaroo cousin, is that it?"

"He's not my cousin, sir; he's married to my cousin."

"Oh, yes. And you feel that this family bond is more important than the crown you swore to serve, I take it."

"It isn't that. . . ."

"Then what is it? Educate me in the rationale of deceit, do."

"We need medicine," said Clive.

"And you feel your Aussie chum can get it for you, is that it?"

"He'll get it for all of us if he can, sir."

"Oh, I'm sure. The fellow's a bloody hero, after all."

"I think you have Doug confused with Saint George, sir. He doesn't slay dragons."

"Another comment like that, and you'll be on report. Your head seems to have been swayed so far off your shoulders you aren't thinking this through at all. Any more influence given to that chap, and we might as well call ourselves coolies and start wearing straw hats."

"Isn't that what we are, sir? Coolies for the Japs?"

"In practice, perhaps, but in spirit, never."

"That's exactly how Doug feels. You're really not so very far apart."

"That is a *ridiculous* statement! Listen to you. . . . He's woven a very tight spell, I must say. Do all the Australians bow down before him?"

"They tend not to bow down to anyone, as a rule."

"Of course. Sons of the soil, rugged individualists, and all that. Well, if the threat of a court-martial can't make you see the light, Lieutenant, I honestly can't find any further use for you."

"I'm not sure I understand, sir."

"Get out. Find another hut."

Clive saluted. Despite himself, he had been stung by the major's words.

"Sir, if you need me for anything . . . "

"I shan't."

"Yes, sir."

Clive's dismissal from the service of Major Reese-Birnham simplified the task set for him by the Australians. With time that he need not account for to anyone, he was able to arrange a secret meeting with a half-dozen British officers, who convened after lights-out in the mess hut. When everyone he had contacted was assembled, he presented in rough outline the plan Doug and Moffet had described to him. There was general incredulity when he finished.

"Absolutely impossible, Clive. Has the old man given his blessing to this piece of madness?"

"The old man and I have parted company."

"Good God; whatever for?"

"My association with the Aussies."

Word of Clive's relation to Doug Farrands had spread among the English following Yoshishito's new work edict. There was an uncomfortable silence for a moment in the hut.

"Can't say I jolly well blame him," said a voice in the darkness, "not if this kind of harebrained scheme is what they want to try. We'd all be mowed down if somebody so much as coughs at the wrong time."

"It's too massive an undertaking, Clive, it really is."

"If you've any influence over this Doug fellow, talk him out of it."

"What was the major's reaction when you told him?—as if I couldn't guess."

"I haven't told him."

"Care to repeat that?"

"Doug specifically doesn't want the major to know about this. He doesn't trust him, not after what happened to the team he came with."

"That was the fault of the bloody little wog whose head he had to stand there gazing at lovingly while the rest of us worked."

"No it wasn't," Clive insisted. "It was someone else, and Doug thinks it might have been the major."

"Poppycock."

"Quite unfair. Bloody ridiculous, in fact."

"Explanation, Clive, please."

"I'm afraid I don't have one."

"You don't mean to say you believe this nonsense?"

"Someone betrayed the Australians. Only the major and myself even knew they were here for those first twenty-four hours, until they were captured. It isn't likely that I'd be the one to turn in a family member, is it?"

Another silence. The officers looked at one another in the gloom.

Clive said, "So you won't take part in this."

"We're not suicidal, and if the old man won't throw his weight behind it, that's that in any case."

"Only if you accept that Reese-Birnham has the last word here," Clive suggested.

The intensified silence told Clive the officers believed precisely that.

"I'll tell Doug what you've told me," he said. "Thank you all for listening to me."

"Better persuade the Aussies to see reason, Clive. They'll be cut to pieces."

Clive was well-liked among the officers, and they were willing to overlook what they hoped was a temporary infatuation with the Australian his unfortunate cousin had married.

Clive said, "I'll pass on your opinion."

"If you think it'll do any good."

The officers began leaving. A few gave Clive further advice on caution before they passed through the doorway. When he was alone, Clive picked up the bundle containing his few possessions. Since packing up and leaving the major's hut, he had been too busy organising the meeting that had just concluded to find other digs for himself. If the reception to his proposal had been more enthusiastic, he might have felt comfortable inviting himself into another officer's hut, but given the skepticism that had been showered on him, he had not had the courage to ask. Clive felt miserable, a man caught between alternatives too profoundly different to merge. He faced a choice, and having chosen, after some minutes of personal reflection, he took himself and his bundle through the British compound and across no-man's-land to the huts of the Australians.

18

ONCE HIS MOVE ACROSS the camp became known, Clive was accused by his fellow officers and the British prisoners in general of bad judgment, at the very least. Some even called him a traitor. There was appreciation among the Australians for what he had done and for the personal difficulties it would engender, and Clive was made more than welcome. These conditions did not last for long. Thirty-six hours after he had moved, Clive was seized, along with Doug and Ted Moffet, by a small contingent of Japanese soldiers and taken to Yoshishito.

"You," said the colonel, pointing to Doug, "you sit there." He indicated a chair in the corner of the office. Doug sat. Clive and Moffet stood before Yoshishito's desk.

"Litter bird brings to me bad news. Two Australia man, one English man, three bad man. Make plan to escape. No escape from Dombi. No escape from mine. Why do you make foolish plan?"

"We aren't aware of the plan you refer to," said Clive.

Yoshishito nodded at a guard, and Clive was struck between the shoulders. He fell to the floor instantly.

"You now." The colonel turned to Ted Moffet. "You tell about plan."

"There isn't any plan—"

Moffet was hit in the back of the head with such force that he fell against Yoshishito's desk before sliding to the floor beside Clive.

The colonel then addressed Doug. "You I do not punish. Two men here, they take your punish for you, half each man."

"No need for that," said Doug.

"Yes! Yes! Verrer much need for that! You are fools! I give to you all food you need, keep away from prisoner hut all Japanese man who like to do hurt! This place civilise! I do this for you, but you wish to escape! You are fools! Now you pay price for fool. This man, that man"—he pointed to Clive and Ted, now lifting themselves from the floor—"they pay price! Take head off both man! Both man say no escape! Both man lie!"

Doug stood up. "No, listen—there was just a bit of a chat about getting away, no plans or anythin', just a kind of conversation, y'know, about how it *might* be possible to get away, nothin' that we really intended to do. It's . . . whaddayacallit . . . "

"Speculation," said Clive, slowly regaining his feet. "Purely abstract, I assure you."

"Both lie!"

"We didn't intend to escape . . . ," Moffet said, his voice slurred. Clive and Doug assisted him up from the floor.

Doug said, "Whoever your little bird is, he's the one that's lyin'. Who is he?"

"Litter bird does not lie. Litter bird genterman."

"It's Reese-Birnham, isn't it? The Pommie officers told him everythin', and he came straight to you."

"You will show respect!" screeched Yoshishito. "Bow head when talk!"

Doug bowed his head.

"Better that way," said the colonel, appeased by the sight. "Now I give you choice. You tell me if litter bird is liar or tell truth to me. If you tell me lie, I take off head, all three mans."

Clive and Doug looked at each other. "We did talk about such a plan," admitted Clive, "but it was speculative, not intended to be taken seriously, you see. It's possible that some of the British officers mistook the conversation for an actual escape plan, but as you yourself have pointed out, Colonel, such a plan would have absolutely no hope of succeeding, not with so many alert Japanese around to stop it, and of course your own brilliant counterintelligence organisation."

"No organisation," said Yoshishito. "Myself only."

"Amazing," said Clive, assuming an awestruck expression.

"Can't fool you, Colonel," added Doug, with what he hoped was an ingratiating grin.

"No," agreed Yoshishito. "No fool me. You two no fool me. Escape plan was real. Foolish plan, but real. You still lie to me!"

"No, really . . ."

"Be silent!"

The colonel lit a cigarette and smoked it.

"Have decided," he said at last, stubbing out the butt. He took three more cigarettes from his gold case. "Bad cigarette," he said, ripping sections off two of the three. "Malay cigarette bad. American cigarette much better. No get any more American cigarette. After war, plenty."

He placed his hands beneath the desk, out of sight, then raised the three cigarettes in his right hand, their ends an equal distance above the line of his thumb and nicotine-stained forefinger.

"Straws . . . ," said Clive.

"No straw; cigarette. You choose, one man each."

"And what happens to the man with the short cigarette?" Clive asked.

"Lucky man get short cigarette. Unlucky man have to smoke long bad cigarette."

No one moved to take one. Moffet was swaying slightly on his feet. Yoshishito became impatient. "All man take one cigarette now!"

Clive chose first, a half cigarette. Moffet reached for the colonel's hand and shakily extracted a mere stub. Nothing could be shorter. "You now," the colonel told Doug, who stepped forward, took the full-length cigarette from the colonel's fingers, and substituted it for the stub in Ted Moffet's hand.

"No, no, you are cheat," said Yoshishito, smiling.

"You said to choose, so I did. I choose this little bloke here. Got a match?"

Yoshishito shook his head. "Give back," he said.

"I don't like to smoke," said Doug. "I want the short one."

Yoshishito pointed to Moffet. "This man, take head off. Lucky for you I only take one. Could take three. Generous mood today. Learn lesson. Not lie to me. Now go."

"Colonel Yoshishito . . . ," Clive began, but the colonel barked at the guards, and Moffet was dragged from the room.

"We ask with utmost humility that his life be spared. . . ."

The colonel held up a hand to silence Clive.

"Not understand how generous my decision, you both. You tell lie, all three. Only one die. Be smiling this does not happen to you. No reason to be sad. Other man will die, not you."

"He didn't do anythin' to deserve it," said Doug.

"Told lie. All mans told lie. Litter bird always tell truth to me."

"What makes you think so?" said Doug. "Could be he's the biggest liar there ever was, eh? Could be foolin' you, he's such a good liar."

Yoshishito shook his head, smiling indulgently. "Many things bad, British Empire. Arrogant mans, always to think better than Asian mans. But English genterman always tell truth, not like you."

"What gentleman?" said Doug.

Yoshishito's smile broadened. He unlocked a drawer of his desk and drew from it a thick volume bound in leather, its spine embossed in gilt letters: WHO'S WHO. He opened it at a page designated with a bookmark, turned the volume around, and invited both men to peruse what was printed there. Clive read it first, slowly, then let Doug scan the entries.

"Whole bunch a Reese-Birnhams," said Doug, puzzled. "What's it mean?"

"Book of English gentermans," explained Yoshishito.

"Yeah, but . . . "

"Our major Reese-Birnham," said Clive, "is first cousin to Sir Hugh Reese-Birnham. Sir Hugh Reese-Birnham is the prime stockholder of Bandax Mining Incorporated. Sir Hugh pulled strings, I assume, to place his military cousin in charge of Dombi, which is, you might say—or was—his."

"This place belongs to the major's cousin?"

"Now belong Nippon," said the colonel. "Major Ris-Birm genterman. Does not lie. You both lie, other man too. Only take head off that man. You be happy."

It was, Doug and Clive realised, an order. They said nothing.

"Go now," Yoshishito commanded, slamming shut the volume of *Who's Who*. "You learn from this. I hear lies tell to me, man dies. You live, both. No more tell lies. Learn lesson."

After evening tenko, Yoshishito made a speech.

"Today, verrer bad thing. Plan to kill Japanese mans, go free in ship. Foolish plan. Three mans make plan, only one man die. Price to pay for foolish plan. Verrer generous, only one man die. Next time, no plan. All mans die next time. You work hard, work be happy, plenty food for all prisoner. No need for plan. To where you escape? Ocean too big. Here you get food all time, plenty food for prisoner. You see now what happen, you try escape."

Ted Moffet was escorted by guards to the middle of the parade ground, then beheaded. His head was placed on a spike over the main gate, alongside that of Baginda Perak and what little remained of the heads of Keith Ramsey, Athol Harris, and Trevor Costigan.

Following the execution, Doug and Clive could barely bring themselves to explain what had happened. News of the reason for Ted Moffet's execution spread through the Australian side of the camp, and a riot seemed imminent.

"That bastard Reese-Birnham's gotta get done!" was a call heard often in the Australian mess before lights out.

"We can't be absolutely sure it was the major," said Clive.

"Bullshit. His fuckin' cousin owns the fuckin' place. Fuckin' Reese-Birnham's just a bloody caretaker! No wonder he doesn't want anyone comin' in and blowin' the place up! He'll probly get a fuckin' knighthood if he keeps things nice and tidy till the fuckin' war ends!"

"He as good as murdered Ted Moffet, and Ted was a bloody good bloke!"

"When's the last time a fuckin' Pom got his head lopped off, eh!"

"Never!"

"Whaddaya gunna do about it?"

This question was put to Doug.

"I dunno," he said. "Got any suggestions?"

"Kill the bastard!"

"Not without some kind of hearing first," Clive said.

"He's fuckin' guilty; anyone can see it, even a bloody Pom!"

Doug held up his hand.

"Don't start flingin' shit at Clive just because he's a Pom. He's the only Englishman here, with us, not over there with the rest of 'em, so pipe down."

"What about bloody Reese-Birnham!"

"We'll confront him," Clive offered, "Doug and myself, and give him the chance to explain himself if he can. It's only fair. You can't judge a man on circumstantial evidence, no matter how strong it appears to be."

"Clive's right," said Doug. "The major gets to say a few words in his own defense. If he can convince me he hasn't done anythin' shitty, you blokes are gunna have to take my word he's innocent. Everyone agreed on that? I'm not gunna go over there unless you agree, so let's see a show a hands. My way, hands up."

Most of those present raised their hands.

"Right," said Doug. "We'll be back before lights-out."

Doug and Clive crossed no-man's-land and went to the major's hut. Several British officers were gathered there.

"What are you doing back here, Lieutenant Bagnall? I was told you now reside on the Australian side of the compound."

"Got a bone to pick with you," said Doug, smiling.

"You might wish to hear what we have to say without witnesses," Clive suggested.

"Rubbish," said the major. "Say what you have to say, and be quick about it."

"Did you tell that little Jap bastard about the plan to escape?" Doug asked.

"There was never any plan," said the major, "just a wild scheme to bring pain and suffering down upon us all. An absolutely idiotic idea, straight out of a child's adventure book. Foolish and irresponsible beyond measure."

"But it was you that told Yoshishito, right?"

"Of course not. Is this what you also believe, Lieutenant?"

"Yoshishito himself dropped several hints, sir."

"Nonsense. Would you care to name these so-called hints, in the presence of the witnesses you were so anxious to dispose of a moment ago?"

"Certainly, sir. Are you the cousin of Sir Hugh Reese-Birnham, majority shareholder in this mine, or are you not?"

Clive noted that several of the officers exchanged looks. The major's expression hardened. "What are you talking about? Are you suggesting I have some kind of proprietorial stake in the operation of this place? That's an outrageous accusation, and you'd better offer proof of it if you wish to be taken seriously."

"Answer the bloody question," said Doug.

"One more example of insolence from you, and I'll have you thrown out!"

"In Yoshishito's office," said Clive, "there's a volume of *Who's Who,* which states quite clearly that you and the person already mentioned are first cousins. Is *Who's Who* correct, or should you sue the publisher for misrepresentation of the facts?"

"All you blokes listenin'?" Doug asked the officers.

"My connection with Sir Hugh is coincidental," said the major, "and has no bearing on the ridiculous charge you have the gall to bring against me."

"So he's your cousin."

"Yes."

"And you told Yoshishito about the plan to get away from here by ship, didn't you?" Doug insisted.

"I did no such thing!"

"And you're the one that dobbed in me and me mates when we came to blow up your precious fuckin' mine, aren't you?"

"Get out, both of you. . . ."

Doug took a step closer to the major. One of the officers barred his way, murmuring, "Steady on. . . ."

"You've got blood up to your fuckin' elbows," said Doug. "You're a lyin' dingo bastard. . . ."

"Throw them both out," the major said.

"No need," said Doug, stepping back. "We don't like it here, do we, Clive?"

"Regrettably, no."

"We think it stinks in here, as a matter a bloody fact. Too much lyin' bullshit, eh, Clive? Never smelt so much a the stuff."

Clive said to the officers, "Yoshishito calls the major his 'little bird.' I just thought you fellows might like to know. You should also be aware that the major has on separate occasions told both myself and Corporal Farrands that the bauxite deposits on Dombi are running out, making the destruction of the place a more or less pointless task. I wish to state, here and now, I don't believe the major's story. It was a ploy to delay Doug's chaps from destroying the mine. Do you deny making that claim, Major?"

"I have never made any such ridiculous statement. The Bandax mine is good for another half century at the very least. . . ."

"Thank you for confirming my worst fears about you, sir. Gentlemen," Clive addressed the officers, "the man leading you is a liar and, I truly believe, a traitor. If anyone is taking minutes of this meeting, I'd like my statement to be taken down verbatim."

"Clive," said one of the officers, "you're doing yourself no good at all."

"Are you all deaf? The major is a liar and a traitor. Aren't you going to do anything about it?"

"Lieutenant Bagnall," said the major, "you're to consider yourself under house arrest pending a general court-martial over the statements you have just made. Take him into custody, someone, please."

An officer approached Clive and reached for his arm.

"This is absolutely absurd . . . ," said Clive.

Doug punched the officer in the jaw.

"That one too!" barked the major. "They can share the dock together!"

Doug and Clive began moving toward the door. The officers held back.

"Look at 'em," said Doug. "Bloody officers, and they can't even grab hold of a bloke. I reckon you poofters need a nice strong sergeant to help you, eh? Go on, call for someone to come in and lend a hand, if you want a fuckin' riot. The Aussies expect us back in a coupla minutes. If we don't turn up safe and sound, they'll come and tear you bastards to pieces. They know everythin' we know. . . ."

"I suggest," said an officer, "that we sit down together and resolve this like civilised people. You can't come in here and expect us to believe every word you say; it's simply too ridiculous. . . ."

"No it isn't. Reese-Birnham's a little dickey bird for the Japs. You blokes oughta be the first ones that want his guts on the table. Look at him. Look at his face. Don't you know a guilty look when you see one? What's the matter with all a you, eh?"

"Clive," said one of the officers, "come back tomorrow without your friend, and we'll discuss these issues in a sensible manner."

"Get a sergeant," ordered the major. "I want both these men placed under house arrest. Will someone kindly do as I say!"

Doug and Clive had reached the door. Doug pointed a finger at Reese-Birnham. "I'm gunna do you, mate." They passed through the doorway together and were gone.

The officers looked at the major.

"I want court-martial proceedings begun immediately against those two."

"Bit difficult, sir, in a prison camp. Don't know that it's actually possible."

"A lack of precedent is no excuse! Arrange it immediately, if you please."

"Yes, sir. Sir, I suggest you don't stay in your hut tonight. The Australians are capable of attempting to reach you under cover of darkness, especially Farrands."

"Thank you for your concern, Captain, but Corporal Farrands does not send any chills up my spine. The fellow's a lunatic, yes, but a blowhard. It's just a pity he's managed to convert one of our own chaps to his way of thinking. Begin preparations for a court-martial, as instructed. If there are any difficulties, I'll settle them with Colonel Yoshishito's permission."

This statement produced a sudden silence. The major added, "Since a court-martial within the precincts of a prison camp has never been conducted before, it will have to be cleared with the Nips, that's all. A formality, you see."

"Yes, sir."

"Conditions are bad enough without madness gaining the upper hand."

"Yes, sir."

Walking back toward no-man's-land, Clive said to Doug, "That settles it, I'd say. Christ, the cheek of the man, accusing *us* of being liars . . . What the hell kind of a person *is* he?"

"A gentleman, that's what. Lookin' after his posh cousin's place while the Japs are runnin' it. He's a fuckin' caretaker, like I said. He doesn't give a shit what else happens, so long as the place is handed back to Sir fuckin' Hugh all spick-and-span."

"It's unbelievable. . . ."

"Nah. Rich bastards, they don't think like you and me do. Different bloody world when you've got the quids, mate."

"You realise there'll be the devil to pay if we tell all your Aussie cobbers what's happened."

"Yeah," agreed Doug, "oughta kick up a stink, all right."

"What I mean is, should we be the ones responsible for triggering what might turn into a bloody confrontation? Now that we know Reese-Birnham's whispering in Yoshishito's ear, we can simply avoid further trouble by not telling any Englishman about our plans, assuming we make some more."

"Clive, I bet it hurts you in the guts to talk that way about Poms, and I appreciate what you're sayin', but I don't see how I can go back to me own side and bullshit to 'em. They deserve to know everythin' we do. If trouble starts up because of it, that's just too bad. The major's the one that made it happen, not us."

"I disagree. We can tackle this situation more intelligently than that. You want to see him dead, don't you?"

"Too right I do. He's killed five good blokes. Killin's too good for a shithead like that. He's low as a bull ant's bumhole."

The open space of no-man's-land was before them when Clive stopped.

"Listen . . . "

"To what?"

"Listen!"

Doug heard it then, a distant droning of aircraft engines.

"Ours or theirs, you reckon?" he asked.

"Ours, I think. Good God, you don't suppose we're about to be bombed. . . . They wouldn't do that, would they? You said yourself the operations against the mine were covert, because of the prisoners all around."

"Yeah, but that didn't work, did it?"

The aircraft engines were louder now. Sirens began howling for the first time since Doug and Q team had been routed.

"But . . . Christ almighty, Doug, we're all of us still here . . . in the line of fire."

Prisoners began emerging from their huts. Clive and Doug hurried across to the Australian side of the camp.

"They're ours!" someone yelled. "They're gunna fuckin' bomb the fuckin' place!"

"Take cover, you bastards!" called another voice.

"What bloody cover!"

There was not a single slit trench in the entire camp; the only digging permitted had been for the establishment of latrines. There were no underground shelters at all, and the huts themselves were no more impervious to flying shrapnel than if made of tissue paper. Doug noticed for the first time that the moon was full, the sky cloudless.

"Perfect night for it," he said. "I bet they can see this place like it was daylight."

"Wonderful," said Clive. "Precision bombing. Any idea how we might survive what's coming?"

"Better hope they can hit the mine and nothin' but."

There was a general movement of men under way already, as the sound of the approaching bombers grew steadily louder. British or Australian, most prisoners began running toward the fence surrounding the camp, this being farthest removed from the obvious target—the main shaft building. The electric lights along the fence had been switched on for several seconds by Japanese personnel panicked by what was drawing nearer. The sirens suddenly stopped. Hoarse commands in Japanese were heard from various points along the perimeter of the camp.

A machine gun began stuttering a short distance away, driving back prisoners who had approached the fence too closely in their rush to escape from proximity to the mine. From the Imperial Army outpost to the east of the camp came the steady pounding of antiaircraft fire, and the sky above Dombi began erupting with sudden puffs of smoke and the lazy arcing of bright incendiary rounds. The planes these were directed at were still not visible, but the droning throb of their engines was palpable, part of the air itself.

Doug took off the Digger's hat that identified him as an Australian and thrust it into Clive's hand. "Look after that for me, will you, Clive?"

"Look after it?"

"Yeah; don't let it get blown to shit, all right, or yourself, either."

Doug was turning away, beginning to run back toward the English side of the camp.

"Where the hell are you going . . . !" Clive called after him.

"Nowhere! Take care a me hat!"

He was gone, swallowed by the waves of men moving in Clive's direction. Clive stood for a moment, wondering if he should follow, when he heard the first shrill whistling of descending bombs and threw himself flat onto the ground seconds before the first stick began thudding across the southeast corner of the camp, in the direction of the shaft. The earth shook with jarring suddenness beneath his chest, and Clive felt fear for his own life come flooding into his heart. His fingers clutched at dirt, as if he might burrow beneath it to safety.

Now more bombs were crashing nearby, like a colossally booted army ordered to quick-march, their detonations overlapping, until every part of the air and ground shook continuously. Clive heard the screaming of men hit by shrapnel as they ran for shelter that did not exist. Then the bombing pattern changed, the army of explosions hurrying across to the mine itself. Clive stayed where he was, in case further bombs should fall outside the target area.

Before he had gone very far, Doug found himself virtually alone. Every man was running in the opposite direction, away from the mine, and the open corridors between the huts were soon emptied. Doug was counting on the one thing he knew the major possessed in abundance—an excess of pride—to keep him in his hut when everyone else began running away. There might be an officer or two remaining there with him, and if that was so, Doug would simply have to turn tail to wait for another opportunity. He had been trained by Alpha Force to disarm and kill with no weapon other than his bare hands, but Doug had always felt the training was something of a joke, with its strictly choreographed moves and countermoves; he trusted only his tommy gun, and that was buried in shit.

Most of the explosions now were concentrated on the immediate area of the mine shaft, as the bombardiers found their range and delivered their loads with increasing accuracy. Several huts had been blown apart completely; others had toppled into the craters where their neighbours had stood. A few had caught fire and were blazing brightly. Doug saw a snake drop from a smoking roof and go writhing across the ground. A shower of atap and bamboo embers descended onto his shoulders as Doug ran, his body bent over, toward his objective.

The major's hut was not hit, nor any of those nearest to it. Doug stopped and surveyed it from cover but could see no signs of occupancy; maybe the major, if he was there, was very sensibly lying on the floor. Doug ran across to a window and peered into the hut, but the darkness there revealed nothing. He swung himself over the sill and dropped to the floor, then began searching for Reese-Birnham.

On hands and knees, he crossed the room, feeling rather than seeing the palliasses beneath his palms. At the doorway to the room he and Clive had vacated no more than five minutes before, Doug paused. The air was becoming difficult to breathe as smoke came drifting through the curtained outer doorway. Two men lay facedown on the floor beside the bamboo table. Doug recognised the major and one of the officers who had been present. He could see no blood on either man's clothing.

"Sir, I think we're burning. . . ."

"It isn't us; it's coming in from the outside. . . ."

"It might be best to leave anyway, sir. . . ."

"No!"

The officer had lifted himself partway from the floor, anticipating that the major would agree with his suggestion, and was on his way down again when he saw Doug coming toward him in a crouching run.

"Sir . . . !"

Doug hit him as hard as he could, his fist colliding with the officer's temple so forcefully that Doug thought he might have shattered a knuckle. The man, halfway to rising again, slumped heavily to the floor, and Doug rolled over him to reach the major.

"You! What the devil do you mean by this . . . !"

"G'day . . . ," said Doug, reaching for the major's throat.

The neck inside his clutching fingers was narrow, scrawny; the major was no longer a young man. Doug squeezed, ignoring the pain in his knuckle. He was going to kill a man, with deliberate intent, and he did not know how many minutes it would take, or how many were available before the officer might be able to pull him away. Doug and the major lay on the floor together, separated by the length of Doug's arms. The major's legs kicked feebly. His eyes were beginning to bulge, and his mouth, wide open, exuded a startling odour of decay. Despite the continual rain of bombs, Doug could hear the awkward sounds of strangulation that came from the major's mouth. The major's hands were clawing weakly at Doug's cheeks and tugging at his hair.

Sooner than he had expected it to happen, Doug felt the other man's body sag. He made his fingers relax their grip and felt for a pulse in the major's neck. He could feel nothing, but his fingers were themselves in such pain from returning blood that he doubted they were sensitive enough to determine Reese-Birnham's condition. The officer was beginning to stir just a few yards away. Doug had to be sure he had done what he had come to do. He took the major's head in his hands and twisted it sideways until he felt the distinct snap of at least one vertebra. The officer was watching him now, with fear in his eyes. Doug released the major's head and stood up. The officer did not move, but his eyes followed Doug to the doorway and watched him leave. When he was alone, the officer realised that he had urinated.

Clive became aware of a great silence but could not be sure of when it had begun. There were no more explosions, and he could hear the sound of retreating aircraft for some time before he raised himself from the ground. Doug's hat lay a few feet away, but Clive could not recall how it had come to be in his possession. He bent over to pick it up and remembered Doug's sudden vanishment across no-man's-land, and no sooner did he think of this than Doug himself appeared, jogging through the smoke of burning huts toward him. He took the hat from Clive and placed it on his head.

"All right, Clive?"

"Yes, I think so. . . . What an incredible mess . . . " Above them a familiar whistling sound filled the air.

"Down!" Doug yelled, and they fell as one man. The whistling grew louder, seeming to last much longer than that of an ordinary bomb. It suddenly ceased, its whistle replaced by the thud of distant impact, but no explosion followed.

"Fuckin' dud, sounds like," said Doug.

Then the earth heaved itself up against his chest. He felt the explosion through every part of his body. It was a detonation muffled by its passage through the earth, an underground explosion.

"Ten-thousand-pounder," said Doug. "I've heard about 'em. . . . Big buggers that go deep, then explode. Takes a single bomber to carry just one of 'em."

"The mine . . . ," said Clive. "They dropped it down the mine!"

They picked themselves up and ran to the place where the main shaft building had stood. It was gone completely, replaced by a massive crater. From beneath the ground came a continuous rumbling.

"The tunnels are collapsing," Clive said. "Hear it?"

"Whole bloody place is comin' apart down there. It'll take 'em years to dig it out."

Other men had joined them, placing their hands on the earth to feel the destruction continuing beneath their feet. "Ten-thousand-pounder, that last one, I reckon," Doug told them. "Big bugger. The whole place is rooted."

"Beauty. Hey, you blokes, the fuckin' mine's caved in!"

"Too bad there weren't any Poms inside."

"That's enough a that," Doug said. "Nobody's goin' down that shithole again."

"You know," said Clive, "with the mine gone, there's a chance to mend the rift between the English and the Aussies. The work schedule, the wharf or the mine, that was the entire bone of contention. Now there won't be one anymore."

"Dream on, Clive."

"Why shouldn't there be an end to the bad blood? The mine's the thing that created it, and now it's gone."

"It's the major that created it, and he's gone too, but the Poms aren't gunna be happy about it."

"Gone? You mean he was killed?"

"Yeah, stone dead."

"You've actually seen his body?"

Doug nodded.

"Well, well," said Clive. "Bit of poetic justice, don't you think?"

"Nothin' poetic about it, mate. I did it myself."

"Did what?"

"Killed him."

"Oh, God, you didn't. . . . Are you having me on?"

"Strangled him. Another bloke saw me do it, too."

"Well . . . I mean to say . . . he damn well deserved it, I suppose, the way he carried on, acting like a little tin god . . ."

"Clive, you better get back over on the Pommie side of camp, if you know what's good for you. The shit's gunna fly over this."

"Don't tell me where I should be, thank you very much."

"Your choice, mate."

"Indeed it is."

They stared at the crater. Doug had heard that there were big craters like this on the moon. He wished, for a brief moment, that he might be there among them.

Forty-two Australians died in the bombing raid, and fifty-three Britons. The Malay kampong, located at a distance from the mine, was untouched. The tallies were submitted to Yoshishito in a predawn tenko. A general groan rose from the ranks of the prisoners as the colonel, obviously unhurt, mounted the steps to the parade ground platform. The public-address system was defunct, the mine's diesel-electric generator house having been demolished by a bomb, and the colonel had to shout to make himself heard. The open space before him was covered by the broken bodies of the dead, placed there in ranks.

"Now you see what your countrymen do!" he screeched. "No care about you! Kill so many! Only seven Japanese mans die! All these mans die! Too many! All to make mine die too! You will dig out mine, every mans! Mine will not die; only you will die! All die to dig out mine again soon! New prisoners come when you die! Take place of dead prisoners! Mine live again soon this way! Now you dig hole, put dead prisoner in ground, all mans! Soon you dig out mine!"

He strutted from the platform.

The burials required all of that day. No food was served, as a punishment for what the bombing raid had accomplished.

No one seriously believed Yoshishito's threat to make them dig out the mine. Even as late as the afternoon, more of the tunnels belowground could be heard, and felt, collapsing. Every man took a turn at the digging of graves, and the cemetery was expanded to three times its former size by nightfall. The Japanese guards kept at a distance, watching their prisoners from beyond the fence, which had sustained no damage at all.

At sunset, two British officers approached Doug as he set another cross of bamboo at the head of another fresh mound of earth.

"Corporal Farrands."

"Yeah?"

"Tonight," said the first officer, his voice prim with anger and distaste, "after tenko, no-man's-land."

"I'll be there."

"Make sure you are," said the second officer.

"Get stuffed."

The officers turned and marched stiffly away. One carried a swagger stick, a sight Doug found pathetic.

Clive approached him, having seen the encounter from a short distance off. "What did they want?"

"Sort of issued a summons, I spose."

"Invitation to a beheading, more likely."

"No one's gunna whack me head off, Clive."

"You're a bit sure of yourself, aren't you?"

"I know it'll take more than a mob a cardboard cutouts like them to do me in."

"You know, there's a moral argument to be made for what you did. If Reese-Birnham had kept his mouth shut and let Q team blow up the mine, there wouldn't have been any need to mount a bombing raid. All these fellows would still be alive."

"Yeah, Clive, I know."

Following evening tenko, the prisoners drifted toward no-man's-land, and by the time full darkness had come, the open ground between the two halves of the camp was swarming.

"Nice turnout," said Doug, shouldering his way through the crowd to reach the invisible line of demarcation, where no one stood.

"What you might call a captive audience," Clive said.

They stood at the front of the Australians. The same two officers who had approached Doug that afternoon came to him again.

"Evening, Peter. Evening, Colin," Clive addressed them. They ignored him.

"Corporal Farrands, we have a signed statement from an English officer, to the effect that shortly after the bombing began last night, you murdered Major Ridley Reese-Birnham, of His Majesty's Armed Forces. Do you deny the charge?"

"Nah; I killed him, all right."

"Beauty, Doug," called a voice behind him.

"Bastard deserved it," said another.

The first officer asked, "You don't deny the charge?"

"I already said so."

"In that case, no court-martial need be convened to determine your guilt or innocence. There will be a hearing to pronounce sentence, however. Your presence will be required for that."

"Now listen," said Doug. "You blokes can tell me I oughta be cut in little pieces for what I did, but I don't give a stuff what you think. I don't care what rank you are, or if you think the major was the most terrific bloke in the world. I didn't think so, see. I reckon he was a traitor and a coward, and a fuckin' hypocrite to boot, and I don't intend feelin' bad for a single minute over what I did to him. He asked for it, and I gave it to him, and if you don't like it, too fuckin' bad."

This statement was greeted with cheering from the Australian ranks, a churning silence from the English.

"You won't attend the sentencing, I take it," said the second officer.

Doug said, "You can take it and stick it up your arse."

He turned away from the officers before they could turn away from him. Clive stayed where he was; despite himself, he was wrenched by sympathy for the English point of view. The Australians were already falling back from no-man's-land, surrounding Doug like a king's escort.

"Your man is in more trouble than he cares to admit," said the second officer.

"He's not my man," said Clive. "He's very much his own man. That's the one thing you seem unable to appreciate."

"He's marked for reprisal, we warn you," said the first officer.

"From what quarter? Yoshishito?"

"We intend approaching him, certainly," said the second officer.

"Within the hour," said the first.

"You must do as you see fit, of course," said Clive.

"You do realise you're in the very worst kind of difficulty yourself."

"Me?" Clive raised his eyebrows. "Why's that?"

"Because you've sided with those unspeakable morons!"

"That's a bit harsh, Peter. They're just not like the English, that's all. Hardly cause for a court-martial."

"Come with us now, and we'll see what we can do."

"No. Absolutely not. I stand by Doug. The major was a bastard, however you want to see him. He betrayed four Australians to the Japs. He's as responsible for their beheadings as if he'd swung the sword himself, and he's ultimately responsible for everyone killed last night in the raid."

"This is pretty much a last opportunity for you, Clive."

"Keep it."

Clive turned away and followed the Australians back toward what remained of their huts.

"I thought he'd see sense," said the first officer.

"I didn't," said the second. "He's lived there, you know."

"Australia?"

"Yes. Seems to have gone native."

"Pity."

19

AT MORNING TENKO, YOSHISHITO STOOD on the parade ground platform with the two British officers beside him. There was an air of confrontation between the English and Australian sides, and Clive was reminded of ancient battlefields, where opposing armies confronted each other in full view, before charging at the enemy with swords upraised.

"Australia man number one!" screeched Yoshishito. "You come here now!"

Assuming this was a reference to him, Doug stepped forward and stood before the platform. Yoshishito pointed a short bamboo cane at him.

"You say truth now! You kill Major Ris-Birm, yes?"

"No."

"No?"

"I killed a little bird."

The Australians began to laugh. Yoshishito allowed the laughter to continue for a while, then held up his cane for silence. When he had it, Yoshishito howled, "You come to me here for punish! Come now!"

Doug climbed the steps onto the platform and stood before the colonel. Yoshishito struck him on both sides of the head with the cane. It was plain to everyone watching that the blows were light, mere taps, despite Yoshishito's lengthy backswing.

"You are disgrace! You are criminal! You make shame on Australia mans! Now go!"

Doug returned to the ranks.

Yoshishito continued. "Mine no good now for take out bauxite! Never good again! Bad for all prisoner! No work here any more time! Now go worse place! Go Nippon! Yes! All change, quick, quick, speedo! You go there, work more hard! Go in ship! Ship torpedo maybe! Same drop bomb on you, same torpedo you! No care about you! Now you pay! Ship go two, three day! You leave on ship then!"

He left the platform, and tenko was done with, the ranks breaking formation without being told to by their sergeants. Even the English, usually well disciplined in matters of appearance, began milling about in confusion. The officers were stunned at Yoshishito's mockery of punishment for the murder of the major, and the lower ranks were disturbed by the news that they would soon be on their way to Japan.

Walking away with Doug, Clive said, "I gave you a fifty-fifty chance of beheading. Did those swats with his cane hurt as little as it looked?"

"Barely touched me."

"I think Yoshishito has a soft spot for you."

"Or a hard spot. Never can tell."

"Good God, I hope not, for your sake."

"Better move fast if he wants me virginity. I'm goin' on an ocean voyage."

The camp fell into a state of excitement and alarm over the sudden changes that had taken place. While no prisoner regarded Dombi with nostalgia, many who had been held in captivity elsewhere knew it had been a better camp than most. There was also the much-discussed question of possible torpedo attacks. There were five vessels in the harbour, four of them already filled with bauxite. The fifth ship would provide transport for the prisoners. The Australians joked often about their convict ancestry and the sailing ships that had brought their great-great-grandfathers to the penal colony at Botany Bay. Australians in prison ships seemed natural somehow. The English were less sanguine. The topic of Reese-Birnham's murder and Doug Farrands's escape from meaningful retribution was lost in the general anticipation of a completely new chapter in the life of every man.

There had been two photo-reconnaissance flights observed over Dombi since the bombing raid, a Spitfire at a height impossible to reach by antiaircraft fire. Each time the plane had circled twice, the merest speck in the sky, before flying away.

"They know what's happened here now," Clive said, discussing the immediate future with Doug. "They'll know the mine is finished and put two and two together with regard to us. When the convoy sails, it'll almost certainly be left alone. Their pictures will tell Allied intelligence the last ship in the harbour is empty. That's the one we'll all be on. Those aerial cameras are quite amazing. They'll be able to tell."

"Bullshit, Clive. They'll try to sink every ship that leaves Dombi, same as ever."

"You're very pessimistic, for a chap who's got away with murder."

"I haven't got away with anythin' yet, and neither's anyone else. Your bloody cameras aren't gunna tell what ship's carryin' what, so they'll have a go at all a them."

"I can't accept that."

"They sent bombers against the mine and killed a bunch a blokes, didn't they?"

"Only because they had to, for the sake of winning the war."

"And they'll do the same again, with torpedoes."

"So you fully expect we'll all be sunk."

"Yeah."

"You don't seem terribly upset."

"I feel like shit, if you must know. Val's got a kid I've never seen. I want like anythin' to get home and see that kid, and her, but there's no guarantees, mate. Wantin' somethin' bad enough won't get it for you. Pure luck, that's all that's gunna do it, for you and me and every other poor bastard that sails away from here, and we can't all be lucky, so I might as well not moan and groan about what happens next, because there's not a bloody thing I can do about it anyway."

"I think that's the longest speech I've ever heard you make."

"Reckon I could be a politician?"

"Not really."

All prisoners were marched along the railway line, flanked by Japanese guards. It required most of one morning for every man to reach the harbour. The line continued along the wharf

and up to the gangway of *Katori Maru*, an aged vessel
streaked with rust. The prisoners ascended the gangway in
single file and were directed to the open hatchways of the two
empty holds. A Japanese officer directed Australians to hold
number one, Englishmen to hold number two.

Clive simply counted himself among the Australians.
"Thank God we're separated. I can imagine the bloodbath if
we were all lumped in together, willy-nilly."

The holds, reached by climbing down narrow perpendicu-
lar steel ladders, were bare metal, the temperature at the bottom in excess of one hundred degrees. There was an
inadequate container of drinking water in each, but no toilet
facilities at all in either; however, this was regarded as good
fortune, since it meant the hatches would be left open, allowing prisoners access to the *benjo* boxes overhanging the ship's
sides. These crude wooden structures contained a plank with a
hole some fifty feet above the waterline. For comfort in the
hold, every man would have the softness of whatever clothing
he possessed and the body of his nearest neighbours. *Katori
Maru* was filled to capacity with more than seven hundred
prisoners.

Loading was completed by late in the afternoon, and the
ship was eased by tugboat away from the wharf to join the four
bauxite-laden vessels already facing the harbour entrance. At a
prearranged time, the submarine net guarding the entrance
would be lowered, and all five ships would slip through to the
open sea under cover of darkness, to be joined at a designated
time and place by their armed escort for the journey to Japan.
It was a system that worked as well as might be expected, and
sometimes worked very well indeed; there were convoys that
went undetected for the entire three thousand miles, while
others were harassed by Allied submarines virtually from the
moment they left the harbour at Dombi. On average, six out
of ten ships plying the Dombi–Yokohama route succeeded in
making landfall.

At dusk, several buckets of warm rice were lowered by
rope into both holds. Every man took one tin cupful and ate
with his fingers. When the rice buckets were emptied, they
were retrieved. Throughout the afternoon there had been a
constant stream of men using the ladders to reach the *benjos*

on deck. It had been decided that the *benjos* on the port side should be allocated to Australians, and those on the starboard to the English.

With nightfall, a guard bellowed down into the hold, "No more *benjo*! You go *benjo* daytime now! No *benjo* dark!"

"What if we have to have a fuckin' shit, mate!"

"No more *benjo* dark! Go shit on mans close you, haa, haa!"

Soon after this exchange, the anchor chain was heard rattling into the chain locker for'ard, and *Katori Maru* got under way, her engines turning over at slow speed as she crawled from shelter to the dangerous waters of the Banda Sea.

"Here we go, then. Off to see the fuckin' wizard, eh?"

"Hope the torpedoes hit the Poms."

"There won't be any comin' our way, mate. The king give a special order about that because a me. I'm gunna marry his daughter, see."

"Bloody handy."

"Can I be a fuckin' bridesmaid?"

"Sorry, you've gotta be a virgin; king's orders."

"How do I get to be one a them?"

The hold filled with exaggerated laughter. When it died away, the sound of singing could be heard from hold number two; the English were filling their metal prison cell with "Rule Britannia." The Australians immediately began singing "Waltzing Matilda" to drown them out. The English retaliated with "Land of Hope and Glory," so the residents of hold number one shouted a song of their own concoction:

On the good ship Lollipop
It's a short trip to the knocking shop
And the tarts there saaaay,
No naughty unless you can paaaay.
There's a tart there with a mouth like a shark,
When she sucks you she leaves a dirty great mark,
And the other tarts saaaay,
We can suck you in the very same waaaay.

Guards began shouting down at the prisoners in both holds, and when they were ignored, the hatch covers were rolled into place, over much protest from below. The temperature, which had been dropping steadily since sundown, began building again from the moment all fresh air was excluded. The singing stopped. *Katori Maru* was well out to sea by then and revealed her sailing characteristics. She was, as one Australian put it, "like me old Aunt Fannie on a Saturdee night—all over the fuckin' place."

Soon the rolling and pitching increased, and those men without sea legs began vomiting in the pitch darkness. From that moment all jollity, real or forced, stopped.

"Looks like it's gunna be a bastard of a trip," Doug said to Clive, "submarines or no bloody submarines. You all right?"

Neither could see the other, but they rubbed hips occasionally as the ship ploughed through moderate waves.

"Yes, so far. Good thing I had a bit of sailing practice on . . . what was the name of that pearling lugger again?"

"Irish Rose."

"Ahh, yes, the property of the manly but sensitive Moxham brothers. What a wonderful thing nostalgia can be. I suppose they're both in the army?"

"Les is. Ken's dead."

"Really? How did it happen?"

"Got into a bit of a fight with him."

"You did?"

"Yeah. Happened on a boat."

"You killed him?"

"Nah, he got taken by a shark. We both went over the side, but Ken was the tasty one, I spose."

"You're joking, aren't you?"

"No, mate."

"Good God . . . "

"I reckon I'll get a bit of shut-eye now."

"Of course."

Doug leaned back against the trembling steel behind him. He could feel the engine's vibrations through his spine and sense the sliding mass of dark water beyond. Mention of Ken had reminded him of the Territory, and that meant he could not turn his gaze, enfolded by blackness, away from the pictures that began rushing at him from both sides of his eyelids. Within a very short while he wished he could allow himself to cry for all the things that had been taken from him, but Clive was right beside him, their bodies touching, and he did not want to appear weak, before Clive or anyone else.

He had become leader of the Australian prisoners, for whom military rank, or the lack of it, was of little consequence. Doug was not comfortable with the role, but he didn't want to let anyone down, now that he had been chosen by circumstances to be what he was. Tears, even those shed in darkness, would have been a betrayal of his unofficial rank. No one in the hold truly understood the kind of man he was, not even Clive. Doug was unsure himself if he understood exactly who lived behind the face that once had stared back at him from speckled shaving mirrors and the curved surfaces of beer glasses. He did not know why Val had married him. He had never asked, and she had never said. He would have given a lot to feel her soft hip touching him instead of Clive's unyielding bone. He was a prisoner, a killer of men without ever having intended to be, and a target now of other prisoners, those in hold number two. Like them, he was also the unwitting prey of submarines somewhere beyond the shuddering hull of *Katori Maru*, prowling like sharks, like crocs, for his mortal flesh. He supposed his soul had been taken long before.

The hatch covers were rolled back at dawn, and the sudden upwelling of foetid air awakened every man who had been able to fall asleep for all or part of the night. Sea breezes washed through the hold like a rain shower, fresh and cool. Men began assembling at the bottom of the ladder to visit the *benjos* on deck. The upward movement of men had to stop every few minutes to permit those who had attended to their needs to return below; the Japanese would allow no more than a dozen or so prisoners topside at any time.

When Doug's turn came at last, he clambered up the ladder, his bladder complaining mightily at every movement, and was able to void himself into the sea a few minutes later. He tried to move his bowels while he was there, but they were locked solid. He came out of the doorless *benjo*, moving his feet slowly, as if seasick, to forestall a quick return to the hold. The day was bright and clear, and he saw that the POW ship and the four bauxite ships had been joined sometime during the night by a Jap cruiser and two destroyers. He then looked around the deck and found himself looking into the surprised countenance of Ishi Murikama.

"Duck . . . ," said Ishi, his jaw dropping.

"Ishi, mate . . . Bloody hell . . . Bit of a fuckin' coincidence, eh?"

"Duck . . . you prisoner?"

"Nah, signed up for a luxury cruise, y'know. Cold beer, hot women. Never turned out that way, though."

"You make joke . . . I see you, I say, not Duck, but *is* Duck! Duck!"

"Better keep your voice down, Ishi. Might not be a good idea, lettin' people know we're friends, all right?"

"Frens . . . yes!" Tears had begun dribbling down Ishi's tanned cheeks. "My fren all time, back long time, now also, still frens . . . yes!"

"Hey, you'll never guess who else is on board this tub. Go on, have a guess."

"Guess?" Ishi's brow creased mightily. "No guess," he said.

"Clive."

"Crive?"

"Yeah, down below. He'll be comin' up in a minute to piss. Watch out for him."

"Crive prisoner too?"

"Nah, signed up for the same rotten cruise. Seen any subs out there yet, Ishi?"

"No sub, no sub! Sub come, torpedo come—*boooooom!* No more *Katori Maru*. No more Duck, no more Crive. All go down, be with fish."

"Listen, I'll be in touch. Talk with you some more, all right?"

"Talk more, verrer good. Crive come up now?"

"Yeah, he'll be up. Be seein' you, Ishi."

Doug climbed down the ladder into the hold and found Clive in the line waiting to ascend.

"You're never gunna guess who's on board."

"Surprise me. My bladder won't allow concentration at the moment."

"Ishi."

"Who?"

"Ishi Murikama. The *Irish Rose*. Am I joggin' your memory yet?"

"Ishi? The pearl diver?"

"He's right up there, waitin' to say hullo."

"You aren't pulling my leg, are you?"

"Fair dinkum, Clive. Go up and have a chat."

"Is he . . . different?"

"You mean has he got a picture a Tojo tattooed on his chest? Nah, it's the same old Ishi, and he's tickled that we're on the same ship."

"Bloody amazing . . . ," said Clive, moving several steps closer to the ladder.

"Listen, Clive, me guts are like concrete. Have a shit for me while you're up there, all right?"

Doug moved away, and Clive immediately felt that everything he had been told was a stupid joke. It was incredible enough that he and Doug had crossed paths, but for Doug to suggest that Ishi Murikama was aboard *Katori Maru* was teasing of the silliest kind. He climbed the ladder.

Doug returned to his position against the hull and waited for Clive to return. Despite himself, he began wondering if it might not be possible to utilise Ishi's presence to the advantage of the prisoners. He pictured an organised takeover of the ship—there seemed to be very few guards aboard, hence the limited number of *benjo*-users at any given time—and a dash by night toward the south.

Clive returned and sat down beside him.

"I could hardly get him to shut up. One of the guards came over and wanted to know what was going on, and Ishi had to pretend he was yelling at me for spending too much time in the *benjo*. The guard told him it's not his job to do that. He's just a sailor, you know, not in the military. He's glad his bad eardrums kept him out of the war, and says thank you."

"Wasn't me gave him the bad eardrums, and I'd say he's in the war, all right."

"Well, anyway, what an incredible thing to have happened."

"Doesn't do us much good, even with a mate aboard."

"You never know. He might sneak us some extra rations."

"For seven hundred blokes?"

"I suppose not. He was tremendously glad to see us both, though."

"Reckon he's glad enough to help us take over the ship?"

"Pardon? You can't be serious."

"Why not? We were gunna break outa the camp and pinch a ship, weren't we, all the prisoners? Well, here we all are, on a ship together, and the Japs put us here. Funny when you think about it."

"Doug, that plan was never more than a gleam in your eye."

"But most of it's already happened. If Ishi could let a few of us outa the hold at night, we could take over this rust bucket and make a run for Aussie."

"While our armed escort steams blithely away into the distance, utterly unaware they've lost a ship."

"Might work if it's dark enough."

"Well, it isn't. We're just five days past a full moon, in case you hadn't noticed. And it's too much to ask of a fellow, to go against his own people."

"Just askin'."

"I don't mean to sound discouraging, but things like that don't happen in real life. It's a fantasy."

"Nice to think about, though, gettin' away."

"I know. When the hatch cover came off this morning, I couldn't help but wish we all had wings. I could imagine us all flying up from the hold like a flock of pigeons and winging our way home."

They stared at the oblong of sky above.

Rice and water were lowered, the buckets emptied and pulled up again. The men yarned and dozed and made trips up the ladder to the *benjos*. There was no midday meal.

"I was going to write a book about the major, you know," Clive confided.

"What for? What'd that bastard do that's worth writin' about?"

"It was going to be a study in noble failure, all about his losing the battle for Dombi against the Japs and then trying to run the camp to the best of his ability afterward, as a kind of compensation. Of course, in the light of what we found out, he's hardly a suitable subject anymore. For one thing, if I told the truth about him, the Reese-Birnhams would probably have me arrested and put on trial for libel."

"Real rich buggers, are they?"

"A very old, very influential family. Army and government and banking, for generations. They wouldn't like it if I slung some dirt in their direction. Listen, Doug, you'd better keep pretty quiet about what happened on Dombi. There could be serious consequences if the story begins circulating when the war's over."

"What, mean to say you expect I'll be alive?"

"You have as much chance as any of us, and better luck than most, I'd say. A survivor—yes, I'd definitely call you that."

"Ripper."

"Anything happen to put you in a bad mood? Apart from the obvious, I mean."

"Put your hand here." Doug indicated the steel wall behind them.

Clive placed his hand against its scaling rust. "Well?"

"Feel the water rushin' past on the other side?"

"No; just the engine's vibration."

"Well, I can feel the water. It's sayin', 'I'm out here waitin' for you lot.' That's what I hear. I'll tell you somethin', Clive—I don't like bein' over deep water."

"But you're a sailor, on and off."

"Coastal waters, nice and shallow. I don't care how many sharks and crocs there are, so long as the water's shallow. Deep water under me bum gives me the shakes."

"I'm shocked, really."

Doug said nothing for several minutes, then announced he was going to the *benjo*. Watching him climb the ladder, Clive felt panic strike him momentarily; for the briefest moment he thought he would never see Doug again, and contemplation of a world without Doug Farrands in it depressed him tremendously. For the first time since leaving the Territory, Clive gave consideration to returning when the war was done. Where else could he find two finer friends than Val and Doug? It worried him that Doug had become morose of late. Clive supposed it was some kind of delayed reaction to the events on Dombi, and perhaps even to the death of Doug's little girl, a subject that had never again been raised between them after that first meeting in Reese-Birnham's hut. Clive wished there were some small thing he might do or say to cheer up his friend, but he could think of nothing practical. He sat with his back against the hull and listened to the unlovely growling of his stomach.

When he had finished in the *benjo,* Doug looked out across the water and saw that the two destroyers formerly in escort had departed; only the cruiser remained, and he knew that every ship in the convoy had become a very plump duck in the sights of any submarine commander who might be following its progress. It was late afternoon by then; in a few hours at most, the sea would be dark enough to hide the slender wakes of periscopes and the thrashing turbulence that streams from high-speed torpedo propellers. He felt a little sick. Darkness would come too soon.

"Duck, I watch, wait for you."

Ishi was standing several feet away, not looking at him, pretending to inspect the lumber and lashings of the *benjos.*

"G'day, Ishi. Where'd the destroyers go?"

"Go two hour. Need somewhere else for fight, captain say."

"Been in the war much, Ishi?"

"Sunk two time now. Save two time. No die. Wish war go stop now. Finish all sink, all die. No more sink. Go home, everybody. See famery, be happy."

"Yeah."

"Duck, night come, hatch put over, captain say."

"We had a bloody hard time of it last night, Ishi. Why do they need to put the hatches on? We won't do any more singin', if that's what did it."

"No sing. No for that. Make you die if torpedo come, captain say."

"They want us to go down with the ship if she's hit?"

"Captain say no mans live, so hatch put over. Keep you in ship, ship go down."

"Very nice."

"Captain hate submarine. Torpedo come, all you die, he say."

Ishi suddenly walked away. When Doug looked, he saw a guard approaching, gesturing for Doug to get below. He climbed back down into the hold.

"Destroyers are gone. Ishi says there's a fight goin' on somewhere else."

"So there's only a cruiser left watching over us?"

"That's all."

"Oh, bugger."

Doug's news was passed around, and the atmosphere in the hold became subdued, as the implications of a convoy virtually unescorted became clear. The mood of the men brightened a little when their evening rice was lowered to them, then plunged into anxiety as the hatch covers were set in place again after the sky grew dark.

"Anyone know where they keep the fuckin' life jackets?" someone asked, and was told to pipe down.

Sitting beside Doug in the pitch darkness, Clive could feel waves of tension flooding from him. He had never considered that Doug might someday show signs of fear, but Clive was himself haunted by thoughts of sudden death smashing through the thin steel wall separating prisoners from sea, and he assumed every other man felt much the same way. The silence in the hold was one not of weariness but of apprehension. Utter helplessness was, Clive decided, the most frustrating of feelings.

Eventually Clive slept. He dreamed he was in London, walking along the Serpentine, as was often his pleasure on idle Sundays. As he walked, he became aware that he was being followed, but was afraid to turn around. His discomfort grew, until he forced himself to turn suddenly and confront the follower. It was Doug. Clive woke up.

He turned in Doug's direction, breath rasping in his throat.

"All right, Clive? You sound a bit rough."

"Yes . . . bad dream, that's all."

"Sleepin', eh? Lucky bastard."

"When this is all over and done with—the war and everything—I think I'll go back with you, if that's acceptable. To Australia, I mean. After what happened back there—on Dombi, that is—I don't know that I could ever be comfortable again in England. I never thought I'd feel this way, frankly. I suppose I'm a pretty poor kind of Englishman to even contemplate such heresy, a traitor in my heart, something like that. I can't help it, though. There's nothing left there for me. There wasn't when I left in '39. But now there's something in your country, do you see what I mean?"

"Redlands. You own half."

"No, not that. It's—"

The blackness around them suddenly was filled with the sound of a colossal explosion, followed by an overwhelming reverberation. Clive imagined that it must feel this way to be inside a cathedral bell while it is rung. The clapper had hit with tremendous force in another part of the ship, and the sonorous tone of its impact continued long after.

"Torpedo!"

Every man was on his feet, yelling for the hatch cover to be removed.

Another explosion, louder than the first, came to them, and their panic increased.

"Shuddup!" Doug shouted. "Shut your bloody traps!"

There was some semblance of quiet for a moment.

"They both hit aft in the engine room, sounded like. They're not gunna put more'n two torpedoes in a shitbucket this size if they can help it, so no one's gunna get blown to bits. We just need to get out and start swimmin' before she goes down. Coupla the blokes nearest to the ladder, get up there and see if you can't roll the hatch cover back."

"She's goin' down already—feel it?"

Katori Maru was settling by the stern.

"Get your arses up there!"

But the hatch cover was already rolling back. Before the first men on the ladder were halfway up, the hatch was wide open.

"The bastards aren't gunna let us drown, after all," Doug said to Clive, then shouted, "One at a time on that fuckin' ladder! There's plenty a time for all of us to get out if you don't bloody panic!"

Clive said, "I'm trying to think if I saw any lifeboats on deck."

"There's a few aft, I think, but nowhere near enough. This tub's only supposed to carry a coupla dozen crew, and I bet those buggers are already pissin' off in 'em."

Clive resisted the urge to elbow his way through the jostling men to reach the ladder, its narrow frame and rungs already swollen with bodies clambering up on both sides. The ship was settling deeper by the stern, and the shouts of men waiting to climb the ladder became more urgent and profane.

"How long before she goes under?" Clive asked, trying to keep his voice steady.

"Dunno; depends on how big the torpedo holes are and whether the crew closed the engine room's bulkhead doors before they buggered off. I reckon she'd be goin' down a lot faster than this if they hadn't. We'll get out with everyone else, mate, no worries. The hard bit starts once we're in the drink."

The sound of further explosions came to them from a distance, and the sky framed by the hatch began glowing redly. Doug counted eight more torpedo hits on the rest of the convoy during the minutes while he and Clive waited.

"Right," he said. "I reckon we've been heroes long enough. Go for the ladder before it tips too far over."

They joined in the jostling crowd at the ladder's base and soon were climbing it on opposite sides. The ladder had already tilted nearly fifteen degrees from vertical and was becoming more difficult to ascend. Both had their hands stepped on by men ahead of them. The sky outside was becoming brighter as fuel oil from ruptured tanks caught fire. The sound of screaming was everywhere, a universal chorus behind the continuing explosions and shouting and swearing. Doug and Clive were covered with sweat by the time they reached the edge of the hatch. By then the ladder was tipped twenty degrees.

The sea was burning in dozens of places, the nearest a half mile or so away, the red glow reflected back down from the undersides of its own roiling clouds of smoke. Men were standing about on the tilting deck, unable to decide what they should do to save themselves. The hatch cover on number two hold had been rolled back also, and men were streaming from it as fast as they could climb the ladder. Doug went to the side of the ship and peered over. Hundreds of men were already in the water. There was no sign anywhere of lifeboats. Heads bobbed like corks on the waves. Some men were swimming away from the ship; others simply floating where they had landed after jumping.

"Shall we?" Clive asked.

"Might as well," said Doug.

They climbed the safety railing and prepared to jump.

"Crive! Duck!"

Ishi Murikama was pulling at them. "You come, you come!"

"Ishi, you little beauty. Was it you that opened up the hatches?"

"Open up, yes! All sailor gone! Go verrer fast! Torpedo *booom*, sailor gone, five minute! No look to hatch! I open! Frens come out now!"

"Thank you," said Clive. "Thank you a thousand times. . . ."

"Come, come, no jump yet. Come see."

He led them aft. The deck between the wheelhouse and the stern was already awash, but Ishi waded directly into it, beckoning them impatiently. No other men had gone aft because of the water slopping over the deck there. "Come, come! No wait!"

"What's back here, Ishi—a boat?"

"No boat; all gone. Other boat."

The water was up to their waists before Ishi located what he had come aft to find; he thrashed in the water for a moment, then lifted a long, thin rope above his head. He handed this to Doug. "You pull, pull, boat come."

Taking the rope, Doug yanked at the wrong end and realised it was tied to the deck. He pulled hard the other way and felt something at the rope's far end move toward him. He could not see it despite the reddish light all around.

"There!" Clive was pointing. A small life raft was skipping toward them. The water was around their necks now, although they had not moved since Ishi found the rope. Ishi, no more than five feet high, was already swimming.

Doug yanked hard to bring the raft within grasping distance before his feet were lifted from the deck. Ishi was the first aboard. Doug pushed Clive up and over the plump canvas side, then swung a leg inside the raft. Ishi was slashing at the rope with a sheath knife. Clive pulled Doug aboard at the same instant the rope parted. The raft immediately began drifting away from *Katori Maru*.

Men were jumping from the deck in increasing numbers as water ran for'ard from the stern, now completely awash. The bows were raised above the waterline, revealing patches of barnacles and weed. Another explosion from a distant ship came to them, shock waves passing through the water a little behind the blast conveyed through the air. The raft shivered as it was touched.

"There's room for more than just us," Doug said, and took hold of a paddle wedged under a thwart. Clive took the other, and they maneouvered closer to the nearest swimmers. *Katori Maru* aimed her bows at the sky and began slipping backward beneath the waves. The last few men aboard jumped too late and were dragged under by the powerful suction created as the ship left one element to sail stern-first into another. Their screaming was cut short as they were pulled down.

"Jesus . . . Jesus . . . ," Clive heard Doug murmuring as they slashed at the water with their paddles.

The sea was ablaze across fully one third of the horizon in all directions, the air filled with distant screaming and the steady roar of burning oil slicks. The cruiser was dashing between lakes of flame in search of submarines. Clive could see only one other ship afloat, and that also was burning. It was a vision of maritime hell.

"Come on, mate, up and in, as the actress said to the bishop."

Doug pulled a swimmer into the raft. Seeing this, others began splashing toward them. Within a very few minutes there were nine men aboard something meant to accommodate four, and many score surrounded the raft, pleading to be allowed into it. Those nearest grabbed hold of the safety rope around the raft's edge, and more men took hold of those men, until the raft became the center of a floating formation. It could no longer proceed in any direction, could only drift and maintain the lives attached to it.

Other rafts could be seen, silhouetted by fire. Lifeboats, presumably manned by Japanese, worked their way among the shifting oil fires. The cruiser was turning in a tight arc, when her stern suddenly fountained outward in a blast of water and smoke, and the arc straightened immediately. "Lost her rudder," said Doug. "That sub captain's a cheeky bastard, takin' on a cruiser."

"You buggers in there," called a voice from the water, "how about lettin' a few of us climb in and get dry for a while! Share and share alike!"

"Yeah, come on, there's blokes out here covered in fuckin' oil!"

"Fair enough," said Doug. "Everyone gets a turn in the raft."

"Throw that fuckin' Jap out first!"

Doug held up his hand. "Wait a minute! This Jap's the one that opened the bloody hatches after all his mates pissed off! Every man here owes his life to this bloke, and if he gets the short end from anyone just because he's a Jap, I'll personally do the bastard, all right?"

"Come on! Come on!"

Doug slipped into the water, followed by Ishi and Clive. Three men took their places. Doug turned to watch the cruiser's progress and saw it steaming at full throttle away from the fires. It vanished into the darkness beyond in less than a minute.

More and more men attached themselves to the outer perimeter of the floating web around the raft. Another raft drifted nearby, similarly festooned, and the shouting that passed between them established that both groups spoke English.

"Listen!" Doug shouted to make himself heard above the general moaning and swearing. "This isn't gunna work for too much longer! There's too bloody many of us! Soon as someone sees a lifeboat anywhere near, even if it's full a Japs, give us a shout and we'll try and take it over. There's gotta be more of us than them, ten to one at least, even if every Jap sailor got off all the other ships that got hit! They're outnumbered! Don't forget that! Any lifeboat that gets seen gets taken over! Some of us are gunna drown before too long, so keep your bloody eyes peeled!"

The rotation system replaced those men in the raft with more from the water, forcing Doug, Ishi, and Clive farther from it by the progression of those men at the outer edges of the circle to its centre.

"We have to stick together," gasped Clive, the taste of oil lapping into his mouth, "the three of us, whatever happens."

"Too many mans," said Ishi. "No good this. Go find some other."

"Yeah, but find it with your eyes first," Doug said. "Don't just go swimmin' off and hope to find a boat."

"Find boat, had boat, now boat gone," Ishi said. "Too many mans. Nex time stay far way, jus three mans in boat."

"Three men in a boat," said Clive. "That's bloody funny."

"No funny, no funny all mans in boat. Boat too small."

"No, I mean, it's a famous book—*Three Men in a Boat*. Really, it's very well known. Jerome K. Jerome . . . Quite a good read, actually . . . "

"Clive," said Doug, "concentrate on what's happenin' right here and now, all right?"

"Certainly."

They were passed eventually to the edge of the floating formation. In their passage through the rings of men, Doug had heard both English and Australian accents, but by the time a fight erupted aboard the raft, he was too distant to identify the troublemakers by nationality. It was evident a battle for supremacy was in full sway, the men already in the raft being determined to stay there.

"Christ . . . stupid bastards," said Doug.

"This is not going to end well," Clive predicted.

"Too bloody right it won't."

Clive thought it was like witnessing a poorly lit, indifferently photographed scene in a film from the back row of the balcony: a fight scene, in which there were no dramatic close-ups of flying fists and angry faces. There were the sounds of scuffling and curses, and sudden lurches of this body or that as they were pulled into the water or fought off arms reaching toward them from below. It all seemed curiously unrelated to his own predicament. He was at least fifteen yards from the fray, and it was not real; at any rate, it was less real than the unreality of finding himself immersed in a warm and filthy sea, with little chance of survival. He was involved in a hideous adventure, without heroes or heroism, and it seemed likely that all participants would die. Beneath him was nothing but water, above him nothing but air. Only the arms of Ishi on one side and Doug on the other prevented him from thinking the whole thing a maddening dream from which no avenue of escape presented itself.

"Duck, you see . . . !"

Ishi was pointing to something that floated nearby. Clive could not identify the object, but he allowed himself to be detached from the raft's circumference of humanity and steered quietly by Doug and Ishi toward the floating thing. It turned out to be a heavy spar, ten feet long, eight inches by eight, its surface rough and splintered with use.

"Put under cargo," Ishi said, "so make not move, big storm."

"A wedge, you mean," said Doug. "Nice and private."

The raft and its attendant population was already drifting away. Their departure had apparently gone unnoticed.

"No good, mans fight," said Ishi. "Mans fight, soon all mans die. We no fight, no die. Stay not die that way."

"That's it, mate. You're a bloody philosopher, Ishi. Hangin' on all right there, Clive?"

"More or less. Can you see any lifeboats?"

"Saw some before, but they were a long way off. Probly Japs."

A brilliant explosion, many miles away, suddenly lit up the sky. Seconds later, they felt the strength of it through their lower torsos, as the blast was conducted at a slower rate through the water. A series of shattering detonations followed, each one revealing the world from horizon to horizon.

"There goes the cruiser," said Doug. "No one's gettin away from that alive. . . ."

Clive watched Ishi's face, as best he was able. Japanese by the hundreds were dying, and he wondered about Ishi's feelings, but he saw nothing reflected in his eyes that he could not imagine seeing in a mirror held before his own face. Britons and Australians by the hundreds would die as a result of the submarine attack, and Clive was grateful that he was, as yet, not among their number.

"Lucky to be alive . . . ," he burbled.

"Amen," said Doug. "Let's get outa the water, gents. Me hands are turnin' into prunes. Ishi, you first, mate. Up and over."

Ishi straddled the spar as if it were a horse. Doug followed, then assisted Clive onto his wooden perch. The spar sank several inches below the water but was bouyant enough to support their combined weight. They watched the last of the cruiser's ammunition being consumed by fire and could not quite believe the display was over when darkness again invaded that section of the horizon. All the fires were behind them now, although they could still see the raft and its patch of floating heads and hear the continuing sounds of the struggle for survival occurring there.

Clive was suddenly grateful for his separation from the raft. He was much better off with these two men than if he had stayed behind with the rest of the prisoners. He wondered, staring at the back of Doug's drenched shirt a few feet in front of him, if the Australian was experiencing some greater sense of loss over the inevitable deaths of his own kind; but as was usual with Doug, whether one faced him or not, it was impossible to know what he truly thought or felt. Clive had survived the sinking of *Katori Maru,* and he would, in the company of his two friends, survive whatever might follow. He was a prisoner no more, and he had never felt more alive. The most surprising aspect of his current state was the acceptance, if it should happen, of death. Clive felt a kind of exultation over his discovery and hoped that it was not the result of some insidious madness that typically seizes those in adverse circumstances.

The spar was drawn on a powerful current past more debris and bodies, most of them so badly burnt or oil-covered that it was impossible to distinguish the Japanese from their former prisoners. The sea was a liquid graveyard, its floating dead drifting among funeral pyres, themselves adrift. Sometimes, from out of the darkness, the sounds of screaming came to the men on the spar, then those screams were left behind, replaced before long by others. The air remained thickly redolent of burning oil, and the smoke from drifting fires obscured the stars.

"See boat! There!" Ishi was pointing to the left.

"Might be Japs," Doug warned. "Hang on for a bit and let's see."

They could hear shouting and groans from the boat, now less than a hundred yards away, but not until the distance had been halved were they able to distinguish phrases in English coming from the boat, which, they now saw, was surrounded by as many bobbing heads as the raft had been.

"No room at the bloody inn, looks like," said Doug.

"We should stay with them anyway," Clive said, "just in case they're rescued. A big crowd like that's going to be seen a lot easier than us."

"Rescued by who? Every ship's gone down. Hey, you blokes! Got any first-class cabins?"

"Who's that?" a voice answered.

"Blackbeard the fuckin' pirate. Who're you?"

"Come over here if you're afloat and can reach us! We can't manoeuvre at all!"

"Right-oh!"

Doug and Ishi and Clive began paddling. When they reached the nearest floating men of the hundred or so surrounding the lifeboat, someone in the water said, "G'day, Doug! Made it out all right, didja?"

"A healthy turd always floats, mate."

"Is that Farrands?" came a voice from the lifeboat. It was an Englishman, not an Australian, and his accent had the clipped accent of an officer.

"Yeah!"

"Who do you have with you?"

"Clive Bagnall and Ishi Murikama!"

"A Jap?"

"Not *a* Jap! *The* Jap that opened up the hatches and gave every one of us bastards a chance, that's who!"

"Lieutenant Bagnall, are you there?"

"Yes!"

"You may join us if you wish. You'll have to take your turn in the water if you do."

Doug shouted back, "What about me and Ishi?"

"I can't answer for the safety of the Jap! We only have your word on who he is! As for you, you're not welcome!"

"Eh?"

"You know the reason, Farrands! Don't come any closer! We don't want any part of you!"

"How many Aussies in that boat?"

"A handful, no more, and some in the water! The rest of us are English! You're not wanted here, Farrands!"

"Peter!" Clive called. "Is that you?"

"Yes! You can take your chances with us if you choose to!"

"Give Doug a chance too, you bugger!" yelled the Australian beside the spar.

"I have a Jap pistol here," called the officer. "If you attempt to come aboard, Farrands, or even if you join those in the water, you'll be shot!"

"Save the bullets, you whacker! I'll stay where I am!" He

turned to Clive. "Go on, mate, hook up with this lot if that's what you want."

"I'd prefer to keep riding our piece of wood."

"Ishi?"

"Stay here. No trus not to hurt."

"Clive, last chance."

"No."

Doug shouted, "Hoo-roo, you Pommie bumhole! I hope you have a fuckin' mutiny!"

"Go to hell, Farrands!"

"Nah, I'd meet you there!"

He began backpaddling to separate the spar from the floating men. Clive and Ishi joined him, and the gap widened.

"Be seein' you, Doug," said the Australian in the water. "Watch out for yourself."

"You too, mate. Don't take too much bullshit from the Poms unless you have to."

"Reckon I have to for right now. I'll buy us both a beer back home, eh?"

"Beauty."

The spar was moving past the floating men. From here and there among them came words of encouragement.

"Home for Christmas, Dougo!"

"Can't help you, mate! There's not enough of us!"

"Don't worry, you lot!" Doug said. "We'll beat you all back to Aussie and have the booze and sheilas standin' by!"

The spar and the lifeboat drifted swiftly apart. Within five minutes the men in the water were no more distinguishable than an oil slick, the lifeboat at their centre a blob of deeper darkness against the sea.

"You didn't have to stay, Clive."

"I most certainly did. Are sharks liable to nibble our toes if we keep our legs dangling in the water?"

"I've smelt your feet, Clive, and if I was a shark I'd clear off."

"How reassuring."

"No piss," said Ishi.

"What?"

"No piss in water. Shark come for piss, same blood. No piss."

"There y'are, Clive. Advice to bear in mind."

"I wish I hadn't asked."

The last of the fires were several miles away now, their light reflecting from the pall of smoke suspended above them like that of far-off cities beneath storm clouds. The night breeze was mild, and the waves, which rose no higher than the waists of the spar's riders, were positively warm. The farther they were swept from the area of the sinkings, the more vast both sky and sea became, until it seemed that the length of wood and the three men upon it were suspended like a twig between infinite hemispheres of air and water. They could find no words to encourage each other.

"Try and stay awake, everyone," Doug said. "If you fall off we mightn't be able to get you back in the dark. I never asked before, Clive, but can you swim?"

"I can dog paddle a bit, that's all. I was never keen on sports, you see."

"Keep a good hold on the wood, then, or hold on to me, if that's easier."

"I'll be perfectly all right. I'm not about to doze off, you know, not after all that excitement."

Time was a concept impossible to measure, given the circumstances, but Clive estimated it was about eighty minutes later when he first heard the engines.

"Listen . . . "

"Submarine come," said Ishi.

"Where?"

"See nothing . . . "

"There!"

Clive pointed across the water to a slender length of blackness, its conning tower standing square against the silvered waves beyond.

All three men began shouting at the object, at least a half mile distant, which clearly was heading against the current, back toward the scene of its kill. They could not see if any seamen were standing watch on the tower, and the breeze blew their shouting back into their faces. Within minutes the submarine was gone, the throb of its diesels diminishing rapidly.

"Bugger," said Doug.

"Shout too small," said Ishi.

"Might be more about," Doug suggested. "I can't swaller one sub doin' all that damage. Be ready to screech your guts out if we see anythin'."

But there were no other submarines; or none that came near enough to be seen. Clive judged the time to be well past midnight, possibly as late as two A.M. He was fairly sure he hadn't fallen asleep on the spar at any time, but there had been one occasion when he found himself toppling toward the water, only to bump his shoulder against Doug's back and be brought upright again, in a state of confusion and embarrassment.

"All right back there, Clive? You can sit in the middle if you want to."

"That isn't necessary, thank you."

"Don't want you fallin' off."

"I was not falling. I was . . . rearranging myself."

"Well, watch it. A bloke can get very wet that way."

"Point taken, I'm sure."

Clive fell from the spar before dawn and was awakened by the shock of salt water entering his nose. Doug dragged him back to safety without a word. Clive was surprised to see the faintest of light along the horizon. They had drifted all night. He searched for signs of smoke and found them at last, grey smudges low in the sky, almost hidden by the retreating night. They grew more distinct as he watched. There was nothing else to see; no other raft or lifeboat or piece of flotsam bearing prisoners or crew. They were utterly alone, and the new day's light showed how very shabby they were, their ragged clothing touched here and there by oil, salt caking in the seams, their hair standing on end, whiskers thick with grime.

Clive was appallingly thirsty. He was aware that his stomach was empty, but the clamouring of his innards could not compare to the stricken state of his throat. The waves lapping at his belt and thighs was torture, the sounds of salt water producing in his thoughts the very taste of fresh. He studied Doug's back and decided not to mention the subject of thirst. Doug's shoulders were slumped with weariness and dejection. Ishi, a few feet ahead of Doug on the spar, gave an impression of alertness, his head turning back and forth in search of ships that might rescue them.

"See anything, Ishi?" Clive croaked.

"No ship. All gone."

"I suppose that puts us well and truly up the familiar creek, does it?"

"Pretty much," said Doug. "Might get lucky, though. Could rain. That time a year. The Wet's goin' good and proper down in the Territory right now. We could cop some out here; you never know."

"Is it . . . " Clive hesitated, then began again. "Is it a myth about sea water driving you mad if you drink it?"

"Couldn't say," said Doug. "Never had to try it out meself. How about it, Ishi? Can you sip a bit a sea water now and then and not go ravin' bonkers?"

"No good, no! Too salt! Make you more thirst, then have more, then go mad. No drink. I no drink, you no drink. Nobody drink."

"That settle it for you, Clive?"

"Rather."

The sun began edging up from the line of the sea, bulbous and malevolent, a brilliant orange hue. It separated itself from the horizon with startling swiftness and proceeded into the air like an agitated balloon, its circumference appearing to quiver. Clive found himself hypnotized and had to force his eyes away from it. He suspected, passing a thickened tongue across his cracking lips, that the day ahead would prove far more torturous than the night that had preceded it.

When the sun stood at fifteen degrees above the horizon, their faces felt its warmth; when it stood at twenty-five degrees, their exposed forearms become very warm to the touch, and at forty-five degrees they became afraid of what they would experience when it approached the zenith at noon. Their shoulders already were baking, their heads heavy and aching beneath the bombardment. No one spoke.

His submerged thighs and dangling legs were chafing against the rough edges of the spar, and Clive began to worry about blood seeping into the water, attracting sharks. He placed his hands between wood and flesh and enjoyed several minutes of comfort, but it became far easier for him to lose his balance that way, and so he resumed holding on to the spar, with one hand placed before him and one behind. He had allowed a little urine to escape his bladder, but was afraid to mention that this had taken place. It had occurred more than a half hour ago, and he was beginning to hope there had been no sharks near enough to detect it, when Doug muttered, "Fuck . . . company's arrived."

A dorsal fin was cutting through the water less than twenty yards away. Clive almost fainted with fear; he was terrified of what might happen as a result of his incaution.

"Only a tiddler," Doug said, "probly less'n five foot."

"Big enough to bite . . . ," Clive whispered.

"Just keep your eyes on him. Nothin' to worry about unless he comes a lot closer and starts rollin' onto his side. They do that before they rush in for a bite."

The shark circled three times, each time moving closer. "Curious little bugger," said Doug. "Might mean trouble."

Ishi's sheath knife was in his hand, ready. The shark circled a fourth time, then turned toward them and disappeared beneath the surface.

"Legs up!"

They lifted their legs onto the spar, almost upsetting themselves from their narrow perch. Clive saw the shark, its back a beautifully mottled grey, pass directly beneath them. "Oh, God . . . "

"Keep 'em up," Doug warned. "He'll be back for another go."

The shark surfaced, about ten yards distant, and began circling again.

"Legs down again, before we bloody well tip over. Get ready to yank 'em up if he makes another run at us."

The shark was halfway through its second circling when Clive, to relieve his fear, took his eyes from the fin and saw the lifeboat. It was less than a half mile away, he estimated, and he could see no occupants aboard. He blinked several times, convinced it must be some kind of mirage, something born of wishful thinking. But when he looked again, the lifeboat was still there, bobbing on the sea swell, whitely inviting.

"B-boat . . . !"

He pointed. Doug and Ishi stared. The shark chose that moment to begin another attack, and its intent became clear only when the men took their eyes away from the impossible boat and began looking for the fin. "Legs up!" Doug yelled, and their combined reaction was so abrupt the spar spun on its axis and deposited them all in the water. The sudden thrashing of limbs and agitated water scared the shark away, and they climbed back onto the spar, considerably shaken. The shark surfaced again, having presumably passed beneath them while they struggled to regain their seats.

"Start paddlin'," Doug said. "The noise'll piss him off, but keep your eyes on him anyway."

They scooped water backward with cupped hands and began slowly to approach the lifeboat. Apart from a line of oily scum along the waterline, it appeared undamaged. Hope and fear combined to lend their arms greater strength than any of them would have thought possible before the appearance of the shark or the boat, and before long, with their escort still in attendance, they nudged the spar against the lifeboat's hull. It was empty; there was no sign it had ever been occupied. Its bow bore several Japanese characters, which Ishi interpreted: "*Shikoku Maru*. Bauxite ship."

They scrambled aboard over the stern, one at a time. Doug shoved the spar away, saying, "Bite on that, you bastard."

The shark circled the lifeboat once, then vanished. Ishi was opening the tiny doors of a locker in the bow. He brought out a five-gallon tin and shook it, producing the delightful sound of sloshing water. Unscrewing the lid, he offered the can to Clive.

"After you, Ishi . . . ," Clive said, summoning gallantry from a place very deep inside himself. He insisted that Doug drink next and realised, as he watched his friend's Adam's apple bobbing, that he had held himself until last because of the urine he had allowed to pass into the sea. The water, when his turn came at last, was tepid and slightly foul, but he could not have gulped it down with greater appreciation if it had been from the freshest spring.

"More can, two more . . . !" Ishi exulted, pulling them from the locker. After placing his head inside the tight storage space, he declared, "No food too."

"Can't have everythin', mate. Got somethin' better anyway."

Doug laid his hand on the unstepped mast and tightly furled sail lashed along the thwarts. A tiller was wedged beneath them.

The enormity of their importance dawned on Clive. "We can steer . . . ."

"Too right we can. Help us get this bugger stepped, and we can get some canvas up. I reckon if that bloody shark hadn't come along and got us all excited, we mighta drifted right past this little beauty. I was half asleep myself."

"I pissed," Clive confessed. "I couldn't help it. I pissed and brought the shark."

"What, are you claimin' credit for all this? I was pissin' long before you were, Clive. How about you, Ishi? Did you piss?"

"No! I say no piss, you piss both! Verrer foolish mans!"

"Sorry, mate; don't have your control."

Doug and Ishi stepped the mast and hooked the boom, assisted clumsily by Clive. The rudder was assembled and fitted into place, the sail rigged and raised, and the lifeboat became invested with movement by the wind. The canvas cracked, the boom shifted, lightly thumping an unwary Clive, and the craft was under way. Clive stared past Doug, manning the tiller, to the miraculous whiteness trailing behind. No longer adrift, they were under way, making passage.

"I suppose . . . south's the direction to go," Clive suggested.

"You can't miss Aussie if you do," Doug agreed. "Ishi, you wanna be a prisoner a war, or you wanna try and reach Japan?"

"Nippon too far. Be prisoner, your house."

Doug and Clive laughed, then were reminded of their own recent confinement.

"I wouldn't like to hand you over to the authorities, Ishi. I don't trust any bastard that gets paid by the taxpayer. Tell you what: if we can do it, I'll take us up the Flyin' Fox River, right up to me own front yard, and you can do what you said—be a prisoner at my place. What you reckon, Clive?"

"I think that's a rash promise to make, considering we must be five or six hundred miles from Australia. You couldn't really navigate by dead reckoning to the mouth of the Flying Fox, could you?"

"You never know, Clive. I'm gunna have a stab at it, though. Five quid says we hit Aussie within a hundred mile either side a where the Flyin' Fox runs into the sea."

"Assuming you can do it, how will you know which side you're on?"

"Clive, you're talkin' to a Territorian. I know the coast along there like I know me nose. Your fiver's gone, mate, trust me."

"I'm not convinced."

"You will be. How many days' water you reckon's there, Ishi?"

"Five, sis day. No drink big. Take litter bit. Sip, sip. Go five, sis day."

"We could do it by then."

"We don't have a compass," Clive pointed out.

"Got one in me head," boasted Doug. "South by southeast, and there she'll be—home."

"I sincerely hope I lose my five pounds."

"No worries. Any bastards lucky as we've been, we'll get there all right, you wait and see."

20

THE WIND PICKED UP BEFORE noon and became stronger by
the minute. Clouds began massing along the horizon behind
them and to the west. Doug was smiling as the boat skimmed
along. Ishi remained impassive, and Clive grew steadily more
nervous.

"I suppose this is a good thing, all this wind?"

"Won't get anywhere without it."

"But it's beginning to look a bit ... threatening, isn't it?
Isn't that a storm coming up behind us?"

"Yeah."

"And isn't this the monsoon season? That means it won't be
a normal storm, doesn't it? We're not going to be hit by a
typhoon, are we?"

"Might. Doesn't look like one to me. God, I'm starvin' hungry."

"Please don't mention food. It makes my stomach twist
itself about."

"We're better off with water and no food than food and no
water. We could last the whole trip that way and end up
nothin' worse than real skinny."

"Assuming your five-day prediction is correct."

"Might do it in four if this wind keeps up."

The sky darkened quickly, and the boat raced across the
waves with a considerable amount of thumping and bumping.
"Shame she's not bigger," said Doug. "She'd ride easier. She's a
fast runner, though, a real little sprinter when she wants to be."

Ishi took over the tiller. The mast was heeled over at
twenty degrees by then.

"Shouldn't we be shortening sail ... or something?" Clive
asked.

"No more'n you'd wanna shorten your dick, not while we're makin' this kinda progress, mate. This is perfect."

The waves became higher, the boat's progress more speedy and turbulent. Clive did not feel sick, but he attributed this to the emptiness of his stomach rather than to any ability to withstand the constant jerking about he suffered.

"I should be taking my turn steering, I think."

"When it's a bit calmer, Clive. Ishi and me have got the experience."

Occasional bursts of light rain came and went, but these passed virtually unnoticed; every wavetop sent a fine spray over them constantly. The taste of salt on the lips was unavoidable, but all three men avoided bringing out the water cans to wash the taste and the stinging away. They had drunk only twice each since finding the boat, and Clive in particular was suffering already from thirst.

"Can't help thinkin' about those other blokes!" Doug yelled over the thumping of the hull against waves. "This kinda weather'll separate 'em in about five minutes! They were only hangin' on to each other with their hands, most of 'em. Only the ones inside a raft or a boat are gunna have any kinda chance!"

"That submarine we saw! It might have spotted some of them!"

"Coulda done! I bloody hope so, for their sake!"

The squall continued until nightfall and beyond. Doug and Ishi shared turns at the tiller through the hours of darkness. They took brief snatches of sleep as they squatted in the foot or so of water that had accumulated in the bilge, staying low enough to avoid the boom, should it swing suddenly in a change of wind direction.

Their flesh was bruised and raw by morning. The wind did not slacken; the sea did not become smooth. Doug began steering what he judged to be a more directly southern course, since it was clear they were being pushed eastward at too rapid a pace to maintain his original heading. The first can of water was three-quarters empty.

"How long is this likely to keep up!" Clive asked, bailing water with his cupped hands, along with Ishi.

"Could be days!" Doug called back. "It's better this way than no wind at all! We've probly come a hundred and fifty mile already, maybe more! I reckon we're on the edge of a big storm north a here. She better not come too far south, or we're liable to get swamped."

"If it's going to continue this way, I insist on taking my turn back there!"

"Take over then, come on. No time like now to learn a bit a seamanship."

Doug surrendered the tiller to Clive.

"Keep her headed kinda crossways against the waves. If you go along the same way as they're goin', that means you're headin' east, and we don't want that."

"Shouldn't be too difficult," said Clive. "I don't know why you didn't let me before."

"Me neither." Doug grinned. "Give us a shout when you're ready to hand it back."

Clive enjoyed his first twenty or so minutes of handling the tiller, then became aware of the strain building in the muscles of his shoulders and arms from the effort of maintaining the boat's correct angle to the waves. After an hour he was in torment but would not admit it. Doug kept grinning at him, and Clive was not about to give him the satisfaction of falling down on the job. He set his mouth and took a renewed hold on the tiller and squinted into the flying spray, his head filled with scenes from romantic fiction: He was one of Captain Bligh's crew, set adrift in mid-Pacific to face the elements in a vessel too small for any chance of survival. He was being manly and brave; he was doing his share. But he had been a prisoner of war for almost two years, and his strength was low.

Doug took the tiller from him. "Thanks, mate. Good job for a beginner. Grab a drink a water, why don't you."

"I will," Clive said, "and I'll send the maid down to fetch us some supper."

"Bonzer! Double helpin' of everythin' for me, tell her."

"I shall."

Clive volunteered twice more for duty at the tiller, and fell asleep from exhaustion during his second stint, allowing the lifeboat to begin yawing dangerously. Ishi grabbed the tiller. Doug manhandled Clive into the bilge, his head against Doug's stomach to protect it from banging against the hull. They raced onward into the twilight.

Clive awakened slowly. He had dreamed he was in bed, a very uncomfortable bed without a mattress, with a pillow that lurched and shifted beneath his head as if trying to interrupt the dream. Eventually the pillow succeeded, and Clive opened his eyes. He saw the canvas sail above him, snapping in the wind, and beyond the sail and masthead were long reaches of cloud, and between the fingers of cloud, stars were gleaming.

"Time for a drink," suggested the pillow, and Clive sat upright.

"Sorry, didn't mean to lie all over you. . . ."

"Kept me guts nice and warm," Doug assured him. "Help yourself," he added, offering the water can. "This one's just about empty."

Clive gulped the last of the water, then set the can back inside the locker with the two full containers. "If it rains we can fill that with rainwater," he said, recalling scenes from the cinema. "You just arrange the sail to funnel water into the tin."

"Taste bloody awful if we do," Doug said. "The sail's stiff with salt. Need to let it get washed off first before we try that."

The sea was rolling, but the whitecaps that had accompanied them all day were gone. The breeze was enough to keep the sail taut without tipping the boat half over. Violence was absent from the scene. Clive felt better just looking at it.

"Calmed down a bit while you were snorin'."

"I don't snore, as a matter of fact."

"Yeah, you do. Doesn't Clive snore, Ishi?"

"Verrer loud. Make sound make me look up, look for plane."

"Very funny. Are we navigating by the stars now?"

"Tryin' to. They keep gettin' covered up. We saw the sun go down, so we know we're headin' pretty much south. Can't help but hit Australia sooner or later."

"Christ, I'm hungry. . . . I don't suppose any flying fish came skimming across us, hit the sail, and fell down into the boat."

"No, Clive, nothin' like that happened. A sheila came by with a big basket full a posh food, though. Said she was your fairy godmother, and would we mind lookin' after the basket till you woke up, which we did. We looked after it very well. Real good tucker your fairy godmother dished up for you, Clive, wasn't it, Ishi?"

Ishi rubbed his belly and made soft growling sounds of satisfaction.

"She said it'd be flyin' fish next time, mate, but you've gotta be awake to grab the little buggers."

"If humour were food," said Clive, "we'd still be starving."

The squall, whatever its disadvantages, had protected them from the sun. Their third day on the open sea began as the first had done, with an ominous sunrise of orange. Their circumstances had changed for the better in those forty-eight hours, with a firm hull beneath them now, a sail bending above, and one and three-quarter cans of drinking water available; but the sun, as it rose again like a surly giant, told them they would suffer before long.

By noon, the second water can was half empty, and Ishi insisted on a strict rationing of the remainder from then on. "No more big water. You no sip, sip. You glug, glug. No more do. Sip, sip." He held up four fingers. "Take water, one day."

"Four sip sips a day," said Doug. "Hardly enough to keep a lizard goin'."

"What kind of progress have we made, do you think?"

"Hard to say. Coupla hundred mile, probly. We're on the slow train now, not the express."

"Any chance of the doldrums—brassy sky and no wind, becalmed on a painted ocean—that kind of thing?"

"Not this time a year. We'll keep movin', all right; it's just how fast that worries me."

During the afternoon, a fifty-foot whale began accompanying them, sometimes uncomfortably close to the boat. Clive stared at its scarred and barnacled back, captivated by the sheer size of the thing, the steady undulation of its length as it skimmed below the surface for a hundred yards, then rose again, its blowhole spouting a fine spray every few minutes. Its massive flukes, uplifted at each dive, had the grace of a Burmese dancer's hands, water streaming from them in fine curtains until they sliced into the waves again, leaving a brief trail of bubbles steaming behind. Doug and Ishi told stories of whales they had encountered during their years in the pearling trade, but Clive barely listened; he stared at the lumpish creature gliding through the clear waters like a misshapen dirigible and thought it the most wonderful thing he had ever seen.

The whale abandoned them just before sunset, to be replaced by another common miracle. As the sky darkened to the east, clouds along the western horizon turned to lustrous purple and gold, riven by a startling shade of pink. The colours were almost too rich for the natural world, and Clive could not take his eyes from them. He had seen many brilliant sunsets during his years in Delhi and Singapore, but this surpassed them all. He wondered if its beauty had been enhanced by Clive's own hunger and the shifting perceptions his condition generally brought about. It would be a shame if that were so. He could be sure of nothing anymore. He watched this royal display until the sun was below the planetary curve, its light withdrawn from the sky. It seemed inconceivable that after seeing such things as the whale and the sunset, he might have to die.

Clive's sense of universal allness having been primed through the day and evening, it was natural that it be expanded further during the night. The stars had never seemed so numerous and scintillating, so very near to hand. They crowded down from above to shower his face with their frigid light, and Clive came close to weeping from a sense of misplaced joy. He could not be sure when or why he had decided there was a definite chance the boat would not complete its voyage, but the sadness that comes with such acceptance was inside him now, and the world, during the course of a single day, had become a different place. Clive stared at the hemisphere of spangled emptiness that had revealed itself. As the boat dipped and rose with the waves, so the stars in their billions arced slowly back and forth across his field of vision, like some massive pendulum. All of space, to the farthest edge of darkness, was fashioned to measure the passing of time, or so it seemed to Clive, and he felt its silent ticking and waited for the mysterious chiming he was sure would precede his demise.

"Penny for 'em, Clive."

Clive was hugely irritated at having his thoughts intruded upon and for a moment was angry with Doug for having spoken. "Nothing," he said, and attempted to return to the matchless place he had been cast out from, but it was gone, every particle of the magic erased.

"Three men in a boat," said Clive, "that's what I'm thinking about."

"I think of baby," said Ishi. "Verrer litter baby."

"Your missus give you one, Ishi, did she?"

"Now have two baby—boy, girl. Litter girl."

"Same with me," said Doug, "or was. Lost the girl."

"Girl die?"

"Yeah, while I was gone."

"Sorrer to hear. Sad thing."

"Gunna start a family yourself someday, Clive?"

"Oh, I might; you never know."

"That's what we're here for, in the end."

"It's not an absolute rule, you know, not an obligation to God."

"Spose not, but it's better that way."

"Even if you risk tragedy?"

"Yeah, even then."

"I wouldn't feel comfortable, bringing children into a place where there are stupid, senseless wars. . . . No, I won't do it until everything changes."

"You might be an old bugger by then, Clive, with your middle leg about as useful as a rubber cricket bat."

"I'll do as I see fit, thank you."

"Better to be father man," Ishi said.

"There's plenty a blokes that don't have families," Doug said. "Nothin' wrong with that, so long as a bloke's got a mate. Gotta have somethin' in this world."

Clive wanted the conversation to pass on to other topics or cease entirely, and he wanted a big plate of egg and chips and bacon and toast and a steaming-hot cup of tea and scones and butter and strawberry jam and later on a cigarette or two. His stomach rebelled at the memory of these things, causing him more pain than any other thought could ever have done.

Clive thought of food and the soul's redemption; Doug thought of Redlands; Ishi thought of his wife and children; and the lifeboat cut a narrow path through the night, leaving in its wake the phosphorescent glimmering of its passage.

◦   ◦   ◦

The third tin of water was broached on the fifth day. No one talked anymore, since there was nothing to talk of. The boat pursued a southerly course with no sound but that of its hull slapping the waves, wind cracking the sails, and the occasional grunt or moan from its passengers.

Doug had promised landfall on the sixth day, but at the end of that day, with less than a gallon of water remaining, there was no land in sight. Moreover, the wind, against Doug's prediction, had died away to nothing. The sail hung like a sheet on a clothesline, so little affected by the air around it that the boat turned slowly in circles as it was carried along on the currents.

The pain of hunger was not forgotten, but it had receded, overshadowed now by doubts over reaching Australia. It was somewhere beyond the horizon, but they saw no cloud formations above it, nor any bird that habitually dwelt on land. Doug himself began to wonder if they had not come too far west and were drifting due north of the Gulf of Carpentaria. He said nothing, shamefaced that his breezy confidence had not been borne out. Each man's skin was burnt to a nut brown, and the salt in their filthy hair and whiskers gave them the appearance of great age. Their bellies had collapsed after almost a week without food, and they were too weak to do anything but sit or lie in the boat, their heads aching, bodies too weak to do more than breathe and circulate blood.

They experienced, on the sixth day, a variety of hallucinations. Ishi imagined on several occasions that he could see the snow-whitened cone of Fujiyama hovering in the sky, and he wanted to weep over its beauty but could not, there being not the least amount of excess moisture in his body for tears. Doug was surprised to see Aborigines walking across the water, at least a dozen of them, thin dark figures carrying spears and dilly bags and small children; one of the men carried a dead wallaby on his head, and another swung a long goanna by its tail. When they had finished crossing the water, they would build a fire and throw their catches into it, then strip off the burnt skin and feast on crackling meat, running with the juices of freshness. Good tucker, said Doug, but his lips did not move. He wanted the Aborigines to come to the boat, but they walked right past, several hundred yards away, without once glancing in his direction. He was tempted to get out and follow them toward land, since he didn't doubt that land was what they were walking toward.

For Clive, the appearance of the white arches above him was proof he had died and was entering the portals of heaven. They were at least a mile high, built of gleaming white stone, and each arch was buttressed by another, identical arch. It was not a wall of arches that the boat was passing beneath, but a maze of arches that spread across the sea in all directions, causing Clive to wonder which arch he must pass through to enter heaven. There were thousands of them, towering silently so very far above him, graceful and superb, curving down to be lost in ethereal mist: the architecture of the sublime. Clive was surprised he was being allowed into heaven, but grateful that permission had been granted. Were Doug and Ishi coming too? Were they all dead and drifting to heaven together?

He looked across at Doug and saw him attempting to swing a leg over the side of the boat. Clive thought this was foolish, since it was the boat itself that was taking them all to heaven; to step out of it now might mean spending an inordinate amount of time in some watery limbo, and Clive didn't want to enter heaven without Doug's company. Alarmed at the prospect, he stirred himself and slapped Doug hard across the thigh. Doug turned to face him, his eyes unfocused. "They're gunna have good tucker over there . . . ," he wheezed. Clive assumed he meant the nectar of heaven and said, after licking his lips several times, "But we aren't there yet, so don't get out. . . ." Doug considered this statement, nodded, and collapsed alongside Clive.

With nightfall and the loss of direct heat, they revived somewhat. No one spoke of what he had seen throughout the day. They drank the last of the water and felt a little better for a while. Then they slept. Many hours passed, then the wind began to freshen, and the sail flapped, waking the men. The boom shifted, and Clive, nearest to the tiller, grabbed it.

"Which way is south?" he asked.

Doug couldn't say. He knew they had been turning in circles during the windless hours, because the sun had risen to port but had also set to port. He had no idea, on this cloudy and moonless night, where south might lie. The lifeboat was under way again, but without a direction in which to steer, they might sail back the way they had come.

"We have to choose," said Clive. "We can't just do nothing. What's everyone's best guess on which way south is?"

"There," said Ishi, pointing.

Doug said, "Why?"

Ishi had no reply.

Clive attempted to let some deep instinct within him divine which way safety lay, but no small voice whispered into his ear. He said to Doug, "I thought you had a compass in your head."

"It's on the blink, mate."

"Suggestions, anyone?"

There were none. A silence followed, lasting for several minutes.

"Anyone else hear that?" Doug asked.

"Hear what?"

"Listen . . . planes!"

The sound became louder, aero engines at a considerable altitude.

"Ours or theirs, do you think?" asked Clive.

"It's Japs," said Doug. "When I was on ack-ack duty in Darwin, they used to come in at night sometimes, so you'd get used to the sound. It's definitely Jap bombers, and you know what? There's only one place they'd be goin'—Darwin!"

"But we can't see them! Can you tell which way they're going?"

"Give us a bit of hush!"

They listened to the steady droning overhead, already becoming fainter as the planes passed.

Doug pointed. "That way."

Clive said, "They may be returning from a raid, not going toward one, in which case we need to go in the opposite direction."

"We woulda heard 'em before this if they went on a raid and're just now comin' back. Nah, that's the way to Darwin, I'm bloody sure of it. If we're near enough, we'll hear the explosions when they drop their bundles, might even see a bit a fireworks if they hit a petrol supply dump or somethin'. Keep your eyes and ears open, but turn that tiller right now, Clive. I've got five quid ridin' on this, remember."

A tense period of waiting followed, then flashes of light appeared on the horizon, almost dead ahead, followed seconds later by the barely discernible thump of detonating bombs.

"You beauty! Told you!"

It was in fact the sixty-fourth Japanese raid on Darwin—a flight of nine bombers, two of which would be shot down. It was the twelfth of November, 1943, and there would not be another air attack against the Northern Territory for the remainder of the war.

The planes passed almost directly overhead on their return flight. Doug stood up in the boat and shook his fist at the droning above him. "Thanks a lot, Tojo! Couldn't a done it without you, you bastard! No offense, Ishi."

At dawn, they saw Australia, a long hazy line separating sea from sky. A scrap of smoke hanging in the air told Doug where Darwin lay, and he took over the tiller to steer well clear of the harbour before anyone saw them and came out to investigate. The mouth of the Flying Fox lay forty miles east of Darwin.

"You owe me five quid, Clive. I reckon I deserve a ten-bob bonus, meself."

"You'll get a bonus if you can get us up the river to your place. That'll be a bit tricky, won't it, going against the current? I remember it was pretty fierce, the one time I saw it in flood."

"Depends on how hard she's been rainin' lately. If the level's down and we go in with the tide, we might be able to tack upriver and be at Redlands sometime this arvo. Might be lucky. Been pretty bloody lucky so far, haven't we? How many blokes do you reckon have sailed home from the war, right up to their own house?"

"How many blokes are facing a court-martial for willful murder of a British officer? And how many will face further charges if they hide a Japanese prisoner on their property?"

Doug grinned at him, unwilling that his spirits should be quashed by reason.

"In for a penny, in for the full fuckin' quid, eh?"

She had found M'linga outside her door every morning since the birth of Wilf. He sat about fifteen yards from the house, beneath the same tree, as if on guard duty of some kind. He did not speak to her, even when she had gone across to him and attempted to begin a conversation. Brian had explained to Val that M'linga often was not there, even if his body was. M'linga was the oldest Aborigine Val had ever seen, his skin as seamed with age and weather as gnarled bark. His hair and beard were a dirty yellow-white, and his sightless eyes were a perfect match for them. She saw him at other times throughout each day, but never once managed to catch him in a state of motion; M'linga seemed always to be either standing or, as was more usual, sitting, never in between these two positions of repose. It was as if he disappeared and reappeared at will and conducted all bodily movement while invisible.

Val knew it was Wilf who drew the kadaic a man to her door. The nonsense Brian had admitted to, concerning the child's parental link with Gulgulong, had been amusing when Val was first told, but it was clear that M'linga and Ranji and the rest of the tribe believed it literally. Val had herself employed humour to wean herself from annoyance over the whole silly business, by referring to Wilf as Blighty's Boy, but this tactic had backfired when Ranji responded, " 'Bout time you seen what's what, missus." She had immediately told him in the most straightforward language she could use, short of swearing, that Wilfred Timothy Farrands belonged to herself and Doug Farrands, and not to any crocodile or Pitjantjatjara. Ranji had smirked a little and walked away.

All in all, Val was becoming tired of having uninvited company hanging around the place, but she allowed them to stay because they fed themselves and did not get drunk, and because it was plain that Brian was deeply involved in whatever plans they had for Wilf, who remained oblivious to the contest for supremacy over his curly head. For Brian, Val would tolerate Ranji's mob and M'linga's pretentious silences for a little longer. In a way, it was the irritation they gave her that had prevented Val from sinking into a depression after what happened to Judy, and so she felt she owed them something for that too. The circumstances at Redlands were a balance of obligation and tolerance, but Val was unsure how much longer it could be maintained.

Brian came to her late one afternoon. Since the arrival of Ranji's mob, he had spent more time with them and less time with the cattle. He was running up the track from the Flying Fox crossing, and he seemed very excited.

"Better come an see!" he called, still running.

"See what?"

"Boat comin' up the river!"

Val had never heard of such a thing. Doug hadn't taken the dinghy down to the sea or suggested that anyone else ever had. She supposed someone had attempted it solely because the Flying Fox was down this Wet, at least fifteen feet lower than usual for November.

"What kind of boat?"

"Dunno; just a boat. Got blokes in it."

Val picked up Wilf. She took him everywhere now. Once, too tired to carry him while she went for a walk, she had left him in the house, and when she had come back, lubras were inside, surrounding his bed like crows around helpless prey. She had chased them out, but not before noticing among their number Beth, the speechless woman who had been her father's bed warmer. Wilf was unharmed, and Val, once her temper cooled, saw that curiosity had been what drew them inside to admire her baby, nothing more.

She went with Brian down to the river. Many yards of chain on both banks were exposed by the water's unseasonably low level. Most of Ranji's mob were already there, the women chattering, the men silent. Val waited to see the boat. It was obviously still some way downstream, and she wondered how news of its coming had preceded it. The bush telegraph never failed to puzzle her with its prescience and accuracy; she knew there would indeed be a boat by and by, and it would certainly have blokes aboard.

"Know who they are?" Val asked Brian, who wore the kind of grin she had not seen on his face in quite some time, not since the death of Judy, in fact.

"Yeah," he said, his eyes dancing.

"Who?"

"Big surprise. Can't say, but."

"It isn't more Yanks, is it?"

"Nah, not them. You'll see."

Val watched the gathering at the river's edge, and she watched the curve that hid from view the seaward reach of the Flying Fox, and the longer she waited, the more nervous she became. She knew, having absorbed some of Brian's excitement, that it would not be just anyone, but she could not for the life of her think who might be visiting Redlands in a boat, of all things.

When it finally appeared, its oil-smeared bows nudging into sight around the bend, she was disappointed; she had expected some kind of vessel that would excite anyone who saw it, but the fifteen-foot boat slowly approaching was very ordinary in appearance, if less clean than most seagoing craft. There were three men aboard, all incredibly filthy, and Val became nervous again. These were no casual visitors who had simply taken a spin on the water and ended up there. They were thin and unshaven and hairily unkempt, their clothing little more than rags.

One of them raised a hand and waved. "Val!" he shouted.

How did he know her name?

A second man was also shouting to her. Val turned to Brian for an explanation, but his face was toward the boat, and he was waving back at them.

"Dad! Eh, Dad! G'day, Dad!"

Val felt the blood draining into her legs, leaving her light-headed and dizzy. The river seemed to tilt sideways, and she thought for a moment she might faint, and she held Wilf closer to her so he would come to no harm if she fell. She even made up her mind to fall backward, if fall she must, to protect him. But she did not fall, or stagger, or reveal her confusion in any way as the boat drew closer and the grimy sail was lowered.

Doug was shouting something else now, but she could barely make out the words over the thudding of her heart.

"What . . . what'd he say . . . ?"

"Says to put the billy on and get some tucker started, 'cause they're a bunch a starvin' bastards."

PART FOUR

21

REWARDED FOR ITS PRIVATIONS with ample food and a hammock in which to rest, Clive's body succumbed to a malarial attack that lasted more than a week. He was often delirious for hours at a time and would hold fragmented conversations with men he had known while a prisoner of the Japanese. Val, who tended to his needs more often than anyone else, heard the major's name several times.

"Who's this major he keeps talking to?" she asked Doug.

"Dunno," Doug told her. "Probly some joker he used to know. You can't believe anything a bloke says when he's feverish."

"He's not saying anything, really, just mumbling about this and that."

"Good."

"What do you mean, 'good'? He's sick."

"Malaria comes and goes. Just keep the water tricklin' into him, and he'll pull through."

"Says you, the medical expert."

"Look, after what Clive's been through, a bit a malaria while he's in a friend's house is the next-best thing to a bloody holiday. He'll be all right."

"I want to get a doctor to him."

"No doctors."

"Mind telling me why?"

"Just do what I said, all right?"

He was not the same man who had left the Territory. He was easily irritated and seemed at ease only with Clive and Ishi Murikama, even to the exclusion, sometimes, of Brian and Val. He played often with Wilf, and would not discuss Judy, deeming that incident "buried," although Val had seen him standing by his daughter's gravesite several times.

Val supposed the changes in Doug were natural enough, considering what had happened. He had told her the story over several days, in disorganised chunks of understatement, but Val suspected there was more to the events on Dombi than Doug was admitting to. Clive was the one who could supply those missing pieces, but Clive was more or less in a state of collapse. It was Doug's insistence that no doctor be sent for that finally gave Val pause. Ishi could easily be hidden while a doctor attended to Clive, so that was not the reason he wanted Redlands kept in isolation from the world. It was as if Doug had no intention of returning to that world himself. He expressed no wish to report to the authorities in Darwin and declare himself and Clive survivors of the submarine attack, which seemed to Val nothing less than dereliction of duty. She could understand his taking a few days, or even a week, to recover from the trip across the Banda and Arafura seas, which had brought him home; in fact, she was so impressed with this feat that she wanted to make it known to a larger audience, including anyone in the Territory who had ever regarded Doug as a no-hoper who had married a woman of property. But he wouldn't hear of it.

"That's my business, the whole thing. Other people can keep their sticky noses out of it."

"You and Clive might get medals for bravery or something."

"Yeah, and Ishi gets put in an internment camp for the rest a the war. No, thanks."

"Don't mention Ishi; just tell them about you and Clive."

"Look, I don't give a shit if no one knows about anythin', so stop tellin' me what to do. I'm not bloody interested, and that's that."

"But, Doug . . . you can't just not report in, or whatever they call it. You can't just wait here for the army to come looking for you."

"They're not gunna be lookin' for me, or Clive. So far as anyone knows, we drowned after the ship sank. We're dead men, both of us."

"You're bloody well absent without leave."

"I don't give a stuff if I am."

"Is that why you hid the boat?"

The lifeboat from *Shikoku Maru* had been taken farther upriver from its highly visible landfall beside the track and moored in Blighty's Pond.

"Could be."

"I want to know what's going on."

"Nothin's goin' on."

"Doug, you're a great bullshitter but a terrible liar. I know you. You'd love to go to the pub and tell everyone how you sailed a little boat six hundred miles, right up to your own front door. You'd have a good old skite about it to anyone who'd buy you a beer. That's what the Doug I used to know would've done by now, and got a doctor for his mate while he was about it!"

"No need to get snakey."

"Did Clive do something wrong that you're protecting him for? Is that it?"

"Clive? He wouldn't break the rules if you paid him."

"But you would, wouldn't you?"

"You mind your business."

They glared at each other across Clive's hammock.

Val said, "If he isn't better in one more day, I'm riding into town for a doctor. I'm not losing my cousin who I love dearly just because of some silly secret you think you have to keep from me."

"Suit yourself," Doug said, and Val saw the anger leave his eyes, replaced in an instant by the shadow of some other thing.

He stood and went outside. She wanted to run after him and kick him square in his skinny backside. Beside her, Clive shifted restlessly, new sweat breaking from his brow in thick beads. Val passed a damp cloth across his face. The simple fact of his presence again at Redlands was a miracle of sorts, wrought, it seemed, by the casual and cantankerous hand of her own husband and the Japanese to whom he had long ago given the gift of a pearl. It was impossible, but it had happened. Val wanted to comprehend every nuance of the miracle, but Doug denied her a more complete understanding. Ishi Murikama seemed to know nothing that did not bear directly on the sinking of the convoy and the incredible sea crossing that followed. He often sat with Val and took his turn at nursing Clive, and he appeared the very soul of openness and gratitude; she detected no hint of secrecy there. It would have to be Clive who told her.

Brian was walking around with Wilf in his arms when Doug approached him.

"Watch out for that nipper. Drop him and I'll scone you."

"Hafta beat M'linga first, but. He'd do more'n just scone me; probly cut me guts out, I reckon."

"What's all this bullshit Val's been tellin' me about Ranji's mob thinkin' Wilf's theirs? You don't go for that, do you, Bri?"

"Not theirs," said Brian. "Blighty's."

"That's even more stupid. Look, a croc's one thing, and a kid's another. He's Wilf Farrands, not Boy b'long bloody Gulgulong. He's your own half-brother, not somethin' the tribe found out in the bush. Give him here."

Brian handed the baby to his father. "Not doin' him no harm," he said.

"Where's Ranji?"

"Flyin' Fox," mumbled Brian.

Doug went marching to the water's edge, with Wilf held uncomplainingly against his chest. Ranji and M'linga were both there, where the track was cut by running water. The river was still down, and Doug was beginning to worry about intruders driving straight across it without having to fire a shot and wait for the dinghy. There had been thunderstorms aplenty passing overhead since his return, but they carried more noise than rain. Doug went directly to the men.

"See this kid? He's mine and me missus', not Gulgulong's, not Pitjantjatjara. He's a whitefella, not blackfella or crocfella, all right? You blokes just keep your distance from him from now on, or you can all clear out and stay that way."

"Wouldn' wanna do that," said Ranji.

"I know you wouldn't, but you bloody will if you don't stop this Gulgulong bullshit."

"Nah, I mean you," said Ranji, smiling. "You wouldn' wanna tell us blokes to go bush, not with the water low like that."

"What's the water got to do with it?"

"Some bugger comin', we can say when. We go bush, some bugger sneaks up on you, but. Don't want that, eh?"

Doug glared at him. He had never much liked Ranji at the best of times, but now it seemed that he knew Doug's secret, the way Abos got hold of such stuff from God knew where, and was willing to use it as a bargaining tool.

"Nobody's gunna come visitin' Redlands," Doug said. "Val says no one's been out here since those Yanks stopped comin'."

"M'linga says they're gunna come."

Doug looked at the scrawny figure beside his strapping middle-aged son.

"What blokes are comin'? Ask him."

"He's not talkin' much today. Don't feel like it when he's not welcome, but."

"Course he's bloody welcome," said Doug. "All your lot are welcome, just so long as you don't keep up this Gulgulong bullshit. Tell you what—seeing as you're all special pals with Gulgulong, how about sendin' some a your blokes out to his pond and settin' fire to that boat I brought home, eh?"

"Nice little boat. Why you wanna burn it up?"

"It's a Jap boat. We're at war with the Japs, so the boat gets burned, see."

"You got a Jap mate. Wanna burn him too, eh?" Ranji laughed.

"Anyone sees that boat, they're gunna look for Ishi, and I don't want anyone lookin' for him, because he's a good Jap, so you get that boat burned down to the waterline and sunk good and proper, and tell your mate Gulgulong to bite the balls off anyone that goes snoopin' around the pond."

"Get me old man to tell 'im," said Ranji, his face serious again.

"Fine, just so long as the boat never gets seen again. And do it at night, so nobody sees the smoke and thinks there's a bushfire startin' out here. Do it tonight, eh, Ranji, no waitin' around."

"Orright."

"Thanks, mate. Tell M'linga I need to know if someone's comin', anyone at all."

"He orready knows, but. He'll say when."

"Plenty a warnin'."

"Yeah, so they won't getcha."

"Not me, me Jap mate."

Ranji nodded, smiling again. Doug knew he was fooling no one.

It became a tribal activity that same afternoon; even the children took part in the gathering of dead wood to fill the lifeboat. The mooring line was used to pull the boat ashore, and when it was fully laden with firewood, it was shoved out again into the centre of Blighty's Pond to await the coming of night.

"Oughta keep it, Dad," suggested Brian. "Bigger'n the dinghy, an you can sail it."

"Nah, I want it gone. You can do the honours, once it's dark. Reckon you can chuck a firestick fair and square into that lot from shore?"

"Easy."

"The job's yours, then. Listen, don't tell Val about it. She's got her hands full with Clive, so no need to go botherin' her."

"Orright."

Doug went back to the house. The sun was low in the sky by then, and he saw Ishi scratching at the earth with an old hoe.

"Make garden," Ishi explained, as Doug came to stand with him.

"Garden, eh? Me missus has had a go at a couple a them over the years. Never came to much, though. Course, she's a city girl."

"Val give to me seed." He held up several paper packets. "Pea, corrifower, grin bean. I make all grow big."

"Beauty. Look, Ishi, we're gunna have to burn the lifeboat, so no one ever sees it and starts wonderin' if there's a Japanese sailor somewhere around here."

"Yes, good thing to burn."

"No need to tell me missus about it. Brian and his mates'll take care of it tonight."

"Your son, him? Abo boy?"

"Yeah, he's mine. Used to have an Abo wife, sort of. I wasn't much older than Brian at the time. She died, though."

"Better you have wife same white you now."

"Dunno 'bout better. Makes life easier, I spose."

Every member of Ranji's mob was gathered at Blighty's Pond by sundown. Brian was showing off, throwing a lighted firestick around like a juggler, prancing conspicuously before one of the youngest lubras (Doug judged her age at around thirteen) and tossing the firestick into the air, to catch it again by its unlighted end. There was plenty of talk along the water's edge as full darkness was waited on, and a general air of excitement, fueled by Brian's antics. Doug had never seen him so animated. Val had told him, during one of their attempts at conversation, that Brian had admitted to her he had a sweetheart, someone called Jess, but he wouldn't introduce the girl to Val. Doug would be able to point her out now.

Brian tossed the burning stick higher than before and stood in an exaggerated pose to catch it, when he was shoved aside by Ranji. Brian fell to the ground, and the stick fell beside him. Ranji picked it up and flung back his arm to throw the stick out onto the boat. Doug was beside him by then, his fingers around Ranji's wrist.

"Don't go pushin' my boy around, mate. I don't like it."

Ranji shook Doug off and threw the firestick. It flew across the billabong, trailing sparks, and landed among the kindling piled to the lifeboat's gunwales, igniting it instantly. The crowd's attention was divided between the blaze and what appeared to be imminent confrontation between Doug and Ranji over Brian.

Brian took Doug's arm. "Don't matter," he said. "Fuck 'im, eh?"

"Yeah," Doug agreed. He supposed Ranji, as leader, had wanted the ceremonial role of firestarter for himself and had got it the simplest way. It wasn't worth raising a rumpus over, not when Doug needed Ranji's cooperation in keeping visitors away from Redlands.

Now everyone was watching the flames rise. The unstepped mast and furled sail were alight, the coiled rigging smouldering. The incident with Ranji was forgotten as the trees surrounding Blighty's Pond were illuminated by the floating pyre and the fire's roaring filled the night air. It was a wonderful sight, and Doug wished Clive were well enough to witness it.

Then the flames began to slacken; without further wood to replenish it, the fire was dying, before the hull itself could fully catch alight. There were sounds of disappointment from the crowd. The boat soon was a crucible of sparks, nothing more.

"Not gunna sink," said Brian.

"Better get me gun and we'll put a few holes in her," Doug said. "See if you can't sneak it past Val without her knowin'."

Brian set out for the house. Doug couldn't help but notice that the young lubra went with him. He saw that Ranji had noticed this also, and Ranji knew that Doug had seen. Doug turned his back on Ranji to watch the boat. It had been exciting for ten minutes or so, then an obvious failure; he should have tipped kerosene over everything beforehand. Still, it was not a problem that a few rounds of .303 couldn't solve.

Clive had the dream again, the one in which he was strolling along the Serpentine; turning to see who followed, he saw Doug. But when his eyes opened, he saw Val instead, standing by the table, lighting a lamp.

"Where . . . where's Doug?"

"Outside somewhere. Feeling better?"

"I've been sick again, haven't I?"

"Very sick. Doug says malaria."

"Sorry to be a nuisance. It's all been . . . a bit much for me."

"Of course it has." She sat beside him. "All that time getting knocked about by the Japs, then being torpedoed, and having to come all that way in a little boat with no food. It's a wonder you got here at all. And the other thing too, that couldn't have helped."

"No," Clive agreed.

"Would you say it was the worst thing? Worse than the camp and the torpedoing and everything?"

"Is what worse?"

"The other thing that happened. You know."

"Could I have some water, please?"

Val dipped a mug into the water bucket and helped Clive hold it while he drank half. "Doug doesn't like talking about it much," said Val. "He said you'd give me the details."

"He did?"

"If you're feeling strong enough. Are you ready for some food?"

"Not yet." He wiped a driblet of water from his whiskered chin. "I suppose you mean about the major."

Val nodded, hoping this was the correct cue.

"I didn't think he could keep it from you forever," said Clive. "Ishi doesn't know. He wasn't there, you see, at the camp. Poor old Doug."

"What do you mean, poor old Doug?"

"He . . . he felt he had a genuine right to do what he did; that's the thing to bear in mind."

"Yes," said Val, her tone neutral.

Clive reached for the mug and this time drained it without assistance.

"He's in the most awful pickle now, of course. You can't do that to a major in His Majesty's Army and expect to get away with it. God knows what we can do. He can't just stay here and hope everything blows over. There were bound to be other survivors. Some of them will talk, the English ones anyway. . . . I would have tried to stop him, Val, but he went charging off and simply . . . did it. There were bombs falling everywhere. . . . It was all very confusing at the time."

"But what exactly did he *do*, Clive?"

"Do? Why, kill the major. Strangle him and break his neck to boot, he said. Not that Reese-Birnham didn't ask for it, but an official inquiry after the war would have served the same end, I'm sure. I would have testified against the major myself, given the chance. But you know Doug. He was incredibly angry over what happened to his friends."

"I'm going to make some damper for you, Clive, something nice and simple you can eat and not get sick, all right?"

"Thank you. I'm going to be peckish in a little while, I think."

"Tell me all about everything. From the beginning. Doug tells stories in dribs and drabs, but you don't. That's why you want to be a writer, I expect."

"Not anymore. God, I couldn't write this story. . . ."

"But you can tell me, Clive, can't you?"

Clive could, and did, and was done with the telling when Brian arrived.

"Feelin' better, eh, Clive?"

"Yes, quite a bit. Where's your dad, Brian?"

"Arr, out there, I reckon."

"Tell him I want to see him," said Val.

"Right-oh."

Val saw a black face peering shyly around the doorway.

"Who's this? I bet I know."

Brian was trying to shoo the girl away.

"Don't be so rude and ungentlemanly," Val told him. "Invite her in."

"She dudn wanna come in."

"Jess? You come in and don't mind what Brian says."

The girl sidled around the doorway but would not fully enter the house. Brian used the attention Jess had attracted to herself to locate the rifle. He was halfway to the door when Val asked, "What's that for?"

"Dad wants it."

"For what?"

"Dunno." Brian was shooing Jess out again, moving himself closer to the door.

"Just a minute, Brian. I want an answer. . . ."

Brian dashed through the doorway, taking Jess and the rifle with him.

"Mysterious goings-on," said Clive.

"Too bloody mysterious for me. Will you be all right on your own for a bit?"

"Of course."

Doug took the .303 from Brian and placed three shots just below the boat's waterline. It began sinking, and the embers contained within the hull hissed as the water level rose to extinguish it. The blackness of the billabong had risen almost to the gunwales when Val arrived.

"What do you think you're doing?"

"Sinkin' the boat—what's it look like?"

"I want a word with you, away from this lot."

They went a short distance from the water.

"You bloody stupid idiot," Val said.

"Why?"

"Clive could've used that boat. He could've sailed into Darwin, once he was well enough, and told them he spent the last few weeks making his way along the coast."

"Tell who?"

"The military, the police, anyone who's at all interested in what happened to those prisoners you were with. He could've bluffed his way out and never mentioned you and your friend Ishi. He can't do it now, can he? There was a way out of this mess for Clive, but you had to burn it, you . . . fool."

"That's a bit rough on a bloke. . . ."

"He told me everything! You couldn't see your way clear to letting him off the hook, could you! You have to take everyone with you when you jump into the shit, don't you!"

"Steady on, Val. Listen—"

"You listen! You murdered an officer, and now you seem to think you can just wait around for the stink to blow over. You've gone completely barmy—"

"For all you know, every man aboard that ship died at sea—"

"And for all you know, some of them didn't! Oh, I can't look at you anymore. . . ." She turned away from him. Doug squirmed; he'd known Val would find out sooner or later, because she was clever and intuitive, but he hadn't expected it would be this soon. He could kick Clive for spilling the beans this fast, but he supposed it was because Clive was still a bit dizzy from the malaria; he couldn't blame him really. In all honesty, he could only blame himself, for everything.

"Might blow over," he said. "You never know."

"And just how are you going to explain how you came home again? Have you worked that one out?"

"Not yet."

"I didn't think so, but you went ahead and burned the one thing that might have helped Clive bullshit his way out of things. Christ, Doug!"

"I'm sorry. . . ."

"Oh, you're sorry; that helps Clive a lot. You'll all have to hide away in the bush till the war's over and hope they all *did* die, nasty as that sounds."

"I'm not hidin' anywhere."

"You don't think so? Then go into Darwin and give yourself up."

"Fuck that."

"So you're hiding."

"All right, I'm hidin'. What's done's done. I can't unkill the bastard! I wouldn't even wanna! He got what he asked for, the shithead!"

"And now the rest of us'll pay the price!"

"Well, I can't bloody help that now, can I!"

Doug began walking back to the house, furious with himself for having no solution to the problem he had deepened by burning the lifeboat. He hoped Val wouldn't follow, with her sharp words and recriminations. He didn't want to go into the house and face Clive, either, not until his temper had cooled.

Passing near Blighty's Pond, he heard the sounds of a fight and a woman's scream. He ran toward the water and found Brian scuffling with Ranji, receiving the worst of the blows both were trying to inflict. Doug stepped between them. "Eh! Eh! What the fuckin' hell's this! Ranji, you wanna pick on someone your own bloody size."

Ranji said nothing but made no further attempt to hit Brian.

"Bri, what's this all about?"

"Arr, nothin' . . ."

"Don't go givin' me bullshit when I asked for an answer!"

"I dunno!" Brian yelled.

Doug felt like hitting someone.

Beth, mute half-sister to Brian's mother, came forward and pulled at his sleeve.

"What?" said Doug.

Beth pointed at the young girl Jess, who stood with everyone else, waiting to see what might happen next, and Doug understood at last.

Val was there now. "What's going on here?"

"Squabble over a sheila, that's all."

"Brian, are you all right?"

"Yeah."

"Come with us," Val said. "Bring Jess. Who were you fighting?"

"No one."

"It was Ranji," said Doug.

"Ranji? He's too old for a little thing like Jess. Jess, you come along with us."

But the girl hung back, and when he saw this, Brian hung back also.

"Brian," Val said, "I don't want to see you getting into stupid fights, so come on."

"He's not gettin' her!"

"Nobody's gunna let him," Doug said.

Ranji came toward him. "Dudn matter what you reckon. Jess, she's promise."

"Promise?"

"Promise to me. She's mine, gunna be me wife."

"Bugger off. You're at least fifty, mate. Let a young shaver like Bri have a slip of a thing like her, eh? That's the normal way."

"Pitjantjatjara law sayin' she's mine. You bugger off. You tell him to bugger off too." Ranji was staring with contempt at Brian.

Doug faced Ranji, and Val expected a fight to begin at any moment. She had never heard Ranji so openly contemptuous of Doug and Brian.

Doug said, "Brian's only half Pitjantjatjara, so he doesn't see things that way."

"Jess, she's full-blood," said Ranji, "and me, so you bugger off, both a you."

"No, mate, you bugger off. I want the lot of you gone from here by sundown tomorrer. Anyone that wants to stay, like Jess maybe, they can do it, but you're gone, Ranji, and I mean gone for good."

"You carn tell me what to do."

"Don't see why not. You just told me what to do, didn't you?"

"We arn goin' nowhere," Ranji said, as Doug turned away from him. "This place, all fuckin' place, all Abo place, not white! Bugger off!"

"Come on," Doug told Val and Brian. "He's startin' to rave."

They continued toward the house, Jess's thin wrist in Brian's tightly gripping fingers. Val could tell the girl was unsure what she should do.

Ranji yelled, "Gunna get what Perce Burridge got, you don't bugger off!"

Val immediately turned around. "What did you say? What did you bloody say? You killed him, didn't you! I always thought you did, you bugger. Just because he knew about your precious stones! Why don't you have a go at me, then, eh? I've bloody *been* there! Why don't you kill me too, you murderer!"

Ranji glared at Val for a moment, then turned away and pushed past the tribe to vanish among the trees. Val said to Doug, "I knew it was him . . . I always knew. . . ."

Doug put his arm around her shoulders, but she shrugged him off, too angry still over his burning of the lifeboat. They returned to the house without another word between them.

Brian and Jess went into Brian's shed. Val was irritated by their giggling as they slipped from view, and was glad that they would not be present while she and Clive and Doug argued over what could now be done to save Doug from prison, if not execution. She regarded Ishi Murikama as a pawn caught up in the larger game taking place around him.

Inside, Ishi was sitting by Clive, sharing the damper Val had made and dandling Wilf on his knee.

"Tell Clive what you did," Val said to Doug.

"Is something wrong?" Clive asked.

"I sank the lifeboat," Doug said. "You coulda used it to get away from here."

Clive considered this blunt admission of wrongdoing.

"But I don't want to get away from here," he said. "Why would I want to do that? I can't sail worth a damn, in any case. You wouldn't want me to drown, would you?"

Val sat heavily in a chair and placed her head in her hands. "Oh, Clive, you're hopeless."

"I beg to differ, naturally. What was all that shouting out there?"

"Barnyard cockfight," Doug said. "Nothin' to worry about. The old rooster's buggerin' off tomorrer."

"I'm sure all that will mean something to me when I'm feeling better." Clive smiled. "I feel a bit like the proverbial kitten for now."

"You take it easy, mate."

Ishi, still in ignorance of events on Dombi, was told of the murder of Major Reese-Birnham. When the story was done, he shook his head.

"You mus not be here, your home," he said. "Soon they come, take you."

"They think I'm dead, Ishi, and you and Clive too. Nobody's comin' till after the Wet anyway."

"Call this a Wet?" said Val. "Anyone could wade across the Flying Fox and still keep their underpants dry."

"Ishi's right, Doug," said Clive. "None of us can stay here for very much longer."

"Clive, there's nowhere else to go, unless you wanna live on lizards out in the bush. You'd fuckin' die in no time. We all would."

"We could always . . . surrender ourselves and hope for a fair court-martial."

"You're not the one that did it—I am, and I don't reckon they'd give a bloke like me a fair go, not when it's some important English bastard's cousin I did. Nah, bugger that. I'd hafta be an idiot to think they'd find me not guilty."

"You don't know that for sure," said Val.

"Actually, he's right," Clive said. "He'd hang. I'm sorry, Val. I'd love to offer a sunny picture, but there simply isn't one to be had."

"Then we've got to go," Val announced.

"Go *where?*" Doug insisted.

No one could give him an answer.

"Ishi," said Clive, "would you be a sport and help me out to the *benjo?* I think I'm going to be a bit shaky on the old pins for a day or two."

"I come with you. Grandfather, same thing. Go to *benjo,* have to come also."

When they had gone, Doug said, "I'm sorry, Val. I buggered everything and everyone. Didn't mean to, dinkum I didn't. I dunno what else I coulda done, though. . . ."

Val watched him. He seemed as young as Brian, and as gauche, with his brow wrinkled, his eyes downcast, utter confusion evident in his face. Now that she understood the reason for his moodiness since coming home, she could allow her own anger to subside; it served no useful purpose, in any case.

As Doug had said, simply and with piquant inadequacy, What's done's done.

She stood and went to him. "Stand up," she said, and when Doug did so, Val put her arms completely around him, then punched him lightly in the kidneys until he put his arms around her too.

"We're still all right," she said, her face against his shirt, "aren't we?"

"Too right we are, love. I couldn't bugger that up if I tried."

"Well, *don't* try. You might be underestimating yourself for once."

Doug laughed. Val lifted her face and was kissed with the usual reluctance. He would never learn how to kiss her properly, but it didn't matter. He was her husband, and he had done what he had done and, like Samson, brought down the temple, her skinny man who couldn't even kiss. The baby began to cry, and they separated, Val to pick up Wilf, and Doug to stare with growing intensity at the familiar walls around him.

22

~

BRIAN HAD NOT YET BEEN ABLE to persuade Jess that whitefella hammocks were a comfortable and safe alternative to sleeping on the ground. She had sat on the hammock in his shed just once and been spun onto her small behind; since then she would not even touch it. Jess didn't even like Brian's shed, since she was used to sleeping in the open and making love with him there. The shed was a box such as whitefellas put things in to keep them away from the sun and air, and she had gone inside Brian's box on the night of the burning boat solely because he guaranteed Ranji would be unable to follow them there. She went directly to the antbed floor and stayed there, and refused Brian's offer to snuggle next to her, so Brian, annoyed that he would have no jiggy-jig, retreated to the hammock, and both eventually fell asleep.

When he heard the latch being lifted, Brian assumed Jess was leaving to use the thunderbox, but the shape revealed in the doorway when it opened was not hers, and it became larger, not smaller, as it entered the shed, its outline made clearer by the first light of dawn behind it. When he saw, through sleep-blurred eyes, that the shape was lifting its arms above him, Brian rolled over and was deposited on the floor, and the hammock, springing and snapping in the air above him, was what took the blow from Ranji's nulla-nulla, absorbing it and directing the club back up toward the roof.

Brian heard Jess give a yelp as he cast about for something to use as a weapon. Ranji swiped at him a second time, and again hit the hammock, this time with such force that one of the hooks was torn from the wall. Brian reached for his knife

belt and slid out eight inches of Sheffield steel as the ropes and
mesh of the hammock fell around him like a net; if he could
not stab Ranji now, he would be held like a trapped animal,
easy prey for a clubbing that would not stop until he was dead.
At the same instant that Ranji lifted his nulla-nulla to strike at
the rope-strewn boy at his feet, Brian lunged with the knife,
reaching behind Ranji's legs to slash at the Achilles tendon
above the left heel. The blade's sudden bite caused Ranji to
hesitate, and Brian struck again, deeper this time, and Ranji
knew he had been crippled forever in one leg. He shouted,
hopping backward toward the doorway, blood running over
the foot that already was made useless. His shoulder rammed
against the doorjamb and he spun outside, still hopping, the
club forgotten in his hand. Brian watched him hop and lurch
across the yard toward the tribe's camp, but he did not find the
sight amusing, as he once might have. Today there was room
inside Brian only for hatred, hard and unstinting.

He entered the house and took Doug's rifle without waking anyone, then followed the trail of blood to the camp.
Brian knew exactly what he would do, and the act would be
every bit as liberating as his unflinching acceptance of the ceremonial scars across his chest two years before. Ranji had
treated him like a boy, and Brian was not a boy. Ranji would
never understand that, not while he wanted Jess, and Jess
would never belong to anyone but Brian, with or without
Pitjantjatjara law. Now everything would be sorted out and
done with, whitefella style, so it need never be touched again.

Ranji was half in and half out of the gunyah he had built
for himself, his hands clasped around the crippled ankle, his
cries bringing men and women from the rest of the camp to
see what had happened to him. To Brian, he no longer
seemed the embodiment of leadership, a man to fear; Ranji
was a whimpering fool who had grown too long in the tooth to
demand anything from anyone, even if he was the son of the
kadaicha man.

Ranji's audience stepped back from him as Brian
approached, throwing the bolt on the .303, his face rigid as
ironbark. He did not stop to share his thoughts on the matter
at hand, or to seek any kind of tribal consensus for what he
was about to do; all of that was irrelevant, given Brian's anger

and strength and sudden self-righteousness. He raised the rifle and aimed at Ranji's heart, then pulled the trigger. Ranji was shunted farther back inside the gunyah by the force of the bullet, and there lay still, killed instantly.

"Funny bugger, eh?" said Brian, ejecting the spent shell; it hit the red earth and bounced against his naked toes. Brian shouldered the gun and turned back to the house.

Doug was outside, waiting. "What're you shootin' at this early?"

"Ranji."

"Eh?"

"Come at me with a nulla-nulla when I was sleepin', so I cut him, then I shot him."

"Jesus, Bri . . . you didn't hafta."

"Yeah I did. Old bugger, he sneaked up on me, woulda killed me too."

"Shit. Now there's gunna be blood on the moon. Gimme that."

Brian handed over the rifle. Ishi and Val came outside. Jess was peering from the doorway of Brian's shed.

"What happened?" Val asked.

"Stay here," said Doug, and he started for the camp.

By noon, the tribe had arrived at an appropriate reaction to Brian's act. There was really just one way to punish him for murder, and that was the way that had been a part of tribal law since the Dreamtime. M'linga, escorted at either elbow by a woman, came to the house and stood at the door until Brian went outside. A staccato conversation in Pitjantjatjara followed, and Brian translated the gist of it.

"Gotta get a spear chucked at me." He grinned, not at all disturbed at the prospect.

"Spear?" Clive said.

Doug explained. "If an Abo gets murdered, the one who did it's gotta stand and let someone chuck a spear at him. He's got a fifty-fifty chance of gettin' away with it."

"What, you mean, just stand still and be a target?"

"He can bob and weave a bit, but his feet can't move. If his feet move, he's a coward, and he'll get speared to death anyway."

"He doesn't have to do it," said Val. "It's a stupid way of doing things. Brian's not a full-blood, so he doesn't have to."

"Wanna send for a barrister from Darwin to defend him?" Doug asked.

"No need for nunna that," said Brian. "I reckon I'll come through orright. Guess who's gunna chuck the spear?"

"Who?"

"M'linga," said Brian, his grin widening.

"But he's blind, isn't he?" Clive asked.

"Yeah," said Doug, "but he's Ranji's old man, so he's the one that's gunna want Brian dead the most."

"Well, yes, but . . . he's blind, for heaven's sake. How can he possibly hit anything with a spear? Of course, I'm glad it's him, not someone who can see, but it does seem a little peculiar."

"Bri," said Doug, "it's up to you. Stand up to the spear, or if you don't feel like it, I'll just tell M'linga and the rest to piss off."

"They'd sneak back an get me anyway if you done that," Brian said. "I got a chance with the spear. Reckon I can dodge it."

Brian spoke again with M'linga, who turned away and was assisted back to the camp.

"Gotta go over there in a liddle bit an do it," said Brian, his expression cocky.

"I'd wipe that smile off me face if I was you," Doug advised. "You didn't do anythin' smart. Dunno what you're actin' so proud about."

"He come at me, snuck up on me," Brian said.

"Yeah, but once you had him on the run, you shoulda left it at that. Now you're in the shit because you had to show everyone what a big tough man you are."

Brian was not pleased to be criticised in front of Jess and various adults. He said, "Ranji oughta bin done long time back. Oughta bin you that done it, too."

"Me?" said Doug. "Ranji's never been anythin' but cheeky to me."

"You dunno nothin', you don't."

"'Bout as cheeky as you're gettin' right now."

"Ranji, he's the one took me mum off you," said Brian.

"What?"

"He's the one took Mandy and run off with her all that time back. Me mum."

Val saw that Doug was literally speechless for a moment.

"Brian," she said, "is this true?"

"Yeah. Ranji done it, took her away to Arnhem Land, then he left her there an she got sick real bad."

"How do you know this?" Val said.

"Crikey, everyone knows it, always has done, eh."

"Includin' you," said Doug, finding his voice.

"Yeah, course."

"Why didn't you ever tell me, then . . . ?"

"'Cause Ranji, he said he'd cut me guts out. He reckoned you gimme to the tribe, so you never wanted me, so I hadda keep it a secret like the rest of 'em done all that time. So . . . Ranji's the one done it to you, Dad, an I killed him. He was a bugger, that bloke. Did that to me own mum an dad. . . ."

Doug walked away and sat beneath a gum tree.

"Don't anyone go over there," said Val, "especially you, Brian."

Brian, his revelation having caused more pain than joy, retreated to his shed and closed the door on himself and Jess.

Clive said, "One of the first things Doug ever told me, back in '39, was how Mandy was taken away by someone. He said at the time he'd like to have killed whoever did it, and now Brian's done exactly that. But it's too messy for irony, isn't it, really. . . . How could Bri possibly keep such a secret and live alongside the fellow he knew his father would have liked to kill? It seems quite bizarre to me."

"Don't bother asking," Val advised. "It's the Territory."

She went inside the house to decide if she was jealous over the effect a long-dead woman had clearly had on Doug, while Clive explained to Ishi what had happened.

The ground chosen for Brian's test of courage was not far from the house, an open piece of land fringed by gum trees. Everyone from the house, and every member of the tribe, was present.

Doug took Brian aside. "Don't move around if you can

help it," he advised, "and don't open your bloody mouth at all. The old bugger's probly got ears like a bat."

"No worries." Brian grinned. He was looking forward to a victory dance after M'linga's spear whistled uselessly past him. Jess would be proud of the way he had dodged the spear, and they could both be happier than before, with Ranji gone from the world. The spear chucking would be the end of it; once it was dodged successfully, there would be no further recriminations.

"Never mind your no fuckin' worries, you little idiot; just listen to what I tell you for once. You stand there quiet as a bloody mouse, and you might live. Wipe that smile off your face!"

"Jeez, Dad, no need for that, eh. He couldn't hit a tree if they put him next to it, I reckon."

"Get over there and shuddup."

Brian swaggered to the place that had been allotted him, a circle drawn in the earth, not more than two feet across. He stood at its centre and waved to Jess, standing to one side with the lubras. M'linga was led to a spot ten yards from Brian. A long shovel-nosed spear was placed in his hands, its end fitted into a woomera. M'linga lifted the weapon and had its tip nudged in the direction of Brian by one of the men assisting him.

Everyone became perfectly still, utterly noiseless. Brian pulled several faces for the benefit of Jess, then concentrated on watching M'linga, who stood with the spear upraised, his throwing arm held back, ready for the least clue to Brian's exact whereabouts. He moved not at all, despite the flies crawling across his skin and the weight of the spear and woomera supported by his skinny arms. A minute passed, then two, and M'linga did not so much as twitch. Brian became impatient with the delay and relaxed his tense posture, placing both hands on his hips, spreading his feet to the edges of the circle. His grin was returning; it was obvious M'linga had only the broadest idea where to throw the spear.

"Garn, y'old bugger!" he taunted. "Takin' all bloody day!"

"Shuddup, Brian!" Doug yelled.

M'linga reacted to neither voice. He stood as before, the spear ready for throwing, no part of his body moving. It had been at least four minutes since he had adopted his stance.

Brian gave several excellent imitations of birdcalls to give M'linga a hint of his whereabouts, but still the old man maintained his position, not even twisting his head slightly, the way a blind man was expected to when listening intently for sounds to orient himself by. Watching, Doug felt as he had on the morning of the first executions he had witnessed on Dombi, when the sword had seemed to be held upraised forever but then had fallen so swiftly.

"No bloody fun, this . . . !" said Brian, and M'linga threw the spear. It appeared to reach in a long black line from his extended arm and the woomera to Brian's stomach, and then the line was broken as Brian lurched backward, angling the spear's end toward the sky as he fell. The tip had passed clean through him. His eyes and mouth were wide as he touched the earth.

Doug reached him before anyone else. Brian could only gasp and gasp, each breath weaker than the one before. Doug lifted his son's head onto his knee and held Brian there while the life began leaving him. He could say nothing, offer no comfort; anyone could see the boy was close to death. Brian's eyes would not focus. Doug was unsure if he knew his father was there. Doug took his son's face in one hand and turned it a little, so their eyes could meet, and it was then that Brian died, the full weight of his body sagging against the spear point beneath him. The wound was so terrible several pints of blood had gushed from him before his heart stopped beating, and it was in this pool of redness spreading across red earth that Doug knelt, with his son's head on his knees and wordless grief rising up within himself.

Clive watched as Val went halfway to Doug and Brian, then stopped. From where Clive stood, the spear that had transfixed Brian seemed also to have struck Doug, so still was he, with his boy's head cradled on his lap. Val went closer and knelt with her husband. Doug's face was blank. Val could tell Brian was already gone. Blood was soaking into the worn hem of her dress, its redness greedily invading the sun-bleached cloth. Val watched the first fly alight on Brian's cheek. Doug brushed it stiffly away, but another came, and then dozens, crawling into every crevice of the wound in Brian's side. In the Territory, there could be no moment of dignity following death, no passage between worlds that was not immediately sought out and visited by the maggot-bringers.

The Pitjantjatjara were leaving, gathered around M'linga like a royal entourage. Clive watched them withdraw from the area without a word, their few belongings already bundled for departure. He saw Ranji's body, carried between two men, and assumed he was being taken elsewhere for whatever ceremonial burial was befitting the son of a man like M'linga. Clive noticed also that Jess was among those departing. The girl had not approached her dead lover, had simply accepted that he was no longer an alternative to tribal life, and gone with the rest. She did turn back once, but Clive was the only one to see this.

Ishi stood with both hands against his chest, his eyes pouring tears. "Sad to see . . . Sad to see . . . ," he whispered.

Doug would not be helped with the grave. He spaded earth for the rest of the day and by sundown had a hole prepared a few yards from Judy's marker. He sawed through the spear's shaft and drew the barbed tip all the way through, then carried Brian unassisted to the grave and climbed down into it with his son, then laid him down.

"Can't get out, mates," he said, extending both hands up to Clive and Ishi. They each took hold and pulled him out. Clive could feel the tremor that ran through Doug's arm. Val had said, earlier in the afternoon, "He isn't strong enough for all this," and Clive was inclined to believe her. They stood at the four corners of the grave and looked down at Brian, already lost in the shadows of evening there.

"Clive," said Val, "do you know anything that would sound right?"

"Let me think . . . yes, I believe so. Might be a bit rusty." He cleared his throat.

"Under the wide and starry sky
Dig the grave and let me lie.
Glad did I live and gladly die,
And I laid me down with a will.

"This be the verse you grave for me:
Here he lies where he longed to be;
Home is the sailor, home from the sea,
And the hunter home from the hill."

Doug picked up the spade and began covering his son.
When he continued without obvious intent to share the task,
Val said, "I think we all have something to contribute here."
Doug handed the spade to her. When she had done enough,
she passed it to Clive, who passed it to Ishi when the time
came, and so Brian was buried by them all. It was dark by
then, and there was the sound of approaching thunder from
the north. Val could tell by the feel of the air that any backlog
of rains was about to be made up and interest paid on the
period of withholding.

She gave Clive a nudge and watched him begin walking
back to the house, along with Ishi. "Want to be by yourself?"
she asked Doug.

"Dunno what I want anymore."

They stood together. There was lightning along the horizon
now. "Gunna come in strong," Doug said. "Get the river up
nice and high; that's good."

"Yes."

"Been worried about it bein' so low."

"So've I. It'll be up to the usual place by tomorrow night, I
expect."

"Yeah, probly. Val?"

"Yes?"

"I know how it musta been for you now, when Jude died,
only you were on your own, so that musta been worse'n this."

"I had Brian . . . ," Val said, then stopped.

"Yeah, well, now we got each other," Doug said.

"And Wilf," Val reminded him.

"And Wilf. If Ranji and the rest of 'em hadn't believed all
that shit about Blighty, they never woulda been hangin'
around the place for Bri to get in trouble with. Christ, what a
stupid way to die. . . . I've lost two now, Val, and both of 'em
woulda been all right if we lived somewhere else. . . ."

"But we live here. Wilf'll be all right. It's just been bad
luck."

"They better not come around again, lookin' for him, spoutin' their crocodile bullshit. . . . I'll shoot 'em if they do, I swear it."

"They won't come back now."

"They better not."

Val went to the baby, who had lain throughout beneath a nearby tree, and picked him up. "We'll go inside now," she said, "and get something on the stove. You come in when you're ready."

She went into the house, reaching the doorway just as rain came sweeping across the bushland to begin its familiar hammering upon the tin roof. The noise increased within seconds to a relentless din that made conversation inside the house impossible. Doug came in after just a few minutes, soaked to the skin, his hat a sodden mess. He sat at the table and stared at the lamp Clive had lit, and was grateful for the rain that rendered all further opinion and sentiment redundant.

The return of the Wet brought with it an air of gloom that settled over Redlands like a shadow. It rained unrelentingly for two days, and at the end of that time Clive and Ishi declared it was not right to infringe upon the privacy of a married couple any longer, and they began putting Brian's shed to rights, so they might occupy it together. Doug made no objection, and Val was relieved that they had chosen to do it. Doug was poor company at the moment, and his mood had little to do with the weather. Some part of him was gone, an essential part, without which he was not Doug anymore. Val hoped it would return, as a similar part of herself, gone for weeks after the death of Judy, had eventually found its way back to her. She left him alone when he made it clear he did not want to be spoken to or fussed over, and spent time with the other men, helping them clean out the shed.

There were two dry days, then the rains came down harder than before. Doug went to the Flying Fox and saw that the level was higher than he had ever seen it before, so high that he was obliged to drag the dinghy from the river so it wouldn't be swept away by the still-rising waters. Both ends of the crossing chain were already hidden by the rushing red froth creeping up the sides of the anchor trees on either bank. Doug felt safe as he watched the torrent sweeping by; it was a barrier between himself and the world he had chosen to ignore, with its rules and punishments and limited understanding of himself and what he had done. He did not trust that world, but he trusted the Flying Fox to keep him separated from it until such time as he could think of a solution to the dilemma he had created. Doug could not imagine, for the present, what form such an escape plan might take, but he was sure it lay ahead of him, ahead of them all, like a track through the bush that no one else could see, a hidden avenue to freedom.

The one symbol of his homeland that Clive would have preferred to have with him was an umbrella. He was beginning to find that the shed he now shared with Ishi was as intolerable, when lived inside for hour upon hour, as the house had been. His only alternative to listening while rain beat on the roof, and holding stilted conversation with his friend, was walking, and that required an umbrella as part of one's necessary equipage, along with a fly net for one's hat. But there was no such thing as an umbrella at Redlands.

Then Clive was reminded of his chest of books, the very same chest he had brought with him from England in 1939. The chest stood where he had last seen it prior to his leavetaking for enlistment in the army; Val had covered it with a cloth and used it as a corner table to support her few poor knickknacks of decoration, and Clive did not resent its use for such pedestrian purposes, but now he needed access to those books.

"I need a bit of distraction, Val, a damn good read, in fact. Do you mind if I disturb your table?"

She helped him remove every object and the lace-trimmed cloth beneath them. Together they lifted the lid of the book chest, and together they smelt the odour of decay that came wafting from its interior.

"God . . . What happened?"

"Oh, Clive, I'm sorry. . . . I tried reading some of them after you went away, but they were all over my head, so I shut the chest and never looked inside it again."

Every book had been reduced by white ants to a block of pulpy material, rotten with digestive juices and confinement in a damp place. Clive was devastated by the loss, Val contrite. "I feel awful, Clive. Were they very valuable? Some of them had really nice leather covers. I should've taken them out regularly, but I forgot."

"It's all right," Clive told her. "There weren't any first editions, nothing valuable, just a lot of old friends, so to speak. It can all be replaced. Poor old Marcus Aurelius," he said, lifting out a thoroughly destroyed volume with a little of its binding still intact. White ants fell from it in outraged legions. "Pong a bit, don't they?" said Clive.

"It'll have to be taken outside," said Val. "Everything'll have to be burnt, even the chest, I think. The inside's all rotten too. I feel awful."

"Oh, don't worry; it's a reminder of the temporary nature of things, a pungent metaphor, if you will. No great loss. Shall we take care of it now? It isn't raining, for once."

They dragged the trunk outside, away from the house, and doused it with kerosene, then Clive threw a match into it. His library was consumed within minutes, the gutted volumes eaten by flame. The chest, nicely dried by the fire inside it, began burning too, and that was when Doug came running into the yard from the bush, yelling at them to put out the fire. "Want everyone to see it?" he said, throwing soil over the trunk.

"It isn't making all that much smoke," said Val, "no more than the stove does. Stop making such a fuss."

Doug stepped back and watched the trunk burn. "That's what I shoulda done with the boat," he said. "Plenty a kero, and she woulda burned down to the waterline."

The burning trunk was somehow cheering to Doug, and when the sides were gone, he kept turning the bottom over to keep it going as long as he could, until only embers remained. Doug continued staring at these long after Val and Clive returned to the house.

On a day that promised to be rainless, Doug said, "We're low on tucker. Who feels like helpin' me cop a water buffalo for din-dins?"

He appeared quite animated at the prospect of a hunt, so Clive volunteered to join him, and Ishi too, until he learned that the expedition would be conducted on horseback. "No ride horse. Too big high from ground. Fall off, be kill. No thank you verrer much. Stay here, help cook buffaro when you come back."

The rifle was loaded, a variety of knives were distributed between Doug and Clive, and they set off toward the lagoon, leading a third horse to use for bringing the meat home, should they be successful.

"You know," said Clive, "this is my very first bash at hunting."

"Probly won't be the last. We're runnin' outa food pretty fast now, with all those mouths and no trips into town for a while yet."

"And when the Wet has gone, and the track to Darwin is usable again?"

"Then Val goes and gets us the stuff we need. Can't be you or me, or Ishi."

"And thereafter? How long do we keep this up?"

"You tell me. I've stopped makin' plans and decisions. I got meself into trouble that way. Now I'm just gunna take it as it comes."

"I'm trying to decide if that's fatalism or something more prosaic."

"More what?"

"More like simply not giving a damn anymore."

"That's it. I don't give a damn anymore."

"Doug, you can't sidestep everything that's eventually going to start coming down the track to your place."

"Maybe not."

"So a bit of planning for the Dry might be a good idea at this stage, while we still have the opportunity to make plans."

"You make 'em, Clive. I've had it with plans."

"You have a wife and son."

"They'll be all right. They haven't done anythin' wrong."

"As a matter of fact, Val will be in all kinds of bother if it's found out that she's been harbouring a couple of soldiers absent without leave, not to mention one of the enemy. She could very well be sentenced to a prison term, under wartime regulations. You can't simply ignore what might happen."

"You find a way out, and I'll listen."

°   °   °

The idea of visitors to Redlands had always been associated in
Val's thoughts with the track leading across the Flying Fox. That
was the direction from which white visitors had always come and
the direction she associated with Darwin and every other aspect
of civilisation in the Top End. She was not prepared, then, for the
arrival of anyone from any other point of the compass. Doug and
Clive had not been gone more than an hour, and Ishi was with her
in the house, when a voice outside called, "Hullo in there!"

Val pointed to the bed. "Hide . . . ," she whispered, and
Ishi dived for cover beneath the dragging sheets. Val went to
the door and opened it just a few inches. Constable Royce
Curran of the Territorial Police was outside, mounted on one
sturdy horse, leading another by a rope. When he saw Val he
swung down from the saddle.

"Morning, Val. You look a bit surprised to see me."

She glanced behind her at the room, wondering if any evidence of Doug's return and occupancy was there to be
absorbed by a policeman's eyes. There seemed to be no such
thing, and everything belonging to Clive and Ishi was inside
the shed. If she refused to invite Royce inside, he would
become suspicious; bush courtesy demanded a cuppa and a
chinwag at the very least.

He stamped mud from his boots as he approached the
door. Val stepped aside to allow him through.

"Where'd you spring from? I wasn't expecting to see anyone till the Dry."

"I've been east of here the last few days," he said, taking
off his hat. "Crossed the Flying Fox about fifteen mile up
from here. Wasn't running too bad then, but I bet she's roaring down now."

Val busied herself with the kettle and stove, keeping her
back to him.

"Noticed all your horses are out of the pen," Royce said.
"Haven't lost them, I hope."

"Brian's got them. He's out checking up on the cattle."

"You can lose them in this weather, all right. Silly buggers
get bogged down somewhere and don't have sense enough to
get themselves out. Why'd he take three nags?"

"Exercise. It's bad for horses, not getting worked."

"Still working hard, Brian?"

"Yes. He's a good lad. I'd be lost without him."

She faced him while the kettle boiled, watching his eyes roam around the room.

"Reason I was out and about," Royce said, "is Ranji's mob. Old Pop Bailey at Mellindy Downs sent a message on the pedal wireless. Hopping mad, he was. Said Ranji's mob came through and speared one of his bullocks. I found what was left, but Ranji and the rest had cleared out days before. Did they give you any trouble before they left here?"

"No, not at all."

"How long ago did they leave?"

"Oh, about a week, just before the rain came back."

"Any particular reason why they left?"

"They didn't say; just packed up their things and went walk-about. You know how they are."

Royce stood and went to the bed, where Wilf lay.

"Nice-looking kid, healthy-looking."

"He's a little beaut. Hardly ever cries."

"Bet he misses his dad."

"You can't miss what you've never known."

"Heard anything from Doug at all?"

"Haven't been able to get to the letter box. It's on the other side of the river."

"That's right. So it is. So, no word."

"Nothing. Why, have you heard something?"

Royce came back to his seat at the table. "I have," he said.

"Don't keep us in suspense, then."

"It's what you might call unofficial notification. I haven't got the actual papers on me, of course, and it's army business, not police business, but word gets passed around, so you can take it from me as fact."

"Take what from you?"

"Look, I hate to be the one, but you should know now, before the post gets to you, that Doug's been listed as missing."

"Says who? Missing where?"

"Well, at sea."

"He's a soldier, not a sailor."

"I know that. The fact is, a lot of prisoners were being

taken by ship to Japan from some prison camp or other—did you know he'd been captured?"

"No."

"Well, he was, and later on he was part of this prisoner of war convoy that was torpedoed by the Yanks. They didn't know there were prisoners aboard any of the ships they sank. The Japs didn't bother marking any of them, so they got hit along with the rest. There were survivors, about a hundred and eighty, I think it was. They were picked up by a couple of the subs that sank them. English and Aussies. Doug wasn't among the ones saved, Val. He was seen alive after the sinking, but he wasn't picked up later on with the rest."

"I see. So there's no proof he's dead."

"No actual proof, no. That'd be pretty hard to come by, under the circumstances. He's officially listed as missing, in any case, but ... well, I don't have to point out to you just what that means after all this time. The torpedoing took place more than a month ago now, did I tell you that?"

"No, you didn't."

"There'll be some kind of official notification coming to you, but with the Wet like it is, that mightn't be for some time."

"Thanks for letting me know."

She poured tea into the pot and set it down on the table, then fetched two cups, aware that Royce was studying her closely. She wondered if she was behaving in the way a distraught wife ought to, but could not bring herself to begin playacting with tears.

"Haven't got any sugar left," she said, sitting opposite Royce, her face rigid.

"You'll be glad to get back into town for a bit of shopping, then."

"I will, yes."

Royce said, "You don't believe he's dead, do you?"

"When I see his body, not before."

"That's not going to happen, Val. He disappeared at sea."

"I'll think what I want to think."

She poured tea for them both. Royce picked up his cup.

"Who's buried in the new grave out there?"

Val waited until she had poured a cup for herself before replying.

"That's Ranji. He died last week."

"How?"

"Heart attack, I suppose. He just fell over."

"And M'linga let you bury him here?"

"Why wouldn't he?"

"I don't know; it's just not something I would've expected an important kadaicha man like M'linga to do with his son. I would've expected Ranji to get taken away and buried in some secret Abo place, with a bit of a ceremony to send him on his way."

"They had a ceremony. I don't know what it was all about."

"What, Brian didn't explain it to you?"

"He said it was Abo business and I didn't need to know."

"And then they packed up and left."

"Yes."

"So now Ranji's mob is without Ranji. Suppose they'll call it M'linga's mob now."

"They might do; I wouldn't know."

"Not drinking your tea?"

"Haven't got the taste for it."

"The news about Doug."

"Yes."

"There's more news about Doug, but I don't know if I should tell you."

"Tell me what?"

"This isn't official, either, you understand, but it came from someone I know in the military, a reliable kind of bloke, so I tend to believe it."

"Well?"

"Doug's in trouble, if he's alive. A lot of trouble. I haven't heard of anyone being in this kind of trouble before, frankly. It's nothing typical, nothing humdrum."

"That's Doug for you. What's he done, made off with the regimental silver?"

"Killed an English officer, they say."

"Oh, bullshit."

"Might be, might not be. This bloke I was telling you about, he's got all the inside information. A lot of the Pommies that got picked up by the subs talked about what Doug did when they were all in captivity. They all tell the same story, Val."

"What story's that?"

"They say Doug killed this officer, a major, because he blamed him for certain deaths among the Aussies. So far none of the Aussies rescued have said tickety-boo about the allegations. They remember Doug, they say, but that's all. The English are lying bastards, they're saying. Doug didn't kill anyone. Think Doug could do a thing like that?"

"No."

"He killed Ken Moxham not so long ago."

"That was an accident."

"Well, they gave him the benefit of the doubt. Ken's body never did turn up, a bit like the way it is with Doug, assuming Doug's dead."

"Isn't that what everyone's saying, that he's dead?"

"They are, but you're not. I tend to think like you do, Val. If there isn't a body, there's no proof he's dead, sea or no sea. Doug was a pretty fair sailor, wasn't he?"

"What's that got to do with it?"

"If he found himself a lifeboat, he's the kind of bloke who'd have a go at rowing home. That's how I see Doug."

"You didn't say he found a lifeboat."

"I don't know that he did. The sub captains saw quite a few drifting about, though. Some had Japs aboard, and they got left there. Only room for Allies on an Allied sub. Too bad for the Japs, eh. But there were other lifeboats, empty ones, probably launched too soon, and they just drifted away. Sailors in a panic, they're liable to do that. Anyway, there were one or two of these boats drifting about, as I say, and they weren't small boats, either, some of them. Some had masts and sails all neatly lashed inside. A bloke like Doug, if he found a boat like that, he'd definitely have a go at reaching home, wouldn't you say? Six hundred miles north, that's where it happened. Reckon Doug'd be able to sail that far?"

"I don't know. I doubt it, not in monsoon season."

"But the monsoon's been kind this year so far. No whopping big storms or anything like that. It was pretty calm around the time of the sinkings. See the way my thoughts are turning, Val?"

"He'd be here by now, if that happened."

"Not if he got shipwrecked somewhere along the coast. He

might be slogging along through the mangroves, heading home all tattered and torn, like a hero in the flicks. Can you picture it?"

"Not really."

"You'd better hope it's true, because your cousin's with him, they say."

"What cousin?"

"Have you got more than one? The English one, Clive Bagnall."

"Clive? You're making it up."

"Just telling you what's been told to me. Like something in a book, isn't it? Best mates bump into each other in prison camp and drift away together when their ship goes down later on. I reckon those two'd fight like tigers to come home, knowing their cousin and wife was just six hundred miles away."

"I'm not pouring you another cup."

"That's all right, Val; I'm not too keen on tea without sugar."

They both heard a rifle shot in the distance.

"Who might that be?" asked Royce.

"Brian. He said he'd get us a buffalo to eat if he could. That's why he took the extra horses, to bring the meat back."

"I've had buffalo. Bit tough, in my opinion."

"Not if you get a young one. Anyway, beggars can't be choosers."

"Just you and Brian, you won't be able to get through much buffalo meat before the rest spoils."

"I'll salt down what I can."

"They never did find that Yank."

"What Yank?"

"The one that came here to buy meat, then disappeared."

"Nothing to do with me."

"I didn't say it was. It's funny about this place, though, how people come and go in funny ways, starting with your dad. If Doug was to show up, and Clive too, that'd be pretty incredible for some other place, but not for Redlands."

"I'm not even going to comment on that piece of stupidity. If you want to go down to the Flying Fox and see if it's low enough to cross, you can use the dinghy."

Royce stood. "That's the trouble with being the bearer of

bad news. People get a bit upset, and then they blame the messenger, don't they? Human nature, I suppose."

Val went to the door. Royce followed and unhitched his horses. They walked around the bend to the river, Val hoping that Ishi had sense enough to give them plenty of time to be out of sight before leaving his hiding place beneath the bed. The river was still swollen but had fallen several feet from its record height of several days before.

"I don't think I'll risk it," said Royce, "thanks all the same."

"What'll you do now?" Val asked, suddenly afraid that he would suggest staying the night.

"Go back the same way. My black tracker's still out at Mellindy Downs. Broke his leg when his horse slipped in the mud. Fractured femur, can't ride at all for a month or so, I'd say, so he's stuck out there with Pop Bailey. I wonder what he could've told me about the ground hereabouts if he'd been with me. He's a bloody good tracker. Tell you anything you want to know about who's been where and how long ago and if they're still hanging around. He'll be jake again by the time the Dry comes, though. I'll bring him by and introduce him to Brian."

"All right."

They began walking back toward the house. Reaching the yard, Royce swung up onto his horse. "Just so's you don't get the wrong idea," he said, "if what I've heard is true, then Doug did something I personally wouldn't want to charge him over. But I'm not the prime minister, or some army bigwig, so what I think doesn't count. If Doug's alive somewhere, he's in trouble, and the trouble's only going to get worse. A story like this, with hundreds of witnesses, you can't keep it bottled up for long. If he comes back, Val, you tell him he'd better make himself scarce, or else give himself up and hope for a fair court-martial."

"He didn't get one when Ken Moxham died."

"That wasn't a court-martial; that was a hearing."

"Same thing, different name. He got the shitty end of the stick, in any case. He'd never give himself up now."

"That's his choice." Royce looked across at Brian's grave. "Why'd you bury Ranji so close to your own kid, Val? I wouldn't have put a stranger right next to my own family like that."

"Brian dug the grave. Ask him, why don't you?"

"Sure it isn't Doug that's buried there?"

"It isn't Doug."

"Or your cousin?"

"It isn't Clive."

"But it isn't Ranji, either, is it?"

"Why don't you dig it up and find out."

Royce grinned. "Haven't got the energy. Be seeing you, Val."

He rode away into the bush.

Val remained alone for the rest of the day. At nightfall, Doug suddenly dashed through the door. "Had to wait and see if Royce stayed around, watchin' the place through binoculars. He's gone, though; tracked him for miles just to make sure."

He picked up the lamp from the table, took it to the open door and swung it back and forth several times, then came back to Val. "You musta sweet-talked him like a good 'un."

"I didn't sweet-talk him at all. Royce isn't an idiot, Doug; he knows something's going on. Those prisoners you left behind, they survived, a hundred and eighty of them, and they talked; the English ones did anyway. You're wanted for murdering the major."

"Shit!"

They listened to the sound of hooves as Clive and Ishi led the horses to the pen.

Buffalo meat in considerable quantity was brought into the house. Val insisted that the men help her salt the best pieces. When this was done, Clive called for a meeting that he insisted on referring to as a council of war.

"I'm not at war with anyone," Doug said.

"That's beside the point. The military might of England— and, for all we know, Australia—is slowly being brought to bear on you."

"The Aussie government wouldn't let the Poms hang me."

"Are you sure? Is the Australian political system really so independent? You said yourself that when England whistles, Australia jumps."

"Clive's right," said Val.

"So what am I supposed to do, eh? Give meself up? Nah, not on your nellie."

"Go into hiding and hope that you're officially declared dead. Then, at some later date, you can create another identity for yourself. You'd have to leave the Territory, though. Big cities are the best places to hide. You simply become a face in the crowd. I recommend that you grow a moustache too, just to be sure."

"I don't like moustaches, and I don't like big cities. Visitin' 'em's one thing, but livin' there'd be like livin' in hell."

"But living," Val said, "not dead. Pull your head out of your bum, for God's sake."

"All right for you to talk; you're from the big smoke. You'd probly like to go back, wouldn't you?"

"I could do it tomorrow, and so could you."

"Well, I'm not gunna."

"Grow up!"

"This is my place, and I'm not gunna leave!"

"It isn't your place! It's my place and Clive's place!"

"I meant the Territory, not Redlands."

"You have Wilf to think of," Clive reminded him.

"How about you, mate? You're absent without leave. Gunna get yourself another name, like you want me to do?"

"If I have to, yes."

"And what do we do with Ishi? Can't just make up a new name for him and expect him to live in Sydney with no worries."

"I give myself up," offered Ishi. "Prison camp here, not so bad."

"That won't work," said Clive. "If you give yourself up, Ishi, they'll want to know how you got here, and they simply won't believe you came alone. No, we're all in this together. One saved, all saved."

"So we're rooted," said Doug.

"You do surprise me," Clive said. "On Dombi you concocted the most amazing plans for escape. They were pretty impossible, but at least you used your head to think of ways to let hundreds of men get away. Now there are just three of us, and you're ready to throw in the towel."

"Four and a half, including me and Wilf," said Val.

"Still a small number," Clive insisted.

"Like I told you today," Doug said, "you think of a way outa this, and I'll do it."

"Honestly, Doug," said Clive, "getting your cooperation is like getting blood from a stone."

Val felt a strange humming in her head, and the wrangling going on around the table faded from her ears. Blood from a stone. The stones she had found once, and never again—Kukullumunnumantje. The stones no one could find, unless it was decreed that one should, as she, for unknown reasons, had been allowed to do. Gulgulong had decreed it, according to M'linga, because Val was to bear him a son. It was ridiculous, but it had happened. The place of stones had been shown to her wandering feet, revealed to her when lost and alone, and forever after hidden away again. Would Gulgulong allow her to find the place a second time? How did one ask a crocodile to intervene on behalf of a wanted man? How did one tell the man his salvation might be found through the good graces of a crocodile?

"Val?"

She turned to Doug.

"Thought you'd gone off on a moonbeam or somethin'."

"I'm going to bed." She stood up, effectively ending the discussion. Clive and Ishi went out to the shed.

"What's up?" Doug asked.

"Nothing. I have to think."

"So I hafta shuddup."

"Yes, please."

"Jeez, a bloke has to put up with some bloody insults."

"This bloke," said Val, "should be grateful he's got a smart missus."

"Not bad-lookin', either," said Doug, sounding vaguely hopeful as he watched Val undress.

Val knew he was not seriously interested in making love; he was simply attempting to convince her he was the old, joking Doug she had married, but it was not a convincing performance. "If you can't leave me alone to think," she told him, "you can join the others in the shed."

"See what I mean? Insults."

Val lay on the bed and attempted to reconcile opposing cultures, a century and a half of dissonance and antagonism. She was not successful, even when Doug finally fell asleep beside her, but she did decide, before falling asleep herself, to proceed with a plan that did not take into account the fact that she was a white woman of the twentieth century; she would forget all that and ask Gulgulong to help her. After all, the worst he could do was refuse.

Val waited until the men were elsewhere, the following afternoon, before taking one of the less palatable chunks of buffalo meat Doug and Clive had brought home. She shouldered it on a pad of gunnysacking and began walking toward Blighty's Pond, surrounded by an attentive cloud of flies determined to get their share before the croc got his.

Gulgulong had been suspicious at first of the thing that sank into his billabong. It had been burning when it came to his attention, the way the bush around the waters he inhabited sometimes burned. Gulgulong did not like fire and had kept away from the thing, even after the flames went out and it continued to float above him. The three gunshots that had made it start sinking also caused Gulgulong to stay clear; he had heard gunshots before and associated them with the men who had come hunting him over the years; one bullet had passed through the fleshiest part of his tail, and he recalled the pain that had stayed with him thereafter.

The thing settling in the water was a boat. Gulgulong had attacked several of these in the course of his life and eaten the humans aboard that he had dumped into the water with his sudden lunging against and overturning of their craft. Humans were his preferred food, when he could get them, since they were without defensive claws or teeth and were easily subdued once he dragged them below the surface of the water, down into his world. Gulgulong was two hundred and thirty-one years old and had eaten nine humans.

As time passed and he became accustomed to the boat resting in the mud at the bottom of his pond, Gulgulong approached it and crawled inside the hull. It accommodated most of his length, and he became used to treating it as a place in which to wait for prey during the daylight hours, since it received plenty of warmth as the sun passed overhead, beaming its light down into the water. He often dozed while inside the hull, knowing that he would still be able to hear the sounds of any living thing that might approach his domain. He was asleep when Val came to him, but he was awake by the time she set down the buffalo meat. Gulgulong could sense it even through water, and he rose toward the surface very slowly, with just the slightest flicking of his tail, to investigate what his instincts told him was an unusual offering.

She stood back, once the meat had been dumped onto the muddy bank, afraid to stand beside it, even though she suspected the crocodile would prefer something dead to something living. She knew he would come by the tremors running along her skin and the cold sweat that began seeping through her dress. Val felt the hairs rising on her neck, and from that moment breathing became difficult. She watched the surface of the pond, a broad expanse, overfilled by the storms of recent days. Somewhere beneath the sun-dappled surface of the water there lay the remains of a boat, and the reptile god of the Pitjantjatjara, whom she was about to make her own god, if supplication and an offering were considered by Gulgulong acceptable substitutes for genuine conversion, true belief. Her fear was that the crocodile would know her faith was born of desperation, not acceptance of his godhead, and so would refuse her meat and her entreaty both. She wished very much to believe, but could not, unless the creature spoke to her or drew hieroglyphics in the mud with his claw.

And he was coming. The water shifted imperceptibly, the shadows beneath the upside-down reflections of clouds darkening slightly, creating the faintest surge as the shadow that was longest became a physical thing, its outline lost in distortion and cloud. Then his back rose into the air, and his eye sockets of yellow with their slit pupils saw her waiting there, and the craters of his nostrils twitched open to breathe air for the first time in almost an hour. He observed the human and the meat, its odour now powerfully inviting despite being too fresh for immediate consumption. Sometimes humans did this—brought meat to him—and he always knew, with the cunning of his years, whether they brought it as bait, to lure him within striking distance, or whether they simply wished him to have the meat. The human standing beside the meat was not hiding, not waiting to attack him, was afraid of him, the fear radiating from its shape in rippling waves he could almost taste in the air. He would take the offering, rather than the human, since it was already dead and would not require killing and a lengthier wait before the time came to eat it.

Val took several more steps backward, away from the buffalo meat, as Blighty who was Gulgulong began moving toward her, the long snout creating a soft bow wave that fell behind in a gentle V. Now he was in the shallows, the tremendous bulk of him lifting from the water, the fat belly growing broader as he raised himself up, the stubby legs waddling now, the pudgy claws sinking into mud as he came cautiously forward to receive his due. His snout split along the rough line pegged with yellow teeth, became jaws wide enough to grasp a fallen tree. He reached for the meat and took it into his mouth, tossed it once to fit it farther back toward his cavernous gullet, then turned slowly away from the human.

"Help him . . . ," said Val, finding her voice as the creature began its retreat.

Gulgulong stopped and turned his massive head in response to the sound of the human, but he sensed no danger from the noise and continued walking back into the water. When the bank shelved steeply away from his claws, he swam, and when the water beneath him was deep enough, he sank from view into the welcoming murk of his home and the new throne that had come to him from *Shikoku Maru*.

Val waited until the last ripple had passed from the water, then she forced herself to turn away and begin walking. She did not stop shaking until she was back in the yard.

23

WHILE HUNTING THE BUFFALO, DOUG HAD SEEN NOT ONE OF his cattle. In the days that followed, he insisted that business be taken care of in the form of a muster, to establish that the herd was multiplying rather than decreasing. Val admitted that Brian had become negligent after Ranji's mob set up camp close to the house, but she was opposed to Doug's riding around the countryside in full view of anyone who happened to be passing by.

"Like who?" Doug said.

"Like Royce Curran. He's already dropped by once, in the middle of the Wet. He could show up again."

"Yeah, but he'll go to the house, and I'll be miles away, lookin' after the cattle."

"It's too risky."

"Look, we put a lot of money and time and effort into that herd, and I'm not gunna let 'em go bush and get poddy-dodged by some other bastard."

He would not be talked out of it. Clive accompanied him as they began a broad sweep through the bush around Redlands to bring the herd together. The weather was fine, apart from the usual afternoon downpour, and in four days fifty-nine cattle were moved toward the rough pen Doug had built in 1940, about two miles from the house. Doug estimated that there should be at least twice this number, and they began searching farther afield, spending days at a time in the bush with a pack-horse and supplies.

One morning, Doug came across the tracks of a shod horse.

"Someone's been here in the last coupla days."

"Royce Curran?"

"He'd be slinkin' around a lot closer to the house if he was watchin' out for me. This is someone else. I reckon he's pinchin' me cattle, whoever he is."

They began following the hoofprints, a task easy enough even for a white man, given the dampness of the earth, and in the early afternoon they heard the distant crack of a stock whip.

"That's him. We'll move in nice and quiet."

Soon the tracks of the horseman were joined by those of many cattle, and Doug was exultant. "Got the bastard! Come on, mate."

"Is he liable to be armed, do you think?"

"Clive, you're in the Territory, not bloody Texas. He'll be armed with some really bad excuses, that's all."

"What if he recognises you?"

"Not likely to be a local, stealin' from Val. Probly someone from south a here."

They caught up with the cattle thief as an afternoon storm began darkening the sky. At least three dozen cows and bullocks were being driven through the bush by someone Doug could not identify at a distance. The rider's attention was on the cattle ambling ahead of him, and he did not notice the two men closing on him from behind until Doug was just ten yards away. When the rider turned, Doug saw who it was.

"G'day, Les."

Les Moxham's face reflected guilt and surprise in equal measure. Clive rode his horse around to the other side of Les, effectively boxing him in if he should attempt to bolt.

"Thought you were in the fuckin' army, Farrands."

"I thought the same about you. Funny how two smart blokes can both be wrong. What're you doin' here, Les?"

"Got a discharge. Sole survivin' family member. They reckoned I oughta be back home raisin' beef for the blokes overseas. Meat's war work too, y'know."

"If it's your meat and not some other bastard's. They your cows, Les?"

"Yeah; gettin' 'em sorted out."

"They're mine."

"Haven't got your brand on 'em."

"I've been busy, been away fightin'. They're mine, all right."

"Prove it."

"We follered your tracks off my land, so that makes these cattle mine. Get goin', and don't come near Redlands again."

Les placed an uneasy smirk on his face. "Been hearin' stories about you, Farrands. Aren't you sposed to be dead or somethin'? There's talk about you killin' some English bloke."

"Not me; must be someone else."

"Nah, it's you, all right. Turned up again, eh? How'd you manage that?"

"Piss off, Les. Keep your trap shut, and I won't report you for thievin'."

"I don't reckon you're in a position to report anythin'." He turned to look at Clive. "Got your Pommie mate with you too. Heard stories about him as well. Sposed to be a fuckin' traitor to his country. You two are in the shit, or didn't you know?"

"You just keep your mouth shut."

"Heard somethin' else too, when I come back. You're the one that chucked Ken overboard and the sharks got him, they say."

"That's right. He started it, and the sharks finished it."

"You got away with murder that time. Won't happen again."

"You can tell people you saw me, Les, but they won't believe it. I'm dead at the bottom a the sea, and so's Clive."

"Not if I say you're not."

"Who'd believe a lyin' dingo like you? Garn, get out of it, you fuckin' thief."

Les struck at Doug with his stock whip, but Doug flung up an arm and took the blow across his sleeve. He grabbed the lash and pulled hard, unseating Les from his saddle. Doug threw the whip into the nearest tree.

"Go on, move! If I see you again, you'd better be on a bloody fast horse."

Les remounted and edged away from Doug. He disappeared among the trees.

"Well," said Clive, "I'd say that's torn it. He'll tell everyone in Darwin."

"Might not."

"Doug, you know he will."

"Yeah, spose."

"Are you going to get away from here now? Will this do the trick?"

"It'd leave a bad taste in me mouth, knowin' a shit like Les was what made me bugger off."

"The party responsible isn't the point. Sooner or later someone would have spotted you. It happened to be sooner, and it happened to be Les. Now we have to leave, and don't ask me not to tell Val what's happened."

"Let's get these cattle turned around and headed for home."

"Doug! For God's sake! It's finished, don't you understand?"

"Look, Clive, if I hafta leave me own place because a that bastard Les, I'm takin' what I can with me, and that means cattle. We'll take 'em down to Alice Springs through the back blocks where no one's gunna take any notice, and we'll sell 'em."

"That'll take weeks."

"We'll go with what we've already rounded up. It's probly three quarters of the herd, and they'll be worth a few bob. We haven't got any other cash. You wanna walk all the way south to Adelaide, or ride the train?"

"What about Ishi and Val?"

"They'll come too. 'Bout time Ishi learned to ride a horse."

"But he's Japanese, for heaven's sake."

"We'll darken his skin a bit with tea, make him a Malayan or somethin'."

"Ridiculous."

"Less talk, more action."

Doug started turning the cattle around as rain began to fall.

Val thought the scheme was riddled with flaws, but it was the first time Doug had embraced the notion of leaving the Territory, so she agreed with everything he said, and helped prepare four saddle packs and bedrolls. Clive gave Ishi lessons in riding while Doug attended to the hundred-odd penned cattle. Two days after the encounter with Les Moxham, they were ready to depart. Doug went to the graves of his son and daughter and stood there a moment alone, then was joined by Val.

"I feel like I'm runnin' out on 'em."

"You're staying alive. We can come back one day."

"You don't believe that. This is the last time we'll ever stand here."

Val said nothing.

Doug turned away. "Better get movin', I spose."

They joined Clive and Ishi and rode slowly out of the yard. Val looked back, but Doug would not, as the house was left behind.

"Ready to see the real Australia, Ishi?" Doug asked.

"Ready to see, no ready to ride."

"You'll be all right; just take it slow and hang on with your legs if she starts to gallop. Nothin' to it, after a while. There's seven hundred miles between us and the Alice. You'll be a jackeroo by the time we get there, mate."

Ishi's head was covered by a big hat with a double thickness of fly netting dangling from the brim to the neck of his shirt, effectively masking his face from view. He had refused outright to stain his skin with tea, stating that he was "not Abo man."

When they reached the holding pen, Doug bent down from the saddle and unhitched the wire-and-stick gate. He rode slowly into the pen and began urging the cattle out. Val and Clive started the leaders in a southerly direction, and in five minutes the pen was empty. This time, as they began moving again, Doug looked back, not at the pen but at the tracks they were leaving behind. Royce Curran's black tracker might be laid up at Mellindy Downs with a broken leg, but a blind man could follow their trail with ease and would be able to do so for weeks afterward, thanks to the Wet and the muddy earth the cattle were slogging through.

Doug was not a praying man, but he hoped harder than he had ever hoped before in his life that the men who came after them would be slow to start and quick to tire. He had been a fool to wait so long, a fool to wait at all. The four of them should have begun as soon as Clive was over his malaria.

Maybe that way there would have been five, or even six, if Jess had summoned the nerve to come along with Brian. But then Ranji would have followed and made mischief. They would have had to leave the girl behind. It was all a useless exercise, Doug knew, this reworking of events already done with. He had been a stupid bastard, and Brian was dead because of it. At least Ranji was also dead, the long ago kidnapping and waning and dying of Mandy avenged, by way of her son. Doug had played no part other than to witness events perpetrated by others. It should have been him who killed Ranji. Nothing in life ever worked out the way it should, and Doug heard, at the back of his thoughts, a voice telling him that this latest plan would also go disastrously awry. He knew he would have to live with the voice, because even if they got away with it, sold the cattle and went south and became different people, he would hear the voice whispering to him for the rest of his life, as he waited for the hand of authority to fall upon his shoulder.

She supposed it had nothing to do with Gulgulong at all, this sudden burst of sanity from Doug, but Val could not help wondering if her gift of meat, less than a week before Doug announced they were all going south, had somehow shifted the matrix of invisible influences that govern the doings of men. Such ponderings were unanswerable, of course, and she knew she would wait many years before speaking of what she had done. Doug would laugh at her, and Clive would express admiration for so novel and outrageous an act. It would become part of family history. Wilf, who rode before her on the saddle in a bag stitched from a blanket, would never understand how she could have done such a thing, because Wilf would, in all likelihood, never remember the Territory and know its unique contradictions.

Picturing all this, Val realised she must be genuinely hopeful of escape, and her spirits lifted a little. They had barely begun their journey, and already it was an accomplished event in her imagination. Val smiled at herself. Kukullumunnumantje was somewhere near, hidden by Pitjantjatjara magic, or the will of Gulgulong, or perhaps mineral deposits that skewed the needles of compasses; she would never see it again, in any case. The stones were fast becoming one more piece of unfinished business they were fleeing, leaving behind forever. She would never know the full truth behind the death of Perce Burridge; never know if Redlands might one day have become a flourishing cattle station, vindicating Perce's faith in the property; never know if she might have found a kind of happiness growing old and dying as a bush wife; never know what, if anything, the Pitjantjatjara had in store for Wilfred Timothy Farrands—Boy b'long Gulgulong.

It was Clive who saw them first, three black figures among the trees ahead, one of them a woman. Doug saw them next and rode to the front of the herd with Clive.

The woman was Beth, the two men also part of M'linga's mob.

"Waitin' for yer," said Beth.

"Thought you couldn't talk," said Doug.

"Can now. M'linga says."

"Oh, he does, does he? Why's he waitin' for us?"

"Not him. Royce Curran an some bloke."

"This other bloke, has he got a drover's coat and no stock whip?"

"Yeah, thassim."

"Bloody Les Moxham," Doug said to Clive.

Val rode up. "What's happened?"

"Royce Curran and Les are up ahead, waitin' for us. He musta gone straight to Royce at Mellindy Downs and not bothered goin' back to town at all."

"Can't we go around them?" Clive asked.

"Could do, but they'd just follow along till they caught up. We're easy enough to track with this lot."

Beth said, "M'linga wants yer to come with us."

"Beth," said Val, "you can talk?"

"Can now," said Beth. "M'linga says I done me punish."

"How nice of him."

"He wants to see all a yers now. Gotta come, he says."

Val said, "Doug, what if we leave the herd and make a run for it? Royce doesn't have a tracker who can ride. We might be able to lose him, with just four horses."

"Might do."

The two men with Beth spoke to her, their voices angry, abrupt.

"Gotta do what M'linga says," whined Beth. "Get me in bloody trouble if yer don't. Take me talk away again, he will. Garn, do us a favour, eh?"

"We haven't got time for M'linga," Doug told her.

"Gunna help yers all," insisted Beth. "Gunna save yers."

"How?" Val asked.

Beth pointed to the east. "Kukullumunnumantje," she said.

"What on earth's that?" Clive said.

"A place . . . ," said Val, "a special place near here."

"Yes, but I mean to say, what good is it to us, going there?"

Doug was grinning at Val. "You've been droppin' pennies in a wishin' well, haven't you?"

"I might've been. I'm going there."

"Do you know somethin' I don't?"

"I know plenty you don't. Are you coming? It's a way out."

"What way?" said Clive, perplexed. "How? What are you talking about?"

"Gotta leave yer horses," said Beth. "Gotta walk, an bring the baby."

"This is part a that Gulgulong bullshit, isn't it?" said Doug.

Val was dismounting, lifting Wilf from his perch. "Yes, it is. It's for Wilf, but the rest of us can have a piece too, because we're with him."

"Piece of what? Would someone kindly explain?" begged Clive.

"A piece of getting away," Val told him, but Clive still didn't understand.

Ishi joined them at last, having been unwilling to make his horse travel faster than a walk. "Bad thing happen?" he asked, seeing the faces of his friends. "Or good thing?"

"What about these bloody cattle?" Doug said, as Val began walking.

"Them two," said Beth, pointing to her escorts, "they look after 'em. Gotta go where M'linga says, eh. Come on, silly buggers."

He knew they were coming, could sense their approach, the two whitefella men and the whitefella woman, and in her arms, Boy b'long Gulgulong. There was a Japfella too, who had never been part of M'linga's vision, and his presence among the whitefellas, who he had known for many years would be coming to this place at this time, was disturbing. He should have seen the Japfella too, a long time ago, if the Japfella was coming. It made him uneasy. The thing that was happening now should have been in no way different from the thing he had seen behind his eyes so many years before; that was M'linga's strength and his power—that he could see the things to come before they arrived, and see them clearly. He spoke no word to anyone of his doubts.

Words were placed in his ears; the whitefellas and the Japfella were very near and could be seen from the highest stone. They had left their horses and cattle behind, as instructed. M'linga had seen no horses or cattle behind his eyes, so they could not come. The Japfella was there because M'linga had given to a woman the task of bringing the party to Kukullumunnumantje. It should have been the work of a man, but M'linga had relented and given back to Beth the tongue he took from her when she spoke of secret things to the white-fella Perce Burridge. The secrets had killed that whitefella, but his daughter, the mother of Boy b'long Gulgulong, had been shown the secret anyway and so had become a special whitefella woman, which meant that her cousin, the whitefella from behind the sky, and her husband whitefella were also special, by reason of their association with the woman who had been granted permission by Gulgulong to see the remembering stones of Kukullumunnumantje.

But the Japfella should not see the stones. Beth should have used her new tongue to warn him off, but she had not, and now the thing that was happening was happening the wrong way. It was the fault of Beth, and the fault also of M'linga, for not sending a man with the authority to make the whitefellas do what M'linga wanted. He had chosen Beth because she was the half-sister to the blackfella woman who had given birth to Brian. He had done it to let them know he was not happy to have speared the whitefella's son. The things that he had foreseen, and the things that he had done to make those things happen the way they should, formed a line drawn upon stone, a line that wandered here and there, wrapping itself around many things along the way, like a snake embracing its prey, and finally the line had turned in upon itself and was going around and around in smaller circles within circles, and where the line came to an end was this time, this place, and there was no escaping from it.

When she saw the rounded outcropping of red stones, Val stopped. This was the exact approach to Kukullumunnumantje she had made four years earlier. Now it was before her again, the strange agglomeration of rounded stones piled haphazardly, one upon another, like a collapsed stack of gigantic cannonballs. The trees she stood between were the same trees, and the stones carved away a patch of the sky in exactly the same way. She knew that if she went around the stones to the left she would find the same narrow path upward, to the higher levels.

She turned to Doug, who stared at Kukullumunnumantje as if seeing the giant's castle at the top of the beanstalk. "Christ . . . ," he said.

"Told you," said Val.

"I've never seen anything like this," Clive said. "It's . . . quite incredible."

Ishi was watching the dozen or more Aborigines lined up along the crest of the stones. He had no particular fear of them, since they were the same tribe he had been on nodding acquaintance with since living at Doug's place, but he felt a peculiar trembling of the skin across his shoulders and down his spine. He followed the others as they approached the jumbled stones. The shivering would not go away.

"Up here," Val said, and they scrambled up the narrow defile, Val leading the way with Wilf tucked under one arm. When they stood on the midlevel of stones they were not above treetop level, but they climbed no higher, because that was where M'linga sat, his blind eyes turned in their direction. He spoke, and Beth translated.

"M'linga, he says you come 'cause he make you come. Says you hadda come even if yer never wannid to."

"Why did he want us to come here?" asked Val.

Beth addressed the question to M'linga, who replied through her.

"'Cause."

"Are we supposed to hold off the police with gunfire from here?" Clive asked.

"They can't find this place," Val told him. "They won't even come near. We just have to wait here for a while, and Royce and Moxham will go away."

"You seem very sure. Why wouldn't they be able to track us? The cattle are less than a quarter mile away, for heaven's sake."

"They just won't. They can't see this place, Clive. It's invisible unless M'linga says you're allowed to see it."

"I beg your pardon?"

"Don't worry about it," Doug said. "Let's just see if she's right."

Doug began climbing higher, and Clive followed him.

"This place, you say is magic?" asked Ishi.

"Sort of," said Val. "I don't understand it myself, but I was here once before."

"No come get us here?"

"No," Val assured him. "They can't get us here."

"Why Abos do this?"

"I don't know that, either, but they think Wilf is . . . theirs, somehow."

Doug and Clive had reached the highest stone. Three Pitjantjatjara men were already up there, scanning the bush to the west, where the cattle could be seen.

"Royce comin'," said one of the men.

"Arr, shit. Comin' here?"

"Comin'. Got other fella with'm."

Clive said, "So much for Val's invisibility theory. They're simply following our tracks."

"Looks like it, doesn't it?"

"Are you going to use that?" Clive nodded at the .303 slung over Doug's shoulder.

"Nah; that'd make me a real murderer, like they say I am."

Doug called the news of Royce and Les's approach down to Val.

"What?" said Val. "They can't!"

"They bloody can! I can see 'em myself now!"

When Beth told M'linga two more whitefellas were coming, he stood up, so shocked was he that further mangling of his vision was about to take place. It had never been intended this way. The pictures behind his eyes had lied to him, and he did not know what this meant or what he should do to make the things he had seen happen as they should. He could do nothing but stand and await the coming of this shattered event, as its prey will await the jaws of the snake.

Royce had seen the blacks spying on them while they waited for the herd to pass by, and had changed his plans, knowing that M'linga's mob would probably go straight to Doug. Les had agreed that they should go directly to the herd, but when they reached it they found the cattle under the control of two blacks, who simply stared at them and said nothing when questioned by Royce. Les had scouted around during the questioning and found tracks leading from the herd to the east.

"They're on foot, runnin' away!" he called.

They followed the tracks. Royce could not see why Doug and the rest had abandoned their horses. It made no sense, given their predicament.

When they came to the stones, Royce was confused; he had never known of the existence of this formation, and he had been covering this part of the country for years; how could he possibly have overlooked such an unusual place?

"There he is, and the Pom!"

Les was pointing to the top of the jumble of rocks. Doug and Clive stood there with several blacks, making no effort to conceal themselves. Now Royce was doubly puzzled; if Doug had wanted to, he could have led Royce a merry chase around and among rocks like these, but he clearly was not interested in doing so.

"Got the bastard now!" Les said, hurrying forward.

They dismounted. The tracks led directly to the defile, and this led directly to M'linga and most of his people, and Val and a Jap. Doug and Clive were descending from the rock above. Royce took note of the rifle over Doug's shoulder and unsnapped the flap on his holster, although he doubted he would have to draw his pistol.

"G'day, Doug. You're looking healthy for a dead man. You too," he said to Clive.

"How's it goin', Royce? I see the dingo went and whispered in your ear."

"Les is just doing his duty. You know what you're charged with."

"Got you now, smartarse," said Les, stepping forward to snatch the rifle from Doug.

"Might, might not," Doug said. "Royce, I wouldn't trust this bumhole with a gun."

"You can bullshit all you want, Farrands," said Les. "You're stuffed this time."

"That right?" Doug asked Royce. "Me missus told me you reckoned what I did might be a crime, but it was justified, things bein' the way they were. That how you feel, Royce?"

"Might be, but I'm a copper too, and the copper has to take you in, all four of you."

"Not Val," Doug said.

"Val too, for harbouring you lot. Sorry, Doug."

"How 'bout lettin' Ishi go? He wasn't even in the Jap military; he's just a sailor."

"Sorry. He'll be all right in a detention camp; better off than you, probably."

"I'm not gunna go with you, Royce. I'm not standin' trial in front a some bunch a bastards that think they've gotta go by the book and put a rope around me neck. I won't do it."

"You're under arrest, Doug, and that's that."

Val said, "Beth, tell M'linga that Royce wants to put us all in jail, including Boy b'long Gulgulong."

"Who's Boy b'long Gulgulong?" Royce asked, while Beth gabbled in Pitjantjatjara to M'linga.

"This is him," Val said, holding up Wilf.

M'linga said a few words, and suddenly every spear among his people was aimed at Royce.

"Now wait a minute," said Royce. "Don't make this worse than it already is."

"It can't get any worse for us, mate," said Doug, "but it can get a lot worse for you. Just forget about this, eh? Once I'm outa the Territory, I'm outa your hair."

"I can't do that."

"Yes you can," Val said.

"No he can't," said Les, "not while I'm here as a witness.

You let these buggers go, Curran, and I'll make sure you stand
trial too, see if I don't."

"Les," said Royce, "thanks for all your help; now pull your
head in and leave this to me, all right?"

"You're gunna hafta shoot me, Royce," said Doug. "I mean
it."

Val hoped he didn't, but said nothing, waiting to see how
Royce might react.

"Doug, Val, everyone," said Royce, "just start walking back
to your horses."

Val said, "We're staying right here, and there's nothing you
can do about it."

"I can send Les for help," said Royce.

"He'd have to go the long way round," said Doug, "past
Mellindy Downs. Might reach Darwin in three, four days."

"Pop Bailey's got a pedal wireless at Mellindy," Royce
reminded him.

"Got you by the short 'n' curlies, Farrands," said Les, grinning.

"Bastard," Doug said in return. Val heard the defeat in his
voice. Everything that was supposed to have gone right for
them at Kukullumunnumantje had gone wrong.

Ishi suddenly began running toward the rock path they had
all climbed.

"Stop!" Royce called after him. "Stop right there!"

Les ran to the edge of the stones, working the bolt on
Doug's rifle. Ishi was already out of sight. Val could hear the
sound of his sandals slithering down the rocks.

"Les!" shouted Royce. "Put that down!"

Les was aiming the rifle at a point below him. Royce began
to run. "Les! No!"

Royce ran straight into Les from behind, a split second
after Les fired. The rifle was knocked from his shoulder, and
then Les began to fall. The impact of Royce's body slamming
into his own had pushed him from the top of the curved
stone he stood upon. He reached for Royce as Royce reached
for him, but their fingers sliced past each other. Royce saw
Les open his mouth to shout, but no sound came. His boots
were seeking purchase on the smooth stone that curved away
so abruptly. He passed beyond the curve, still traveling backward, and then he was gone. The sound of his body hitting

the smaller rocks below was quite distinct. When Royce turned, all three whites and half the blacks were already streaming down the pathway, but he could not move, could not chase after them. He hadn't meant to shove Les over the edge, had only wanted to upset his aim before he could squeeze the trigger.

"Hey, Royce!" Doug called from below. "Better come down here!"

Royce picked his way carefully down the path. Ishi Murikama lay sprawled on the earth, halfway to the trees, the back of his shirt bloodied. Val was kneeling beside him.

"He's dead," said Clive. "Your friend killed him."

"He wasn't my friend . . . ," said Royce, turning to Les Moxham, similarly laid out by death, his head twisted at an awkward angle.

"Broke his neck," said Doug.

"An accident," said Royce.

"Yeah, but that," Doug said, pointing to the body of Ishi, "that's murder. Ishi was worth a hundred bloody Les Moxhams. Why'd you let him keep me rifle?"

Royce was unable to excuse that oversight.

Doug said, "Come over here, mate; I want a private word."

Royce went with him. When they were beyond hearing range of everyone, Doug said, "This place is called Kukullumunnumantje. It means wisdom stones, or somethin' like that. It's where all the Pitjantjatjara knowledge is stored, everythin' they ever learned. That's what they believe, anyway. You need to spend a bit a time here, Royce, and see if you can't soak up some wisdom. What you need to get wise about, mate, is what happens next. See, I'm gunna bury me Jap mate, and then me and me missus and me Pommie mate and me kid are gunna walk away from here, get back on our nags, and ride south. After we sell the cattle in Alice Springs, we're gunna take the train down to Adelaide, then we'll disappear. That'll take six, eight weeks maybe, plenty a time for you to set every copper in the Top End after us if you want. But to want that, you'd hafta think I did somethin' wrong, somethin' bad. I killed a bastard, and I meant to do it, but it wasn't wrong. That's why I don't feel bad about goin' away and startin' out somewhere else. But I can't do that—the three of us and Wilf can't do it—unless you let us. That's why you need a dose a wisdom, to help you make up your mind."

He walked away. Royce went over to Les and wondered if he should ask for help in burying him or take him to Mellindy Downs. He picked up Doug's rifle. Its stock was shattered by the fall, the gun ruined. He let it drop, then sat with his back against the stones and watched as Doug and Clive began scooping a shallow grave for their friend among the trees.

Now M'linga understood. The Japfella had been removed from the world to bring it into accord with his vision, so balance had been restored; but he felt no satisfaction. The presence at last of Boy b'long Gulgulong at Kukullumunnumantje should have given M'linga happiness and an answer to the riddle of his vision, a reason for the boy being so important to the Pitjantjatjara, but no such reason had been revealed. And then there was the dead whitefella and the whitefella p'lice, neither of whom should have been there. Only one of them had died, like the Japfella, to make M'linga's vision reflect back from the world, and M'linga was reluctant to order the death of the whitefella p'lice just to make things the way they should be. Nothing was as it should be, and M'linga suspected that his powers as a kadaicha man were slipping from him like water through opened fingers.

His vision had been true, but he had not been able to make the world the way it was supposed to be. Only part of the vision had happened as foretold, and that was a bad thing, an incomplete thing, and incompleteness was a sign that the world was collapsing. M'linga knew this was because whitefellas had come into the place behind his eyes for the first time, and they had destroyed everything inside his head, just as they took delight in destroying the world that can be touched and tasted. The songless men had strangled his songs. Boy b'long Gulgulong had tricked M'linga, made a fool of him, because Boy b'long Gulgulong was white. M'linga had led his people into a world where the ancient songs would have no strength anymore, where the whitefellas, with their emptiness and silence, would become stronger than they. The world was being turned upside down, and he was himself responsible. His shame was without boundaries, like the songlands that soon would be no more. He should have known that the death of his own son at the hands of a white-blackfella was a sign that the songs were in danger, but he had ignored that sign, and now the world he had known was dying.

When Ishi was buried, M'linga approached Val, with Beth beside him. He spoke to Val for some time, then turned from her and lay down on the ground, not far from Royce Curran.

"Says you can take the littlie with you," Beth translated. "He wasn spose to come here like M'linga thought. A mistake, see. Snake went down the wrong hole. M'linga says . . . he says the world's all smashed up, not like it's spose to be. Happen jus now, he says. So you can take the littlie away."

"Thank you," was all Val could think to say.

"Says he's gunna die soon," Beth added.

"He's . . . very old."

"Dusn matter how old. Made up his mind, he says. Gunna go soon, 'cause everythin's busted an smashed up."

"I'm sorry."

"Your dad," said Beth, becoming shy, "he wasn so bad. Was orright to me."

"Did he . . . did he kill himself, like they say, or did someone else kill him? Can you tell me now, without getting punished?"

"He done it to himself. Drunk lots a beer, then he done it to himself, dinkum he did. Ranji was jus skitin' to yer. He never done it."

"Thank you."

Doug came over to Val, and Beth wandered away. Every member of M'linga's mob seemed to have absorbed some of their leader's disappointment, and a kind of torpor was invading their features, their very movements. They began lying down, as M'linga had done, and soon not a single Aborigine was standing. They made no noise or fuss over this new way of behaving, simply adopted M'linga's example.

Royce was obliged to stand. He could feel some of what appeared to ail the blacks creeping into him from the stones he had been leaning against. He wanted to sleep, despite the occurrences of the day, and forget everything, a state of mind so alien to his usual self that he was a little afraid of it.

"We're goin' now," Doug said.

Royce nodded, unable to think of any suitable response. He did not know what he intended doing later that day, or weeks from now, or years, concerning Doug Farrands. His mind would not function, would not choose a path for him to follow. He envied Doug in a way, since Doug knew exactly what he intended doing. Doug had a wife and a child and a friend. Royce had none of those things, but he was not envious, merely appreciative at last of the man he saw as Doug Farrands, a very complete man in his way. And he wished for Doug the kind of life he might well have wished for himself.

"Good-bye," Val said, and again Royce nodded, including Clive in the gesture. Clive raised a hand, then all three, with Wilf held against Val's breast, turned and began walking. They did not hurry, and they did not look back.

He watched them leave, and continued watching until the trees hid them from him.